More Than Need You

MORE THAN WORDS SERIES BY
SHAYLA BLACK

MORE THAN NEED YOU
More Than Words, Book 2
Written by Shayla Black

This book is an original publication by Shayla Black.

Copyright © 2017 Shelley Bradley LLC
Print Edition

Cover Design by: Rachel Connolly
Photographer: Sara Eirew Photographer
Edited by: Amy Knupp of Blue Otter

Excerpt from *More Than Want You* © 2017 by Shelley Bradley LLC

ISBN: 978-1-936596-45-4

PRAISE FOR *MORE THAN WANT YOU*

"Highly recommend! Shayla Black delivers once again with this passionate and sexy novel... A beautiful love story with a twist that you'll never see coming!"

—Meredith Wild, #1 New York Times Bestselling Author

"Amazing! Everything I didn't even know I needed or wanted in a romance novel. Hot. Spicy. Addicting."

—Rachel Van Dyken, #1 New York Times Bestselling Author

"Sexy, passionate and oh-so-clever! An intriguing love story!"

—Lauren Blakely, #1 New York Times Bestselling Author

"You'll hate him and then you'll love him! A sexy read with a surprising twist."

—Carly Phillips, New York Times Bestselling Author

"I'll play house with the hot real estate mogul Maxon Reed any time! Shayla Black's fans are gonna love this new series!"

—Lorelei James, New York Times Bestselling author of the Need You series

"More Than Want You is a delightful mix of heartache, passion and twists. Maxon and Keeley are my favorite kinds of characters—flawed and lovable—and their story is one you don't want to miss."

—Georgia Cates, New York Times Bestselling Author

"Wickedly sexy, totally delicious, and an absolute page-turner. Maxon Reed had me swooning and completely stole my heart."

—Chelle Bliss, USA Today Bestselling Author

ABOUT *MORE THAN NEED YOU*

I'm Griffin Reed—cutthroat entrepreneur and competitive bastard. Trust is a four-letter word and everyone is disposable...except Britta Stone. Three years ago, she was my everything before I stupidly threw her away. I thought I'd paid for my sin in misery—until I learned we have a son. Finding out she's engaged to a bore who's rushing her to the altar pisses me off even more. I intend to win her back and raise our boy. I'll have to get ruthless, of course. Luckily, that's one of my most singular talents.

Nearly sixty days. That's what I'm asking the gritty, independent single mother to give me—twenty-four/seven. Under my roof. And if I have my way, in my bed. Britta says she wants nothing to do with me. But her body language and passionate kisses make her a liar. Now all I have to do is coax her into surrendering to the old magic between us. Once I have her right where I want her, I'll do whatever it takes to prove I more than need her.

FOREWORD

There are infinite ways to tell someone you love them. Some of the most powerful don't require words at all. This was the truth rolling through my head when I first conceived of this series, writing about a love so complete that mere letters strung together to make sentences weren't an adequate communicator of those feelings. For this series, music was my go-to choice.

I *love* music. I'm always immersed in it and spend hours a day with my earbuds plugged in. I write to music. I think to music. I even sleep to music. I was thrilled to incorporate songs into the story I felt were meaningful to the journey. I think of it this way: a movie has a sound-track. Why shouldn't a book?

So I created one.

Some of the songs I've selected will be familiar. Some are old. Some are newer. Some popular. Some obscure. They all just fit (in my opinion) and came straight from the heart. I listened to many of these songs as I wrote the book.

For maximum understanding (and feels), I seriously recommend becoming familiar with these songs and either playing them or rolling them around in your head as you read. Due to copyright laws, I can't use exact lyrics, but I tried to give you the gist of those most meaningful to Britta and Griff's story. I've also made it simple for you to give them a listen by creating a Spotify playlist.

Hugs and happy reading!

BLACK – Pearl Jam

WINDOWS – Angel Olsen

UNCHAINED MELODY – The Righteous Brothers

PICTURES OF YOU – The Cure

WHERE I STOOD – Missy Higgins

DIDN'T YOU KNOW HOW MUCH I LOVED YOU – Kellie Pickler

FOR A LIFETIME (Vox mix) – Lustral

BREAKING TIES – OceanLab

GOOD RIDDANCE – Green Day

KE KALI NEI AU (The Hawaiian Wedding Song) – Andy Williams

CAN'T HELP FALLING IN LOVE – Elvis

LIES – Trifonic

WRAPPED IN YOUR ARMS – Fireflight

THANKS

I never would have survived this book without the support of some of the dearest people in my life, whom I often thank. These people help me laugh, hold my hand, and talk me off the ledge when I threaten to find a sane career. My wonderful family—William and Baby—as well as my friends—Rachel, Shannon, Jenna, Isabella, Lexi, Kris, Liz—I could never do everything without you amazing people in my life. Hugs and squishy smooches!

DEDICATION

This book is dedicated to everyone who's ever loved someone with their whole heart and wished that, despite the odds, it could somehow work out...

AUTHOR'S NOTE

Thank you for choosing to read this selection in my More Than Words series. MORE THAN NEED YOU is book two. If you like reading series in order, please start with MORE THAN WANT YOU. However, the books in this series are companions, not serials, meaning that backstory, secondary characters, and other elements will be easier to relate to if you have read all installments in order but the main romance of each book is a stand-alone. Therefore, you do not need to read all the books to understand this second-chance love story.

For those of you who have read MORE THAN WANT YOU, the timeline of MORE THAN NEED YOU overlaps by ten days. Britta and Griff's story begins before the end of Keeley and Maxon's journey. So while you read the reunion and happy ending of the elder Reed brother and his sunshine in book one, you'll see some of their time apart early in this book.

CHAPTER ONE

Griff

HOW THE FUCK DID I get here?

It's nine thirty at night. By now, I'm usually curled up in bed with my laptop and some work…or another meaningless one-night stand. Instead, I'm rushing down Highway 30, the breeze from the open window whipping through my hair as I speed through the nearly hour-long journey toward Kihei. After more than three years, I'm going to see the one woman I haven't managed to forget.

And the son I never knew I had.

Holy shit, I'm a father. That still hasn't truly registered since I found out ten minutes ago. Now I can't reach them fast enough. I dodge a slow tourist and run a yellow light. Yes, I'm breaking multiple traffic laws. And I don't care. I just need to get there.

Then what? a voice in my head whispers.

I have no idea what I'm going to say to my ex-girlfriend, Britta. Well, that's not exactly true. I intend to figure out why the hell I never heard about her pregnancy. Once, I loved that woman. I lived with her. I wanted to marry her.

Then I got stupid. And she let me.

Everything has been fucked up since.

I push the past behind me and try to think ahead. My first priority is to finally meet our boy. I'll insist on it. My brother says Jamie looks a lot like me. Based on Maxon's pictures, I agree. And I can't wait to meet him.

1

I've missed so much—pregnancy, birth, first year, first steps, first words… I'm shocked by how badly that fact is grinding up my guts. Kids were never on my radar. They were cute—for someone else. I wasn't interested in wiping noses or butts. But after one look at the picture of that little boy with my face and his mother's blue eyes, I felt stunned. And I felt protective. That snapshot of him smiling at the toy truck he clutched in his chubby fist completely changed my world. It fired up my determination not to miss another day of James Tucker Reed's life.

Oh, he doesn't have my last name yet. But he will. I'm going to do whatever it takes to make damn sure of that.

In my pocket, my phone buzzes. I'm hoping it's not a client. Though it's true Realtors are never really off the clock, especially when one sells multimillion-dollar estates, I am not in the frame of mind to deal with work right now. Thankfully, when I glance at the display connected via Bluetooth to my Porsche 911 Carrera convertible to see who's calling, I'm not surprised by the name that's popped up. I've been expecting this.

I close the window and press the button to talk. "Hi, Keeley."

"Griff, is your meeting with Maxon over? What happened?"

Our reunion a few minutes ago was the first time I've spoken to my brother in over three years, so it's momentous. We used to be close, best friends and business partners—before I fucked everything up. Tonight's reconciliation wouldn't have happened without Keeley and her grudging agreement to dabble in a little corporate espionage and spy on Maxon for me. She also fell for him, despite the fact he hadn't yet grown past his clueless douchebag stage. But I found out tonight that he fell for her, too. I'm not telling Keeley anything about my brother's determination to win her back and persuade her to marry him just yet. She needs time with her family in Phoenix to think. Then, if she decides to return to Maui—and Maxon—I'll help my older brother with his sweeping romantic gesture to slide a ring on her finger.

"Yeah. Maxon and I talked about the split, the major reasons we stopped getting along. Actually, we talked about a lot of things." And it felt damn good after so much ugliness and strife. "We made up. We've decided that, instead of being competitors, we're going to pursue the Stowe estate together. And if the arrangement works well, we'll think about making the partnership permanent once more."

"That's great!" She sounds genuinely happy for me...but I hear the sad note in her voice. "It must have felt so fantastic to be with Maxon, talking business again, catching up..."

"Yep." I sort through the meeting in my head, think of details that might cheer her up. "He seems different. I have you to thank."

Keeley doesn't say anything for a long moment, which tells me something about her mood. She's never subdued.

"Don't thank me. I really hoped he'd figured out what was important, but, Griff...I can't change him. He has to want to be a different man. Just like you did."

She's absolutely right. But Maxon truly seems to have grown as a person. Hopefully, she'll come home and see that.

Keeley sighs. "It's so great that you and your brother are talking again. At least something good came out of the mess I made with him. Please be happy. After everything that's happened, you deserve it."

She's being kind. I don't deserve shit. I also know that arguing with Keeley about this is pointless.

And how is it possible my GPS says I still have another thirty minutes before I reach my destination?

I think back over the last few weeks, everything that's happened... Then a realization hits me. She's been my confidant and best friend for more than two years. So why would she stab me in the back like this?

"You knew I had a son, didn't you?" I rake a hand through my hair. "How fucking long have you kept that from me?"

"So Maxon told you about Jamie?" she breathes. "That's good. You need to—"

"How long?" No answer. The interminable moments are shredding my admittedly thin patience. "Goddamn it, Keeley..."

"Almost three weeks. I'm sorry," she rushes to add. "I hope you'll forgive me for not telling you."

That's asking a lot. Keeley knows I have deep trust issues. I haven't told her the whole reason why, though.

Hell, I haven't told anyone.

"Three fucking weeks?" I bark. "What the hell? He's my *son*. Why would you keep him from me?"

"If I'd told you the minute I found out, you would have confronted Britta immediately and messed up everything I was building with Maxon for you and… I really only did what I thought was best in the situation." She pauses. "Wait, it sounds as if you're in your car. Please tell me you're heading straight home."

I hear what she's saying. She's probably even right. Everything would have blown up in my face if I'd jumped Britta's case three weeks ago. There's still a high likelihood it will tonight. On the other hand, all I can think of is that if I had known sooner, I might have endured a little less misery and might have been involved a bit more in Jamie's childhood.

"I value my best friend too much to lie."

Unlike some people. The subtext hangs there.

"C'mon, Griff. I would never intentionally hurt you. You know that."

Fuck. I do. I have to take a deep breath, count to five, and remind myself that Keeley is nothing like the people I used to know. Once I have, I wish I could take the biting words back. You'd think after the misery I've brought down on myself by failing to trust that I might have learned. But no, my knee-jerk certainty that someone is fucking me is sometimes instant and unavoidable. In the back of my head, I expect people will shit on me. So I strike before they do. Sometimes before I even think. Damn it. I have to stop the bitterness that's been rotting me for half my life and start handling it, along with my shock and frustration about Jamie. The first step is to apologize to Keeley.

"I do. I'm sorry." I wince. "I'm an ass. You know this about me."

"Sometimes 'ass' is putting it nicely. At least you listened and didn't hang up."

For me, that's progress. Refusing to hear a word of their defense was the disservice I did to Maxon and Britta just over three years ago. "I'm trying to learn."

"I know. Tonight has been a lot for you. But not everyone is as forgiving as I am. If you're heading to see Britta because you want to meet Jamie, you can't handle this like a dumb ass." Her voice softens.

"You're right."

"When Maxon first told me about him, I didn't say anything because I genuinely believed that if we could get your brother on your side, he wouldn't interfere if you tried to include Jamie—and Britta—in your life. But three weeks ago, you would have barged in, temper blazing, and asked questions later. Maxon would have become a roadblock. And you would have destroyed any path to being with the people you need most."

I tap my thumb against my steering wheel in agitation. Keeley is right. My head knows it. The rest of me is still reeling and I can't quite admit it aloud. "What do I do next?"

"Turn your car around and go home."

"Not happening. I'm already years late as it is."

"But now isn't smart. You haven't had time to process the shock."

"Waiting to meet my son isn't the answer!" But even if I lay eyes on him tonight, how do I compensate for not being there for him since birth? "I've got to make this right ASAP."

Keeley sighs. "I'm sure in your shoes I'd feel the same. Just go easy on Britta. Don't assume the worst."

I'll do my best. "Maxon swears Britta tried to tell me about the baby. I don't know how or when or…"

"I think you need to believe him."

After failing to trust my brother about the business deal that broke us up, I can't call him a liar now. "Okay, so Britta tried to tell me."

How did I not hear or understand her?

"Maxon said she wrote you a letter."

"That's a pretty fucking impersonal way to tell a man he's about to become a father."

"What choice did you give her, Griff?"

There Keeley goes again, shoving the inconvenient truth in my face.

After our breakup, I rejected Britta's phone calls and deleted her urgent voice mails. Her only alternative was to put a stamp on a missive and drop it to me via USPS.

God, I was such a stupid fuck. I wish I had a do-over on the craptastic days that blew up my life.

"I never got the letter. I have no idea what happened to it." But I'm beginning to have my suspicions.

"I told Maxon that." She pauses. "When you left your brother a few minutes ago, did you mention that you were heading to Britta's house?"

"Not in so many words but I'm sure he can read between the lines."

Another pause. I know Keeley; she's gearing up to ask something big. "How will you feel when you see her again?"

Isn't that a great question? Before I saw Britta last month at a restaurant with some Hawaiian dude in a suit who all but fondled her in public, I would have sworn I was over her. Immune. I was good at lying to myself. But that night, when I saw him touch her, I wanted to rip his face off with my bare hands. What ate at me more was that Britta didn't notice me at all.

"I spent a long time thinking she betrayed me to help my brother close a huge deal behind my back. Now that I know she didn't, I owe her an apology. More than one, really. But I'm so fucking furious." Not at her but at life. At circumstance. At all the things I can't go back and change. Mostly, at myself.

I try to shake it off. Tonight is about Jamie. How I feel about Britta doesn't matter anymore. We've both moved on—in theory. She has a new boyfriend, and I'll try to get along with this dude and refrain from committing murder.

No promises.

"When you see her, listen. Don't make snap judgments. Hold your temper. Breathe through your anger. Yelling at her will accomplish nothing. In fact, take the rest of your drive to collect your thoughts. If you want to be a part of your son's life, it's important for you to be strategic."

I hear the soothing, rational note in her voice. She uses it when she's trying to talk me off the ledge. That's been a lot these last few years. I'm grateful every day she was answering the phones for that useless therapist I was seeing for a while. Keeley is way smarter than the bad doctor. She's helped me so much. And she always gives the right advice...even when I don't want to hear it.

"Thanks. I'm on it. How are things in Phoenix?"

"Fine. It's good to see Mom and Phil. They're so tan from their trip to the South Pacific. The pictures they snapped are gorgeous!"

"You're envious?"

"Yeah," she spouts as if that's obvious.

"Um, you live in Hawaii." When she laughs, I smile with her until we both sober. "Are you coming back?"

She's quiet for a long moment. "I don't know. I suspect your brother and I both need to do some thinking. I can't get a clear head when, every time I turn around, I see places we've been and..." She sighs. "I'm sure it sounds silly, but I'm not ready to handle it."

"Not silly at all." I remember the devastation of being on this goddamn island and stumbling into someplace every day that reminded me of Britta and what we used to share.

"Thanks. I left you a little something in your CD player when you dropped me off at the airport."

I hesitate. "Should I be afraid? It's not more meditation music to humping grasshoppers, is it?"

Keeley laughs at me again like she can't decide whether to slap me upside the head or simply be amused. "No. It was cicadas, and we don't know that they were humping, goof."

"We don't know that they weren't, either. It sounded like an insect orgy."

I hear a whole lot of *what am I going to do with you?* in her laugh. "You know music helps me interpret feelings—or give advice—when I can't find the right words. So stop giving me a hard time and listen to what I left you, okay?"

I'm sure it's something meaningful that will try to move me forward,

7

etc. She knows I find that shit painful. Why won't she let me wallow like a good friend would? Because that's not her style. Probably why she *is* my friend.

"All right," I grumble. "I will."

"I wish I was there to make tonight easier on you. I really am trying to help."

"I know." And I would have been lost without her friendship years ago. "Thanks."

"Don't lose sight of what you want out of the conversation. Stick to topics that will help your cause."

In other words, don't get stupid and flay Britta open with my sharp tongue. "I won't."

"Uh-huh. Let me put it in Griff-speak. Keep your shit together or you're not going to get what you want. Call me later."

"I will. Seriously, thanks for everything."

"You can thank me by straightening out your life and finally being happy."

Wouldn't that be nice? Sure. I'm just not holding my breath.

I PASS THE NEXT FEW miles of the drive to the music Keeley left me. I should have guessed she'd find the perfect song for the occasion. Her knowledge of music is insane, spanning genres and decades. You could scratch off what I know about it with a penny. I never really paid attention to all the melodic angst on the radio until her. Now I admit, I like it.

She left a sticky note on the case that reads THINK ABOUT THIS FOR ME, PLEASE? I can't refuse.

The opening strums of guitar on the first song are iconic. Then Eddie Vetter's voice shouts a little "Hey." I already know this song is "Black" by Pearl Jam. A lot of people think this tune is sexual. If you listen to the lyrics, it's depressing as hell. But it also describes where I'm stuck. Once, my earth totally revolved around my sun, Britta. After the split, the air I tasted and breathed took a turn, all right. A nosedive into hell. My bitter hands are still chafing beneath the clouds of what was everything to me. All my pictures, my memories, have been washed in black. Keeley's "subtle" way of saying I've been mourning for three years.

No shit.

I skip through the last of that long track and move on to the next. The first notes of an unfamiliar melancholy tune hit my speakers, and I grab the CD case and give it a read. This tune is called "Windows" by someone named Angel Olsen, who has a haunting voice. By the end, she's telling me I've been blind and I've been dead and it's time to open up a window and let some light in.

I snort. Keeley is never shy when she has something to say.

The third song I recognize before the end of the first word. "Unchained Melody" by the Righteous Brothers. The tune is sweeping and epic. In the first three lines, I already feel as if the lyrics have stabbed me and left me to bleed out. Yes, if I'm being really honest—and Keeley knows this too fucking well—I have hungered for Britta for a long, lonely time. A few lines later mirrors exactly what I'm wondering deep down. Is she still mine?

But I already know the answer. She must hate my guts. I unwittingly walked out on her when she was pregnant. Why wouldn't she?

I turn off the music in the middle of the song. I'd rather drive in silence than fantasize there's a smidgeon of hope for Britta and me while Bobby Hatfield croons on in his perfectly tuned whine.

But cutting off the audial distractions leaves me alone with my thoughts. Until Keeley and her goddamn playlist, my primary focus has been on Jamie, not the woman who gave birth to my son. Not the woman who once held my heart.

What if there's any chance at all, deep down, that she *is* still mine?

Jesus, I have to stop this emotional shit. I can't see Britta without my head screwed on straight. My only goal is to meet my boy. *Focus there, dumb ass.*

I turn on talk radio and tune out the political pundits. At least they aren't trying to yank my heart out from between my eyes. I'm already intimately acquainted with that feeling. It set in after Britta and I ceased being a couple and hasn't let up since.

Minutes later, I pull up in front of her house and examine it with a frown. It's small but nice. Pale blue facade, clean white door, well-maintained yard. A glance tells me it's under fifteen hundred square feet. I know this neighborhood. It's decent and not terribly expensive—at least by Maui standards. I'm grateful Britta has given my son a solid home. I'm glad my brother—not her boyfriend—has been subsidizing this roof because there's no way she could afford this place without one of them.

That's going to change. In fact, everything is.

I park on the street. Despite the long driveway and carport, I have nowhere else to leave my high-priced wheels. Everywhere I look is packed with vehicles—sedans, sports cars, jeeps. Old and new. This many people couldn't live in a house this small.

Is she having a party? On a Thursday night?

With a frown, I step out of my Porsche. The Hawaiian breeze has a hint of cool nip that reminds me it's February. I try not to think about the fact that Valentine's Day is next Tuesday. I'm sure someone invented this crappy lovers' holiday to mess with single people's heads. Every year, I find some random woman who also can't bear the loneliness without someone to pretend with. Last year's shitbaggery started in some tourist bar and ended up in a ritzy hotel with empty orgasms and regret. I was home by two a.m., in the shower and trying to wash away my sins.

As I climb the stairs to Britta's porch, I focus on the here and now. Somewhere in that house is my son…and his mother.

With Keeley's advice in mind, I draw in a calming breath and head to the cheerful front door. The little glow of the porch light illuminates the piece of paper someone has taped in the middle. WE'RE OUT BACK. COME THROUGH THE SIDE GATE. IT'S UNLOCKED.

The scrawl doesn't look anything like Britta's writing.

I grind my teeth together and head back down the stairs to find the side gate. Weaving between the cars strewn across the driveway, I find my way to the fence and see a break, the wooden door standing slightly ajar.

What the hell is going on? I have no idea as I push it open.

Across the yard, stretched between a pair of swaying palms, is a big, homemade banner that stops me dead.

CONGRATULATIONS ON YOUR ENGAGEMENT, BRITTA AND MAKAIO.

Holy. Fuck.

Maxon warned me this might happen. Still, I reread the sign, rooted in place. My body thuds. My head races. My blood boils.

I want to fucking kill someone despite the fact that, logically, I know she doesn't belong to me anymore. But my reaction is purely primal.

It tells me that whatever we might have had is gone, along with my foolish hope.

Working to take my fury down ten notches, I breathe deep and tell myself to be practical as I scan the yard. I don't see any children. Is Jamie already asleep? Maybe so. It's ten thirty. Don't little kids go to bed early? I didn't consider that sooner. Damn it.

Now what do I do? I'm hardly in the mood to stand here and toast the bride.

Britta isn't hard to find since she's the only blonde among a sea of native Hawaiians in bright, tropical prints and sandals, clinking glasses and smiling.

From a distance, I see she's wearing a pencil skirt in a sedate gray that clings to a curve in her hips she didn't used to have. Her ass looks lusher, rounder. Her hair, though wrapped up in some classic twist, looks longer or thicker—something.

The lust that hits me is stronger than ever.

Jesus, when am I going to stop wanting her?

She's talking to a pretty brunette who's about her age. The striking woman hugs her, joy evident in her huge smile. Britta replies. I can tell because she still talks with her hands. She's graceful, as always. Not surprising. She entered college on a dance scholarship.

I remember watching her move on stage for the first time. The beauty of her movement stunned me, the way she was aware of her every muscle, the complete control she had over even her smallest gesture. Pale tights and a flowing scrap of chiffon flirting with her thighs gave me a hard-on from hell. I was her boss at the time. She'd just begun to work for Maxon and me. I appreciated her smarts in the office and her talent on stage, sure. But more than anything, I wanted those slender thighs wrapped around me while I fucked her. I told myself to back down. She was still young. Everything about her screamed hands off. I didn't listen. I corrupted every bit of her purity. Then I walked away, leaving her with a pregnancy she hadn't planned for, and myself with a mountain of fury and regret.

I wonder how much she's changed. Maxon told me that I broke something in her. Fuck.

Is she bitter now? Withdrawn? How much does she hate me?

How many beds has she slept in since mine?

I swallow the question down. I have no right to ask. Besides, do I really want to know?

I keep staring at her, watching her slender shoulders as she laughs gently. I hear the sound rising above the din of conversation. It's good to hear her happy even though I'm so fucking sad.

No one has noticed me. I need to approach her, think of something rational and non-confrontational to say. Or turn around and come back tomorrow, when she doesn't have a whole bunch of company who will gawk at me the minute I demand to see my son. When she isn't celebrating her pending union to another man.

But I can't make myself leave. I just stare, willing her to look my way.

Suddenly, she stiffens. I see the moment she becomes aware of my presence. She tilts her head toward her right shoulder. The cock of her ear and the jut of her chin follow. She pauses for a sliver of a second, as if she's not sure she truly wants to know if I'm just beyond her line of sight, making her senses flare.

"Britta," I call out to her.

At the sound of my voice, she whips her head around, as if she's heard a ghost and is eager to dispel the notion I could be standing ten feet behind her.

Our eyes meet. My breath stops. God, she's still so fucking beautiful to me.

In that moment I know one thing: no matter what's happened or how long it's been, I want her back. Whatever Britta thinks, she's still mine.

A gasp falls from her lips. She drops her drink, her face going pale in an instant.

The woman she was speaking to frowns in concern and grabs Britta's shoulders, shooting me the evil eye.

Yeah, I'm the bad guy here. Everyone knows it, even me.

I take a step toward her, and that seems to pull her from her daze. She waves off her concerned friend and darts in my direction, bearing down on me with something between shock and fury.

Her eyes are still a stunning shade of blue, almost turquoise, like the warmest ocean waters near the shore. They're the first thing I noticed about her. Blue-eyed blondes aren't terribly unusual, especially in Los Angeles, where I spent my childhood. But everything about Britta is different. Her eyes are slanted and slightly far apart, framed by heavy lashes. The effect is exotic, sexual. Her pillowy mouth sucks me in next, bent with an exaggerated bow on top and a puffy curve on the bottom. I still dream of that mouth. I remember every time I kissed it, every pleasure it ever made me feel. Tonight, she's exaggerated her pouty lips with a soft gloss that makes me want to tell everyone else at this gathering to fuck off so I can eat it from her now.

No one else has lips as enticing or soft as Britta Stone. Believe me, I've looked. A lot. I can't un-remember the way her eyes flared wide for me when her mouth opened to let loose the gasp of orgasm she could no longer keep in. It was one of the sexiest things ever. Even now, I sometimes close my eyes and stroke my cock to her memory.

Any wonder seeing her in the flesh is making me harder than hell?

Any wonder I'm now determined to have her back?

"What are you doing here?" she demands.

How did I find her house or why did I choose this moment to invade her life again? I'll spare her the boring details of both and focus on my first priority. "Somewhere in the back of your head, you must have known this day would come. I want to see my son. Where's Jamie?"

Her eyes widen in shock. Her chest caves in, as if my words are more of a battering ram than a question. She braces her left hand over her heart. She's wearing a round diamond solitaire on a simple gold band. The sight of another man's ring on her finger enrages me.

Someday, somehow, someway, I'm going to replace it with my own.

"Griff…"

When her face goes taut, I know she's fighting worry. And maybe tears. I want to do something—hold her, reassure her I don't mean to take Jamie away, wrap her in my arms and kiss her until she forgets about the world.

But when I reach for her, she jerks away. "Don't. Why would I know this day would come? He's two and a half, and before tonight you never showed any interest—"

"I found out he exists an hour ago. It took me three minutes to coax your address out of my brother and fifty-two minutes to drive here."

She stares at me in blinking shock. "You and Maxon…talked?"

"Yeah. Face to face. We buried the hatchet. Starting tomorrow, we're co-listing the Stowe estate."

She gapes at me. Ah, yes. Clearly, my brother's assistant has just realized we'll likely be seeing each other every day for weeks—potentially even months.

"Oh." She doesn't sound thrilled.

I don't expect her to be. I'll make everything between us right as soon as she lets me. But I doubt she wants to hear that now.

"So…" Her voice warbles. "Maxon told you about Jamie?"

"He seemed to think I knew. You wrote me a letter when you found out you were pregnant?"

"Eventually. As a last resort."

I want to curse. "I didn't get it."

Britta flattens her full lips into a grim line. I can tell she's not sure whether to believe me. "Well, I-I...tried. I—"

"I know. I'm not blaming you."

On the far side of the yard, I see the woman she was talking to earlier tapping a man on the shoulder. He turns. It's the suit I saw Britta with last month. A glance tells me that he and the brunette are related. Siblings? She's speaking rapidly, trying to discreetly point my way. The man looks over, seeking Britta out with a stare. His eyes zero in on us. The fiancé. He's a complication I don't need, but I'll deal with him in due course.

One problem at a time.

"It doesn't matter now." She sounds wary. "You don't need to get involved. Jamie is happy and healthy and—"

"It *does* matter, Britta. He's my son. I *am* going to get involved."

"What kind of father will you be?" she challenges. "I know yours way too well. And you're so much like him..."

Dear ol' dad is a prick and a half, banging my teachers and knocking up his secretaries, treating everyone in his life like second-class citizens whose existence should revolve around him. That's not me. Well, not anymore.

"I've stopped having anything to do with that bastard."

"Good for you. But you still don't know anything about being a parent." She shakes her head at me as if willing me to understand. "Leave us alone, Griff. Makaio is good with Jamie. He's patient. He makes time. He—"

"Isn't Jamie's biological father. *I* am. I want to see him. I have the right to my own son."

What little bit of color flushed her face during our exchange drains out again. "You don't. He's not yours legally. Your name isn't on his birth certificate."

I intend to right that wrong ASAP. "His first name is my middle name. He's mine. We both know it. You've admitted it. Let me see him."

Behind her, the fiancé hustles across the yard, looking determined to figure out who I am and why I've come.

A vertical furrow appears between her brows, which slash down as she scowls. Yeah, she's pissed. But I also see her eyes watering. Her hands are shaking. "No."

"You're really going to keep him from me?"

Unaware that in a few seconds three will become a crowd, she glares at me. "You can't barge in now. I'm finally happy. I have a good future in front of me. You shattered me once, and now you're going to crash back in and ruin everything? Go shack up with another of your brother's ex-girlfriends and leave me the hell alone."

I deserve that. Tiffanii was a giant mistake.

She tries to turn away. I grab her wrist. God, touching her again is everything. No way am I letting her go. But the boyfriend is bearing down. I only have a few seconds alone with her. "Britta—"

"Hey." Her fiancé tries to act casual as he approaches. He's my height, similar build. He's good-looking in a Hawaiian calendar boy sort of way. "Is everything all right?" He plants beside her and lays his hand on the small of her back, claiming his territory as he sends her a questioning glance.

I let her go—for the moment.

"I'm fine." She drags in a breath and manages to compose herself. Most people would be fooled. But her voice shakes.

I wonder if he notices. I wonder if he has any idea she's lying.

"Griffin Reed," I finally say. I don't extend my hand for him to shake. I won't pretend to be his friend when I already know he's my enemy.

He stiffens slightly. Yeah, he knows who I am. But the guy doesn't look at me as if I'm a threat or silently warn me that if I lay a finger on Britta he'll take me apart limb from limb without an ounce of remorse. Stupid bastard. That's how I'd be looking at me if I stood in his shoes.

"Makaio Kāle." He doesn't hold out his hand to me, either. "Why are you here?"

"To see my son."

He frowns. Obviously, he's not thrilled. But I also see the moment he realizes he doesn't want to step into the middle of a matter between Jamie's biological parents.

"Can you give us a few minutes?" Britta asks, flipping her blue eyes up at him. I see the pleading there.

I hate the thought that she would silently beg this man for anything. She's only supposed to look at me like that when we're naked and I'm deep inside her and I'm fucking her so slowly she can't quite come but she can no longer contain the need, so she bites her lip to beg me with needy whimpers.

"All right. I'm going to say good-bye to my sister," Makaio says reluctantly. "I'll be nearby if you need me."

I smile at him. *Don't worry. She won't need you for anything ever again, pal.*

"Thanks, babe," she says softly. "I'm going to walk Griff out, too."

The endearment she speaks to him wrenches my heart. So does her proclamation that she intends to get rid of me. I know she said both to put me on notice. She wants me to believe she's invested in this guy. And maybe she is on some level. But I'd bet every dime I have that if we were alone, I could make her melt.

With a nod, Makaio walks away. Her stare lingers. I see the moment she realizes her safety net is gone.

She draws in a bracing breath and gestures me toward the gate.

I turn stubborn and shake my head. "I want to see my son now."

"He's asleep, and I won't wake him. And you were *not* invited to my engagement party. Don't ruin this for me."

I glance around. People are staring, and the party is beginning to break up. My first instinct is to press Britta further, but her voice is trembling again. I can tell she wants to nudge me toward the gate but doesn't dare touch me.

The me of three years ago would have pounced on her weaknesses and used them to turn her inside out until she gave me what I wanted. My old man taught me to cue into others' emotions and manipulate them to achieve the ends I sought. The me who's finally learned some empathy senses that Britta needs me to back down for the night. If I don't ease up, she'll only be more resistant in the future. Besides, I have an hour's drive home and an early meeting tomorrow morning. Tactical retreat is in my best interest.

I'm in her head. I've planted the seed that I'm back and I'm not going away. I'll let her stew on that knowledge.

"All right," I relent. "I'll go."

Britta's wary expression tells me she's looking for the catch. "Really?"

I pluck my keys from my pocket. "Yes."

For now.

Her visible relief makes me feel vaguely guilty. "Thank you."

She knows I'm showing her mercy. She should also know that I may not show much more of it until I'm a part of my son's life.

I wonder if she has any idea that same concept applies to her? Certainly not yet, but she will.

"Britta, let's be clear. I don't want to take the boy from you. I don't want to upend his world. I simply want to be a part of it. We're starting while he's young. I'll ease into his life a little at a time, whatever is easiest and best for him. I think you and I should meet tomorrow, maybe for a drink after work to discuss—"

"No."

"You're not free then?"

"I won't be free ever again. I'm engaged."

That fact torques my gut. "When did that happen?"

She looks down, away. "I said yes about four hours ago. Makaio called everyone, and they surprised me with the banner and food and..."

Fuck.

"I'm not asking you on a date," I bite out. "I'm asking you to sit down so we can be adults and discuss our son."

"If you really want what's best for Jamie, you'll vanish. He's a little boy and he won't understand your sudden role in his life. Makaio will be a good father. Go back to your twenty-hour workdays, your meaningless flings"—she marches out the gate and lays eyes on my deeply impractical two-door sports convertible with a scoff—"and your bachelor-pad sports car and disappear again. We're all better off that way."

"You will *never* convince me that my son is better off without me."

The front door creaks open. Makaio and his sister make their way outside. He eyes me the entire time he's escorting her to a beat-up sedan. Then a few more people pour out the door, clearly the in-laws to be. Neighbors head out next, wandering toward their houses. Everyone is staring. I curse. Everything else I want to say will have to wait. This isn't the time. With an audience isn't the place.

I lean in, close to her ear, trying to ignore the hint of jasmine that always clings to her and drives me mad. "I will not go away because it's convenient for you. And I won't leave you alone simply because I hurt you or you don't like the way I rattle you, Britta. I'm back. And I'm never leaving again."

CHAPTER TWO

"How did it go last night?" Maxon asks me early the next morning.

Funny how natural it feels to resume the habits we shared three years ago, like checking in first thing each day. As I got on the stationary bike for a spin at six thirty, I rang him. He picked up right away, obviously already getting aerobic himself.

Now I hesitate replying. Once, Maxon was the person I trusted most. Well, as much as I trusted anyone. I know now he didn't do me wrong and I utterly overreacted. Keeley and I have talked a lot about trying to believe the best in people, rather than assuming the worst. She keeps telling me I have to take a leap of faith if I ever want to be happy.

Trusting my own brother seems like a good place to start in learning how to jump. Besides, I owe him.

"Disastrously." I fill him in on the reunion, including the reason for Britta's impromptu party.

"What are you going to do?"

Is he really asking me this? As if he doesn't have the same instincts? "What would you do?"

"Well…" Maxon pauses again. "Keeley is always telling me I should listen and empathize and—"

"Let's be real here."

Maxon sighs as if he hates to admit the truth. "If I had a son I wanted to know by a woman I was estranged from? I'd figure out how to ingrain myself in every level of her life until I wore her down and she gave me what I wanted."

"Bingo."

"I'd be calling an attorney to find out what my rights are and how to exercise them fully."

"I've already left him a voice mail," I assure my brother.

"I'd also be learning her schedule."

"Yep. I plan to work on that today. In fact, I'll be quizzing you later."

"Every time I saw her, I'd insist that I want to meet my son."

I nod. "That goes without saying."

"Then, I guess that's it—if all you want is to have Jamie in your life." He pauses. "But you want more. You want the woman."

"Of course I do. What would you do in that case?"

When he hesitates, I wince. I probably hit a sore spot. I have no doubt he feels lost without Keeley.

"In your shoes, I'd do everything humanly possible to separate Britta from Makaio."

I grin. "I'm already thinking of a strategy."

"But I'm trying to think less like a cutthroat bastard and more like a reasonable human being," he says as he breathes through his run. "For Keeley."

"I get that. I'm just not convinced the Mr.-Nice-Guy thing will work. I'll try, but I'm prepared to be more…persuasive if she won't listen."

"I think relentless might be a better term."

"Probably. I walked out on Britta when she was pregnant. It doesn't matter that I didn't know. What she remembers is that I left her to give birth alone. Now, I have to convince her how badly I want Jamie. I also have to give her opportunities to see me as something other than the enemy. Once she's reassured of that, I'll start working with her on us."

I would prefer to claim both of them simultaneously. If she thinks she's marrying Makaio, I have to change her mind *and* her heart. On the other hand, I know Britta. If I press her too hard too fast for something more than co-parenting, she'll shut me down. She doesn't trust me at all. I have to fix that, and it will take time. But I also can't let her believe I'm only back in her life for Jamie's sake. Which leads me to something I've been thinking…

"You know, for the duration of the Stowe contract, I think you and I should work really closely together. In fact, we should work out of the same office."

Maxon jumps on my train of thought a split second later and barks out a low laugh. "Oh, Britta will hate my guts for agreeing to this."

But my brother *does* agree. That's what's important right now. "I'll make her very happy in the end."

"You can't walk away from her this time. I'll kill you myself," he vows.

"That's absolutely the last thing on my mind, I promise you."

"So you really still have feelings for her?"

"Yes." I don't have to think about it. I know. In fact, I knew the second our eyes met last night. Whatever she once felt for me may have utterly changed, but despite the years and my parade of faceless flings, I love Britta. I've always loved her. I was too stubborn and too stupid to tell her that when we were together. For now, I can only add that to my pile of regret.

"We converted your former office into a storage and conference room, but we could do without it for a while."

I smile. "Excellent. You know, Sheila is having a grandbaby soon," I say of my assistant. "She's been eager to visit her son and daughter-in-law in Seattle. I think she's earned some time off."

"A month or two ought to do it." Maxon laughs.

Of being in the same office with Britta and of her being my assistant, too? "Agreed."

If I have her in my sights all day, I can work on her slowly. Maybe we'll tackle projects and have lunch together. I'll look for opportunities to see her after hours. Once I meet Jamie, I will insist we do things as a family…and encourage our natural connection until she no longer has any interest in marrying another man and raising our son with him.

"We just have to secure the listing first," Maxon points out. "Can you show up about eight thirty? I'll go over the preso with you. We'll figure out how to split it up, then make our pitch at ten. I think George and Vivienne Stowe will be pleasantly surprised."

I hope. Since I fucked it up yesterday, I'd definitely like to make them happy clients now. "Perfect. Maybe you can ask Britta to help me clear out my former office afterward so I can move in again?"

"I could do that. I really hope it works out for you two."

"Thanks. Once you've spoken to her, I'll take it from there."

"Cool. Now that we've got business behind us, um…have you talked to Keeley lately?"

"Last night. Nothing has changed since you and I met over dessert."

"I wish I could talk to her." My brother sounds glum that he can't.

"Don't rush her, man. That's not how she works."

"I know."

And he clearly doesn't like it.

"There's every chance she'll come around. Don't worry. I'm supposed to talk to her later, so I'll keep you posted. If nothing else, I have to pay her back for the CD of music she left in my car."

At that, Maxon laughs. "That woman and her songs… Do I dare ask?"

I fill him in on the first few tunes she laid on the disc. "Then it got worse. You're better with music than me. She passed on this damn tearjerker, 'Pictures of You?'"

"The Cure?"

I'm vaguely familiar with that band. When we were kids, we had a Goth babysitter who was obsessed. "Yeah. But this version was stripped down. All acoustic."

And poignant as hell. Stab me now with the lyrics. Something about remembering her standing in the rain and running to her to be near. Yeah. I close my eyes, imagining that. Fuck. The next verse I see all too clearly, too. Her falling into my arms, crying for the death of her heart. I remember that awful morning we split up so sharply it eviscerates me even now. My anger, my righteous sense of betrayal, my need to lash out.

I wish I could take every bit of it back and that Britta and I could go on as if it never happened.

But it's way too late for that.

"Huh, you'll have to share that version," Maxon suggests. "I'd like to give that a listen. What other songs? Because I know she left you more than a handful. That's how Keeley rolls."

"I had to turn it off after that wrist-slashing emo ballad. I'll try the CD again later."

I couldn't handle more after seeing Britta and leaving her house feeling infuriated, slightly defeated, and worried like hell I'd never have the chance to tell her I'm sorry, that I still love her, or that I want to make her happy. She's not ready to hear any of that now.

Did she give Makaio a celebratory fuck last night? Or fuck him as a fuck you to me? If I let myself believe that, I'll only add to my growing fear that I'm going to be miserable for the rest of my life. I blame myself mostly…but I kind of blame Keeley, too. Before her, I was an emotionless bastard and I weathered any twinges of sadness with booze and pussy. It's hardly an original tactic, but it was effective enough. Now? That shit won't fly anymore.

"When you listen to the rest, brace yourself," Maxon recommends.

"Yeah." Even now, I'm working like hell to tamp my shit down. But I feel it simmering just under the surface. "See you in a couple hours."

I'll see Britta then, too. I hope she doesn't rip my balls off before I can make her understand.

I ARRIVE AT MAXON'S OFFICE—IN the building we used to share—at ten minutes before eight. It's like déjà vu parking in the lot I shared with my brother for over six years. I see he's already here. He's doesn't lease the same car he did when we were partners, and I will totally have to rib him about driving his SUV day to day. I own one, too. I can't show property in a two-seater. Admittedly, his Range Rover convertible number is pretty sweet. But...

As I climb out of the car with my coffee and briefcase, I shove my phone in my pocket and lock up, then stride for the front door. I see the tall wooden sign in the grass out front. It used to have a white background where we had REED BROTHERS PROPERTY ASSOCIATES carved out and painted a really flashy, masculine blue. Maxon didn't replace the sign, just covered it with a canvas he's tied to the legs, so it reads MAXON MAUI REALTY. I snort. I thought it was a stupid name when I first heard it. I think it's a stupid name now.

I'll be sure to rib him about that, too.

Most of all, I don't see anyone else in the lot. We'll have a few minutes before Britta arrives.

I push the door open, and Maxon looks up from his desk. It's still the same furniture in the same location. I've seen this sight a hundred times, but seeing it again now is like a revelation. A homecoming. I smile.

Damn, it feels good to be back. In fact, I feel more like me than I have in years.

"Morning," I call out.

"Bro..." He goes back to tapping on his keyboard as furiously as he's able.

I take a sip of my brew as I approach and drop into the chair opposite his desk. "I see you're still a lousy typist."

He lifts one hand from the computer long enough to flip me off. "I see you're still an insufferable asshole."

I grin. "Oh, I haven't even started yet. Let's talk about that mom-mobile you're driving."

"That's a nice fucking vehicle," he argues.

I scoff at him in mocking tones. "Sure, if I was taking a passel of kids to school on my way to join the ladies' coffee klatch before my run to the grocery store..."

"Bite my ass. At least I'm not driving an overpriced phallic symbol that looks like compensation for what I don't have behind my fly."

I bark out a laugh. "What's behind my fly has never been the problem. You're a Reed. You should know that."

"Okay, true enough. Besides, I think your 'personal number' is even scarier than mine."

I shift uncomfortably in my seat. I have no doubt he's right. "So, what do you want to tackle first?"

Maxon sips his coffee and puts on his older-brother expression. "Before we dig into the presentation for the Stowes, we should talk."

Uh oh. Here comes a lecture.

"Lay it on me."

Because he will, regardless.

"We need ground rules, man. I'm all for giving you time with Britta so you'll have the opportunity to meet Jamie and maybe the three of you can finally be a family, but there are a few things you can't do."

"Like sexually harass Britta at work. I know."

"Exactly. I don't think she's the type to sue, but right now she enjoys her job. I'd like to keep it that way. I've done her enough favors over the last few years to keep her from quitting the instant she realizes you're officing here. But those favors will only go so far. If you push her too hard or too fast, she'll resign."

"You think so?" That doesn't sound like Britta. "She values loyalty more than almost everything."

Another reason getting her back will be an uphill battle. She probably thinks I left her to boink Maxon's ex, Tiffanii, the moment they broke up. Nothing could be further from the truth.

"She does but she already threatened to quit earlier this week."

"Really?" That shocks the hell out of me. "Why?"

"Britta thought I was grooming Keeley to be your next lover and she *hated* that idea."

I smile. Britta being jealous is good news. It means she still gives a shit what I do. "Ironic, isn't it?"

"That Keeley was really in your camp and you two decided to make her my downfall? Yeah. How did you never fuck her? God, I wanted to in the first ten seconds."

I shrug. "I needed her digging in my head and trying to straighten me out so badly that I just didn't see her sexually. It...wasn't there for us. How have you never touched Britta?"

Because I want to every single time I see her and I always have.

Maxon shakes his head. "She's like another sister to me. Besides, she's always belonged to you."

I'm eternally grateful for that, especially since I'm the one who stepped over the line. "Thanks. You could have been a real bastard and repaid me in kind after I slept with Tiffanii, but then I would have had to kill you." I'm half joking. Kind of. "I'm sorry about your ex."

He shrugs. "I was mad at first. Then I realized I was only pissed off because you went behind my back, not because I actually cared about her."

Thank God.

"The other thing we have to be clear about is this: the Stowe estate is going to be high-maintenance. We have to stay focused."

"Of course."

"Your dick leads you astray. You lose concentration about everything but sex. And Britta is your Kryptonite. You can't let her mess with your brain. Or we're screwed."

I want to argue...but he's got a valid point. Historically, I've been a fuckup when I let sex twist my cock into knots. It started with my one and only school play at fifteen. I got banned from the set for caring more about the contents of Sarah Morrison's bra than the background I was supposed to be painting. It continued when I interned for my dad in high school. I knew he was banging his secretary, AnnaBeth. She was happy to do me, too. I didn't say no. She was twenty-three, stacked, and loved giving blow jobs. One afternoon, I totally zoned out while she had her head between my legs, and I missed a phone call that my father wanted me to attend a meeting on his behalf. We lost the account. No one took me seriously after that. Dad fired me.

"I'm aware," I tell him. "The good news is, this isn't about me getting laid." Well, not exclusively. "I have to stay focused all the way around or I'll lose out to Makaio. What's up with him, by the way?"

"He's not right for her."

"No shit." I am.

"He's a banker. Nice enough guy." Maxon shrugs.

Maybe too nice. "Does he have any balls?"

"I haven't seen them. But he treats Britta decently and he seems good to Jamie. I can't say anything negative there."

Maxon is being fair. It's my problem that I hate it. "Does he love her?"

"I haven't seen them together lately, but my impression was that he has definite feelings for her."

I've been hoping she couldn't possibly return those feelings, but I have to find out what I'm truly up against. "Does she love him?"

"No."

His swift, emphatic answer fills me with dizzying relief. "You're sure?"

He nods, slowly at first but the gesture picks up speed and conviction. "This past Monday when she threatened to quit? That same day, she admitted…" He sighs. "God, you can't ever tell her I told you this."

"Sure," I promise. Anything to hear whatever secret of Britta's he's keeping.

"She admitted she still loves you and thinks about you every day."

A big smile spreads across my face. I want to fist pump, let out a whooping holler of joy, hug someone. The only person here is my brother, who would poke fun at me for all three. Instead, I opt for the truth. "Well, it's mutual."

"Now you just have to convince her."

"Yeah." I already know Britta won't make that easy.

Waiting for her to arrive is making me nervous. To pass time, I check my emails on my phone. Predictably, Keeley has sent me a YouTube link to a song. Because I really need more food for thought. It's called "Where I Stood" by Missy Higgins. I read my bestie's accompanying message:

This one's an emergency. Now that Britta is engaged, you need to give this a listen before you decide what to do. Reverse the genders. You'll understand.

Dreading this more than a little, I drag out my earbuds. If I don't give this hear this now, she'll just hound me. And okay, I'm curious.

After a single strum of the guitar, the vocalist jumps in. The first few lines nail me—utterly. I don't like what I've done. Or who I've become. I'm not even sure I know me anymore. But back then, something told me to run, that I should go, that Britta and I should end. Like a dumb ass, I listened.

As the song rolls toward the chorus, I'm amazed that Keeley continues to locate these dead-on tunes that make me think at the same time I want to throttle her for forcing me to feel.

The music changes, and the vocalist admits a terrible, painful truth…just like I should. I don't know who I am without Britta. And I certainly don't know if I could stand another hand upon her…but I left, and I'm no longer the man in her life, so I should.

I listen to the next lines roll around. They seize my breath. I tear the buds from my ear and kill the music. Britta might think that bastard who dares to stand where I stood would love her more than I could.

She's wrong.

A moment later, the front door creaks open. I turn to the sound, disappointed to find a slightly familiar guy with bad eighties hair striding toward us. I've never met him in person, but I know *of* him.

When he hits the threshold, he takes one look at me and shoots me a death glare.

"Morning," Maxon calls. "Come in and meet my brother. Griff, this is Rob."

I stick out my hand. He ignores it.

"You didn't follow through?" he asks Maxon obliquely instead.

On his ridiculous plan to use Keeley to distract me into fucking up a multimillion-dollar deal?

"No." I drop my hand. "News flash, dude. Keeley is my best friend. If anything, I sent her to seduce *your* boss, not the other way around. There was no way she was going to succeed in undermining me."

"What he said," my brother backs me up. "So we've decided to do the Stowe deal together. Are you really going to quit over that?"

He must have threatened to at some point. I wince.

"You stupid motherfucker," Rob mutters. "You're going to split the money and glory without a fight?"

This guy sounds like a kinder, gentler version of my father. The garter snake when compared to the rattler, my dad. But at the end of the day, they're both still snakes.

"Yeah. And if everything goes well, we'll merge firms and go into business together again," Maxon says. "There will be plenty of work for everyone. I'd love it if you stayed."

Rob's face says he could give a shit about the motivational speech. I'm not a fan of the guy's attitude, but if my brother wants him here, I'll try.

"I'm not going to cause trouble," I swear. "You're my brother's marketing guy, right? You do a hell of a job. Don't leave because of me."

"I'm against this." He ignores me and tsks at Maxon. "Griff fucked you over once. What's to stop him from doing it again?"

Ouch. That's a hard blow…but not an unfair one. "I've learned since then."

"We've talked, and I believe him," Maxon insists. "He's family. He's staying if he wants to."

I tend to rate pretty high on the macho scale, but I have to admit that my brother's words give me a warm fuzzy. "Thanks, man."

He nods in acknowledgement without looking my way. "Are you in, Rob? Or packing up your desk and pouting your way out the door?"

The other man hems and haws, shaking his head as if he's trying to reconcile himself to something he really doesn't want. "Son of a bitch… Do we need to go over the presentation before the call?"

"That's next on our agenda," my brother assures as he gestures to the other chair in his office, glancing at the clock on the wall. "Have you talked to Britta this morning? She's not usually late."

Rob shakes his head. "No."

I frown Maxon's way. Britta is always punctual. Worry nips at my gut.

"She'll be here," my brother insists. His phone dings two seconds later, and he plucks the device from his pocket. "She says she just dropped Jamie off at daycare and she has to swing by to see Mr. Kāle, then she'll be here."

"Who?" Rob asks.

"Makaio's father?" I raise a brow at Maxon.

"I guess so." He sounds as confused as I am.

"Why would she see him on the morning you have the biggest presentation of your career?"

"*Our* career. I can't think of a reason." Now he sounds as troubled as I am.

I rake a hand through my hair. "Shit."

"It's probably nothing. Let's start rehearsing the presentation. We'll figure out what she's up to later."

You can bet on that.

After a quick run-through, we hammer out a few issues. I give input based on my conversation with the Stowe heirs yesterday, and Maxon looks grateful for the insight. We're done prepping about forty-five minutes before show time.

Which leaves me to stare at the clock.

I have a good feeling about this pitch. The Stowes will be thrilled. We'll get the listing, sell this mansion that once belonged to the Vermont syrup-maker's widow, and Maxon and I will start doing great things together again.

I'm hoping the future looks even half as bright for Britta and me.

As I pace in worry at how slowly the hands are moving on the clock, I see Rob head to the restroom. Maxon takes a phone call from what sounds like another client. I leave his office and pace the main area, hovering around what's obviously Britta's desk. It must be. Rob's is cluttered with empty soda cans and Snickers wrappers with a few empty bags of Cheetos.

Britta is too meticulous for her workspace to resemble a dumpster. And when I peek at the surface, I hit the jackpot. She has framed pictures of all sizes of Jamie. My heart stops. It's like a visual history of his young life.

The first pic that catches my eye is of Jamie asleep and swaddled in a gauzy blue blanket like a papoose in a wicker basket with sprigs of greenery all around. He looks weeks old at most. I see a picture of him on his first birthday, grinning at a chocolate cake covered in frosting soccer balls, half of which is smeared across his face. There's a photo of him and Maxon at the beach, and another of him and Britta in a go-cart. I spot a still of him and Makaio at the library, solemnly reading a book together. At that, I grit my teeth.

On the cubicle's left wall, she's tacked up more recent pictures—Jamie waving good-bye as he walks into daycare, him playing beside another boy with some Lincoln Logs, my son running across the backyard at Britta's house with a big grin. He's cute, yeah. But the glimpses of everything I've missed and can never experience for myself wrench at my goddamn heart.

A glance toward the far side of her keyboard reveals another photo, this one obviously taken in the hospital when he was born. Britta sitting up in bed looking pale and exhausted but more beautiful than I've ever seen as she glances down at infant Jamie with naked love all over her face, one arm supporting his little body, the other stroking his downy head.

I would give anything to have been there the day my son made his way into the world so I could hold him, protect him. Tell him I love him. I wish I'd been there to give Britta the same devotion, that she'd been wearing my ring, that we'd gone home as a family. I'm shocked to feel tears sting my eyes.

Then I hear the creak of the door behind me and whirl around.

Britta.

She's wearing a black pencil skirt that hugs her body and a tuxedo-style blouse, white with black cuffs and collar. The black-and-white peep-toe heels complete the look. She's accented with red—purse, belt, lips.

The urge to fuck her is blinding and instant. Her chilly expression as she approaches me vows we won't be having sex soon. If she has anything to say about it, not until hell has frozen over for good.

Carrying a stack of magazines, she proceeds to her desk.

"Good morning," I say.

She nods stiffly and tosses down both her purse and the magazines.

They are all bridal publications. Dresses and flowers, smiling beauties and lace, updos and bows. Every edition seems focused on summer weddings. My heart stops. My sister, Harlow, has taken over a year to plan hers. I thought I'd have more time.

"When's the wedding?" I ask.

"We haven't set a date. Could you excuse me? You're standing in front of my chair."

I take one step to the side. "I was just looking at your pictures of Jamie."

"I'd rather you didn't," she says as she sits at her desk and proceeds to ignore me, tucking away her purse, spreading out her magazines, and turning on her computer. Then she tunes me out.

She's definitely withdrawn this morning. Dark circles under her eyes tell me she hasn't slept much. That makes two of us. Despite the fuck-off vibe she's giving me, I catch Britta sending me a sidelong stare when she thinks I'm not looking.

"Too bad, angel," I murmur the endearment I once called her for her ears alone. "I made myself clear last night. I know you heard me."

With a press of her sin-inspiring lips, she turns to me. "Can you please think of someone besides yourself this once? Consider your son, the upheaval you'll create in his life. He's too young to understand. He's too impressionable to—"

"I didn't demand that he call me Daddy right now. I said I'd like the opportunity to be a part of his life, whatever you and I can work out like rational adults." I settle closer, brace my forearm across the back of her chair, and bend close to her ear, trying to ignore the sultry jasmine scent that wafts up and stiffens my cock. "I think the bigger problem is you. Jamie doesn't know a reason to hate me. But you do."

That finally has her gaze darting up to mine as she rolls her chair sideways, a good foot away from me. Our eyes meet. *Zing.* I know she feels it, too. There's no way she doesn't.

Britta's face closes up as she jerks her gaze back to her scarred wooden desk. Does she think that will somehow make me go away?

"You don't affect me one way or the other. I'm protecting my son because I know you too well to believe you'll stay for long. Then I'll be left to pick up the pieces—again—when you decide to ditch all your responsibilities and chase your next piece of ass."

"Let's get one thing straight right now," I growl. "I left because I thought you'd elected to help Maxon betray me with the estate for that obscure prince. Our breakup had *nothing* to do with another woman."

She rolls her eyes. "So you just happened to decide to move Tiffanii in with you the day after our breakup because she was merely a good friend? And you never had sex with her?"

It's a trap question. I'm damned if I tell the truth and damned if I don't. "You really want to do this now?"

"No." Britta closes up. "I don't want to do this at all. What you did with your brother's ex doesn't matter to me anymore."

Liar. I love Britta, and it's hurting me to know she's been with at least one other guy. I was supposed to be her first, her only.

I have to live with the regret of fucking that up, too.

"Tiffanii meant nothing to me." As soon as the words are out of my mouth, I realize they're so lame they're counterproductive.

"At the time, she seemed to mean more to you than me, so—"

"No." I spin her chair to face me and brace my hands on the arms, caging her in her seat. "Never. She told me a lot of lies, and I was in a bad place then, so I was stupid enough to believe them."

"And then she just happened to fall into your bed, onto your penis, with a camera nearby. That's one set of pictures I would have liked better if they'd been blurry. But gee, thanks for sending them over and proving once and for all what an asshole you are."

I hear the words she's speaking, but I can't process them. "Pictures?"

She huffs and stands, pushing me a safe distance away. "Seriously? Stop. I'm talking about the shots of the two of you in bed that you sent your brother via email shortly after we split up. You *knew* I'd see that message first." With a shake of her head, she really looks at me. "If you wanted to make sure I was going to fuck off, you waking up and making love to me, then packing to leave me while I was in the shower more than did it. I stood there dripping and naked in front of you while you called me a backstabbing bitch and walked out. I didn't need pictures of you and Tiffanii in coital bliss or whatever to prove I meant nothing to you."

I still have no idea what she's talking about.

"I didn't take naked pictures with Tiffanii." If I was going to take sexy snapshots with someone, it sure as hell wouldn't be her.

"I saw them. They came from your email address. How do you—" Britta stops herself and shakes her head. "You know what? Never mind. Old news. Water under the bridge. A waste of my time. Like you."

When she tries to walk away, I grab her wrist. I didn't want to do the Tiffanii thing first, but clearly Britta needs me to. "Here's what went down: That morning, while you were in the shower, I found out about Maxon's deal. Since you were his assistant, I assumed you were involved, too. I should have asked. I should have talked to you. But I was furious and not thinking straight, so I didn't demand answers. I just packed, I said a lot of things I wish I could take back, and I left. Tiffanii hunted me down a few hours later to tell me that Maxon had cheated on her and—"

"Try the other way around." Britta scoffs.

"I know." That doesn't surprise me—now.

She tilts her head, suspicion all over her face. "Of course you do. She was cheating with *you*."

"What? No. Fuck no! Listen. To me, she was just my brother's pain-in-the-ass girlfriend. The day I moved out, she came crying to me that she was pregnant, and when she told Maxon, he threw her out and changed the locks. She needed a place to stay until she got back on her feet. I found a crash-by-the-week motel with two bedrooms. She said she'd help with rent until we could each find a place of our own. I spent the first three days pushing down my anger at everything that had gone wrong and establishing my own business while figuring out how to go on without you. I spent the next three days blindingly drunk. I have no idea what happened." That whole chunk of time is simply gone.

"Drunk? More likely in a sex haze." She pinches her lips, looks away. "She must have been damn good."

I'm happy to see firsthand the proof that Britta is no more over me than I've moved on from her. But I can't let her whacked-out assumptions persist. Time to set the record straight. I hope Britta believes me someday.

For now, I suspect she'll find the truth hard to swallow.

I grab her by the shoulders and drag her closer until I see her eyes widen and her soft lips part with a little gasp. Jesus, I want to kiss her so badly, back her onto her desk, lift her skirt, and make her mine again.

I can't, which makes me growl and grit my teeth. "I didn't consciously sleep with that woman for another two months. I only did it because I was so angry." At everything and everyone. At life. "The minute I did, I knew it was a fucking mistake. It never happened again."

"You must think I'm stupid. Maxon told me about the Bora Bora thing."

"I didn't plan to take Tiffanii on a romantic vacation. We both need-ed some time away. As a flight attendant, she could get us on a plane for free. I knew the manager of a small resort willing to rent us a villa for cheap after someone cancelled last minute. So Tiff and I decided to get some R and R as platonic friends. I had no reason to bail until I discov-ered her fucking some random guy on my sofa the afternoon before our departure. Then I grilled her until she admitted she'd never actually been pregnant. She'd only scammed me to get back at Maxon."

Britta doesn't say anything for a long time, just searches my face. She's not sure whether to believe me. I see the pain in her expression, and I know I put it there. I want to kick myself again.

My fingers bite harder into her. "I swear it's true."

"Griff," my brother warns from across the office.

A glance around the room tells me he's staring. So is Rob.

I harassed her in the office. I also made a scene. Fuck.

"Let me go," she demands softly.

"I'm sorry." Slowly, I peel my fingers off of her. "But I'm telling you, I never touched Tiffanii when you and I were together. And I never had a single romantic feeling for her. I made one terrible mistake with her. I've regretted it since."

She looks skeptical. "Then how do you explain the pictures of you two in bed I received six days after our breakup? On your birthday, by the way."

"After that hellacious three-day bender, I woke up naked in my bed with an epic hangover and no recollection of life for seventy-two hours. She had free run of the motel room, so she had access to my camera, my computer… I didn't send you any pictures." I try to stare that truth into her. "I would never have done that to my brother or to you. She must have taken your letter about Jamie, too. I swear to God if I had received it I would have come back."

Britta drags in a shaky breath and crosses her arms over her chest. "It doesn't matter now. Tiffanii might have been the first woman after me." She scoffs. "Or not. But she was hardly the last. The truth is, I don't need you in my life. Neither does Jamie. Leave us alone."

"I won't," I vow softly and force myself to take a giant step back. "But I'll give you some space for now."

She needs to think about everything I've laid bare. I know from experience that being up in Britta's face when she's upset will only make her shut down.

I look at the clock on the wall. "We only have a few minutes before the Stowe call. Do you need anything? Did you eat?"

She's always been notoriously bad about forgetting breakfast.

"I'm fine." Britta tries to brush past me and head for the conference room.

I step in front of her. "Did you eat?"

"I had an errand to run. I'll get some breakfast after the call."

"No." I march into Maxon's office and rifle through my briefcase, fishing out a spare protein bar, then barrel toward her again. "Eat now."

Since this topic isn't open to debate, I head to the little coffee bar situated at the back of the room and make her a cup of tea. Black and weak with a hint of sugar, the way she's always liked it. When I hand it to her, she blinks at me.

"You remembered?"

"I'll never forget."

"Don't do this. It's over, Griff," she whispers, then gives me a wide berth as she heads to the conference room.

I follow her, muttering "like hell" under my breath.

CHAPTER THREE

As NOON APPROACHES, IT'S ANOTHER gorgeous day in paradise. The call with the syrup heirs went well. Maxon and I teaming up surprised George and Vivienne at first, but by the end of the pitch, they saw the benefit.

They want to confer over the weekend, and I'm not surprised. It's way past quitting time on a Friday night in Vermont. They've recently lost their mother, to whom they seemed close. Most people are. Me? I'll do almost anything to avoid the viper who gave birth to me. But the Stowes are grieving and need extra time to think their decision through.

It's cool. I have a good feeling business will work out in the end.

Maxon stands and stretches, smiling big, before he holds out a hand to me. "Good job."

I shake it. "We always made a good team."

Even Rob looks reluctantly impressed. "I'd heard you two together were killer, but damn. You played off one another, had all the answers. It was like a well-oiled machine."

Maxon's marketing guy sounds way more enthusiastic about me being here than he did three hours ago.

"Thanks." I look my brother's way. I can tell it felt good to him, too, being together and doing a deal… We fell back into the old rhythms that kept us on top year after year. I have no doubt we could dominate again.

"We're going to make so much money." Rob now sounds downright gleeful.

Maxon laughs at the guy. "Get the fuck out of here."

Rob glances at the time at his phone. "I'm going to Dairy Queen for lunch. Want something?"

My brother shakes his head. "I'm good."

I shudder at the suggestion. Keeley and her healthy food have rubbed off on me over the last couple of years, and now I rarely want anything else. "Thanks, anyway."

With a wave, Rob exits the building. I see Britta at her desk. She's on the phone, jotting notes, nodding and listening intently. Client call. At her left, a bridal magazine sits open. Tape flags in various colors lay strewn around the glossy pages in a semicircle.

"Got another lunch suggestion?" Maxon asks.

"Keeley introduced me to a little place for vegan and raw foods…"

He swallows as if he might be sick. "And she likes it?"

"Yeah. We actually go there a lot."

He blows out a breath as if he's worried he's taking his life into his own hands. "What do you think?"

"It's good."

I see the moment my brother decides he wants to be close to Keeley if he can't be with her. "All right. She said anything new?"

I shake my head. "Her return ticket is scheduled to bring her home on the sixteenth. I won't know what she's thinking for sure until she tells me whether or not she's gotten on the plane. Try to be patient."

"Maybe I should go to Phoenix."

"We've been over this." I shake my head. "Don't do it." I look over my shoulder at Britta again. "It's like me rushing that one. A stupid waste of effort and breath. Trust me when I tell you it's no easier when the woman you want is right in front of you and you can't have her."

"I see your point." Maxon drops his voice. "Don't confront Britta in the office again."

"Sorry. She wanted to talk about the Tiffanii thing." I feel more than vaguely ashamed. "I told Britta the truth, that I voluntarily slept with that woman just once, but she—"

"Seriously?" Maxon looks stunned. "That's it?"

"Yeah." I fill him in. "I really don't know how you lived with her for two years."

"Now that I know what the hell having an emotional connection with a woman means, I don't either." He grabs his car keys and phone, shoving the latter in his pocket. "Hey, Britta. We're going to lunch. Want anything?"

She looks up at us, her stare seeming to pass me over as if I don't exist. "I brought something. I'll eat here. I've got a few phone calls to make."

As we walk toward the door, I see what's up on her screen. HAWAI-IAN TIME WEDDINGS.

Every reminder that she intends to give the rest of her life to another man twists my gut.

Maxon nudges my shoulder. "Let's go."

I really don't want to, but we've already hashed this. I can't push her now. I've given her the Tiffanii information she wanted. She'll have to decide if she's going to believe—or forgive—me.

My brother and I have a productive lunch and start to talk about other business we've got in the hopper, possible ways we might consolidate it in the future. Maxon has some good suggestions for me. I give him possible insight into things he's working on.

It's like old times…but better.

In the past, we bonded over our mutual hate of our philandering father. But when we didn't have the monster around to give us a common enemy, I turned on Maxon. He turned right back. So this is the more mature version of us. It's nice.

On our way back, I suggest we swing by my business digs so I can move my stuff into my former office, on the other side of the wall from Maxon's. While I'm grabbing essentials, he calls Britta. Even through the window, I can tell the discussion is heated.

When I emerge again with a box of my belongings and a spare brief-case of papers, I toss it in the back of his car. "How did she take the news that I need her help cleaning out the storage room?"

He looks grim. "She'll do it."

But not happily. It's her job, and Maxon is her boss, so she grudgingly agreed.

"That wasn't the question," I point out.

"Let's just say that if you don't act like a pushy prick, we *might* be okay."

Right. How do I not behave like myself?

When we hit our shared office, Rob is at his desk with some noise-cancelling headphones, whipping up something on Photoshop. Maxon gives me a head bob toward Britta, who's in the storage room, loading knickknacks from the table into boxes. Holy fuck, now that I'm really looking at the place, it's obvious my brother has become a pack rat and shoved everything in this room since I left. If the mountain of crap fell on her, she'd be buried alive.

I jog in. "Hey. I'm here."

"Sorry your throne isn't ready yet, your highness." She doesn't even look at me.

I clench my jaw and remember restraint. I've earned her anger. Now I have to be patient enough to let it burn out. "I don't expect you to clean this place alone. It's going to be my office, so I'm perfectly happy to do the heavy lifting. Anything ready for me to carry out yet?"

Britta pauses. Apparently she can't think of a snappy comeback for that. "That box over there."

When she points, I cross the room and grab it, then haul it past her and out the door. "Any ideas where to store this?"

Since most of the box's contents are day-to-day items, she suggests we shove them in the little cabinet under the coffee bar so they're within quick reach.

After that, we start tackling the stuff choking the rest of the room. I can use the long, mango-wood table carved with traditional Hawaiian elements and one of the desk chairs on wheels. But around the perimeter, binder after binder of Maxon's files, stuffed into a half dozen mismatched floor-to-ceiling bookcases, line the walls.

This stuff will take all afternoon to pack.

"Hasn't my brother ever heard of scanning a document and storing the paper off-site?"

Britta actually suppresses a smile. That's the first time since laying eyes on her again I've managed to coax a reaction from the woman that's not hostile. I wonder if she's thought about our earlier conversation. Does she believe me at all?

"I mention that to Maxon all the time. But no. Every six months, we're buying another bookcase and a pile of binders, then pulling an all-nighter to file everything so we can find it again when hell freezes over. I mean, when someone requests documentation," she says tongue in cheek.

I chuckle. Britta always had a dry, sarcastic sense of humor. It's one of the things I love about her.

"Well, now it has to go somewhere else," I point out.

"Do you know anyone who could help us scan and store it quickly? This place has become a cave since we covered the windows with all these shelves. I'd love it if we Craigslisted these units and never saw them again."

"I do know someone. Consider the document storage done. I'll talk Maxon into selling the bookcases, too."

"Thanks."

There's a long pause. We share a lingering look. A flush crawls up her cheeks.

Then, as if she remembers I'm the villain in this story, she looks away, all business again, and shuts me out.

Fuck. "Do we need more boxes?"

"No. You can go. I'll get the paperwork out of here. I don't need your help."

I saunter closer. She has no escape since I'm standing between her and the door, and a bookcase looms at her back. I won't touch her. But I'll make it clear that she can't brush me aside professionally. Personally? Well, she should know that, too. I've put her on notice.

"You're going to get it. We work together now. You're not lugging boxes that, all together, weigh hundreds of pounds. I'll help you pack. I know you like things done methodically, and that's not my strong suit. So you direct. I'll take action."

She glances at me, then casts her gaze to the shelves and the reams of paperwork closing off the shadowy room. "Since it will go faster that way, fine. But don't talk to me."

The last thing Britta and I need between us is silence. "Can we just take a deep breath? I'm sorry if I upset you this morning. Hell, if it helps, I'll apologize again for everything I did when we split up. I wish I could take it all back. Whether it sounds farfetched or not, what I said earlier is true. Every word."

She grabs the nearest flat bit of cardboard and assembles it into a file box, taping the bottom until it's sturdy. "It really doesn't matter."

"It does. And you're fully aware of that. Let's stop pretending. Whatever you want to know about everything I've thought or done before, during, or after us, just ask. I'm an open book. I will lay it all out, no matter what."

She rears back. "Why would you do that?"

Because I love you seems like the wrong thing to say when she's wearing a suspicious expression and some other guy's ring. "If I want to be in Jamie's life, you have to trust me. You have to know I'll be truthful, that I'll be here, and that I'm not leaving. So if spilling whatever details you need to hear will convince you I'm serious and help you believe in me again, I'm ready."

I know she won't ask about my sex life today or even tomorrow. But it's coming. If we're ever going to reconcile, she'll demand to know. And I have to be ready for the fact it will be ugly. Then I'll have to convince her—somehow—that no one before or since has or ever will mean more to me.

Tall order.

Britta doesn't say anything as she mounts a step stool to reach the top shelf of the first bookcase. The labels on the spines of the binders indicate these are the first of the files Maxon stacked up after I left. She thinks she's climbing level with the top shelf on those slender stilettos?

While I admit the view of her gently curved ass is really fantastic, hell no.

"Let me get those."

As I reach around her and grip the first binder in chronological order, I brush against her body. At the contact, she teeters. Automatically, I steady her with my hand to the small of her back. At the touch, fire blazes through me, zipping down from my chest and up from my toes to settle in at my cock and start a vicious throbbing.

Britta whirls around with a scowl, taking me in with one glance. She sees the bulge behind my zipper. I've got no way to hide it. I'm not even going to try.

She pins me with an accusing glare. "Don't touch me."

Because sexual harassment suit. Right.

When I'm sure she has her balance again, I raise my hands in a placating gesture. "All right."

"Don't even think about me."

That's never going to happen, and I won't make any promise I guarantee I'll break in the first thirty seconds. "Come down from there. I'll hand you the binders on the top. You can put them in the box in whatever order you want. No touching."

But fuck, how I want to. The urge to peel off that button-down blouse and see if the bra she's wearing underneath is really as creamy and lacy as this light suggests is ripping my restraint to shreds. I want to see her body. I ache to feel her skin against mine again.

No one has ever been quite as intoxicating—or as soothing—as Britta. It took me three years and an embarrassing number of hookups to realize that no one ever will.

She looks warily between the top shelf, still a tippy-toe reach away, and the box on the table. Then she huffs. "All right."

"I just don't want to see you hurt," I tell her. "And this is one of the few times being six three comes in handy. Folding myself in your old compact definitely wasn't."

She doesn't smile at my lame attempt at humor. Instead, she looks over her shoulder as she descends the footstool. It goes against my grain not to help her. To be clear, I'd also help a two-year-old or your grandma, as well. I particularly don't want Britta stumbling in those crazy-sexy heels, so I stand nearby until she's on solid ground. Then I fold up the stool and hand her binders, one after the other, in a slow procession.

This is my time alone with her. I need to make the most of it.

"I saw the picture of you and Jamie in the hospital when he was born. You looked really happy. And beautiful."

She pauses, one hand poised over the top of a box. I see her thinking. Maybe she's finally deciding to share something with me about my son. Or maybe she's merely willing to tell me what I want to know so I'll fuck off sooner.

"The first time I held him, I was amazed," she murmurs. "That little round face, the eyes he couldn't quite open, and the red cheeks. Your chin. But I... There are just no words to describe the moment he was put into my arms. I felt a love unlike anything I ever imagined." She goes quiet for a moment. "I appreciate you making him possible."

I wish she wouldn't thank me. I had the easy part.

I also wish I'd been there, that I knew what it was like to hold him. "Tell me about his birth. Please."

Though Britta doesn't want me closer to Jamie, I'm hoping she'll cave to my sincerity and share the details.

She lets out a long breath. "He was born July tenth at three twenty-four a.m. It was a Thursday." She shakes her head. "There are parts of the twenty-four hours before that I remember so clearly and others things I can't recall at all. I went to work Wednesday morning. I'd been up for days cleaning, washing, organizing. Nesting, my doctor called it. About lunchtime, I told Maxon I thought I was having contractions again. He didn't pay me much attention. I ruined his fourth of July with false labor. I think he'd found a hot tourist who liked Grey Goose almost as much as he does. But he left her to take me to the hospital for nothing. So the day before Jamie was born, Maxon wasn't keen on blowing off the deal he was trying to close for another nonevent."

I'm a little irritated with my brother for not taking Jamie's birth more seriously—until I remember that he was there, I wasn't, and I should be fucking grateful he took care of them in my stead.

"You insisted on going to the hospital anyway?"

"Yeah, about four thirty. Labor seemed to be progressing." She gives me a wry grin. "And for whatever reason, the minute I arrived, my contractions stopped. My doctor said it's common, but I'd dilated enough that they wanted to keep me for a few hours. Maxon and I played some cards. I called my mom so she could try to move her flight up. Jamie was a week early." Her grin becomes a full-fledged smile at the memory. "He was so eager to be a part of the world. The doctor broke my water at a little after one a.m., which is when everything got real. And painful. Then, after a lot of pushing and sweating and cursing, Jamie came. He's been surprising me ever since. You know the rest."

No, I know facts. Britta added to my library of knowledge about our son. But I want more. I want to know what it was like to be there, holding her hand, watching him take his first breath, let out his first cry. To hold him myself when he first opened his eyes. To greet the child Britta and I made in love together.

I missed everything.

I shove down how much that chokes me up. "What did he weigh?"

"He was a big boy. Nine pounds, four ounces. Twenty-two inches long." The fond curl of her mouth makes my heart swell. It's so obvious she loves Jamie with every bit of her heart. "The nurses called him their little linebacker. He came out with a full head of dark hair and an appetite that wouldn't quit." Then she seems to remember herself—and her animosity. "That's it. I was there for thirty-six hours. Maxon took me home. My mother flew in from Chicago for a week. And we've been fine since."

But not happy? I don't ask because if she's less than sublimely thrilled with her life, she won't admit that to me. "Thanks. I know it must seem awkward, telling me about my own son's birth years after the fact. Believe me, no one regrets my absence that day more than me."

She pauses, as if she can't quite decide whether to open this conversational can of worms. "I called. I left messages. I even went by your office, but Sheila told me you were 'sick' and couldn't see me and…" She waves her words away. "It's done. It's over."

Despite her attempt to convince me the past doesn't matter, I hear pain in Britta's voice.

"I was irrational and angry. I went out of my way to avoid seeing you or hearing about you. And I can never tell you how sorry I am." At the time, I couldn't stand the thought that the one person I'd invited into my life—into my heart—had sold me out for her own gain.

After being taken for a ride a decade ago, I could barely handle the thought that I'd somehow allowed it to happen again.

She gives me a slight nod of acknowledgement but doesn't say a word. Obviously, she thinks that's the end of the conversation.

It's not. "I intend to be a good, steady father to Jamie. I know I didn't learn much about that from my own…but I'm beginning to understand wanting what's best for your kid. I know that's what you want, too."

"Jamie's needs always come first, Griff. They have to."

During our conversation, she's filled up a pair of file-organizing boxes with binders. She pauses to close them up and slap a label on each. I stack them on the far edge of the table so they can be scanned and stored off-site later.

Britta thinks I'm too busy moving the box to pay attention to her straightening her skirt with a little wriggle that has my cock hardening again beneath my fly. But I'm never going to be too busy to see her, watch her, catalog her every movement.

We continue organizing the room, but now it's quiet. That bothers me. So does the seeming lack of air conditioning back here.

But that gives me an idea…

She's so determined to insist that our relationship is dead. Since Maxon gave me the inside scoop, I know she still loves me. Once upon a time, Britta couldn't resist gawking at me. I'm still attracted as hell to her. I'm dying to know if it still works both ways.

Yeah, maybe I should leave it alone, especially since we're in the office and she's just started to defrost. But no guts, no glory, right?

I toe off my loafers and peel off my socks.

"Um…what are you doing?" she challenges.

"It's stuffy in here. Aren't you hot?"

As I unbutton the cuffs of my dress shirt, Britta double-checks to make sure her blouse is still fastened at the neck and tucked into her skirt, covering every inch of skin possible.

"I'm actually comfortable."

Bullshit. I see a sheen of perspiration at her hairline.

Good. I'm about to turn up the heat. "Oh, well… Maxon has to be the only guy on the island who still loves the suit-and-tie thing. Dumb ass. I'll be ready to carry on here in a second."

With a hint of a smile and a raised brow, I tackle the buttons down the front of my shirt, unfastening one after the other—never taking my eyes off her.

By the time it's open to mid-chest, Britta isn't breathing. She's frozen. Staring. Watching my fingers move lower and lower…

Slowly, I yank the tails from my dress pants and pull the shirt open wide.

She snaps out of her haze. "Stop! I have a fan."

Without waiting for my reply, she darts out of the office. I lean around the corner and watch her hightail her gorgeous ass to the coffee bar. I grin as she plucks up the device gathering dust. Nothing about her reaction says unaffected. She might tell herself she hates me…but she still wants me.

A moment later, Britta dashes back into the room, holding the little oscillating fan by the neck. But I'm already naked from the waist up, smiling her way.

She stops. Her blue eyes go wide. If her stare were a physical touch, she would be caressing me everywhere.

I saunter her way and take the fan from her grip. Our fingers brush. A fine tremor works through her body. I'm so damn heartened by her response. She gets to me the same way.

"Thanks." I nod, in no hurry to put distance between us. "I'll get this going."

"Put your shirt back on." Her voice sounds slightly pleading.

I like it.

"Why?" I play dumb. "No one will see me back here except you, and you've seen it all."

"But...I-I don't think—" She sighs in frustration. "This is an office, not a strip club."

I shrug. "I wasn't dressed for physical labor, so I'm adapting. My chest isn't bothering you, right?"

Her stare is still glued to my torso. I'm damn grateful my gym habit and my love of surfing have kept me lean, muscled, and tan.

"Why would it?" She sounds a bit like she's swallowed her tongue.

"Good." I'm working hard not to laugh. "Where's the nearest electrical outlet?"

When she points weakly, I bend to plug the little device in. I can't tell for sure, but I suspect she's staring at my ass.

As I press the button to begin the soft breeze, she shakes her head suddenly as if to clear it. "I'll, um...empty out these bottom shelves. Can you tape me up a few more boxes?"

Is that how she's going to avoid looking at me? Escape the chemistry sweltering between us again?

Good luck with that, angel.

Britta bends to the bottom of the first bookshelf, all but perching her butt on the backs of her heels as she reaches forward for the first volume on the left. The back slit in her skirt parts, revealing the soft skin between her knees and inner thighs. Another inch or two and I'd know the color of her silky panties.

Despite the fan, the temperature in here doesn't feel cooler at all.

My gut clenches. My cock jumps. I'd accuse her of playing my game if I thought she was intentionally trying to tease me. I'm frustrated as hell, but I know I can't tug her into my arms and kiss her—or any of the countless other things I'm fantasizing about. For now, I simply have to console myself with the knowledge that she's aware of me again, not just as Jamie's dad but as a man. Over time, I'll rebuild our rapport and wear her down until she's mine again.

I slap together a few boxes so I'm ready as she hands me more binders from the first bookcase. Finally, we finish emptying the sucker.

After securing that box shut, I stack it with the others. "One shelving unit down. Five to go."

Britta glances my way, trying not to look panicked. I can almost hear her thoughts. *I have to spend hours trapped in a small room with my half-naked ex I have the hots for?* Well, she didn't think the last part, I'm sure. But it's true.

"Maybe we should call it a day," she suggests.

I shake my head. "I have to be productive first thing tomorrow, so we've got to finish now. In fact, we might have to stay late. Want to order in some Chinese tonight?"

She looks horrified by the notion. "No. I'm not a naive twenty-year-old anymore. That trick won't work on me."

What? "That was never a trick, and we genuinely have work to do before I can set up an office in here."

"I have to pick Jamie up by five thirty."

"Oh. Right." Feeling stupid for not realizing that, I lift the storage unit and maneuver it to the corner so it's not impeding windows or the door.

I feel Britta watching every flex of my shoulders, arms, and back. "Yeah. H-he has a…um, playdate. At the park, ah… A boy. F-from our…"

She can't finish a sentence. Since my back is to her and she can't tell…well, I admit I'm preening.

Once I release the bookcase, I turn to her and brush my hands together. "Neighborhood?"

She swallows and jerks her gaze away. "Yeah. H-he's been looking forward to this. I can't miss it."

A million thoughts circle my brain, but the most cogent is that I want to see Jamie. And this may be my opportunity.

I learned to be a ruthless bastard from the best—my father is an absolute artisan at getting his way. So I consider how I can coax more information out of her about where they'll be and use the knowledge to my advantage. "Won't it be dark by the time you get back to Kihei? It'll be tough to play outdoors. Unless the facility is inside?"

"No. The park is well lit. I'll watch him." She frowns. "If you're thinking that's dangerous, I'd never let anything happen to him."

"Hey, I have no doubt you're a great mom." I'm in no way accusing her of endangering or neglecting him. Hell, that's the last thing I'm thinking.

"I really have tried."

"Some years might separate us, angel. But I know you always give your all to the people you love."

Why the fuck couldn't I remember that when it counted most?

"I take good care of him, Griff. I always will."

"I'm sure." I brace my forearm across the top of an empty box and sidle closer. "Let me go with you tonight, meet Jamie. We don't have to tell him who I am yet. We can—"

She's already shaking her head. "He's not ready."

"*You're* not ready," I accuse, then bite back my frustration and a whole bunch of words I'll regret.

"It's been less than twenty-four hours since you crashed back into my life. I haven't had time to decide what's best for my son or figure out who you are now. I..." She frowns at me like she's grappling to cope. "I'm not convinced you're ready to be a father or that you wouldn't walk out again. Or try to take Jamie from me."

I shake my head. "You're his mother. He needs you."

"He does," she agrees. "But you should understand that trust, once broken, is never easy to mend."

Yes, of all people, I know that.

She turns away. I can't argue with her when she's right.

But that's not going to stop me.

CHAPTER FOUR

BRITTA SPENDS THE REST OF the afternoon trying to ignore me. I lay off teasing her because she obviously has a lot on her mind. Watching her eat me up with her hungry little stare was fun and informational. But I've given her a reminder of the crazy-strong pull between us. Now I have to focus on Jamie and finagling a way to meet him. Then I'll work on a future with his mother.

By four, we manage to clear out all the binders and box them up. Maxon only puts up a small fight when I tell him I've arranged for a document imaging and management company to haul the paperwork away in the morning. With his grudging consent, I also post the shelving on Craigslist and I'm not surprised to start getting inquiries within minutes.

As I'm organizing the long table like a desk, Maxon strolls in and shuts the door behind him. "Looking good. Wow, I'd forgotten how much light comes through these windows."

"Yeah, caveman. The chiseling on stone tablets is so two millennia ago."

"Ha ha." He sends me a sour glare. "When it comes to record keeping, I'm particular."

"Dude, you were one binder short of starring in an episode of *Hoarders*."

"At least I had my documentation at my fingertips and I didn't have to call someone else to look up a file."

"Which works out great…unless there's a fire or a flood."

Maxon doesn't have a comeback for that. "Thanks for your analysis, Chicken Little. Looks like you're all settled in. Would you rather have your own desk?"

"Eventually. There's no rush. This works for now."

"Except Britta might want her dining room table back. When we turned this into our 'war room' a couple of weeks ago, she let us borrow it."

I glance at her across the office. She's gathering her things at her desk, her profile tense. She's trying not to look my way, even though I'm wearing my shirt again…mostly.

"She didn't tell me it belonged to her." But the wheels in my head are already turning. She'll get her table back. In fact, I'll be more than happy to deliver it to her house myself.

My brother sends me a suspicious stare. "That smile scares me."

"What?" I ask as innocently as I'm capable of sounding. "I'm just thinking of ways to be helpful."

"And you have *no* other motive. Right…" Maxon grunts. "Did the time alone with her this afternoon help you two?"

I shrug. "I think. We'll see. Thanks for being there during Jamie's birth."

He nods. "I was happy to. And don't change the subject. What's the plan running around in your head? Don't insult me by saying you don't have one."

Britta turns off her computer and yanks one of her desk drawers open, retrieving her red purse. After gathering up her bridal magazines and tape flags, she approaches Rob and says something that makes him smile. Then she sends a wave in my brother's general direction and doesn't acknowledge me.

I look at my phone. It's five fifteen.

"Bye, angel," I yank the door open and call across the office to her.

She shuts the door behind her without replying.

Through the window, I watch her pull out of the lot in her white family sedan and onto the street. "Jamie has a playdate with a kid in their neighborhood. Tell me everything you know about where she might take him."

"You going to crash and see Jamie?"

Smart question. "I have to. Even if I don't get to meet him, the fact that I've never clapped eyes on my own son is killing me."

Maxon groans. "I know that sucks, but you've got to stop trying to make me a Judas."

"Think of it as completing your nephew's—and your brother's—family. I won't be able to share my life with them if I don't have your help, man."

He lets loose a sound that's somewhere between a scoff and a grunt. "You owe me so big, and I expect you to grovel to Keeley on my behalf so you can help complete your brother's family in return."

"Done." My last conversation with Keeley seemed as if her earlier leaning toward staying in Phoenix was beginning to lean back the other way. A few assurances that my brother is very seriously in love with her might help make up her mind.

Maxon smiles like he thinks he's won. I let him believe that. I love them both and would have done everything possible to make them happy anyway.

"You didn't hear this from me..." he mutters in low tones. "But Britta keeps a calendar of appointments in her desk and usually jots down addresses."

I clap my brother on the shoulder. "You're my hero."

It takes me less than two minutes of prowling through her workspace to find what I'm looking for. Rob is too wrapped up in whatever he's doing to care. Maxon pretends to look the other way. It's perfect.

With a dash back into my office, I sweep up my keys and phone, then nod in my brother's direction. "Talk to you later, man."

"Play nice," he calls to my retreating back.

I wave without committing to that. Maxon knows me well, so knows I'm not playing at all.

The Hawaiian sunshine is bright but waning as I fight the island's version of rush-hour traffic south. A glance at the song titles on the case Keeley left me warns me that I should avoid more musical selections designed to rip my guts out—at least for now. I don't need that messing with my head just before I see Jamie.

By six twenty, I reach the park not far from Britta's house and catch a glimpse of the playground. The sun has nearly set when I pull my Porsche into a spot on the far side of the lot, hiding between a big truck and a giant SUV.

After locking up, I hang out against the fence in the shade beneath a few palms. With a view of both the road and the parking area, I kick back.

Two minutes later, Britta pulls up. She hustles out of the car, slinging the handles of a woven beach bag over one shoulder, and shoves a giant bottle of water inside it. She's wearing tight black workout pants and a flowing shirt that matches her eyes. It's a V-neck with embroidery down the front and along the sides. It hugs her body and ends at her hips. And I can't stop staring.

Jesus... She is still the sexiest woman on the planet to me.

Finally, she opens the back door of her car and leans in. She must be unbuckling the car seat. I find myself tensing, holding my breath.

I'm going to lay eyes on my son.

She emerges from the back of the vehicle, holding the boy against her. He lays his mop of dark hair on her shoulder, body limp, eyes closed. I scan him up and down, wishing I was closer, that I could see him more clearly, hold him myself. From the bit I can discern, he's... I don't even have words. Beautiful. Amazing. Everything I didn't know I wanted.

My heart melts. Taking in this moment is like trying to absorb a shock, understand an illusion, and decipher a miracle all at once.

He's bigger than I thought a kid a few months shy of three would be. But I was a big kid, too. Tall and strapping, especially in adolescence. Blue flip-flops shield big feet that dangle beside Britta's thighs. They're obviously long, too, as are his legs and arms. The picture Maxon showed me the night we met up didn't reveal him wearing a cast, but Jamie has a blue one covering most of his left hand and forearm. I'll be sure to find out about that ASAP. He's also wearing blue shorts and a tan shirt with some print I can't discern at this distance.

She kisses Jamie's forehead and strokes his hair as she makes their way toward a nearby bench. On one side of the area is an empty playground. On the other is a vendor closing up shop after a day of selling sno-cones. At a distance, I follow a path along the far side of the lot, thankful for the shadow. Britta is too distracted to see me anyway as she sits on a bench perched outside the sandy area and waits, gently rocking our son.

I'm itching to interact with Jamie. I've known about him for twenty hours and I feel as if I should have met him at least nineteen ago. But if I push Britta, she'll get stubborn, like that time she refused to toss out the houseplant I inadvertently killed. She waited for me to take responsibility for the greenery, dig it up, and replace it. She asked me to take care of it more than once. I didn't have time. No, I didn't *make* time.

I took her for granted. A lot.

That truth smacks me between the eyes. With a curse under my breath, I examine my year with Britta through the lens of more mature eyes. Deep down, I knew I hadn't been great to her. But back then, I hadn't realized what a steaming asshole my dad is or that the way he treats people isn't something I should emulate if I want to keep others in my life. But I was raised to believe that I'd eventually live a life like him and the world would revolve around me.

And what a prick I was.

Jamie's birth aside, I think specifically about the times I didn't come through for Britta—the dinners I worked through, the birthday I nearly forgot, the Valentine's Day I half-assed because I didn't see myself as the romantic sort.

Where does that leave me now? Staring at my kid across a park and wishing I had the right to hug him tight and play with him just to see him smile while I hold Britta's hand and we laugh at his antics.

For now, I have to be satisfied with watching from afar. I feel like a stalker, but that doesn't matter. At least I've seen my son.

Behind me, I hear a car pulling into the lot. Britta turns toward the sound. I slouch behind a tree and watch a woman emerge from her minivan with a boy who's smaller than Jamie. Once he peels out of his car seat, his mother, who looks harried, has to grab his arm to prevent him from darting across the blacktop to reach the playground.

With a huff, the brunette picks up her son. Britta approaches, a still-sleepy Jamie in tow. At the edge of the sand, the women start chatting. I can't hear what they're saying, but the brunette ruffles my son's hair. The other boy hugs Britta's thigh, then seemingly ecstatic they have the playground to themselves, he runs to the slide. Suddenly, Jamie wriggles out of Britta's grip and dashes off after the little guy as if he wasn't dead-ass asleep three minutes ago.

As they reach the first rung of the ladder, the park's overhead lights turn on, illuminating the area with a megawatt LED glow. Suddenly, I can see every expression on my son's face—his smile and little white teeth, the small blade of a nose that will someday look more like mine. And my chin, square and prominent and stubborn.

It hits me that Jamie is the most amazing blend of me and Britta.

I hug the tree to stay upright as his giggle fills the evening while he stands at the top of the slide, pumping his little fists in the air like he's a champion. Normally, I'm a cynical bastard, but I can't stop the smile that creases my face. Britta barks something at him—probably a demand that he sit before he falls—and he scrambles to his butt and pushes off, gliding down the long, yellow slide with a howl of laughter.

I can't remember ever being as happy as my son seems right now. I'm so fucking grateful to Britta for giving him the childhood I never had.

His friend follows him to the ground before they chase each other around the sand. When they body slam onto nearby swings, the moms spring into action and sit them down properly before pushing them gently. Soon it's clear that Britta is holding Jamie back. He's trying to soar in the air, shouting "higher!"

He's a daredevil—something else he inherited from me.

I'm flabbergasted to see so much of myself in my son, given the fact we've never met. I'm also stunned by the incredible responsibility of being a parent. I'm sure I don't know the half of it, but I'm acutely aware that if I intend to be around the boy in the future, I'll influence him, whether I mean to or not. I want to show him only the best parts of me. I want to be the kind of father he can look up to, the kind I always wished for.

It may sound weird because Jamie is still a toddler, but I want my son to be proud of me.

I also better understand Britta's resistance to letting me meet my son. She doesn't know who I am today. She just remembers the guy who seduced her in the office, the jerk who fixated on fantasy football with my brother most of our one Christmas Day together, the asshole who didn't take her out for New Year's because I'd worked a crazy fucking week after tourists suddenly decided they wanted a Maui house right now and stayed glued to my side for twenty hours straight until they got one.

At the time, I'd never seen a man put his woman first. It sounds like a lousy excuse now, but that's the only reason I have for being such a douchebag to Britta. My dad wasn't faithful or nice for a day of his marriage to my mother, not that she's any saint. Probably the reason they're getting divorced. Maxon was a butt to Tiffanii the whole two years they were together. Though, in fairness, his attitude was probably a defense mechanism because she was a bitch to everyone. I thought being faithful to Britta meant I was a good guy. At the time, the important things—consideration, empathy, compromise—didn't register.

I'm grateful Keeley convinced me to become a better human being over the last few years. I'm not perfect. I have a lot of anger. Sometimes, I still slip into old patterns…but I'm trying. Now I have to convince Britta I'll be a model husband and father.

That's hard to do when she'll barely talk to me and refuses to let me interact with our child.

The moms watch their little boys play for the next twenty minutes. Then Jamie charges to the monkey bars and clambers up the three steps to reach the rung above his head. Despite his cast, he swings across with surprising speed and strength. The other boy follows as quickly as he can but has only made it halfway by the time Jamie has jumped down, run around, and is dangling from the first handhold again.

He's athletic, for sure. Like me, he's probably never met a ball he didn't like. Will he also hike, surf, scuba, kayak, and—I gulp—skydive? Okay, I haven't even officially met this kid and already I'm compelled to make sure he learns limits and safety...and tries exercising some sanity when it comes to sports. I never did and I had a lot of broken bones in my youth to show for it. Did some crazy stunt of his result in the cast he's wearing?

On the third trip across the monkey bars, the other kid rubs at his hands and seems to lose interest. Not Jamie. He darts over to the ladder for a fourth trek.

But instead of working lightning fast from one rung to the next again, he kicks a leg up and throws it over the top bar.

"Jamie!" Britta calls as she dumps her bottle of water in her bag and runs to him, worry carved into her face.

The little rascal ignores her and swings the other leg over the first handhold, then yanks himself up until he's sitting on top of the monkey bars—ten feet in the air.

My heart stutters.

"Come here!" She holds out her arms to him, jumping up to snag him down, but he's out of her reach. "This minute, young man."

Jamie gives her a stubborn shake of his head.

When Britta runs for the ladder to snatch him, he scrambles on hands and knees to the middle of the apparatus. The other mom lingers underneath him, awkwardly holding out her arms in case Jamie falls, but she's shorter than Britta. She's also a waif. I'm not convinced she could catch a falling hunk of boy.

Then my son stands, wobbling on two different bars, and holds out his arms like he's pretending he's got wings.

I'm not going to lie. My heart flat stops because I know what's coming next. He's my kid, and I did roughly the same thing when I wasn't much older.

Yeah, he's going to jump.

So I've got a fucking dilemma. Keep my expedition to the park a secret or save Jamie?

No contest.

I push away from the tree and take off, sprinting across the walkway, the patch of grass, then leap onto the sand itself. I skid to a stop under Jamie just as the boy bends his little legs and leaps off the monkey bars like he's Superman.

A split second later, he lands in my arms with a chest-thumping thud. He's breathing hard when he freezes and blinks in surprise.

I look at him. He looks back at me.

Even though my heart is pounding and I feel Britta's shock coming at me in waves, I'm savoring this moment because I'm finally holding my son.

God, I'm instantly in love.

"You okay, little man?" I ask him.

It's almost painful to see how much he looks like me. Pictures were one thing, but our resemblance is more pronounced in person. He has his mother's eyes. He's also got three freckles on his nose, which he's scrunching. He's trying not to pout, but his little lip sticks out as he stares at me in challenge. He's pissed that I didn't let him finish his "flight."

It's not funny at all but I find myself smiling at him.

"Jamie!" Britta calls as she scrambles down the ladder, then rushes over to us. She grabs my son from my grip and pulls him in for a tight squeeze, kissing his forehead one moment, then shooting me a stunned stare the next. "What are you doing here?"

"Apparently I'm saving our son."

"You have *no* right," she all but hisses.

To say that aloud? To be here? To keep him from a concussion?

I have to work hard not to growl at her. "But aren't you glad I was?"

Britta's stare becomes a glare. She casts an embarrassed glance over to the other mom, whose gaze ping-pongs between me and Britta. She's not trying to eavesdrop, but she can hardly help overhearing since we're all standing mere feet apart. I wince.

Okay, I could have handled that better and kept our business a tad more private. On the other hand, I'm not hiding the fact that I'm Jamie's father and I plan to be a part of his life. Britta's friends will eventually know, too. Why not start now?

"In this instance, yes. Thank you," she says curtly, then turns to the brunette. "Sorry to cut this short. I think we need to go."

Is she fucking serious? I've barely seen Jamie.

"Sure. We should go, too." Scooping up her son, the other woman gives me a sidelong once-over and steps away as if I somehow scare her.

I try to smooth my expression. I've been told I can look fierce as a son of a bitch, and the last thing I want to do is intimidate the five-foot-nothing mom of a toddler who's friends with my son. "Griffin Reed." I hold out my hand to Britta's gal pal. "Nice to meet you."

Slowly, she extends her hand, sending a speculative stare between Britta and me. "Emily Marks. Same. I'm glad you were here to save Jamie."

The woman looks like she's trying damn hard to figure out why I've so suddenly dashed—literally—into the situation.

Britta pulls Jamie in tighter against her. He turns into a squirming ball of boy, all arms and legs, determined to have his freedom…and probably climb the monkey bars again.

"I'll call you later, Emily," she tells her friend as she tries desperately to get Jamie under control so they can leave.

"Talk to you then." The woman turns to go, then has second thoughts. "I didn't know Jamie's dad was in the picture. Anton took off when he found out I was pregnant. You're lucky." Then she adjusts the boy on her hip. "Wave good-bye, Cody."

He does so without being told twice. He's wholly unlike Jamie, who seems as strong-willed as I am.

Emily and the toddler in cowboy boots depart, leaving me alone with Britta, who's still trying to contain Jamie. When his struggle to escape nearly has him punching her in the face, I snatch the boy and make sure

Britta is out of the range of my son's swinging arms. It's like trying to hold a herd of angry cats.

"Give him back to me," she insists.

"Once he's calm," I promise, then turn all my attention to Jamie. "Hey. Let's calm down. What's wrong?"

"Let go. I jump!"

"Nope." I shake my head. "That's dangerous, and you scared your mother. Don't do that again."

"Who you?" he challenges me with a fierce little frown.

I'll tell him the truth soon. He may have overheard the conversation between the adults tonight, but he clearly didn't understand. Or wasn't really listening. Either way, I'm slightly relieved. Sure, it sucks waiting to hear him acknowledge that I'm his father, but I'd rather do this right.

"I'm someone who cares very much if you get hurt. So does your mom. You don't want to see her upset, do you?"

"No." His glum little frown tugs at my heart.

"Or crying?"

The frown deepens. "No."

"Then listen to her next time or you and I might have to exchange more words, Jamie. Do you understand?"

He doesn't know me at all, but he gives me a slow bob of his head. "Okay."

"Good." I hug him tight again, vowing it won't be the last time. "Go back to your mom and be a good boy. Can you do that?"

"Yeah." His heavy sigh sounds a lot like a teenager who's been asked to clean his room.

"That's a good man. Give your mother a hug." I return him to Britta.

She takes the boy gratefully and hugs him tighter than ever, shooting me a glance that asks *who are you*? "Why did you come here?"

I send her a reproving stare. "Really? You have to ask?"

Britta swallows—her anger, her pride—and blanks her face. "Thank you. I don't know what I would have done without you tonight."

"Watched him fall." I smile wryly. "I did something similar at his age and broke my ankle. Is that how he broke his arm?"

"He didn't, just got a finger stuck in a door at school. Normally, it would require a simple splint, but asking a toddler to leave the dressing alone…" She rolls her eyes.

"I'm glad that's all it was."

"Me, too. You have no idea. He's gotten so big so quickly. He's never not listened to me like that. I'm still shocked."

"You know me, and you're wondering why he's headstrong?"

She tsks and shakes her head. "Good point. The last three months have been really hard. I thought I'd escaped the terrible twos, but suddenly…"

"He's willful? He bucks authority? He does crazy things for a thrill?"

"Yeah. I don't…" She frowns. "He was such a good baby, too. Never sick. Rarely cried. Liked to eat and sleep, enjoyed his playtime and his baths. He loves it when I read to him. He never minds his car seat but…"

"This is his first step to becoming a man."

Britta looks horrified. "What are you talking about? He's not even three."

"Independence was always a big thing for me. I couldn't wait to grow up, try new things, be my own person." I shrug.

"I'm not ready for that. He's a still a baby."

Not so much. And certainly not for long. It hits me that she's going to need help as he gets bigger and bigger. The last thing I want is her struggling to give him the boundaries he'll require. Or for Makaio to provide them.

Tamping down anger at that thought, I can't resist touching Jamie again, smoothing my palm over his crown. "But growing every day."

"I remember when he fit easily into my arms. Now he's over three feet tall. His pediatrician thinks he'll be about six foot five when he's full-grown." Britta sounds distressed by that fact.

I take a chance and cup her shoulder. "If you let me, I'll help you every step of the way."

That shuts her down instantly. "We need to go. I have to feed Jamie dinner."

When Britta turns away and scoops up her bag, I follow. "I'll take you two out to eat."

"No, thank you. I defrosted pork chops."

"Work with me here. I'm late to acknowledge that I'm a father." I grab her arm and turn her to face me, grateful that Jamie seems focused on some other kids just arriving at the park. "But I won't leave again."

"I don't want to talk about this now." She pulls out of my grip and rushes toward her car again. "It's too soon, too complicated. You made your choice a long time ago, and—"

"I hurt you. And I'm more sorry than you think I'm capable of. I'll tell you that every day until you believe me. But the only reason to keep us apart"—I gesture to Jaime—"is because you're afraid of me or you're feeling spiteful. I've never known you to be vindictive or mean, angel."

"Don't call me that." She fumbles inside her bag for the keys to her car.

I know why she's demurring, but she looks like an angel to me. "Don't leave yet. When can I see him again?"

She finds the shiny key ring and presses the fob. Her hands are shaking. "I have to think about it. I'll see you Monday at work."

I debate whether I should tell her I have an appointment in the morning with a former client who happens to be a family law attorney. That's probably the only reason he agreed to see me on a Saturday. But I keep silent. It's not a threat. I simply want to know my rights—and how I go about getting more. In fact, as many as possible.

When she struggles to open the rear passenger door, I nudge her hand aside and jerk it wide. I could let her put Jamie in his car seat, but this may be my last time to hold him for a while, so I take him from Britta's arms and give him a quick squeeze. Thank goodness he's not fighting me. It feels so good to just touch him, like a part of me was missing but I've suddenly found it.

Then again, that's how I feel every time I look at Britta.

"Give him back to me," she huffs.

By the time she's finished her sentence, I've already set him in his car seat and ruffled his hair.

"I'm just strapping him in," I assure her.

Jamie stares at me uncertainly. I smile back. I know some kids are weird about strangers—as they probably should be. But I can't deny that I want Jamie to like me. I'm disappointed our first conversation is me scolding him for his acrobatics. But it probably won't be the last such conversation. I wish we'd had more time to bond. I'm hoping that, after today, we'll have the rest of our lives to get to know each other, so he can love me the way I already love him.

But for now, my time with him has run out.

When I turn my attention to securing him safely in his car seat, I encounter a tangle of buckles and straps…and I've got no idea what the hell to do.

After a little fumbling, I manage to fasten the device appropriately. I think.

"Is it supposed to be this tight? He can't move." I step back from the open car door so Britta can stick her head in.

She murmurs something to Jamie, then checks over my work. "Yes. That way he can't go anywhere in case we get in an accident."

That makes sense, I guess, but I don't know how this contraption doesn't give him claustrophobia. "Can I see him tomorrow? Please."

She bites her lip. "I have a ton of housework to do."

"I'll drive over and pick him up. I'll bring him here to—"

"Absolutely not." She shuts the rear door and stands in front of it protectively. "You're not taking Jamie anywhere unsupervised."

"I would never harm him," I protest.

I'm actually hurt. Britta knows me. I may have been a lousy boyfriend in the past, but I'm not violent or mean. I'm not the kind of guy who would kidnap him from his mother. I simply want to be with him.

"You don't know anything about Jamie," she points out. "He has likes and dislikes. He has a food allergy. You can't…" She shakes her head so vehemently she doesn't finish her sentence.

She's getting worked up and digging in her heels, so I need to back off. It's something she did once or twice when we were together. But my angel has grown more spine in our time apart. She's spicier.

I like it.

"Or I can take him out in your backyard while you keep an eye on us. Whatever makes you comfortable. But you've spent his whole life with him. I've had less than five minutes. C'mon…"

She presses her lips together in thought. Britta is a reasonable woman deep down. She wants to accommodate. She dislikes strife. I have hope.

"What am I supposed to tell him?" she whispers. "You can't just show up and be his buddy."

"I was thinking we'd tell him the truth."

Britta grips her car keys and trots around the back of her vehicle. I don't want to, and it's utterly the wrong time, but I can't avoid noticing that her ass looks fantastic in those exercise pants.

Then I realize she's making a mad dash for the driver's seat of her car. "Don't push me, Griff."

I follow, thinking of several things I could point out: I'm not going away, a boy needs his father, letting me see Jamie is only fair. She won't care about any of that. That's my boo-hoo bullshit. I'm a sales guy, so I know better than to expect that to matter to her. I might not be the top producer on the island—that distinction goes to my brother—but I run a fucking close second. What I have to tell her is how *she'll* benefit if I become a part of our son's life. Besides, of course, the fact I'm going to give her the most amazing pleasure for the rest of our days. She's not ready to hear that.

"I can help you with him, Britta. You said it yourself; he's growing fast. That stunt he pulled today might be the first, but it won't be the last. He'll need someone who understands what it's like not to have a healthy fear of gravity and can anticipate when he might exercise his lack of common sense. I've got two decades of that experience. You've never had an incautious day in your life. I can talk to him, temper him, guide him. I—"

She's already sliding into the driver's seat and shutting the door. I hear it lock as she starts the engine.

Britta cracks the tinted window enough to look at me. "I'll think about letting you see him again and advise you on Monday. Bye."

Then she's slinging her way out of her parking space and squealing across the lot, flashing taillights as she heads to the open road, taking my son and my potential for happiness with her.

Yeah, trying to open a dialogue, empathizing, and working through it like a reasonable guy didn't go well. Fuck. Though Keeley put me in touch with my emotions, sometimes they frustrate me because they aren't useful. But what I *do* know? Good strategy sometimes calls for relentlessness. Britta doesn't yet know even half the persistence and liquid savagery running through my veins.

But she will.

CHAPTER FIVE

"ARE YOU SURE ABOUT THIS?" Maxon asks as we stand over Britta's dining room table in the middle of my office. "She's going to be pissed."

"I have to do something." After a mostly sleepless night, followed by an intense workout this morning, then an hour with my attorney friend, I've come to some hard realizations. "I'm not listed as the father on Jamie's birth certificate, so legally Britta can cut me off at the balls where he's concerned if she wants. I have absolutely no rights."

"Now that you're back in the picture, if you negotiate with her, she might fix that."

"Voluntarily? I'm not holding my breath."

"Normally I'd say you're wrong, but…" Maxon frowns. "She has a lot of anger. What's your recourse?"

I give him a cynical grunt. "Well, I could take her to court, force a paternity test, and have Jamie's records altered. But if I do that, I'm almost guaranteed to pay child support for fifteen and a half years so she can resent the hell out of sharing our son with me every other weekend and during holidays. No thanks."

Maxon concedes that point with a nod. "I hear you. I just don't know how you change that."

"I have to find a way to make Britta *want* to share Jamie with me." I'd damn sure prefer to be tucking our son into his crib at night and then tumbling his mother into bed, rather than fighting with her about his custody while she's Mrs. Somebody-Else. My desire dovetails nicely with the fact that, despite her fresh engagement, she will marry that banker over my dead body.

"Sure. But how?"

"In a word? Romance. I was going to wait to pursue Britta until after I secured my rights with Jamie. But that's obviously not going to work, so I'm going to make us a fucking family now. I'm open to suggestions on sweeping her off her feet."

"Do you really want ideas from me?" he jokes. "I've made my own clusterfuck. And what does any of this have to do with Britta's dining room table?"

I laugh. "If I return it to her, she has to talk to me. If I can just spend time with her, show her who I am now, prove I simply want what's best for Jamie—and for us—it might work out." Even if the opportunity to woo her doesn't pan out today, if I get to see my son, I'll still consider it a win.

"Sneaky. I like it. But I'm telling you, she's going to be pissed."

I shrug. "Making Britta happy in the long run may require some short-term…discomfort until she realizes this will be best for us all."

But I'm worried she may have buried the love she once felt for me so far under her resentment I'll never be able to exhume it, much less breathe life into it again.

My brother shakes his head at me. "You've got balls, man."

"And you don't? It still amazes me you spent the night with Keeley, *then* asked her to seduce me the next morning."

"What? It made sense at the time."

I roll my eyes. "That kind of logic only works if you have balls."

Maxon laughs. "Must run in the family. So, um…speaking of Keeley, did you talk to her last night?"

"Yep." I don't say more. I'm having fun with my older brother's frustration. God knows he used to torment the shit out of me when we were kids.

"Don't make me beat the conversation out of you. What did she say?"

When I hear his real anxiety, I let up. I know now what it's like to love a woman you've wronged and be worried she's never coming back.

"She mostly talked about her family. Phil's birthday was yesterday. They went out to dinner."

Apparently, he tried to talk her into job hunting in Phoenix. She browsed some Internet sites and drove around…but she had a feeling staying there would be wrong. The desert is all well and good, but she's missing the ocean. And I think she's missing Maxon, too.

"And?"

I shrug. "She's still thinking."

My brother looks like he's ready to climb a wall. "It's killing me to wait until Thursday to find out if she's coming back."

"Hang in there. You have a solid plan. Everything in place?"

That makes him smile. "Almost. If she returns to Maui and decides I'm the guy for her, I'll make her so fucking happy."

I understand that sentiment. "Fingers crossed, man. You ready to haul this?"

When Maxon nods, we each grab an end of the table and lift. We removed the leaf earlier—a necessity when my brother and his staff were using it as a conference table in their "war" room. Now it's packed away in the back of my black Escalade.

In short order, the table is also stored in my vehicle and we're heading to Kihei. Weekend traffic is heavier than I'd hoped, which means it will take longer to reach Britta and Jamie.

I've got to kill the time somehow… "Want to hear more of the music Keeley left me? I swiped the disc from my car."

Maxon grips his thighs tightly. I understand wanting to know more about the woman you love and yet not wanting to know, in case it's some indication she's going to hate you forever. I went through that with Britta after the split. Burying my head in the sand was easier. Probably why I had no idea she was pregnant.

"Have you listened to more since we talked about it?"

I shake my head. "She's trying to give me a message I'm not sure I want."

He smiles fondly. "That's Keeley. Go ahead. I'll interpret if you need help."

"You?" I raise a brow at him. "Mr. Sensitivity?"

Maxon scowls. "Play the damn CD already."

I bark out a laugh as I pluck the disc off the dash. Maxon removes it from the plastic case and slides it into the player.

I forward through all I've already heard until I come to the new stuff. The next song has a distinctly country flavor. According to the case, it's "Didn't You Know How Much I Loved You" by Kellie Pickler. We listen in silence. I shift in my seat. Keeley definitely knows how to select music for maximum pain. As the lyrics roll on, she sings that she can't get me out of her head, even though I've left her alone in bed. She was fighting mad, vacillating between falling apart to not giving a damn… Jesus, I can almost feel how confused and decimated Britta must have been after the split.

It's not as if I never considered her feelings. I guess…I figured that if she could betray me by helping my brother stab me in the back, she must not care about me anymore. But Keeley knows the mind of a woman way better than I ever will, and she's sending me a message I can't miss.

I was a dick and I crushed Britta's heart.

When the song finally ends, I turn off the player again and stare out at the traffic.

"Ouch," my brother says into the silence only broken by road noise.

"Yeah."

"I see why you're taking Keeley's 'musical suggestions' in small doses."

"The woman always gets her point across, and it's very often not in a straight line. Remember that."

Maxon nods slowly. "It's a little like Mom, but much nicer."

I tense. The only topic I like discussing less than my breakup with Britta is our mother. "Thank god she lives in San Diego. If she and Dad both moved back to Maui, I'm sure there would be some form of family murder in our future."

My brother snorts. "Don't be too thankful yet. According to Harlow, she's looking for Dad. Plus, she's coming out for Harlow's wedding in May."

No idea how I'm going to handle that.

"Well, Mommy Dearest hasn't called me." She's not likely to. "And I am *not* about to call her."

"Boy, she must have pissed you off after I went to college."

You have no idea...

Instead, I shrug. "As I've gotten older, I just see them both for who they are."

Maxon pulls at the back of his neck. "Me, too. How did we turn out halfway normal?"

"Did we?" I ask—and I'm only half kidding. He and I are both massive bastards, though trying to reform. Our little sister, Harlow, seems like she's in a better place, at least over the phone. But I haven't seen her in a couple of years. So who really knows?

"Good point."

Twenty minutes later, we're pulling up in front of Britta's house. The windows are open. I hear the buzzing hum of a vacuum.

As we climb out of the car, I snag the table leaf in my grip and head up the steps toward the door. Halfway up the yard, Maxon grabs my arm to pause me. "Don't do anything stupid."

"I already did. Now I'm here to fix it." Then I shake off his hold.

With a sigh, he follows to the porch. I raise my hand to the bell.

Moments later, Britta pulls the door open. She's wearing a white sports top that bares most of her flat stomach and a pair of black spandex shorts that start below her navel and end at the tops of her thighs.

My eyes nearly bulge from my fucking head.

"Maxon," she greets happily, then looks at me with a frown. "Griff. What are you doing here?"

He nudges me to reply. *Thanks for smoothing my way, big brother.*

"Um, I changed my mind. About the desk. I'm going to bring in my own. Maxon told me the table belongs in your dining room, so we decided to bring it to you and clear out the space." I hold up the leaf. "If you'll tell us where you want it…"

She gives me a wary look, opens the door wider, then points to an open area on the hardwood floors behind some stools lined up at a breakfast bar. "It goes over there."

Maxon nods. "Got it. We'll get the table back in place. Two shakes."

He turns away, and I know I'm supposed to follow and help him, but I'm still staring at Britta. She crosses her arms over her exposed middle self-consciously. All she does is show me more of the cleavage she didn't have before childbirth. The delicious curves of her hips are impossible to miss in these shorts. I know I should stop gawking but…damn.

"You get more beautiful every time I see you." The words slip out.

She frowns and lifts a hand to smooth out the messy bun she's sporting and the red bandana knotted at the top of her head. That goddamn engagement ring of hers picks up the sunlight and glints in my face.

"I-I…" She blinks at me like she's not sure how to reply. "Don't—"

"I'm not lying to you, just telling you my observation. And now that I've opened my big mouth, I'll go help my brother."

I turn away before she can say another word. But I feel her eyes on me as I walk to the back of my SUV, where my brother is waiting for me with a barely suppressed grin.

"Smooth," he remarks as he grips one side of the table and starts easing it out.

I grab the other side. "Shut up."

He chuckles as we lift the heavy slab of wood. The legs are tall, so we have to slide it clear of the SUV's hatch. Then we flip it over and cart it to Britta's door, settling it in the spot she indicated. It looks as if she's already stored the leaf elsewhere.

I glance around the house. It's faintly tropical, earth tones with splashes of red here and there. And it's spotless. That's my angel. She likes things organized and simple. She has bins of toys tucked away in corners. The kitchen isn't fancy but it's functional. The whole place has a homey vibe.

It reminds me of her.

I wish I lived here with Britta and my boy. I'd miss the ocean view from my condo, but to see those two every day, I'd give the beach up in a heartbeat.

"Where are the chairs?" Maxon asks.

"I stored them in the spare bedroom. I'll grab them." She heads down the hall.

"Let me help you." I follow, watching the graceful sway of her hips. "Where's Jamie?"

She stops and whirls on me. "Napping. Don't push me."

I hold up my hands. "Just asking."

"You were supposed to keep your distance until Monday."

That was never going to happen, and I won't apologize when I'm not sorry for finally trying to make us a family.

With a huff, she turns her back on me and opens the first door on the right. There's a double bed with a woven gray comforter and a pair of white closet doors in one half of the room. The dining room chairs are lined up like soldiers between the two. In the other half of the room is a corner desk with a faintly modern flair and a sleek new iMac. Like everything else I've seen about this place, it's neat and well put together.

"Take this." She lifts the first chair and proffers it to me, holding it between us.

I take it from her grasp. "Got it."

The tension between us is a tingle prickling the back of my neck.

"Thanks." Her hands are shaking. Her gaze won't quite meet mine.

She's visibly nervous. Because I make her feel something. Maxon swears she's still in love with me. If I want Britta back, I need to tell her how I feel. It's something I've historically sucked at. I also have to give her a reason to open up to me in return.

This is my moment. My heart is thudding manically. Maxon stayed in the living/dining room. Jamie is surely sleeping in his crib. And we're not in the office. This chance alone with her may not come around again soon. All I have to do is kick the bedroom door shut behind me.

Anxiety nearly chokes me. But if I'm ever going to win her back, I can't give Britta less than my all now.

I set the chair aside and grab her hand. "I'm not the same man I used to be, I swear."

She searches my face. "Let go."

If I do what she asks, I'll only give her time to build a taller wall between us before I've even begun chipping away at the one she's already got in place.

I cup her hand tighter. "I was a bastard. Three years ago, I didn't value you the way I should have. I didn't love you the way I meant to. I..." Finding the right words is harder than I imagined. "I never meant to hurt you. But I know I did."

She's had a long time to lovingly craft creative curses to rain on my head for the shit I did to her. I'm expecting to hear a litany of them. Instead, hurt flashes in her eyes. "What do you want me to say, Griff? What are you looking for? Absolution?"

"Be mad. Yell at me. It's okay. I'll answer your questions. I'll stand here and take your anger. Whatever will prove I'm serious. Whatever you need to feel better."

"I don't feel anything at all." She wriggles free and turns to retrieve another chair.

Liar.

So she doesn't want to talk? Well, some situations call for more than words. They've never been my strong suit anyway.

I take the second chair from her grip and set it in the corner beside the first. Then I wrap my fingers around her elbow and give a gentle tug. She stumbles against me. Our chests collide. She gasps. Her head snaps back. I pull her body closer to mine. Our eyes meet.

"Angel," I whisper as I cradle her cheeks in my hands and drop my head. She barely has time to draw another breath before I settle my lips over hers.

Then I'm kissing Britta again after three long fucking years.

A million sensations hit me at once. I inhale her familiar jasmine scent. I caress the velvet of her face, her nape. I hear her rapid intake of breath. Heat burns my veins. I'm melting. Her touch feels so electric. I'm dying. Holding her again is so stunning. Arousal hammers me—heart pinging, breaths sawing, cock hardening. But my feelings aren't the same as before. Now they're desperate. They're so yearning. So deep.

They're the feelings of a man who finally understands love—and has been given a second chance to give it back.

Touching her is also a comfort, like coming home after a long war. I feel as if I've fought myself and exorcised the demons of my past. I'm unshackled but I'm so chained to her that I'll never be free. I don't want to be.

Memories of the hundreds of times I stripped her bare, physically and sexually, and left her blushing and smiling and panting my name bombard me. I'm haunted by the times she told me she loved me and I said nothing in return.

Against me she's frozen in shock. Her body is tense. Her fingers are splayed wide on my chest where they landed when she tried to catch her balance. She's not moving her lips against mine. And goddamn it, I crave her response. I have to know I'm not the only one willing to give us another try.

With a groan, I brush my lips over Britta's again. If anything, she goes stiffer. I breathe against her and try like hell to coax her. I almost back off. But…she's not yelling at me. She's not shoving me away.

I try one more time, giving her a suede-soft slide of my lips over hers. Then suddenly, she trembles under me. Her fingers begin to curl into my shirt. I sense that she wants to give in…but is trying so hard not to.

"Kiss me." I nudge her mouth open and hover. "Just once. I've missed you like hell."

The still moment hangs, suspended. Then finally she exhales and closes her eyes. Her arms curl around my neck. A little moan escapes the back of her throat as she tilts her head, parts her lips for me…

And she invites me in.

With a low groan, I fuse our mouths together and taste that something sweet, elusive, and addictive that's purely Britta. She softens against me and pours herself into our kiss. Every breath, every crush of lips, every slide of tongue—she's with me. She curls her fingers into fists, grabbing my shirt before she uses it to drag me closer. But there's already no air between us.

Emboldened, I dive deeper inside her. One kiss bleeds into the next, endless and urgent. Right now, I don't give a shit if we ever come up for air.

With seeking palms, I slide my way down the bare skin of her waist until I'm gripping her hips and grinding her pussy against my aching cock. Tingles ignite and explode, and I groan into her mouth. I want her to know how much she affects me. She should never again feel less than confident about how desperately I want her. I also realize one other undeniable fact.

I. Am. Hers.

My hands slide down from her hips to cup her pert backside. In one grunt, I lift her against me, spread her thighs around my hips, and rock against her. She turns frantic, eating at my mouth, pulling at my hair, like she's looking for some way to be closer, let me deeper inside. She climbs my body and wraps her legs around me, trying to wriggle against me for friction.

My heart is racing so fast I swear it's going to explode. And I don't care. I keep at her. The only thing that will stop me now is if she says no. And the way our chemistry feels…I'm not sure that word is in her vocabulary anymore.

Holy fuck. This is hotter than anything I've ever felt.

I break away from the kiss to look at her. But I can't stand any distance between us. I brush my lips over her neck. My teeth nip at her lobe. I breathe across her skin. She shivers, opening her eyes just enough to reveal her heavy lids and dilated pupils.

"Griff…" She tilts her head back and shifts restlessly over my erection again with a groan.

In the back of my head, I realize the boyfriend must not be satisfying her, because she's acting like a woman who *needs* pleasure. I hate thinking of that snoozer-loser touching her at all, but the realization that he's inept in the sack makes me smile. If she'll let me, I'll give her all the orgasms she can handle every single day before I heap more on her each night.

"That's it, angel. Fuck, you feel so good."

I slide one hand up to her hair and unwind the messy bun. The blond skeins fall like silk over my fingers as I wrap my hand around them and tug until her neck is totally exposed to me. Then I run my tongue from the hollow of her throat to the tip of her chin.

She shudders in my arms, gasping and panting, kissing a path across my jaw. "Griff..."

Her pleading is so pretty. "You liked that?"

"Yes."

"Good. That's how I'm going to eat your pussy, angel, with long, thorough licks until you feel me all the way through your body."

She whimpers in answer before she lays her lips over mine again, asserting her desire, demanding more of mine.

Oh, she can have it all. Right now. For-fucking-ever.

I spin to my left and dive down onto the waiting bed. I cradle Britta in my arms as she falls under me. Once I'm on top of her, possessing her mouth once more, I unzip the little white sports top with one hand while I work my other into her spandex shorts. When I touch her pussy, something savage pulses through me. She went bare for me when we were together. She's still bare now.

Like she's just been waiting for me.

With a soft swipe, I reward her. She cries out. For a moment, I tear my mouth from hers so I can look at her, pink-cheeked and writhing and lost to desire. I want her so damn badly I'm blind and crazy with it.

At once, I suck her nipple into my mouth as I curl my fingers into her cunt. I suckle and rub her, gratified when her whole body jolts like I've hooked her up to a live wire. She's so wet, her every fold is slick.

Fuck yes.

The bead of her breast is tight, but her clit is even harder. She can't stay still under my touch. Hips rolling, back arching, lips parting...

God, I want to make her come in the next two minutes. I could. All the signs are there. But I've waited too long to be with her again to rush. I'm going to savor every sigh and every groan as she pleads with me to fill her, fuck her, claim her once and for all.

I lean over her slight body and Hoover her other nipple into my mouth. Her breasts are fuller now, but she still responds exactly the same—losing her mind when I get my mouth on these sensitive tips and torture them lovingly.

After another nip to the nub, I tongue my way up the side of her breast and still my busy fingers over her needy clit. She gasps in protest and wriggles, hips shifting, thighs spreading. "Griff…"

This is every fucking fantasy about Britta I've imagined. It's mind-blowing that she wants me, too.

I can almost taste our tomorrows.

"You want me to make you feel good, angel?" At her whimper, I smile. "Say the word. I'll strip you down and get deep inside you. Possess you. I'll give you the kind of pleasure neither of us has had in three years. I'll—"

"No." Suddenly, she heaves a shuddering breath and frantically pushes at me. "No. Let go. Get off!"

She's panicked.

I frown, lifting myself to my knees and easing my weight off her. "Hey. Everything's okay. If you need me to go slower—"

She pushes me away, and I see tears pooling in her eyes. "I don't need you to touch me at all. God, I never meant for that to happen!"

She's trembling and guilt-ridden. I'm confused. And frustrated. Britta was totally and completely kiss for kiss with me. Now, she's scrambling to get away from me as if I'm a leper.

Or like I'm the man who utterly devastated her once upon a time.

I roll to my feet as she turns her back to me and zips up her top. I offer her a hand to help her up. The fingers of the other are still slick with her moisture.

She yanks away from me, scooting to the end of the bed and standing on wobbly legs without my assistance. "Get out."

"What? Tell me…" What spooked her? What is she thinking? What does she need from me?

"Why I'm saying no?" She scowls as she winds her hair back into a messy bun, then drags the back of her hand across her mouth, as if wiping away my kiss. "That's so typical of you, Griff. Never imagining for a moment why any woman would say no to you. Yes, you're great in bed, but I know at least a half dozen places *that's* been." She glances at my stiff cock shoved in my shorts.

I'm certainly not about to tell her six other women are a drop in the bucket. "Britta—"

"No. I had a stupid lapse of judgment, but there's no way I'll ever trust you as a lover again."

Her words hurt more than I thought possible. "Angel…"

She brushes past me and reaches for the first of the dining room chairs I stacked to one side. As she curls her fingers around the spindles, I barely manage to stop myself from wrapping my hands around her waist and bringing her back against me until she melts. But she's said no very clearly. I have to fall back on verbal communication.

"I'm so fucking sorry. I was wrong."

She stiffens but doesn't stop or turn back. She just keeps walking. "I want you out of my house."

"Don't do this." I'm all but pleading.

"*You* did this," she reminds me, voice warbling. "You live with it."

"I've missed you." I dare to sidle closer and cup her shoulder. I wish she'd look at me, but at least I know she's listening.

"I don't care."

"I love you."

I've never said those three words to her—or any woman—in my life. And I mean them now more than I can possibly express.

She freezes, then whirls around and gapes at me, blue eyes wide with shock.

Way to ease her back into a relationship, dumb ass.

"You did not just… No." She shakes her head vehemently. "All you've ever done is things to make me want you and then to make me hate you. It's too late." She lifts the chair as I stand still, lashed by her fury. "Fuck off. And don't touch me again."

"Britta?" I hear another man's voice call down the hallway. It isn't Maxon's.

The fiancé must be here.

I bite back a curse. Terrible fucking timing.

"Hi, Makaio. I'm here." She smooths her hair, looking flustered, then picks up the chair and marches out of the bedroom. "I'm getting the dining room put together now that the table is back."

"Maxon told me," Makaio says. "Why is he sitting on the front porch? Why are you flushed? What's going on?"

"I'm just moving the chairs." Her voice trails down the hall as she glides toward the man she's planning to marry.

Fuck.

I close my eyes. I know how much she hates to lie. Maybe kissing her now was a stupid-ass move. I wanted to remind her of all the passion and yearning between us. I never meant to put her in a position to either wear a hair shirt or confess her "sins" to Mr. Boring. I don't know Makaio well, but if I were in his place, I'd beat the shit out of me.

Since she wants me gone, I have to respect that—for now—and figure out my next step. I know her too well not to understand that she needs time to process what's happened today and decide what that means for her engagement. On the other hand, if I leave now, she'll only be harder to reach on Monday.

Double fuck.

I smooth out the bed, take a deep breath, then lift a chair and shoulder my way to the door.

"I didn't have to use my key to get in. You have to remember to lock the door," Makaio scolds.

The fucker has a key?

"I know. We'd just moved the table into the house and I…forgot."

I grit my teeth. *Because I was too busy trying to seduce your fiancée and remind her of all the reasons she and I belong together, so locking it slipped her mind, tool.*

With sarcasm echoing in my head, I silently shove my way into the hall.

"Hey," I greet Makaio.

It's the most I can speak civilly to the man without sounding like either a jealous prick or the big, bad wolf.

He blinks at me. "You're here, too?"

"Her table was in my office." I sidestep him and carry the chair to the dining room, setting it beside the one Britta just positioned.

She doesn't look at me, simply heads back to grab another chair. I want more time with her, to help her understand that I was serious when I said I loved her. Whatever might help her hate me less.

I just don't know what else to say or do to convince her.

Makaio taps my shoulder as Maxon appears in the doorway, shooting me a questioning glance. "Why don't you and I talk outside? Your brother can help Britta finish up in here."

Oh, Slow-Dick McGraw finally wants to warn me away?

"Sure."

He takes me out back to a couple of cozy Adirondacks on the lanai overlooking the lush backyard. A cluster of palms sways in a cerulean-blue sky. When he gestures me to one of the chairs, I sit. This ought to be interesting...

"I don't know you well and nothing I've heard is good. But I'm also willing to understand that Britta is, perhaps, too colored by her resentment to separate your romantic past from your future as Jamie's father."

I could admit to this guy that I was a prick. But I'm not giving him any leverage to use against me later. I don't know what his angle is, and I'm a little surprised he all but called his fiancée hysterical before he threw her under the bus. I need to feel him out more so I can best determine how to work around him.

"Agreed." I choose the safe topic he's already raised. "I want to be a part of my son's life."

He nods. "When I was a kid, my parents divorced for a few years. They ended up together again, but one of my greatest comforts was knowing I still had the love of them both. I adore Jamie and I'll always treat him well, but I would never try to replace his biological father. I understand that's your role."

I'm happy to hear it. A little grateful, too. But this dude just gave me a big concession. He might not know that I tried to woo his girl a few minutes ago, but seriously. I'm the enemy. Where's his protective instinct?

"I appreciate that. I came as soon as I found out about Jamie, and I intend to be active in his life."

"That will be good for the boy. I'll help you work with Britta on a custody arrangement that's acceptable to everyone."

Did he just offer to help me instead of supporting the woman he's planning to marry? It's stupid on so many levels... But if he wants to play like we're both reasonable men and that I don't want to steal her away, that's fine. Fighting with this guy outright can only make me look like an asshole.

"That's great." I nod. "I appreciate it."

"Of course." He hesitates. "I trust you understand it's definitely over between you and Britta."

That's not what her kiss less than five minutes ago told me.

Yeah, she pushed me away...eventually. But I more than felt the spark. She did, too.

"If you're asking whether I understand she's engaged to you and that you plan to marry her, I grasp that completely." It just doesn't matter.

He gives me a condescending smile. "Good. I've done everything I can to make her happy. I treat her well, I adore her son, and I put a ring on her finger. I'm not sure what your feelings toward her are—if you even have any—but ultimately Britta is a reasonable woman who knows I'll give her an optimal future."

I do my best to listen with a straight face, but it's tough.

So let me get this right... This guy thinks that because he ticked all the boxes off on some mental checklist of what makes a happy wife and that because she's "reasonable," they'll soon be skipping hand in hand down some logical, yellow-brick road to everlasting love?

Is he for real? *Would it interest you to know that I just had my fingers in your fiancée's pussy?*

Usually, I prefer to come at a foe head on. I'd rather fight the rough fight than the underhanded one. But Makaio could be a huge advocate in helping me gain rights to Jamie. I can't afford to turn that down. I feel bad that I'm going to make the asshole choice to take this sap's help while I try to steal his woman. But a little remorse isn't stopping me.

Yeah, I know. You're judging me. Hey, I'm judging myself, too. But I don't see another way to meld the people I love into a real family with me. Jamie deserves his mother and father together. Britta doesn't need a man who expects her to love him because he treats her well and it seems logical; she is entitled to a man who will be passionate about her every moment of every day and always put her first, no matter what.

That will never be Makaio.

"I see your point," I finally say. "You've done everything right."

I just don't think that's going to work for you, pal.

Britta's banker nods stiffly at me. "Good to hear. I'll talk to her about devising a custody arrangement. My father is a retired attorney, and I know they've already been discussing the situation. Of course, Britta wanted to understand her options."

"Of course," I manage to say without sounding cynical at all.

Well, now I know why she went to see the asswipe's dad the other morning. Damn it.

"I'll urge her to think about what's truly best for the boy," Makaio assures me. "Not what serves her bitterness."

Wow, what a dipshit.

I keep my thoughts to myself and I give him a vague nod of thanks.

I need a new plan. I'll bet that, now that Britta knows I can get to her, she's mentally digging a moat and building more protective fences around her heart. I have to find a way back in pronto—and persuade her to share

Jamie with me. But given the passion still sweltering between us, I don't think she'll be able to resist me for long.

I leave with a smile.

CHAPTER SIX

AFTER MOVING MY OWN DESK into my former office late Saturday afternoon, I arrive early Monday morning, ready to go. I throw myself in my chair, looking out the window with a view of the parking lot. And I wait. Undoubtedly, Britta did a lot of thinking over the weekend. The reception I get from her today is going to tell me a lot.

But I have to admit...stupid or not, I have more hope today than I did last Friday.

While drinking Saturday night with Maxon—we both turned down flirty girls at a bar—and while pushing my body to the limit with an eight-mile run on Sunday, I got some clarity about our situation. I could have handled it better. Merely saying I'm sorry for all I did to her wasn't enough. Kissing her, even if she reciprocated, didn't repair the damage I inflicted on us. Telling her I love her was too little, too late. But my heart is in the right place. Some combination of all that—something gentler and less rushed—should bring us closer together.

It goes against my grain to downshift. For Britta, I have to try.

My brother pops his head in with coffee. "You prepared for World War III? You know, just in case."

I'm hoping she's looked at everything I've done these past few days and realizes I'm both serious and committed. But if it's going to take more time and more potentially heated conversation for her to believe me...

"I'm prepared."

"You're crazy. You know that, right? I knew that for sure on Saturday when you kissed her…and whatever else you did—"

"I never said I touched her."

Maxon scoffs. "I've got ears. Whatever was happening in that bedroom was getting raunchy. And when I heard a zipper go down, I had to get out of earshot. Nothing I want to hear less than my brother and the woman I think of as a sister doing the nasty."

"Well, since we have a child together, we obviously have in the past," I point out.

And the fact that I didn't see him all weekend is sitting sour in my gut. How am I supposed to start being a father to the little guy if I'm never with him?

"There's a difference between laying eyes on my nephew and hearing his parents' slobbers of passion."

"No one slobbered," I assure my annoying-ass brother with a pointed glare.

As he laughs, Britta swings her sedan into the lot and parks.

"Speak of the angel…" I drawl.

Maxon looks out the window. "If there are battles, you know the drill. Keep them out of the office."

"I got it. I got it. Go."

As she emerges from her vehicle, she's wearing a black skirt edged in a lacy hem and a gray blouse with puffed sleeves so sheer I can discern the shape of her arms. The rest of her body is frustratingly obscured but so elegant. Sparkling silver shoes complete the cool, sophisticated look.

Fuck, she knows what a turn-on it is for me when she's dressed like a lady…and she lets me undress her like a woman.

Today, Britta is wearing her hair in gentle waves halfway down her back. The breeze tugs at the strands as she slams her car door with a determined swagger. Then she strides to the office's main door, clutching a folder in hand and looking ready to conquer the world.

From her attitude, I'm guessing she's raised her defenses and girded her loins.

That's not good.

"Good luck with that," Maxon tosses my way as he watches her, backing out of my office.

"Thanks," I shoot back sarcastically.

"By the way, George Stowe left me a voice mail late last night. The listing is ours." He grins.

I relish that piece of good news for a few seconds. This is cause for celebration. We can do great things together.

But I'm distracted by Britta. She looks beyond pissed as she barrels across the office. She doesn't even stop at her desk, merely continues her stomp into my office and shuts the door, clutching the folder to her breast like a shield. That fucking engagement ring is winking at me in mockery.

"What happened on Saturday will never happen again," she says through clenched teeth.

Yes, it will. Only next time, she'll be less angry with me. We'll have worked things out. Then I'll get her naked, pump deep inside her until her nails are in my back and she's crying out my name. I'll rinse and repeat a few times, put a smile on her face…then we'll see how she feels.

"Hmm." I'm noncommittal because I refuse to add fuel to her fire. But I won't lie to her face and agree, either.

She narrows her eyes at me. "Griffin James Reed, don't you dare act as if you didn't step way over the line with me."

"I did."

My admission seems to startle her, then she narrows her eyes at me. "But you're not sorry."

"If I upset you, yes. That I got to touch you again and remind you of what's between us, no." When she stiffens and opens her mouth, likely with a comeback, I hold up a finger. "But I promised Maxon I wouldn't drag our personal shit into the office." I glance at the folder in her hands. "So, did you have something else to discuss?"

"That's a convenient excuse. I'm engaged, and you grabbed me and kissed me. You put your hands on me—"

"My mouth, too. Don't forget that. In fact, after I left your house and got alone in my own car, I could still smell your pussy on my fingers. It was driving me crazy. I had to lick them. Savor them." God, she tastes exactly as I recall.

Her eyes bulge, and she turns a hundred shades of red, then whips her stare out the interior window to see if Maxon or Rob could possibly have overheard us. "Don't say things like that!"

"I should lie?" I lean back in my chair.

"You're twisting my words. Don't say sexual things to me."

I shake my head. "I'm not going to candy-coat how much I want you, angel. Or how much I love you."

She rears back as if I've slapped her. "Don't say that, either. You're only claiming you have feelings for me now because you want parental rights to Jamie. I won't let you sweet-talk me into—"

"Let's get one thing straight." I stand and round the desk, approaching her on slow steps. "I still loved you even before I knew about Jamie."

Britta pauses as if absorbing my words. "Funny how you never took the time to say that until you found out about your son. My reply is still the same."

Fuck off.

"Too bad. I won't walk away from Jamie," I promise. "Or from you."

"Why do you always expect that everyone will bend to please you? I've moved on. I don't need you." She clenches her fists with a grunt. "I never lose my damn temper unless you're involved."

"Because I matter to you, just like you matter to me."

"No." She shakes her head. "No. It's because you infuriate me. You can tell me you 'love' me all you want. I don't believe you. I never will. Ugh, you make me hate you."

Not true. I get under her skin. "That didn't feel like hate on your guest-room bed less than forty-eight hours ago."

She blinks, looking as if she's fighting furious tears. "You're throwing my momentary lapse in my face?"

I refrain from pointing out that her "momentary lapse" was closer to five minutes.

"Stop it, Griff. I'm not a naive little virgin anymore. I'm done letting you manipulate me." She slaps the folder down on my desk. "This is the solution to our problem. Read these papers and sign them, damn it. If you ever really cared about me and what I want, you'll do this."

I stare at the spilling paperwork like it's a snake. I round the desk and flip the folder open. The header at the top of the stapled document on legal paper reads VOLUNTARY RELINQUISHMENT OF PARENTAL RIGHTS.

Holy. Fuck.

More words swim before my eyes. GRIFFIN JAMES REED DOES HEREBY IN WRITING EXPRESSLY CONSENT AND AGREE TO THE TERMINATION OF HIS PARENTAL RIGHTS CONCERNING JAMES TUCKER STONE. CONSENT IS PERMANENT AND CANNOT BE REVOKED…

I stop reading. I stop breathing. I probably shouldn't be surprised that she's fighting back…but I didn't see this coming. The gnawing in my stomach is definitely panic. I try to keep myself under control as I close the flap of the folder, covering the document. "No."

Tears well in her eyes, and I see she's trying to will them away.

I soften my refusal by pointing out one detail. "I'm not his father legally, so I have no rights to relinquish. This document is unnecessary."

"Damn it, Griff." She sniffles. "Do the right thing by me for once and sign it so there's no question in the future."

Her insistence hurts. But seeing her so upset is killing me, too. She clearly feels backed into a corner, and this legal maneuver is tearing her apart. It must be. If Britta flat-out hated me, she would be coldly silent. But she isn't the sort of woman to share her vulnerable side easily. So all her upset tells me is that she truly doesn't want to cut me out of Jamie's life.

It tells me she's far more terrified to trust me than I thought.

The other thing this morning says is that Makaio has absolutely no control or sway over Britta. That's great news for me. Sure, he might have lied to my face about his thoughts and intentions, but I doubt it. He's a truth-justice-and-American-way sort of guy. He would view something important, like Jamie's custody arrangement, as too vital to play games with.

Well, I'm not playing games, which he'll figure out...eventually. Britta isn't messing around, either. She's simply trying not to think with her heart.

I need to show her that she can believe in me, that I'll be here for her. I can't do that if I'm unable to spend time with her and our son. So I'll fix that problem—fast.

But I will never, ever sign this document, no matter how much she pleads.

"I'm trying, angel. I'm simply not convinced that me bowing out of Jamie's life forever is best for any of us."

Through the interior window, I see Maxon glaring my way. *Not in the office. Right.*

"You're just going to confuse him. The schlepping him back and forth between your place and mine... He's too young to understand. He doesn't take that well to strangers or new surroundings. You don't know the first thing about kids. Please. It would be better if you let us go."

A tear finally escapes and rolls down her cheek. With a valiant sniff, she tries to call it back, but it's too late. Instead, she wipes it away and blinks stoically, determined to press on no matter how much this is killing her. I'd be happy to kiss her tears away, but I'd rather not be kicked in the balls—by her or my brother.

Of course, I could argue with Britta. I've got a hundred comebacks whizzing through my head. *He's a smart boy. We'll help him figure out any new arrangement. I'll do everything possible to make him comfortable, and I'll ask your advice so the transition is the best it can be. What I don't know about kids, I'll be more than happy to learn...* I could go on. All that does is prolong the argument. We'll never get to the heart of the issue that way.

Clearly, she's torn. Her head is telling her one thing. Her heart is saying something else entirely. I'm going out on a limb—not really—and guessing that after I abandoned her, she mentally combed through every moment of every day we spent together and tried to figure out where it went wrong and how she could have been so mistaken about our commitment, etc. When she didn't find anything she could definitely point to as *the moment*, she resolved never to let her guard down with a man, especially me, again.

Yeah, I've got to fix a lot of shit.

"Why do you think this arrangement would be better?" I ask.

"After Makaio and I get married, I'm going to ask him to adopt Jamie. It would be easier if we all had the same last name."

That will never fucking happen. I agree with her general concept...but I'm determined Britta, Jamie, and I will be the happy Reed family.

"Let me read the paperwork," I manage to say without snarling out my frustration. "Then we'll go to lunch and discuss it."

"I'm not going anywhere with you." She shakes her head stubbornly.

So I guess my idea of grabbing takeout and hashing out the particulars at my place is a big hell no. Maybe that's for the best. I don't know if I can keep my hands off her. As much as she seems to be falling apart, I don't think she could deal with sex now. What's between us is tentative and fragile...but simmering, sparking. If I rush her before she's ready simply because I'm impatient to put the past behind us, before she's had the chance to see how getting back together could be the best path for her—and for Jamie—we'll be done forever.

"We have to talk," I point out. "I can't sign this if I don't understand exactly what you want and why."

Britta casts a side glance to the ceiling. Obviously, she doesn't want to put herself in a vulnerable position when she's feeling weak. I don't know if she's aware how easily I can read her, but it's like I'm tuned into her frequency. She's mad at me, sure. But she's more afraid of what I make her feel and what that means for her future.

"I can't do it today." She shakes her head. "I have an eye doctor appointment."

At least I have a viable delay for signing this crap. "Tomorrow?"

She looks at me in horror. "No. I'm not spending any moment of that day with you."

That day? "Tuesday?"

Britta tosses her hands in the air. "Oh, forget it. What about Wednesday?"

I'm still stuck on tomorrow. What the… I glance at the calendar, and suddenly it's clear. She's protesting having lunch with me on Valentine's Day.

Once upon a time, she was giddy with the thought that I might utterly adore her on this holiday for lovers. I sent flowers, sure. I avoided chocolates since they sometimes give her migraines. And I took her to dinner. During the meal, I spent half the time on my phone. I didn't really pay her much attention until we got home alone. I was hoping to get her naked…but it didn't happen.

Valentine's Day will be different for us from now on. I'll do everything in my power to make her feel like my one and only.

I tap my thumb against my thigh, knowing I've got a decision to make. Either I leave her in peace to share Valentine's Day with Makaio, knowing what they will more than likely be doing that night, or I push Britta now and risk her shutting down.

"This is obviously upsetting you. Wouldn't you feel better if we came to a mutual understanding sooner?"

Yeah, I'm coercing her to have lunch with me tomorrow. Of course it's manipulative. But my statement is true…even if Jamie's custody arrangement isn't going to turn out the way she thinks.

She hesitates, pressing her lips together as if she's not exactly sure what to say. "Oh, all right. Tomorrow. Will you actually read it by then?"

"Absolutely." And I will. I'll simply be looking for every possible way to avoid signing it and every single loophole she might use to trip me up. I see check boxes and conditions and more jargon than I can plow through at a glance. This delay, though it chafes, will give me time to confer with my attorney. "I'll make notes. We'll talk and figure this out. Just…don't cry, angel. I'm not trying to make your life worse."

"It's too late," she murmurs, then turns, leaving my office.

It's a blade in the heart I deserve. But if we're going to move forward, I have to lay a bunch of my cards on the table so we can get past all the blame-laying and anger. That means I need to explain everything, not just our breakup. She needs to know how much I regret not changing before I destroyed us.

BRITTA CALLED IN SICK ON Tuesday. Maxon didn't press her for details, damn him. So all my plans for a quiet—and yes, romantic—lunch go down the toilet. I'm both cynical and suspicious at her no-show. Is she really under the weather…or passive-aggressively refusing to spend even a moment of Valentine's Day with me?

When she calls in again on Wednesday, I become concerned.

As promised, I read the paperwork she gave me. Yeah. Fuck no. Never. Ever. In a million years. It's not just a relinquishment of my rights, it also reads something like a restraining order. If I try to approach Jamie in any way, I'm legally a stranger. Anything more than a casual conversation, and she can call the police and have them arrest me.

It's ludicrous. And it's never happening.

The end of this hellacious hump day comes, and I leave the office. When I climb in the car, I'm ready to press the redial button on my last missed call from Keeley. I need to find out if she's getting on that plane tomorrow morning at eight a.m. If not, I don't know what I'm going to tell Maxon.

But before I can dial my bestie for details, my phone rings. I look at the display on the device and answer with a grin.

"Hey, Harlow."

"Hey, you."

I hear a low note in her voice instantly. "You all right?"

"Me? Yeah…"

But she's not, just like she's rarely forthcoming with her feelings. If

I'm going to get to the bottom of her woe, I'll have to be subtle. "How's school?"

"Great!" she says genuinely. "I'm glad I already finished the course work for my final semester and my dissertation is going so well. I'm talking to some great firms about a job after graduation. It's been hard sticking around to get a master's when I'm beyond ready to join the real world, but I think the sacrifice will be worth it in the end."

"Smart girl. How are your wedding plans coming?"

Harlow doesn't answer right away. "Simon and I have both been busy. He's traveling all the time. I've been neck deep in my dissertation and getting ready to defend it. Mom was helping me with the wedding for a while, but she's completely focused on Marco, her new boyfriend, and finding Dad so she can officially serve his ass with divorce papers and get her half of his money. Have you seen him lately?"

"Dad? Not since the night he flew in, like, ten days ago."

No one was more shocked than me when my father beat on my door late unexpectedly one night after arriving from San Diego, demanding I give him a place to stay while he and Mom legally ripped each other to shreds. An hour before that, he'd ragged on Maxon, called him a pussy. Then he said some things that made me realize that I'd been the same kind of bastard to my brother and I owed him a huge apology.

So I guess I can thank him for the wake-up call, but not much else.

"You can't help Mom find him?" she asks anxiously.

Why would I want to? Granted, Dad is no peach, but she's hardly without blame in this shit storm. "I've got no clue where he is."

"If Mom doesn't find him soon, my wedding may never get planned."

I feel for Harlow...but I'm at a critical stage with Britta and Jamie right now. Between that and business, I can't babysit my dad. "If he turns up, I'll let you know."

"If he doesn't, don't be surprised if Mom calls you," my sister warns.

My gut tightens. I've barely spoken more than monosyllables to her in ten years. Then again, what should I say to the woman who forever fucked my adolescence? "To help her find Dad?"

"Yeah. She's threatening to 'do something drastic,' whatever that means. And you know Mom. The wine posse is backing her up, Chardonnay in hand."

I grunt. I know Linda Reed probably better than anyone in this family. "She's still hanging around with Julia?"

The leech followed my mother when she moved to San Diego a few years back. Thank god.

"Oh, yeah."

I can practically hear my sister roll her eyes. I try not to grind my teeth over the phone. God, how much I hate them all.

"Thanks for the warning. So if the wedding plans get finished, how many weeks until you're Mrs. Butler?"

"Less than twelve. I'm a little panicked. I have to fly to New York for my final fitting at some point. I've been waiting for Simon to come home so we could finish the menu and floral selections. He needs to pick out his tux. We have more phone counseling sessions with the minister. We both thought we'd have time to make a trip to Maui and settle everything in person…but life has been so hectic."

I've never met Simon. I understand a job that seems to eat your life for weeks on end. I often live it. Maxon does, too. But if Britta told me tomorrow that she'd marry me, I wouldn't give a shit what was happening professionally. I would push everything aside to focus on giving that woman the wedding of her dreams. The fact that Simon isn't interested in the details… Well, I know a lot of people would say that guys just aren't into that shit. But for the woman you love, c'mon. Taste some froufrou food, sniff a few flowers. Make her feel important. How hard is it?

From a guy who didn't learn the first time around, what Harlow is describing smacks of a boyfriend who's not really committed.

But maybe I'm wrong. I hope for her sake that I am. I keep my opinion to myself.

"Things will settle down, and you'll get it all sorted out."

"Probably. I just need to not let the details freak me out, I guess." She pauses. "So…Maxon says you met Jamie."

"Kind of. I saved him from a trip to the ER. Don't think he appreciated it." I have to laugh. "At his age, I wouldn't have, either."

She laughs, too. "I'm so relieved I won't have to avoid talking about the cutie pie with you anymore."

"Why did you in the first place?" I have some suspicions.

"Because we thought you knew and simply didn't care. I was so angry I couldn't even talk to you about him. I thought you didn't deserve him. I'm sorry. I didn't realize... I should have given you the benefit of the doubt."

I can't really blame Harlow. I'd like to, but I see her point. In her shoes, I might have made the same choice.

"I'm sorry if that sounds mean," she goes on. "But you really broke Britta's heart, and I didn't want to see you hurt your son, too."

"I understand." I can hardly fault her for trying to protect him.

"Good. I'm glad." She pauses. "I'm flying to Maui sometime in mid-April. The wedding is on Saturday, May sixth. I can't wait to see you. And to finally meet Jamie in person! Maxon sends me the cutest pictures."

"You'll love him. He's beautiful."

"I have no doubt. So...what about you and Britta? You two are talking again?"

"We have a child, so we have to. I'm trying to open the communication between us. And...I'm trying to get her to do more than talk to me."

"Griff, seriously? Maxon said she's engaged."

"She is." But I can't feel guilty. The alternative will make us miserable for the rest of our lives.

She snickers at me like I'm incorrigible. "Actually, I'm pulling for you two. You really seemed to have something. It wasn't perfect, but—"

"That was my fault."

The shock of her silence is almost palpable. "You're admitting you were wrong? Someone record this day in history."

I roll my eyes but take her ribbing in the good nature in which she intended it. "I've grown into a more evolved sort of asshole."

"I'm so proud," she teases.

In the background, I hear someone knocking on her door. "You need to go?"

I hear rustling and guess she's getting up from her chair. A few steps later, she groans. "Yeah. It's Mom."

Without even opening the door, she sounds exhausted by the woman. I understand, but I'm not about to talk to the she-dragon.

"I'll let you go. Call me anytime, little sis."

"Same with you. Love you. Hope everything works out with Britta and Jamie."

Before I can say anything else, she's gone. Ending the conversation is probably for the best since I'm nearly at Britta's. No, she won't be happy to see me, but she owes me an explanation. We'll never work out any arrangement about Jamie and our future if she's going to avoid me.

Three minutes later, I'm knocking on her door. And knocking. I see her sedan under the carport. She should be here. Unless Makaio took her out.

Damning the thought, I'm just about to walk around the house and see if I can peek in through the sliding glass door around back when I hear the click of the lock. The latch gives way and the door creaks open.

Britta wobbles in the portal with her hair pulled back haphazardly, skin somewhere between white and gray. She's tried to belt a pink robe around her middle. It's gaping open to reveal an overlarge oatmeal-colored T-shirt. She's removed everything else—shoes, makeup, engagement ring. Jamie stands behind her, clinging to her thigh.

Whatever remained of my righteous anger swirls down the mental drain. "Are you okay, angel?"

She leans against the door. "It's just a cold. I'll be fine. Sorry we haven't been able to talk—"

A cough interrupts her nasally, scratchy-voiced reply. It sounds deep and productive, and she winces like it's painful.

"Have you been to the doctor?"

She shakes her head. "Haven't felt like it. Maybe I'll go tomorrow."

Where the hell is Makaio? Shouldn't her fiancé be taking care of her?

Whatever. He wasn't important before and he's certainly not important now.

"Have you eaten in the last few hours?"

After a slight pause, she frowns. "Not since midday. It's probably good you woke me up. I need to feed Jamie. Um, we'll talk about everything once I come back to the office, hopefully soon."

If she thinks I'm leaving her and Jamie to suffer alone, she's absolutely fucking crazy.

Gently, I nudge my way past the front door and lock it behind me. Then I kneel down to Jamie, who's staring at me, thumb in his mouth, from behind Britta's shapely thigh. "Hey, big guy. You hungry?"

He looks at me suspiciously, then back up to his mother. When she nods at the boy, he meets my gaze again. "Yeah."

"I'll take care of you. Meet me in the kitchen. Mommy is sick, and I'm going to make sure she gets in bed, okay?"

"What?" Britta balks as Jamie scampers off to dance around the refrigerator. "You can't. I'll—"

"I can't make a can of soup or fix a sandwich? C'mon. You need rest and you don't need to be risking Jamie's immune system. I'm perfectly healthy and I'll handle it." When she still looks uncertain, I cup her shoulder. "You took care of him by yourself for years. I owe you at least this much."

She closes her eyes, obviously torn. But she's too exhausted to fight. "He's allergic to strawberries."

"Got it. Anything in particular he likes?"

"Bananas. Peanut butter sandwiches. Peach yogurt."

"Consider it done. What can I get you?"

"I don't need anything."

I send her a stare of tender rebuke. "Don't be stubborn."

"Seriously. I need to lose those last couple of pounds I gained at Christmas anyway."

Oh, that just annoys me. If she weren't so sick, we'd exchange words about the fact that she'd rather starve herself than ask me for help. Nor is an illness a good time to consider her weight, which seems just fine to me. But right now, getting her back to bed so she can rest matters most.

I curl one arm across her back before I bend and lift her, settling her knees over my other forearm. She shrieks as I nestle her against my chest. To keep her balance, she tosses her hand around my neck. Her body feels like a blast furnace. No doubt, she has a raging fever.

"Put me down," she protests. "I can walk."

"But you don't have to. Relax, angel. I've got you."

I start walking down the hall with her in my arms before she can renew her protests. "Which room is yours?"

"The room I stored the chairs in." She refuses to meet my gaze.

In other words, the room in which I kissed her and tossed her down to the bed and touched her. "You don't sleep in the master?"

She shakes her head. "It's on the other side of the house. Too far away from Jamie. He sometimes has nightmares and…"

"Needs you at all hours?" I scowl. How like Britta to give up her comfort for those she loves. Her health simply won't allow for that now.

After an about-face, I head down the hall again and across the living room, where I spot a closed door on the far side.

Britta sees my destination and starts wriggling with what little energy she has. "I can't sleep there."

"You have to. Listen to me. I've got this."

"You're not sleeping in my bedroom!"

"Is Makaio coming back tonight?" I hate that thought, but I have to be practical at the moment.

"No," she croaks. "He has a big presentation on Friday. He can't afford to get sick."

So he left Britta and Jamie to fend for themselves because he's not man enough to handle a cough or a sniffle? Fucking uptight dick. It probably wasn't "logical" to get sick when he could prevent it. But he'd leave a kid who's not even three alone with a contagious mother who has a blazing fever? I'm not an experienced parent, but even I know that's moronic.

"Then I'm sleeping in your room and taking care of Jamie tonight."

She pushes at my chest. "You can't. He might be upset if he has a nightmare and wakes to find you. When he's afraid, he wants me and—"

"I'll handle it, Britta. Don't be stubborn now. You can't get better if you don't rest."

After a pause, she sighs. "I guess you're right."

I am. She simply doesn't like it.

I give her a nod, then shoulder my way into the master. There's a king-size bed. The decor is somewhere between nonexistent and masculine. Everything is brown and bland and barely used. It looks like someplace Makaio would enjoy.

Gritting my teeth, I set Britta on her feet gently and yank down the comforter to find cool white sheets. I help her into bed and tuck the blankets around her. "Let me see to Jamie. I'll be back in ten."

"Don't worry about me," she calls weakly to my retreating back.

Ridiculous. Of course I'm going to worry about her.

In the kitchen, I set Jamie on the counter and look at him eye to eye. "I'm Griff."

He thumps at his chest. "Jamie."

I teach him how to shake hands, then we make a game out of washing up, stopping just shy of a suds fight—mostly because I don't want his giggling to keep Britta awake.

Then I explain to him that I'll be taking care of him while Mommy is sick before I set a peanut butter sandwich in front of him. He grunts and points at the refrigerator urgently until I realize he's demanding grape jelly with it. Once I slap that on, too, I grab the yogurt and a spoon, then pluck a banana from the basket on the counter and chop it up. A glass of milk follows.

In ten minutes, he's demolished everything on his plate and is looking at me as if to ask *where's the rest?*

Wow, Britta wasn't kidding. He's a great eater.

"What else do you want?"

"Ice cream!"

Of course. One of my favorites, too. I shouldn't be surprised.

I prowl through Britta's freezer, but it's empty of anything that looks like dessert. I sigh. Plan B. I have to feed Britta anyway.

After rinsing Jamie's plate and milk cup, I put both in the dishwasher and pause. The food wasn't fancy...but I just fed my son for the first time. I don't know if he feels like it was a bonding experience. Probably not. But I'm moved and oddly struck by how satisfying it was to take care of him.

After wiping his hands and face clean, I lift him from his booster, then cart him through the front room and into the entry way. I spy Britta's car keys on a foyer table and swipe them. "Want a little adventure?"

When Jamie bobs his head excitedly, I smile at his infectious grin. I'll bet he thinks we're going to do something physical and maybe a little bit crazy. Britta will definitely need my help raising him from here on out.

Silently, we sidle out the front door. I lock up behind me and head to Britta's car. I would take mine, but a car seat in a Porsche convertible just doesn't make much safety sense to me. So I press the button on her car fob, unlock the door, secure Jamie in his place, and head to town.

We're gone about twenty minutes. I make a special trip through the McDonald's drive-thru for some ice cream for Jamie, then we're back at Britta's place with melting soft-serve and one of her favorites.

As soon as I open the door, she's standing in the foyer, looking as if she's barely upright.

"You had no right to take him—"

"Angel, come sit before you fall down." I shut the door behind me and let go of Jamie's hand so I can help Britta to the sofa. I have our bags of goodies in the other.

Thankfully, she doesn't really have the energy to resist.

"I was worried," she says wearily as she sinks onto the nearest cushion.

I grab a blanket from the back of the sofa and toss it over her lap. "I wanted to get something for us to eat and I didn't want you to exert yourself with Jamie. Now give me one second. Our boy had a request..."

She groans. "He conned you out of ice cream?"

I pause. "Is this a regular occurrence?"

"Almost daily." She lays her head against the back of the sofa with a sigh and closes her eyes. "He's good at getting what he wants from me, just like his father."

I send her a faint smile. She can't see me. Hell, she's half-asleep, and I wonder if she even knows what she said. It doesn't matter. I know. And she has no idea yet how right I'm going to prove her.

Eyeing Jamie's bib, I hesitate. I already know he's not great with a spoon. The yogurt was a valuable lesson in toddler messes, so I can't leave him alone entirely with a cup of soft-serve. But I need to get Britta settled. She's grown even paler in the last half hour, and I'm really worried.

For lack of anything better to do, I rip a giant plastic trash bag in half and settle it on the kitchen floor. I strip Jamie down to his Pull-Up and set him in the middle with a plastic spoon and a warning to eat where he's sitting and not to move. He gives me an absent nod before digging in.

I know it's going to be a mess, so I'm just not going to look.

Instead, I grab a bottle of water from the fridge and schlep Britta's takeout over to her as I settle beside her on the sofa. "Hey, angel. I brought you one of your favorites."

I show her the bag from the deli we used to frequent when we lived together. Plain white with cheerful red lettering. Her eyes light up. "Tuna salad?"

"And homemade potato chips." I smile as I set everything up for her.

"Did you get that caveman's all-meat special you used to love?" she teases me.

And it feels fantastic.

I beat my chest. "Me, Ug. You, Ugga."

Even though her laugh is weak, I know it's real.

"That's a yes. Thanks, Griff. And thanks for remembering."

No other way to describe it, her praise makes me feel warm and pretty damn proud. "What else can I get you?"

"Nothing. We'll be fine from here. I can give Jamie a bath soon and he'll go—"

"No. I'll give him a bath and put him to bed. You eat and then you rest."

I must look stubborn because she concedes with a sigh. "All right."

I check on Jamie while I grab my food from the kitchen counter. Yep, it's a mess. I'll deal with it in a few.

As I settle in beside Britta, she takes the first bite and moans. "I'm in heaven."

"You can taste it?"

"I'm congested, but I'd have to be dead to miss this flavor." She takes another bite, and her pleasure sounds almost sexual. "I remember eating these at two a.m. after we'd been out barhopping most of the night. They always tasted so good then, especially when I knew we had to get up early for work the next day."

I remember. I also recall how many times we'd finish our sandwiches, shower up, and fall into bed, frantic and hungry for each other, then make love until damn near dawn.

Why the fuck was I so stupid that I didn't believe the devotion and happiness in my arms?

After I've finished my sandwich, I look over to see she's managed to eat half of hers, along with a few chips. I insist she drink more from the water bottle before I lift her and carry her back to bed.

As I lay her on the mattress, it's clear she's fighting to keep her eyes open. She touches my arm. "I don't know whether to thank you or ask you to stop before I get used to you taking care of me."

"You don't have to do either," I promise. I don't need her thanks, and I definitely intend to be by her side—giving her whatever she needs—for the rest of her life. "Just rest."

Her faint smile slowly fades. "'K."

"I love you," I whisper.

But she's already floating away to wherever her dreams have taken her. I kiss her forehead, resolving to bring some ibuprofen and whatever I can find that's useful in her medicine cabinet as soon as I get Jamie in bed. Then I back out of the bedroom, leaving her to sleep alone in peace.

I also promise myself it's one of the last times in our lives that she'll sleep without me.

CHAPTER SEVEN

I GOT ALMOST NO REST, but the night was still beyond epic. I slept under the same roof as Britta. Not just under the same moon or in the same time zone or even on the same island, which was what I sometimes told myself in the past. But legitimately mere footsteps away.

After giving Jamie a bath and reading him a couple of stories about puppies, I tucked him in. I made sure the kitchen was clean and the house was secure, then I checked on Britta to find her utterly sacked out. I glanced at my watch. Not even nine p.m.

It's late for Keeley, but I take a chance that she's still awake and call her back.

She answers on the second ring. "I haven't heard from you in a couple of days. Everything all right?"

"I had to think."

"What's going on?" Concern rings in her voice.

With a reluctant sigh, I fill her in. I'd rather not say anything but A) she gives great advice and B) she'll only ask me a not-so-gentle avalanche of questions designed to dissect my thoughts. I've only ever been able to keep one secret from Keeley. I often wonder if she's managed to fill in the blanks anyway.

When I finish my recap of recent events, she pauses. "What are you going to do?"

"I planned to romance Britta, but when she got sick, I had to scrap my intimate lunch for two." I'd managed to finagle some private catering on the rooftop of a hotel with amazing views that went on forever. Once we were alone, I intended to be as honest as I could about my life, my past, my regrets. I hoped being that real with her would prove I was a different man and she would change her mind about Jamie, Makaio…everything. "It was a good strategy, but in retrospect, the issue isn't simply my relationship with her but with Jamie, too. Britta needs to see what life with the three of us together would be like. She needs to believe I intend to stay and be good to them."

"You're in her house with your son now," Keeley points out. "It's a start, right?"

"I'm caretaking and babysitting, not wooing and bonding."

"Yeah, but it's helpful. I guess it's not what you had in mind."

"Britta will be well in a few days, and the fiancé will slink back. Then one of those two will heave-ho me out of the house. And I'll be back to square one."

Not making amends with Britta. Not forging a relationship with Jamie.

I'm not tolerating that.

"I know that tone in your voice," she says suspiciously. "You're scheming something."

"I'm not." Yet. But, all right, I'm thinking about it. No masterful strokes of genius have lit my bulb so far.

She sighs. "I'd tell you to stop and win her back with your heart, but I'm not sure you can suppress your ruthlessness for that long."

"I've been trying to do this the right way." But I don't know if it's working out.

"Well, that's a start. I know you'll probably ignore me but… Tread carefully or you'll talk yourself into something reckless you'll only have to repent for later."

"This is a go-big-or-go-home situation."

"Griff…" Keeley warns.

"Think about it. When I walked out on her, it changed her life. It was a huge deal. Can I really approach her quietly, hat in hand, and expect her to welcome me back? I have to be more than sorry. I have to prove I've changed and that nothing is more important to me than her and our son."

"But you can't *force* her to accept that. Her asking you to sign those papers was like caution tape. She's clearly feeling threatened, so—"

"I feel threatened, too. She blindsided me by asking me to relinquish my parental rights, and the terms? Fucking draconian. There's no way I'll ever agree. But if I'm ever going to earn her forgiveness so we can live happily ever after, I can't let this shit make me angry. I have to get smart."

And yeah, maybe a little ruthless.

"You could be right. At the moment, I'm questioning my own wisdom. And I can't help with ideas to win Britta back since I'm not feeling very grand-romantic-gesture. I mean…It's great that Maxon respected the space I asked for." She sounds anything but thrilled.

I laugh. "He asks about you every day. To say he wants you is an understatement, somewhere in the league of me stating that the universe is big. Are you getting on the plane in"—I look at the time on my phone—"eight hours?"

She lets out a tortured breath. "I still don't know. Maybe."

"What do you need so you know for sure?"

"Probably to see Maxon, but that's what I'm most afraid of. I'm so in love with him that I'm worried after one glance, I'll sweep everything under the rug."

"You? Nah. Though I always believed you had better taste in men…" I tease to lighten the mood. After I work a chuckle out of her, I get serious. I owe her for all the times she talked me through my personal shit. In fact, I can never truly repay Keeley. "Look, I know my brother. He…can be thoughtless. He's driven. Like you said, he wants what he wants when he wants it. But I've never seen him actually love anyone— until you. I'm not just saying that. You know few people are as important to me as you, so I'd never lie. I think if you gave him another chance, he'd do his best to capture sunshine and bend rainbows if he thought it would make you happy."

Keeley doesn't say anything for a long moment. "One thing I do know? I don't belong here. Mom and Phil plan to do Mardi Gras in New Orleans at the end of the month. They invited me to come along, but I feel like a third wheel who sits around with a long face and occasionally mooches food."

"I doubt you're that sad." I scoff. "I have an idea. Come home and get your things out of storage. You're supposed to sing at Gus's hole-in-the-wall on Sunday night, right?" When she gives me an affirmative murmur, I go on. "So come crash at my place. See Maxon and hear what he has to say. Sing on Sunday. If you still want to leave come Monday, then I'll get you another plane ticket to Phoenix—or wherever. But at least you'll have your stuff and some closure."

"When did you get so smart, Mr. Reed?"

"Well, a few years ago, I met a really cool chick who was answering the phones for this worthless therapist who was supposed to be helping me sort through my personal issues…"

She laughs. "Well, that girl was in need of a good friend, too. I just don't know why you had to have a hot brother she'd fall for?"

"Maybe…you were meant to be, like, my sister, huh?" I suggest. When she tries to poo-poo that, I lay out the truth. "Without you, Maxon and I wouldn't be speaking. I'd have no chance at all of winning over Britta or my son. I mean, it's still slim, but it's more than I had. Thank you for helping me figure out how to be happy again. Maybe it's time for me to help you."

"You're entirely too silver-tongued, Griffin Reed. All right." She sighs. "I'll come home and see how I feel after the weekend."

Gotcha. I've heard Maxon's plan, so I know that by Monday, she's going to be so thrilled the last thing she'll ever want to do is leave.

I smile as we ring off, then answer some emails from my phone. About midnight, I'm winding down and ready to find my pillow when I hear screaming.

I rush down the hall and fumble in the dark, stumbling into Jamie's bedroom. The boyish space is illuminated by one low-glowing nightlight. I spot the little guy wearing a furious expression, fists clenched, in the middle of his room.

Apparently, he climbed out of his crib. He's big enough, so I'm not surprised.

I drop to my knees in front of him and hold out my arms. He backs away and shakes his head. It's like a dagger in my heart. But I'm pretty much a stranger, and he's a little kid. I need to remember that.

"Hey, buddy." I try to soothe him in a soft voice. "Did you have a bad dream?"

"Mama…" Tears stream down his face.

"She's sick. I'm here. What happened?"

He points at the crib and begins crying in earnest again, then picks up a stuffed animal at his feet. He flails his arms angrily, and the bear flops above his head, then swings against his leg a few times before I pluck it away.

"Let's not hurt the bear. Come here, big guy. Let's talk this out."

This time, I manage to pull him into my lap and hold him. I try to convey calm and give him a sense of security. But I'm fully aware that I know nothing about easing a toddler's imaginary fears.

Across the room, I spot a rocking chair of some sort and lift Jamie, settling him against my chest as I sink in and glide in gentle strokes. It doesn't take long before he sticks his thumb in his mouth, then lays his head on my shoulder and drifts off.

I'm in his dark room, cleverly decorated in blues and woodsy accents, and I'm surrounded by his toys, his scent, his presence. He's done nothing but go to sleep, as small children do. Yet it's a profound moment.

I really am a father. This boy is my son. And what's happened between us is a small, fragile start. But it means everything to me to feel his heart beating against me, have his deep breaths heat my neck, to know he trusts me enough to simply relax in my arms.

It's unlike anything I've ever imagined. I've spent thirty ridiculously self-absorbed years on this planet being angry at my father for being an unfeeling asshole and my mother for being the sort willing to sell her kid out for a modicum of power. I took for granted my brother, my woman. I plowed through so much pussy and threw away phone numbers the next morning without even remembering their names or caring about the time I spent with them. I've done too many things I'm not proud of.

But in this moment, I'm overjoyed because somehow, somewhere along the way, I did this one thing right. If I've contributed nothing to society except Jamie, then at least I gave my best.

Now that he's good and asleep, I should set him in his crib and leave him in peace. But I don't want to let go. Just another minute.

Silence seeps around me, broken only by the sounds of my son inhaling and exhaling. He's limp weight in my arms. I'm not doing anything exceptional except holding him.

Yet it's so moving I feel tears sting my eyes.

I see the fork in my road in front of me so clearly. Down one path lies more of this—moments with my son, with Britta, growing our love, expanding our family. Down the other...well, I know that road. More emptiness. More nameless hookups. More wondering what the hell the meaning of life is.

Fuck no. I'm going to fight with everything I've got to hold on to this family that's mine. It may get ugly and dirty before I'm through, but I will do whatever it takes to claim and care for them.

I lay my son to sleep in his crib with his stuffed animal, a light blanket, and a kiss on his cheek.

I seek my own bed but barely manage to sleep. Too much is swirling through my head.

I jolt out of bed at seven, make coffee, then check on Jamie to find him stretching sleepily. I'm not sure what his morning routine is, but I'll figure it out.

For the first time, he comes to me right away. And when I lift him up, the first order of business is obvious. Jamie's diaper is sloshy and wet.

"Okay, big boy. Let's do this together."

I'm damn glad I have my phone handy. YouTube is totally my friend, and within thirty seconds, I'm pulling up a video for men about changing a diaper. I would feel stupid...but nearly two hundred thousand other guys have watched this clip, so I'm clearly not the only lost sap.

After that, I dress him in clean clothes, make a few eggs—and coffee for me—then I set him down to a cartoon and some toys. I'm struck by one vital question: how does Britta take a shower in peace with a toddler roaming the house who's able to open doors, climb furniture, and maybe even start fires?

Suddenly, Britta rushes into the family room in her oversized T-shirt with her hair in what was once a haphazard ponytail. She looks like hell warmed over, but she looks better than she did last night.

"Morning, angel." I sip coffee.

Her stare volleys between Jamie and me in question. "Everything's all right?"

"Perfect. I just need a shower. Um…how do you watch him while you get cleaned up? Take him in the bathroom with you or…? I'd suggest a playpen, but he climbed out of his crib last night—"

"Again?" She winces, then sighs. "He started doing that last week. Rascal. Any nightmares?"

"One. I handled it."

She glances at him, all ready for daycare. To say she looks surprised is an understatement. "Thanks."

"As soon as we drop him off, I'm taking you to the urgent care clinic."

"No need. I'm fine," she says, then almost instantly doubles over in a coughing fit.

"Obviously, you're not." I want to wrap my arms around her, but I'm trying to respect her personal space while she feels crappy. "They open in ten minutes, so start getting ready."

Britta wants to dig in her heels but doesn't have the energy. While she's throwing on some clothes, she keeps one eye on Jamie so I can call Maxon to tell him what's up and grab a shower. Twenty minutes later, we're all heading out the door. Jamie goes happily to school, and Britta is grumpy all the way to the doctor's office.

I smile. I probably have no reason to be this chipper. I barely slept. But I'm at peace. If I play this right, today could be the first day of the rest of our lives. It's different. It's hectic. It's not perfect. None of that matters. I'm with the people who matter to me.

"What's this?" Britta asks as she plucks up the CD case I left in her car last night when I drove to get her food. I meant to listen to another track but I was enjoying my time with Jamie too much to let anything, even well-intended music, bring me down.

I'm not sure how she'll take this, but I can't be less than honest. "You've met Keeley?"

Beside me, Britta stiffens and sets the case down. "I have."

"We're just friends."

She sniffles into a tissue and rolls her eyes. "It's none of my business."

I want it to be her business. "What would you say to me if it was?"

"That you've never been 'just friends' with a woman in your life."

"Until Keeley, no. But I swear I've never touched her. It would be like touching Harlow to me." I recoil at the thought. "Seriously. I'm just friends with her the way Maxon is just friends with you."

She considers that with a frown. But given my history, it sounds farfetched. I know.

"If you were feeling better, angel, I'd take you with me to the airport this afternoon to pick her up so you could see for yourself."

Now Britta looks alarmed. "She's coming back?"

I fill her in. "I'm hoping that she'll give Maxon a chance to make her happy. They're really in love."

Britta ponders such a long time I'm not sure she's going to answer. "He's been different since he met her. If what you're saying is true, I hope everything works out for them."

But she still sounds a little suspicious. And glum. It's going to work out for us, too. No matter what I have to do.

The doctor confirms that she's got an upper respiratory infection and gives her a prescription. After settling her at home, I pick up her Z-Pak, get her some lunch, tuck her in bed. She thanks me…and doesn't balk when I kiss her on the forehead.

It's progress.

Then I head to the airport.

When Keeley hustles into baggage claim, she looks exhausted from traveling all day, but she's also got a little glow that tells me she's happy to be home. She sees me, then immediately starts looking around, her smile slowly falling.

"Maxon isn't here," I say softly as I hug her. "I didn't tell him in case you changed your mind."

In fact, I've been dodging his calls all morning.

"Oh." She frowns, but I hear the relief in her voice that my brother didn't suddenly stop caring about her. As if.

"He has something he wants to say when the moment is right. You'll see." I grin smugly.

I take her to an early dinner so we can talk more, then get her settled back at my condo. She gave up her apartment when she moved in with Maxon a month ago, so she's got no place to go. Keeley protests, but I tell her it's cool. I'm hoping not to be there for a few days—at least.

I must be watching the time a lot because she laughs at me. "You're anxious to get back to Britta, aren't you?"

"Yeah." I feel my face getting hot. "Sorry."

"I need the rest," she assures. "Go away."

With a chuckle, I leave her at my place. On the drive out to Britta's, I call Maxon. The relief in my brother's voice when I let him know Keeley is back in Maui would be comical if I didn't understand how much it hurts when you have nothing but hope that your woman will come back to you.

Finally, I arrive at Britta's house. I'm ready to talk to her about allowing me to pick Jamie up from daycare. I've got arguments prepared. But when she answers the door, I see she's already driven the nearly hour there and back and brought our son home.

"I was going to get him for you. You're supposed to be resting," I admonish when she answers the door and I walk in to find Jamie on the family room floor, playing with some Lincoln Logs.

"I'm feeling better," she promises, but still sounds raspy as hell. "What are you doing here?"

I scowl. What does she think I'm doing? "Taking care of you two."

"We're good for tonight."

"The antibiotics will take twenty-four hours to kick in. It's been what, eight? Jamie can be a handful and he doesn't need exposure to your germs. You two still need dinner. So...here I am."

"You're offering to cook?" At my nod, she frowns at me. "That's awfully...domestic of you. When we were together, you never wanted anything to do with cooking or cleaning or—"

"Or anything helpful. I know. I've honestly changed. A couple years ago, I realized how bad it is for you to eat out every night, like I did before I met you. So, out of self-preservation, I learned to throw together a few decent meals. I'll cook tonight, angel. I'm not promising that dinner will be spectacular, but it will be edible."

She shuts the door and heads back to the sofa, plopping down like she's exhausted. "You don't have to do that."

"Yeah, I do." Frankly, it's what Makaio should be doing, but I'm not going to diss the bastard to her face. She'll only feel compelled to defend him. And I want to avoid comparisons. Right now, this is about her and me, period. "We'll see how you feel tomorrow. If you're really well then, I'll leave if you want me to."

Britta looks like she wants to accept my offer but knows she shouldn't. "Really, you don't have to. I already fed Jamie a cup of soup and a grilled cheese. I can whip up something for myself—"

"You need rest and at least one more stretch of uninterrupted sleep. I'm going to take care of you two. Jamie and I were buds after his nightmare last night. I rocked him back to sleep."

"He let you?" She sounds stunned.

"Yeah. Took a minute or two to coax him, but..." I shrug. "Look, just promise me we don't have to talk about the papers now, okay? Let me show you I can be a good father." *And a good husband.* But I don't add that aloud. She's not ready to hear it.

"You win. I should say no but I don't have the strength." Britta drops her head back against the sofa, eyes closed. "Where's Keeley?"

"I stashed her at my place tonight. She'll be with Maxon soon, I'm sure."

"And you'd rather be here?"

I have to hold in a smile of triumph. The answer clearly matters to her.

"Absolutely. Keeley helped me through a lot. She's my friend, and I wish her all the best. But I love you. I intend to stay here as long as you'll let me."

She lifts her head and stares like she's shocked I confessed my feelings to her again. "Griff…"

"You don't have to say anything. For as often as you used to tell me and I stayed silent, I've earned it. But that's not going to stop me from saying the words and trying to convince you I mean them. In case you're wondering, I love Jamie, too. It was instantaneous. I never expected that."

After gnawing on her lip, she finally nods. "Isn't that the craziest thing? I loved him before he was born, but when I first saw him…"

"It was unstoppable. In that moment, he became my son. You thanked me for making him possible, but I'm the one who should be thanking you. You carried him, birthed him, nurtured him—all without my help. I'm never going to let you down again."

Britta presses her lips together and stares. I don't know what's running through her head. For once, I can't read her expression or body language. I suspect she's at least thinking about what I've said.

"What can you cook?" she finally asks on a sigh.

I'm disappointed at the change of subject, but I get it. Nothing with Britta is going to happen overnight. "What do you want?"

"Something with chicken sounds good."

"That leaves my choices wide open."

She shrugs. "I'm good with whatever. I'm going to shower."

"Sure. It will be ready when you come out."

After a little poking around, I find the fixings to make her a chicken quesadilla with some homemade salsa. I boil up some instant rice and doctor it with spices to make it a tad more authentic.

By the time I finish, she's walking out of the bathroom, looking squeaky and fresh, with a towel wrapped around her head, wearing a matching cotton cami and shorts that double as pajamas.

It's not sexy. All the essentials are covered, and she's not dolled up in the least. But she's coming toward me with a smile, and that's all it takes these days for my body to flash hot and for me to want her.

Vaguely, I think back to the last time I had sex. Was that only ten days ago? Feels like a lifetime. Yet I'm aware that if you gave me a choice between whatever-her-name-was in the killer stilettos and skimpy dress or Britta in her jammies and turban, I'd absolutely take the woman I love. Even sick. Even though I'm sure nothing will happen between us tonight. I'm exactly where I want to be.

She sits at the table, and I put a bottle of water, her antibiotics, and some ibuprofen in front of her. "Eat up."

"What about you?" She frowns my way.

"I had an early dinner with Keeley since she came off the plane starved. Want me to bathe Jamie while you fill your belly?"

She glances at the clock. "Do you mind?"

I wonder if Makaio ever helps her with my son like this. I suspect he doesn't get involved too much, but I'm kind of hoping he doesn't lift a finger with Jamie. He probably tells himself that he doesn't want to step on Britta's toes. Deep down, does he think my son is baggage? I suspect he does. I'll bet that's why he was more than happy to help me obtain some custodial rights, so he'll have Britta all to himself every other weekend. I don't know whether to be glad or disgusted. Either way, he'll soon be out of the picture.

"Not at all. I love spending time with him. But I learned a valuable lesson last night not to encourage too much splashing or I have a hard time keeping his cast dry. And most of the water in the tub winds up on the floor."

That earns me a smile that becomes a gentle laugh. "Yes. He never does anything halfway. Always full throttle for that kid. He's a lot like you."

"Poor guy." I wink at her, then glance at him over my shoulder. He's moved on to his trucks and is making *vroom* sounds as he rolls one across the hardwood.

Britta forks in a bite of the dinner I've prepared and her eyes widen. She gives me a look of surprise. "This is actually good. You *can* cook now."

Secretly, I'm pleased she thinks so. "Not too hard to follow a recipe. Need anything else before we get started?"

"I'm good. Thanks." She gives me a little smile that makes me feel warm inside. "For everything."

After bathing my son and dressing him in pajamas, I help him brush his teeth, then take him to Britta for a kiss. When she presses her lips to his cheek, he fights my hold to sit in her lap. He wants Mommy, and it's obvious they're close. I have to take him to his room and sit him in my lap to soothe him with a few stories and some pats on the back.

It doesn't take long before he's yawning, little fist covering his mouth, his eyes droopy.

"Night, Jamie."

When I hug him, he presses a sleepy, sloppy kiss on my cheek.

My heart melts, even as my determination to hang on to my son solidifies into steel. No one—especially not some fucking banker—will ever be Jamie's father but me.

I set him in his crib, and he rolls over with his stuffed animal and his thumb. His breathing evens out and deepens almost instantly.

I'm sure I'm hardly the first father to think this about their kid, but he's amazing. He's a little individual. He's got a smile I'd know anywhere. He's got a cowlick in the back of his head, a small splatter of freckles, and a tiny gap in his teeth. I've memorized them all. Everything about him is adorable.

I come back to find Britta on the sofa, curled up with a blanket, head resting on the back. The TV is running softly in the background. She's asleep.

A glance around tells me she's already cleaned up the kitchen. I'd chastise her if she didn't need her rest.

I settle beside her on the couch and flip a few channels, coming to some basketball recap on ESPN. I've been trying to keep up with the college games. March Madness is right around the corner. But I can only smell Britta's light scent—jasmine and clean skin.

With a moan, she rolls and shifts her weight to one hip, clearly trying to get comfortable. Her head slides off the back of the sofa and hangs awkwardly against her chest. She looks damn uncomfortable. If I don't do something, she's going to wake up with a stiff neck or a headache.

Okay, that might not be the only reason I decide to touch her. And yes, I know she's sick. I'm not planning to seduce her...just get a little closer.

I sidle against her and dip my shoulder under her head until she's using me as a pillow. In her sleep, she shifts around, seemingly looking for a more comfortable position. Her hand drops to my thigh.

My entire body goes tense.

I want this woman.

I admit I always want sex. I can probably count on one hand the number of times I've turned it down in my life, and most of them were from a former co-worker's wife. I do have a few boundaries. But what I feel for Britta is beyond desire. She's...comfortable. That sounds unsexy, I'm guessing. But what I mean is, I don't have to pretend with her. Britta Stone is kind, reliable, funny, sensitive, sharp, interesting... My feelings are real, and as I sit here with her head on my shoulder, I realize that no matter how many women I slept with in the thirty-nine months we've been apart, I never found anyone as perfect for me as her.

It's reassuring in a way, the validation that my love isn't mere nostalgia. I can picture her asleep as she cuddles up next to me in thirty years, when we're talking about things like retirement and grandkids and cruises around the world.

Oddly, I'm looking forward to sharing all those adventures with her.

When she shifts her body for the tenth time in as many minutes, I decide enough is enough and lift her into bed. Her sheets are still rumpled from last night, and I tuck her into the cloud of softness, then shut the door so she can rest peacefully.

I'm not really sure what I'm going to do with the rest of my evening. I flip more channels, talk to my brother about a lead he got late this afternoon on the Stowe estate—shockingly fast for a property ringing in at nearly thirty million dollars—and pace a lot, wondering if I should check on Britta again.

Then a phone rings somewhere in the house. It's not mine.

I follow the sound into the kitchen and see Britta's phone lighting up and vibrating its way across the table. A glance at the display has me cursing.

Makaio.

I figured out a long time ago that he's nothing like me, but in his shoes, if my sick woman didn't answer her phone I'd get my ass in the car and head over to her house to make sure everything is all right.

I don't need him here, fucking up my domestic bliss and reminding Britta that she thinks she's moved on.

"Hello," I answer. I don't try to sound unfriendly, but I'm pissed that he won't go the fuck away.

It's unrealistic, since he thinks he's marrying Britta, I know. But he's totally wrong.

"Um…hi. What are you doing—"

"Answering Britta's phone? She's asleep." *Dipshit.* "She's really sick. I took her to the doctor today and got her some antibiotics. She should be better in a few days." *You're welcome, prick.* "No cause for concern."

"You? And why are you at her house?"

"She's far too sick to take care of a toddler, and Jamie is my son. This is a good opportunity to get to know him and let him be comfortable with me while making sure he doesn't catch whatever bug Britta's got."

"Well… I-I…" He sounds as if he doesn't like it and is looking for a logical reason to dislodge me from Britta's place. "It's almost nine thirty. Isn't Jamie in bed?"

"Yep. Now I'm just hanging out in case he has nightmares. I put Britta in the master bedroom so that if he starts screaming, she won't hear. The doctor told her to get plenty of rest. I'm making sure she gets it."

"If I had known she was truly that sick, I would have taken care of her."

Who is he lying to, me or himself?

"Sure. I'm going to sleep now," I brush him off. I just can't talk to this dude anymore. "In the morning, I'll tell Britta you called."

"You're staying the night there?"

He hadn't gotten that picture yet? I try not to sigh. "Yeah. In the room next to Jamie's. I'm there when he needs me."

"Oh. Well. Yeah, if she's really that sick. All right. I'll…um, see them tomorrow."

Hopefully not. "Bye."

I hang up before Makaio can say another word. He's an ass and I don't like him. And yes, I'm jealous as hell knowing that Britta has had sex with him. I can't admonish her for having a life after I left her. I've had plenty since our split. Doesn't mean I like it.

It does mean I'm going to do everything in my power to make sure the rest of her life is with me.

Tomorrow, if she feels better, it's so on.

CHAPTER EIGHT

FRIDAY AFTERNOON, MAXON AND I are conferring in his office. I swiped the carseat from Britta's car, and daycare allowed me to drop Jamie off with a phone call from his mother. But I have no idea how I'll pick him up again at the end of the day. I'll have to work that out with Britta soon, but for now I refrain from calling to check on her in case she's asleep.

"I have a hunch who our potential buyer might be," my brother says, barging into my thoughts.

"For the Stowe estate?" At his nod, I shrug. "Let me have your brilliant speculation."

"Well, the buyer's representative said she was previewing for a wealthy, high-profile client who's been living in Dallas, but he wants to return to his home state and is looking for privacy."

This is the first I'm hearing of this conversation, but immediately one name springs to mind. "Noah Weston."

"Yes. Exactly. He just retired from the NFL."

"Hall-of-Famer, for sure." I nod. "You're right. He's originally from Honolulu, isn't he? But he's been playing in Dallas for most of his career. The guy gets hounded by the press everywhere he goes, so naturally he would want privacy."

"And I doubt money is an object," Maxon drawls. "Holy shit. I always wanted to sell this place, but to a guy like Weston?"

"The cherry on top," I agree. "Any chance he's coming along to view the house, too?"

My brother shakes his head. "His rep is flying out alone next week. She'll let us know exactly when. But apparently, her client just sold his house in Texas and will be ready to make the move quickly. I know the Stowes are eager to unload this place. If the rep likes the property…this might work out."

I'm salivating at the thought. "Hot damn. I'd like the paycheck. And I'd love to meet that guy."

"Me, too. Both would be epic."

We meet celebrities from time to time when they decide Maui would be a great place to keep a getaway. But… "Noah Weston is a man's man and a stud on the field. From what I hear, he's not a douchebag off the field, either."

"Right? He seems cool."

I laugh. "We sound a little like fan girls at a Bieber concert."

"Yeah." Maxon grins. "Good thing Rob took the day off. He, like, worships the guy. He'd be leg humping us for even the suggestion that he might get to meet Weston someday."

"Watch…" I say cynically. "This buyer will be some old oil executive who's had enough of corporate life and wants his slice of paradise."

Maxon chuckles in return. "You're probably right."

A noise at the office door has me whirling around. I'm stunned to see Britta coming in. She's wearing black yoga pants, a tank top with a Shaka sign that reads HANG LOOSE, and some flip-flops. Her hair is in a ponytail. Her face is white as a sheet, except her nose, which looks red from blowing it.

I jump to my feet and rush over to her. She looks even frailer up close, and it's all I can do not to put my arms around her. "What are you doing here, angel?"

She won't meet my gaze. "Just grabbing some work to take home and Jamie's carseat before I pick him up."

"I would have brought it and him out to you." If she'd let me. I frown her way. "You should be in bed."

"I feel a lot better this afternoon. I couldn't lie around anymore. And you don't need to make another trip out to the house. I appreciate everything you did, but I've got it under control now."

"It was my pleasure," I assure her. "I'm happy to spend the evening with you two tonight. I'll cook something more exciting—"

"Makaio is back."

And she let him in. After he failed to take care of her? After he left Jamie to get sick because he didn't want germs? Yep, I see she's wearing her engagement ring again.

Goddamn it.

"Can I see Jamie this weekend?" I won't last a whole weekend without him, and when I visit, Britta will have to see me, too. Maybe she'll remember how good it felt to spend time together over the last few days and decide that Banker Butthole isn't for her.

"I don't think that's going to work out." She swallows nervously. "Iolana, Makaio's sister, is going to keep him this weekend. Um…Makaio wants to take me away since we missed Valentine's Day."

I see red.

It's on the tip of my tongue to ask her if the way I took care of her and Jamie over the last two days mattered at all. I can't, even if I think it did mean something to her. That's why she won't quite look at me. She feels guilty. But the bottom line is, she's still engaged to Makaio Kāle. Until that's off, she's going to choose him every time.

"Am I supposed to be happy?" It's kind of a dick reply. Since I'm feeling like a deeply pissed-off dick, it fits. "I love you and he's not right for you."

She flinches. "That's not your decision."

"I think you still have feelings for me."

"You're wrong." Now her voice is shaking, like she's more nervous than before.

"So what did that kiss on your bed mean, Britta? What was that about?"

"You confused me for a few minutes. But I'm going to marry the man who, despite whatever conclusion you've drawn from these last few days, will stay with me."

I grit my teeth and hold in my temper. The old me would have blown up and walked off, waited for her to apologize. And if she didn't, I'd have needled her until she did because her words hurt me. The me now acknowledges that I shredded her heart and put her through hell. Just walking back into her life because I claim to be a good guy who's gotten my shit together now is unreasonable.

But, fuck, my patience is wearing thin.

"Tell me something I can do to prove I'll never leave you again. Whatever it is, I'll do it."

She shakes her head. "He came to see me after his presentation this morning, took off work to check on me. We talked." She draws in a shaky breath. "He wants to get married on April fifteenth. I agreed."

Her words seize the air from my lungs, then take a sledgehammer to my heart. "Of this year?"

"In eight weeks. Yes."

"Why?"

She still won't look at me. "Will you please sign Jamie's papers and—"

"No."

The last fucking thing I'm going to do is roll over and play dead. Britta's got another think coming if she imagines for one moment that I'm giving up the notion of being a family with her and Jamie.

Finally, she looks up at me, seemingly fighting tears. "It's over, Griff."

"You're wrong."

Until this point, we haven't had a direct discussion about the future I foresee. Between sniffling and coughing fits didn't seem like the right time. Besides, I thought it might work to my advantage to slide in under her radar, show her I'd changed, earn her trust, *then* bring it up when her attitude was softer.

Apparently Makaio isn't as gullible as I thought. And my time to finesse this situation has run out.

Before I can say anything else, Maxon approaches. He's a safe distance away, like he knows he's interrupting something. I'm sure he thinks he's stopping my temper from turning this conversation into all-out warfare.

I might thank him later. Right now, I just want to rip his head off.

"Hey, Britta. Feeling better?"

"Yeah. The antibiotics have really helped." Her gaze slides over to me once more. "I'm going to grab a little work and do it over the weekend. I'll be back for sure on Monday."

I want to snarl. I want to physically stop her from leaving for a romantic weekend with a guy who has a stick so far up his ass I'm shocked it's not coming out of his mouth. And I'm beyond infuriated that I can't do a fucking thing to stop her now.

Maxon slides a gaze my way, probably to see if I've turned volcanic yet. "Sure. Glad you're feeling better. See you then."

"Thanks." Britta rushes over to her desk, looking relieved not to have to see the rage and disappointment on my face anymore.

I cut my brother a glare. *What the hell?* I ask him silently.

He tosses his hands in the air. What was he supposed to do? Something to convince her that Makaio isn't the man for her. Britta isn't listening to me because she doesn't trust me. But my brother... She values his opinion. Hell, she asked him to be with her when she gave birth.

But this isn't his fight. It's mine. I need to do whatever it takes to end this shit.

And now I'll have just under two months to do it.

Fuck.

Britta grabs an empty messenger bag and shoves some papers into it. She checks her voice mail messages, then tucks her laptop into the briefcase.

"Have a good weekend," she says to Maxon.

"Call me if you need me...for whatever."

I hear his subtext; if she needs him for a big brother, a sounding board, a heavy to kick Makaio's ass.

She nods, patently refusing to look at me. "Thanks."

With that, my brother slinks back into his office and shuts the door. The silence between us is almost deafening, except I can hear my harsh breathing. I'd be yelling, but her skittish expression is killing me. And I know Britta. She'd be fighting if she thought she was right.

If she knows better, what the hell is she doing?

"I'm not signing the papers."

"Do what's best for your son," she implores.

"Oh, I am," I assure her. "You should take your own advice. Don't marry a blowhole who chose not to take care of you both properly when you needed him. What good is he if he stays with you and doesn't fucking put you first?"

"I'm not arguing with you about this. It's my choice. I got by without you during the most difficult three years of my life. Stop insisting I need you now."

She shoulders her way past me and bangs the door open. The wind catches the heavy wood and slams it shut behind her. She's gone.

I'm devastated.

I've tried to be understanding, be a good guy, prove I've changed by listening and coaxing her trust. Fuck all that now. I've got to stop acting against my grain. Or I'm going to lose her—and Jamie—forever.

"GRIFF..." KEELEY PUTS HER HAND over mine across the table during dinner and drinks the following night, after I catch her up. "I can only imagine how you felt."

Like shit. Like Britta had pulled the rug out from under me. Like she didn't care at all.

I'm still angry. I've been angry for more than twenty-four hours. The way I feel right now, I don't know if I'll ever not be angry.

But the fact she's gone away with him is killing me, too. Right now, she could be fucking him and not giving me another thought at all.

I swallow a lump of resentment. "I've got fifty-six days and twelve hours to change her mind."

"Well, that gives you time to keep talking to her and showing her you've changed—"

"I've been doing that." I beat my fist on the table. "It's not working."

"It's barely been a week," she argues.

"I can't be sure another eight weeks like the last one will get me any closer to making her and Jamie mine for good."

"I don't know what to tell you." Keeley shakes her head. "After what you put Britta through, you can't rush her. What did you think was going to happen, Griff? That you'd pop up in her life again and she'd be so damn happy to see you that she'd break off her engagement and glue herself to your side forever? That finally telling her you love her after failing to say it three years ago would thrill her so much she'd drop to her knees, kiss the ground you walked on, and forgive everything?"

When she puts it like that, I feel sheepish. "No."

Well, not exactly. But as I shift in my seat, I realize that she's closer to the truth than I'd like.

"I don't know her, so I'm not sure what it will take for her to believe that you're not the same selfish bastard you once were. For me, it's about actions. They do speak louder. Words are cheap. So are promises. But what you do now, how you treat her, whether you put her first…that's important. I'd bet money she made note of the fact that you were there during her illness and Makaio wasn't."

"It didn't change anything."

"Not that she admitted to you. But you haven't let her sort anything out. You haven't been patient."

Fuck patience. It's beyond time to be ruthless.

I need the right plan.

I don't mention that to Keeley just now. She'll only try to talk me out of it in some circular argument I can't win.

I give her a noncommittal hum. "So what will you do when you see my brother again?"

"You don't want to talk about it, I see." She gives me a humorless laugh, and I know better than to think this subject won't come up again during our next conversation. "*If* I see Maxon again. He hasn't even tried to call me since I came back to the island. It's been two days."

"Trust me when I tell you he hasn't lost interest. At all."

"You keep saying that. What is he waiting for?"

I grin. If someone's going to be coupled up soon and it's not me, I'm glad it will be my brother and this amazing woman.

"What was that you said about patience a minute ago?" I raise a brow at her. "Don't worry. It won't be much longer."

"Just because I see him doesn't mean we're going to wind up happily ever after. Stop grinning at me like that. I'm serious."

"So am I." My smile deepens. "And you're wrong. It couldn't happen for two nicer people."

The phone in my pocket vibrates. I'm pretty sure I know who's calling me at nine p.m. on a Saturday night. When I look at the display, sure enough…

"Hey, bro," I say to Maxon.

Keeley snaps to attention and points at my phone. *That's him?* she mouths.

I nod.

"Hi," he says in my ear. "You with Keeley?"

"Uh-huh." No way I'm letting her in on my conversation with my brother and potentially ruining his big surprise.

"Is she all right?"

"Uh-huh," I answer without looking Keeley's way.

"You can't talk? Is that it?"

"Uh-huh."

"But you'll have her there tomorrow night and you won't tell her a thing?"

"Uh-huh," I promise.

"All right. You're saying you've got everything under control and it's taken care of on your end?"

"Uh-huh."

Maxon breathes a sigh of relief in my ear. "Great. Yeah… I'll talk about business to throw her off track. So I got a phone call from our potential buyer's rep about an hour ago. She's arriving in Maui on Monday afternoon. She wants to preview the Stowes' place on Tuesday."

"That fast. It sounds like the buyer is really interested."

"That's the vibe I'm getting. But we need to go out there and make sure the house and grounds are looking their best tomorrow morning."

"Sure. If not, we'll come up with a strategy then."

"To snag this mysterious buyer or our reluctant women?"

I laugh at my brother. "Yeah."

He'll know I mean both.

"You got it."

We ring off, and Keeley looks ready to ask me a million questions. I cut her off. "Business call. We already have someone interested in the Stowe estate."

I fill her in, minus the speculation about who the buyer might be. She listens with half an ear, finishes her wine, then pleads exhaustion. I think she's just sad that Maxon didn't ask to talk to her.

Back at my condo, it's close to ten, but I'm nowhere near ready for bed.

I feel sadness settle over me. It weighs as much as a goddamn elephant sitting on my chest, suffocating me. So when Keeley shuts her bedroom door, my options for distraction are limited, but deep down, I've made up my mind.

I'm going to torture myself.

It's not the first time…but I've indulged in this self-inflicted agony thing more than a few times in the last thirty-nine months. The previous time, I swore it would be the last. Obviously, I was full of shit and I'll probably hate myself for this later. But I'm like an addict. Relapse is just a matter of time.

I can't stop thinking that Makaio might not have been making love to Britta an hour ago. He might be doing it now. Or maybe he's doing it again. And there's not a fucking thing I can do to stop him.

With a curse under my breath, I pour myself a few fingers of Lagavulin 21. I'm old enough to drink, and my Scotch better be, too. I swirl it in my glass. It burns going down.

Am I really going to do this?

I toss back the rest, enjoying the fire blazing its way down my throat and into my belly.

Yeah. I really am.

I make to pour another few fingers of the booze. Oh, fuck it. The shit's only five hundred bucks a bottle. I grab it by the neck, take it with me into the bedroom, and decide to stop procrastinating.

It's time for the ultimate pain I can inflict on myself. Tonight, I've got an added bonus. I swiped the CD Keeley left me out of Britta's car and brought it into my bedroom. I set the bottle on my nightstand and start the next unfamiliar tune on the disc. According to the case, it's called "For a Lifetime" by a band called Lustral.

The song is chill. It's got a sense of…waiting. Like something is about to happen. When the background singers come in and chant the title a few times in something just above a whisper, the tune shows its gravity. I can't stop listening.

I also can't stop my feet from moving forward, into my closet, up to my safe. I scroll through the combination and push aside all the papers I keep and my stash of ready cash. I reach for the black velvet box in the back and lift the lid.

Yep, it's still sitting there. Two carats of princess-cut diamond in rose gold with sparkling pavé clusters set in the thin band to resemble little flowers.

I've kept it for nearly four years.

The minute I saw it, I knew it belonged on Britta's finger and that I was the man who needed to put it there.

At the time I saw it, we'd only been dating a bit more than three months. We had only been having sex for two weeks.

Winter was about to tip into spring, and on a gorgeous day, I took a drive to Wailea with my top down. Britta's mother was in town, and I was supposed to have dinner with them later that night. I parked at an outdoor mall and eyed an Italian place for lunch. As I headed that way, I walked past a jeweler's window. This ring glinted and dazzled. I couldn't stop looking at it.

A voice in my head told me to buy it for Britta. *She's too young,* I told myself at the time. *She's not ready.* Hell, I wasn't, either.

But that voice insisted if I walked past the ring, I'd be making a mistake. So I spent a small fortune on it. And I held on to it, all through the spring, when I felt as if I really got to know Britta. Through the hot summer, when we seemed to forge something deep, so I asked her to move in and she said yes. Through the early fall, when I truly began picturing what it might be like to live with and love this woman for the rest of our lives. With some help from friends and neighbors, I threw her a surprise party for her birthday in October. It was too crowded to pop the question then. But a month later? I thought proposing to her and hearing her say yes would be the perfect birthday present to me.

Damn, I had this great plan… I told her I wanted to take a sunset beach cruise for my birthday. She bought the tickets. Unbeknownst to her, I hired a string quartet. I had a speech planned with a private dinner for two afterward where I fully intended to finally tell her that I loved her and wanted to marry her. And I reserved a swanky suite, along with champagne and dessert.

Perfect.

Except it never happened.

Six days before, I found out about Maxon's secret deal with the Asian prince and lost my shit, ripping our business apart. Ironically, my brother had broken up with Tiffanii the night before when he discovered she'd been cheating with both a pilot and a wealthy playboy. I walked out on Britta, leaving when I had no idea she was pregnant.

November first was the worst day of my life, hands down. Every person and thing that made me happy was gone in the blink of an eye.

With that thought, I strip and get in bed, ring in one hand, bottle in the other. I swallow down another mouthful of the burn while I rub the precious metal between my fingers and imagine her wearing it while I'm making love to her, while she's got on nothing else but the symbol of my possession.

I'm harder than fuck.

The song rolls on. She sings that the world she clings to is the one where she'll walk beside me and she wants to show me what it feels to be complete. She's been waiting for me for a lifetime. Yeah, I feel like I've been waiting for Britta that long, too. The background singers add a panty, breathy vibe. It's sensual. And if I toss a little more booze into my system and close my eyes, I can almost imagine Britta beside me.

Yeah, that's her hand wrapped around my cock. That's my ring on her finger giving an edge to the pleasure of her stroke. Her thumb swipes over the head, circles the crest, teases the hell out of me with the slow pace until my back is arching, my breathing is uneven, and my balls hang heavy with need. Now she's looking into my eyes as she drags her fingertips up and down my shaft, urging me on. The band of her engagement ring slides over my most sensitive spots. She's here with me—in body, in spirit, in heart.

How can I give her any less than my all?

Another few strokes later, the pooling pleasure builds to a crescendo that, just like the song, becomes a climax. The singer cries out in what sounds like pleasured pain. I do the same, basking in the thick swirl of ecstasy.

Then the song ends. So does my glow.

I open my eyes. Blink. Sadness crashes in.

I'm alone in my bedroom with half a bottle of super-expensive swill, sheets that need a change, and a ring that might never be on Britta's finger.

No. Fuck no.

This is pathetic.

What am I doing?

I don't know. Tears sting my eyes. I try to drown them in more booze.

But I can't torture myself like this again. Somehow, someway, I'm going to turn our relationship around. I'm going to show that woman what it would be like to live with me. I'm going to prove I love her. And the next orgasm I have will be with Britta Stone when I've got her between the sheets of our bed and I'm making love to her for the first time for the rest of our lives.

CHAPTER NINE

I SPEND MOST OF SUNDAY with Maxon. Early in the morning, we head out to the Stowe estate. George and Vivienne have clearly already done as we instructed and hired someone to clean up the house and grounds. The photographer took the basic pictures of the estate on Wednesday morning. We uploaded them twenty-four hours later. Two days from now, the potential buyer will come to see the place. If he loves it, we may not need the video and aerial footage. Things are moving fast with this listing.

And slower than hell with Britta. Logically, it's only been nine days since I crashed her engagement party. God, it feels as if it's been nine fucking years. I can't take this shit dragging out any more.

Is she back from her weekend getaway yet? Where did she and Makaio go? What did they do? Did she tell him that we kissed? When he touched her, did she experience even a tenth of the passion we shared?

As we're leaving the listing, I turn my back on the full-frontal ocean views that make this massive estate a whopping thirty million dollars. Yeah, it's beautiful. Under normal circumstances, I would linger, dip my toe in one of the step-down infinity pools, take advantage of the game room, home theater, or billiards table. Or shower in one of the eight spa-like bathrooms. Instead, I'm tied into knots.

I don't think Maxon is in a better head space when I see him head to his car with a grimace.

"What's wrong?" I'm happy to dwell on a problem other than my own.

He blows out a breath. "I think we need a full-time caretaker here. I don't know where we're going to get one."

I can't disagree. It's a huge property, over ten thousand square feet. It's the kind of place you can leave for a week or so. Much longer than that, and some part or another needs attention. "You're right. The Stowes will have a hard time taking care of this from Vermont. We'll have to get creative and find someone."

My brother nods absently. I have some ideas percolating, but I'll keep thinking until something makes sense.

"So…you ready for tonight?" I ask. "Need help?"

"Thanks. I'm good. Everything is a go. I picked up the ring. I signed the papers late on Friday. I've got all the props in place. I called Gus to double-check that he's ready. Tonight just has to get here. You'll bring Keeley by at seven?"

I nod. "You got it."

"Great. Now what are you going to do about Britta?"

I ponder what to tell my brother, then decide if anyone is going to understand my choice, it will be him. "I've tried being nice and understanding and patient."

"You have. For the most part, I've been surprised at your restraint."

"You mean in between the constant warnings for me not to 'harass' her at the office?"

Maxon chuckles. "Except that. So the gloves are off now?"

"Oh, yeah." I debate the wisdom of strong-arming Britta. I don't want to reinforce all her worst opinions of me. I definitely don't want her to hate me. But I also can't keep trying the soft-shoe approach. It didn't work yesterday. Why would it work tomorrow?

"You have a plan?"

"I do." After my miserable self-humiliation last night, I paced my lanai, listened to the ocean crashing in the distance, and took a pen to paper. My options are limited, so I'm taking the best of the crappy bunch. "If you're going to be a bystander, you'll need a seat belt and a shield."

My brother laughs like he's relishing what's coming. "I know you wanted to do this 'right,' but if you're worried about taking the ruthless route, have you considered that Britta might be looking, even subconsciously, for some sign that you're willing to fight for her? Something more than words."

"Keeley said action was more important to a woman. So Britta's going to get it." And I appreciate the validation.

"Have you told Keeley what you're planning?"

"No. And my self-preservation instinct is strong enough not to. But my gut tells me the best way past Britta's defenses isn't going under or around them, like I've been trying. I have to go straight through, mowing them down and plowing ahead." I'm desperate to reclaim the territory I once foolishly abandoned, leaving it vulnerable for the enemy to storm.

Everyone is in for a shock tomorrow.

If I fail, at least I'll know I tried every way I can think of to be with the woman I love and our son.

"I hope it works out for you," my brother says into my thoughts.

Me, too. But I can't fixate on the moment I'll confront Britta without losing my mind. "We have to get you through today first."

My brother nods nervously. "By tonight, I'll either be engaged or ready to jump off a bridge."

"I'm betting on the former, but I'll be there for you either way."

He smiles, then shoots me a sideways glance. "Thanks. It's good to have you back."

"Yeah." I'm not one for mushy moments, but I didn't tell the people in my life what they meant to me before. I can't let this opportunity pass me by without saying something now. "It's good to have you back, too. I'll cross my fingers that when you go to bed tonight, you'll be the happiest bastard on the planet."

"I'm hoping the same for you soon. I may not want you hashing out your relationship with Britta in the office, but I totally want you to get your girl. If you need any help in the devious department…"

I laugh. "When have I ever needed help there?"

He smiles back because he knows the answer is never. "I can't wait to see what happens next."

"Me, too."

MONDAY SEEMS TO TAKE A century to roll around, but it's finally here. After a very interesting evening with Keeley and Maxon, I don't expect to see my brother in the office before noon—at the earliest. When Rob comes in a few minutes before eight, I send him on an errand to put a FOR SALE sign in the yard of a new four-million-dollar listing and to meet the photographer scheduled to take the pictures. If Rob is going to create the flyer, he can work with the cameraman to get exactly the shots he wants. Best of all, he'll be out of the office when Britta walks in the door.

I'm watching the hands fucking crawl around the clock when she finally comes in, briefcase slung over one shoulder, wearing a dress that more than covers everything...but still should be illegal. It's a soft gray knit. The deep V-neck shows a surprising amount of cleavage. It has a wide sash at her small waist and clings to her hips before ending just above the knee. Her shoes are a matching gray patent, sedate yet somehow sexy. She's dragged her hair into an elegant twist my fingers are already itching to unravel. She's eschewed all jewelry except dangling pearls at her ears and that fucking engagement ring she won't be wearing for long. She didn't apply much makeup today. The only thing I notice is that her eyes look wide and exotic. And she's accentuated her bee-stung lips with a deep red color.

It's like waving a crimson cape in a bull's face.

Come hell or high water, I'm going to have this woman under me, in love with me, and bound to me for life. I'd love to bypass the bullshit and strip her down, tell her I've given her my heart as I'm seizing her body. But she shoots me a challenging glare the second she walks in.

"Morning."

That's all she says as she heads for her desk. Something about her has changed. I can't put my finger on it. My eyes narrow as I watch her, but whatever is different is too subtle for me to detect.

"Morning," I drawl.

Doesn't she remember that the cold shoulder only fires up my blood?

As she walks past me, I get a glance at the back of her dress—or rather the lack of it. Other than a thin strap dangling between her shoulder blades, there's nothing to cover her. The shoulders swoop down to a vee that gathers at the waist. The wide sash trails into a bow that swishes across her luscious ass, which the gray knit lovingly cups.

I'll bet you a hundred bucks she's not wearing panties.

I start to sweat as I approach her.

Shit. I've got to keep my head screwed on straight. Temptation fucks with my brain, and no one has ever gotten to me faster than Britta.

"How was your weekend?" I ask.

"Fine. Where's Maxon?"

"With Keeley. They're engaged as of last night. Do you need something?"

For a moment, her expression slips and she looks happy for my brother. Then she remembers she's talking to me. "Not from you. Rob late?"

Oh, she's challenging me. The trembling girl I shocked at her engagement party is long gone. In front of me is a woman who looks ready to give as good as I'm going to give her. It's making me hard as hell.

"Busy. It's just us in the office."

She stiffens but gives no other indication she's troubled by that fact. "Fine. I have things to do."

"In a minute. How's Jamie this morning? How did he do with Makaio's sister?" Logically, I know why Britta didn't ask me to spend the weekend with him...but it pisses me off nonetheless.

Some of the starch leaves her shoulders, and her voice softens. "He's fine. He's happy."

"Good." I nod. I'd like to hold him. I miss my little man more than I thought possible. But he's part of what I'm fighting for. "Thanks." I glance at the clock. "Look, it's not quite eight thirty, so business hours haven't started yet. We need to talk. I want to make it perfectly clear that I'm speaking to you right now not as your boss but as your lover."

"Ex," she insists, the starch back in her spine.

"Not for long."

She raises a cool blond brow at me. "You wish. Sign the papers. Glad we've had this chat. I've got nothing else to say."

She digs into her briefcase, completely ignoring me. File folders come out, which she spreads across her desk in order of priority. I know how she organizes.

When she withdraws her laptop and hooks it up again, I step up behind her and grab her wrists. "You may not have anything else on your mind, but I've got plenty. Let's sit down face to face and talk."

"Not happening." She wrenches out of my grip and sashays to the back of the room, hips swaying, to make her tea.

Are you fucking kidding me? Did her getaway with Makaio make her feel so badass female that she's actively inciting me to verbal combat?

"That's not an option, angel."

She leans her backside against the coffee bar and dips her teabag into her steaming water. Absently, she scoops up a sugar packet on her right. Her expression says she could give two shits what I have to say. "You're going to force me to listen?"

I grit my teeth. I feel my blood boil. God, I want to fuck the sass out of her.

"You're going to want to hear this." I saunter toward her to lean my fists on the counter on either side of her hips, caging her against me. "We're going to make a deal, you and I."

Her eyes widen a fraction before she quickly blanks her expression. "I don't have to make any deal with you, Griff."

I can't stop looking at her goddamn mouth. I'm so close, if I inhaled just right, leaned in a little bit, I'd be kissing her. I'm so distracted by the thought I almost forget to speak. Thankfully, my head up north kicks in.

"If you ever want me to sign those papers so Makaio can adopt Jamie, you do."

Her lips tighten, and she pushes against me. I give her—and myself—a little breathing space. She shoulders her way past me and heads toward her desk again. "Determined to make my life hell to the bitter end, huh?"

"Determined to take the worst possible slant on what I have to say before I've even said it?"

Britta reaches into her briefcase again and pulls out her stack of bridal magazines, all lovingly tape-flagged over the past week and a half. I want to rip them all up. No, that's pointless. I want her to stop planning her life with another man.

"Of course. You hounding me hardly says you're totally in the mood to be agreeable."

"I thought cynical was my department."

She casts me a sidelong glance. Yes, she's always been sexy as hell to me—soft, feminine, heartfelt, corruptible. All the things I'm not. But this Britta with sharp edges is setting off all my predatory instincts.

Stalk, capture, claim.

"You made sure I'm pretty damn good at it, too." She slaps her palms down on top of the magazines and sighs like it's already been a long day and she's exhausted. "What do you want, Griff? Besides the opportunity to be a pain in my ass."

Now that I look at her, she doesn't appear well rested. I see dark circles under her light makeup. What the hell did Makaio do to her this weekend?

I clench my fists, certain I don't want to know.

Determined to press on, I grab Rob's chair and roll it across the floor to her desk. When I sink into it, I gesture to her. "Sit. Let's talk."

She shakes her head. "Just spit it out."

"All right." I cross my arms over my chest. "You and Jamie are moving in with me until your wedding day."

Britta blinks at me in shock before she scoffs her way into an all-out laugh. "You have finally lost your mind. Why would you think for an instant I'd do that?"

Once I threaten her, I can't take it back. It will change the tone of our relationship. Despite my ruthless rah-rah cheer, I'm hesitant to make this ugly if I don't have to. "It would be so much better for us all if you simply agreed. I'm trying to be nice here."

She stills and looks at me like I've lost all my faculties. "I have a house. I have a fiancé who will object. I have my sanity to keep. So unless you've got some way to compel me to move in with you, the answer is an absolute no."

With a sigh, I rise and march to my office. I don't look back, but I hear her tsking and settling in at her desk. Does she think I've given up?

After rifling through my briefcase, I find what I'm looking for. Then I hear something that sounds like a crash. A metallic gong sounds next. I spin around and see her trash can wobbling. What the hell?

I'll get to the bottom of that after the end of this discussion. If she thinks she's going to derail me with some stunt, she's damn wrong.

I close the distance between us with single-minded determination. She looks up as I approach, her gaze chilly. "Griff, I really don't have time for—"

I slap the paper I retrieved on the desk between us. "You're not the only one who can see an attorney, angel."

I watch her face as she scans the document. VOLUNTARY ESTAB-LISHMENT OF PATERNITY BY PARENTS.

She turns chalky white. "What's this?"

"You've got two choices where Jamie is concerned: Either you and I can find a notary public and sign this right now, establishing the fact that I'm Jamie's father. Or I can take you to court, demand a DNA test, and prove I'm his father. Either way, I wind up with rights—a whole slew of them. And I will have your ass in court every minute necessary until I get every one coming to me."

Britta looks stricken, then turns her face up to me with rage. "God-damn it, you son of a bitch! Jamie is mine. I birthed him. I'm raising him. I love him. You took so much from me, and now you want to take him, too."

"I want to share him with you," I correct. "I want him to have the love of two parents."

Bolting out of her seat, she paces the office. She looks like she has daggers on the tip of her tongue, but she knows I have her cornered. Either way, I'm going to be Jamie's father legally. She's going to have to let me visit, spend nights, weekends, holidays with him. She'll have to relinquish the boy to me for days, sometimes weeks.

Frankly, this is not my first choice. In fact, it's my worst-case scenario. It's the one in which Britta winds up married to Makaio, and I'm reduced to seeing my son when the courts allow. But I have to start somewhere.

Now that I've put this out between us, I have a bargaining chip. I have an outcome she'd like to avoid, which I can make possible…for a price.

She shoots me a glare, then runs into the restroom, slamming the door and locking it. I don't think for one minute that she suddenly needs to tinkle. Britta is pissed, and this is her exercising her power over me—to put a door between us. It's temporary, and I'm not sweating it.

I turn to head toward the coffee bar, then glance into her trash can to see what she dumped so loudly and unceremoniously.

It looks like every single edition of her bridal magazines and the stack of tape flags. I frown as I lift one out of the bin. This can't possibly be something she doesn't want anymore. It's chock-full of marked and bent pages, even a few with colorful notes in the margin.

Something is up with this. For now, I quietly slip the booklet back into the canister and grab a cup of coffee.

My hand is shaking. I've played cool, but I seriously have no idea what she's going to say or do when she comes out of that bathroom. Whatever is making her different today is also making her unpredictable. I wonder if the magazines are tied in. Is it possible there's trouble in paradise?

That thought gives me comfort as I brew a mug.

When I turn back, Britta is coming out of the bathroom. Her eyes are swollen. Her nose is red. She looks pissed as hell as she struts across the office toward me.

"If you do this, I will hate you."

It's a hefty threat, but I've already thought of this one.

"You'll hate me because I don't want to be an absentee father?" I saunter closer until we meet in the middle of the room. "Isn't that part of why you've been furious with me for the last three years?"

She grits her teeth. "I needed you then. I don't need you now."

"After the incident at the park a week ago last Friday, I'm going to disagree. I will understand that boy in a way that you can't since you've never been a reckless, testosterone-driven creature."

"Makaio can handle that part," she insists.

"Really?" Okay, so I shove a little condescending note in there. It's not intended to make her feel stupid. I just want her to think about what she's saying...and to stop overestimating her Hawaiian calendar boy's abilities.

"I will handle it. I'm his mother."

"I'll be there, too, because I'm his father. There's only one thing you can possibly do to change that."

Britta scans my face. I see her thoughts racing. I know the moment the realization dawns.

"*That's* why you suggested I move in with you until I get married?" She looks aghast.

"Bingo. You and Jamie live with me for fifty-two days. At the end of that period, if you can look me in the eye and tell me you don't love me and that you would rather marry Makaio Kāle..." I drag in a deep breath. I can hardly say these words. I don't know what the fuck I'm going to do if I lose this giant gamble and actually have to *do* what I'm about to promise. "Then I'll sign the papers you gave me and let you both go. But I'm going to make you spend every one of those fifty-two days—and nights—with me."

She looks at me, shocked. "You can't force me to have sex with you for the next eight weeks."

I shake my head. "Of course I can't. You just have to cohabitate with me."

"But...but I'm engaged to another man."

One who's about to find out that nice guys finish last in my world.

"I don't need the reminder." I clench my fists at my sides. "But if the sex happens between us"—when, as far as I'm concerned—"I want you every bit as willing and ready and wet for me as you used to be. I want you to kiss me good morning before I satisfy you into a pretty blush. I want you to tell me you love me before I lay you down in our bed at night and fuck you senseless. But if the sex never happens..." I shrug as if that possibility is so slim it's ridiculous. "Well, then we'll have spent those eight weeks co-parenting. And if you still don't think I pass muster, I'll let you and Jamie go. Acknowledge me as Jamie's father now or take a gamble that may pay off later. Your choice."

She gapes at me. I see her blink, breathe hard, stare at me as if I'm insane. Hell, maybe I am. It wouldn't be the first time I've been accused of that.

"I can't just...move in with you. What would I tell Makaio?"

"That this is your one chance to get me out of your lives forever. He must want that. He simply needs to understand this is a take-it-or-leave-it opportunity."

"He'll never agree." She shakes her head.

"Why?" I lean closer. "Do you think he'd worry your love for him won't survive fifty-two days with me?" I walk behind Britta, so close I can feel the heat of her body rising. I can see her shoulders square as she breathes. I circle back around and ease even closer, until my face is mere inches from hers. "Are *you* worried it wouldn't?"

Her eyes narrow as she backs away. "I've always known you were an underhanded bastard. It wasn't enough to seduce me out of my virginity. It wasn't enough to turn me upside down by getting me pregnant and walking away. Now you have to pull shit like this?"

"You didn't answer my question," I point out.

When she stiffens, it's all I can do not to put my hands on her, but now isn't the time. And if she agrees to my plan, what's between us is going to get a shitload uglier before it gets better.

If she doesn't agree, we'll have nothing more than a coldly polite child exchange in a fast-food parking lot every two weeks.

That makes me so fucking sad, and I can't think of it right now. I've got game. I'm playing.

"I'm not going to," she spits back. "Your question is absurd."

Or too accurate. But I let it slide for the moment. I have a more important point to make.

"What's it going to be?"

"Jamie c-can't live in your condo building. Do your grounds even have an area for kids to play? I'll bet your unit overlooks the ocean and has a balcony. How can we stop him from climbing the railing? The outlets aren't kid proofed and—"

"Valid points." But she's talking about us living together. That makes me smile. "I'll make alternate arrangements."

"No. My house is familiar to him and—"

"It's an hour from both our work and his school." I shake my head. It's also a place where she can find comfortable places to retreat from me. That's not acceptable. That's not my only objection, however. "Have you ever had sex with Makaio in that house?"

She rears back. "That's none of your business."

"So that's a yes." I grind my teeth together and work on keeping my shit wired tight. "I won't make love to you in a place—hell, in a bed—where he's had you. Period."

"This is ridiculous. You think I'm going to move in with you *and* leave my house? Just because you don't like what I might have done there? Just because you demanded it?"

Pretty much. "What's your answer?"

"Never mind ridiculous. This is crazy!"

"I realize this decision involves others, so you don't even have to know the answer right this instant." I look at the clock. It's nearly nine a.m. I have a mountain of work on my desk, and I can hear my phone buzzing from my office. But nothing is more important now—nor will it ever be—than Britta and Jamie. "You have twelve hours to decide. I expect a phone call at nine tonight with your decision. If you agree to my terms, I expect you to be ready to move in with me at six p.m. tomorrow."

"I'd need at least a few days to gather—"

"The timetable is nonnegotiable." I shake my head. "You either accept or you can sign the form I gave you. If not, I'm taking you to court."

Her fingers curl into fists, and she looks near tears again. "You're trying to ruin my life all over. I don't know why I'm even surprised. So much for you changing and becoming a better man. I should never have bought your insistence that you've learned to be a good guy. Keeley is your bestie and she's taught you so much about compassion and humility and kindness. Oh, I see exactly who you are now. You know what, Griff? Fuck you."

Rob walks in and pauses in the doorway like he knows he's interrupted something intense. He stares between us, his gaze bouncing back and forth. "Everything cool?"

"Fine," I tell him with a bland smile. "Britta and I were just finishing a discussion."

"Um…" Rob obviously feels the tension swirling thick and heavy in the air. "Sure."

He knows I'm lying to him but isn't going to challenge me. Smart man.

Without meeting my gaze, he nods and heads for his desk. "The photographer finished. The shots will be good. She'll get back to us in a day or two."

"Excellent." I stand in expectation and wait for him to get busy.

He proves he's smart again when he dons his headphones and cranks his music, then focuses on his computer and ignores us completely.

I slant my gaze back to Britta. She's breathing hard, teeth gritted, staring at me like she wants to take me apart limb from limb.

If she thinks I'm a bastard now, she hasn't seen anything yet. I'm on a mission. I have a goal. I won't rest until I've accomplished it.

"Fuck me, huh?" I murmur to her. "No, angel. Here's what I think is going to happen. You're not going to be able to resist me because you don't love that asswipe you're engaged to. You might be angry as hell at me right now, but deep down you still love me. And I'm going to prove I love you. Once you're ready to admit it, once all the walls are down between us? Then you're going to be saying sayonara to your banker and I'm going to be fucking you."

CHAPTER TEN

"YOU'RE WEARING OUT THE CARPET," Keeley points out, grabbing the last of her stuff from the spare bedroom in my condo. "What is going on?"

I stare at the time on my phone again—8:58 p.m. Nerves are gnawing a hole into my gut. If Britta doesn't call in the next few minutes, I have to start down a path of administrative forms and legal battles and court proceedings, all of which will net me some grudging visitation with my son. I'd rather have more. But even if she does call and agree to my scheme, there's every chance she'll hate me for that, too.

Makaio didn't just set a quick wedding date. He fucking maneuvered me into a corner to see if I'd fight my way out. I'm sure I counterpunched harder than he expected. I had to. I certainly won't underestimate him again.

As my thoughts circle, Keeley stands in my living room, waiting for an answer. If I spill the details to my best friend, she will give me a tongue whipping about the thousand and one ways I've totally screwed up. And my brother, who's standing impatiently in the doorway, will help her just to speed the process along. Obviously, he's dying to take Keeley back to his place and get her naked. He won't let anything paltry, like my torment, get in the way.

Lucky bastard, getting to spend the night with the woman he loves.

"I'm all right."

I have to be. What's done is done. I can't take the ultimatum back. And I don't want to. So listening to Keeley tell me why I've fucked up isn't helpful. She's way better at untangling my problems once they're deep. I'll call her then.

Keeley's face softens and she approaches me, left hand on my shoulder. I see her sparkly new diamond there. I'm happy for them...even as I'm worried the ring I bought for Britta will simply continue to sit in my safe and gather dust for the rest of my fucking life.

"Are you really, Griff?" Keeley asks.

"Yeah. I'll be in a better place to talk tomorrow. Tonight, I need to get some quiet and think. Don't worry about me. You've barely been engaged twenty-four hours. Think of Maxon. He's desperate over there. Hell, think of our brotherly bonds. They're tenuous now because if I don't shut up and let you leave now so he can do naughty, unspeakable things to you back at his place, he may stop speaking to me."

She rolls her eyes and laughs. "You're so full of shit. Call me in the morning."

"I will." I kiss her cheek. "Do you mind if I talk shop with my brother for a second?"

Keeley looks between us, her fiery hair brushing the tops of her shoulders. She's not fooled for a second, but like a trooper, she bows out gracefully.

With a little wave, she grabs the handle of her smaller suitcase and rolls it toward the door, pausing in front of Maxon to kiss him softly. "I'll wait in the car."

He caresses her face and looks at her as if she's his world.

It's funny. I've seen my brother take apart his adversaries. I've seen him verbally dismantle someone in under two minutes. I've even seen him beat the shit out of an asshole threatening our little sister in high school. But I've never seen him happy, tender, centered.

It's like I'm seeing Maxon for the first time.

"I won't be long, sunshine."

After tossing a smile to us both, Keeley is gone.

The second the door shuts, Maxon turns to me, brow raised. "What did you do to Britta this morning?"

"You want the 'office-friendly' version?"

"Fuck no. I want the truth."

"All right. I forced her to deal with me." I explain my ultimatum.

Maxon's eyes bug out. "You've got balls the size of Jupiter. The gravitational pull obviously sucked your brain from your head. Holy shit. How did she take that?"

I glance at my phone again. Straight up nine p.m. "I'm waiting to find out. But I need to talk to you about an idea... I can't keep Jamie in my condo. Britta has valid points about why. I won't live with her in her house. She has memories of Makaio there. I refuse to compete on what's essentially his turf. So that leaves my options short. I mentally ran through a few and had this thought... So I called George Stowe and talked to him about the caretaker situation. He understood. And he seemed awfully relieved when I said I would do it for free."

"You're going to move Britta and Jamie there?"

"Temporarily. Even if the estate sells this week, it won't close right away. The place will need maintenance until it does. If it doesn't sell quickly...well, at thirty million bucks, it's not as if we're going to show the property every day. Or even once a week. It's also closer to work than Britta currently lives. Jamie will consider it a giant adventure..." Plus, it's romantic. Fuck, it's a honeymoon suite on steroids. I'm really hoping it will help sway Britta to think of me not as the enemy but as her lover again. So we can spend time together as a family.

"Yeah. All right." Maxon nods. "If the Stowes are cool with the idea, I know you'll respect the house. It's probably better than hiring someone with dubious follow-through skills. We'll certainly save money." He shrugs. "I like it."

I'm relieved. "Good. Thanks, man."

Once we get there, I'll have Britta walk the property with me and tell me what kind of kid proofing she needs. Beyond that, I think it's the perfect solution.

Now, most everything is settled. All I'm waiting for is Britta's answer.

I glance at my phone—9:02 p.m. Why isn't it ringing?

"You look like you're going to crawl out of your skin," Maxon observes.

"Remember when you were waiting to find out if Keeley was going to board the plane?"

"It's like that, huh? Sorry. That sucks. I know."

"But you're happy now, right?"

The smile that transforms his face is unlike any expression I've seen on my brother. He isn't just happy. He's completely, utterly content.

I'm thrilled for Maxon. I'm also hoping that if he can find his way to a great life with the woman he loves, I might be able to finagle the same. I don't know how I'm going to persuade her to admit that she still loves me, but I'm working on it.

"I honestly never knew what happiness was until Keeley." He winces. "I'm sure with Mom and Dad serving as my example for the great institute of marriage that I'll fuck up from time to time. But this woman gets me. She knows what's in my heart. She loves me anyway."

Every one of his words settles like a boulder in my belly. Britta gets me. But does she like anything about me at all? I'm trying to tell her how much I care. So far, she's unconvinced.

"That's fantastic. I expect to be your best man." I laugh.

"I don't know." Maxon shrugs. "Keeley was thinking you'd make an excellent maid of honor. She's thinking you'd look great in peach chiffon."

I punch him in the shoulder. "Take her home and make sure she remembers the difference between men and women."

"I've done a pretty damn good job reminding her all day if I do say so myself." He gives me a loopy grin.

"Ugh, I don't want details."

My brother laughs. "We also called her mom and stepfather. They're really excited for us."

"Did you tell our folks?"

"You think they'd give a shit? Mom would want to know when she could come preside over the grand celebration. Dad would tell me I've lost my fucking mind because Keeley can't bring me money, power, or prestige. No. I called Harlow. She was happy for me. She's a tough girl, but I think she even shed a tear. So all that's left is for us to pick a wedding date. Keeley is thinking fall. I won't wait that long."

The topic of overeager grooms brings me back to my problems. I reach into my briefcase and pull out the stack of Britta's bridal mags I retrieved from her trash can. Maybe she's bored with them. But why go to all the trouble to flag certain pages and photos, complete with colorful notes, only to dump it all? I'd suspect that the wedding is off...except she's still wearing her engagement ring and is calling him her fiancé. Nothing makes sense. The whole incident sets off my suspicions.

I'm going to get to the bottom of this.

"Any idea why Britta would ditch these?" I lay them out on the counter. "I had to make a quick stop at the grocery store during lunch, so I looked at the magazines on the shelves. It's not as if there are more updated editions available."

Maxon frowns. "No idea. That is weird, though."

"She's been poring over this stack and combing websites for days. All of a sudden, she's not interested anymore?"

"She hasn't said anything to me. But if I get a chance tomorrow, I'll feel her mood out. She usually talks to me..."

Well, she did until Maxon and I decided to be brothers again. I'm not sure if she'll confide in him now. She must suspect she'd be feeding information directly to a spy of sorts. So she probably won't say shit to Maxon.

"That would be great. If it doesn't work out, don't worry. I'll be leaning on her, too."

He nods. "Shouldn't she have called you by now?"

A glance at my phone tells me it's 9:06. She's out of her mind if she thinks I won't hop in my car and drive over to her place and demand an answer right the fuck now.

As if my very thoughts compelled her, my cell starts to buzz in my hand. Her name pops up on my display.

Here we go...

My brother claps me on the shoulder. "I'll leave you to it. Let me know what she decides."

I nod at my brother gratefully, then tap my thumb over the button to accept the call as the door shuts behind him. "Britta? You're late."

"I have a life."

Yeah, with me.

I try not to clench my jaw. I try even harder not to lose my temper. She feels powerless in this situation, and I'm pretty sure this is her little defiance. It won't last. I'll make sure she feels plenty happy and powerful as soon as she'll let me.

"Everything all right with Jamie?"

As usual, that subject defuses some of her anger. "He's fine. A little fussy tonight." She pauses like she debates the wisdom of saying more, but she finally sighs. "He asked about you."

"I miss him," I say softly.

My chest actually hurts at the thought I won't see him again tonight. If I'm honest, a part of me worried he would forget me in the span of a couple of days. I can't have made a huge impact on his little life yet, so the possibility that I'd have to start all over with him again tomorrow night disturbs the hell out of me.

"Griff..." she begins. I hear the tone in her voice. She's about to ask me to be reasonable.

"I don't want discussion. I just want your answer. What is it?"

"Seriously, this is such a huge upheaval for Jamie and—"

"He's young. Kids are adaptable. He'll benefit in the end because he'll be better off with both parents. I don't want more excuses, Britta. Yes or no? It's very simple."

"I can't leave my house—"

"You can. We'll check on it."

"And my fiancé—"

"He's a big boy."

She sighs in exasperation. "Did you ever stop to think that I'll miss him?"

"No." I'm going to make sure she doesn't have the time or inclination.

"When am I supposed to see him?"

"Have lunch," I toss back. Yeah, there's a hint of sarcasm. "You're still stalling. Yes or no?"

She huffs now. Obviously, she doesn't want to answer me. She hoped to drag me into a debate about the wisdom of this idea or shade my insistence with some detail that I frankly don't give a shit about. Maybe that works with Makaio. On me? Not so much.

When she still fails to answer, I grip the phone tighter. "I've got my attorney on speed dial. Ten seconds before I hang up and give him a ring. And yes, he'll take my call this late. He's also a friend. It's really handy."

"If you're trying to prove to me what a bastard you are, trust me. I already know."

Another argument starter. I'm not taking the bait.

"Five seconds."

She still doesn't reply, and I can all but feel her resistance through the phone.

"Three, two, on—"

"All right, you pushy, insufferable asshole. You've got me for the next fifty-two days. On the fifty-third, I'll be marrying Makaio and I'll expect you to have signed my papers. But I've got one condition."

So she's given this more than passing thought. Good. I expected her to load some ammo into her weapon. I was a little surprised she didn't when we argued in the office, and I can only imagine she was too stunned to think through scenarios that would benefit her.

"I'm listening." I also don't have to agree, but I won't say that just yet. I'll hear what's on her mind and decide if it's worth the brawl.

"You're basically cutting me off from…intimate contact with Makaio for almost two months."

Not basically. I am.

"Absence makes the heart grow fonder. Think of how much you'll have missed him by the time your wedding night rolls around," I drawl.

"Don't be flippant. I'm not letting you come between us, Griff. He's my fiancé. I'm going to see him. That's only fair."

"Fair to whom? The point of our time together is to experience what it would be like if we were a family. If one of us is stepping out, then we're not a cohesive unit. And you can't argue with me on that. Dad always had a mistress on the side when I was growing up. He still does. You've met my family. There's no way you can make a case we're functional."

"You're not. But you and I aren't married," she points out. "I can't shove my relationship with Makaio on the back burner simply to 'play house' with you."

"Can't he do without you for a while? Or are you worried he can't control himself if you're not around?"

"This isn't about sex. He's barely accepted the fact that I intend to move in with you, even temporarily. If I tell him I can't be with him because I have to be faithful to you and our 'family,' what do you think his reaction will be?"

Since he's not a total dumb ass after all, I'm pretty sure he'll understand their relationship is doomed.

"He seems like an understanding guy." I try not to vomit. "I'm sure he wants you to be really sure before you say 'I do.' Besides, you just said this wasn't about sex. Why is it not about that where he's concerned, but when I'm involved, it's about nothing else?"

"Because I'm engaged," she reminds me, exasperated. "I'm committed to him."

"For the next fifty-two days, you're mine. Only mine. After that, if you want to be his again, I won't stop you. Or I can call my attorney right now. What's it going to be?"

If she agrees to this, she can tell herself that I've twisted her arm and that she's only protecting Jamie. But I don't believe for one minute that she wants me out of her life more than she's afraid of sharing our son for a few nights and weekends.

"That's not fair."

"You having sex with him is a nonstarter for me." If she's giving her time and attention to another man, she'll never consider what it's like to live with and love me. "That's the deal. Take it or leave it."

Britta pauses, then finally grits her teeth together, sounding like she wants to strangle me. "God, you're such a bastard."

She can think that all she wants, as long as she's willing to concede this point. Once I have her away from that cocksucker she's engaged to, I'll work on changing her attitude. Since he doesn't seem to give her much of anything, I doubt it will be too hard for me to shower her with everything she needs.

"Does that mean we have a deal?"

"Not so fast. Reciprocation is only fair, Griff. If I can't be with Makaio for the next fifty-two days, then you can't touch any other woman. Or this whole deal is off. I move out. You sign the papers. I keep Jamie. You go away for good."

Does she imagine for one moment that I could possibly have my dick in a knot for any other female? If I did, I wouldn't be up in Britta's business right now. I'd be pursuing that woman. But I get it. Three years ago, I left her and jumped right into a full and busy sex life. She's convinced I have a wandering dick and that she's going to end up with the custody arrangement she wants because she'll trip me up on a technicality. In her head, when I fuck up by fucking someone else, she'll be vindicated and have everything she wants.

That's never going to happen. In fact, she's in for one hell of a shock when she realizes how attentive and focused I'm going to be on her and her alone.

I bite my tongue to hold in a laugh.

"Define touch?" I say both to be very clear and to needle her. "If I buy something at the drugstore and I happen to brush fingers with a female cashier as I'm picking up change…"

"That's not what I mean."

"So incidental contact doesn't count? Okay. My sister is coming in April. I'm going to hug her."

She grunts like she's exasperated. "Now you're just playing stupid."

"You tell me then, angel. Where's the line?"

"What would you consider cheating in a relationship? I'm assuming that sort of thing registers with you. But if not and you need more explanation about what it means to break a commitment by crawling between someone else's legs, I'll be happy to show you a picture. I have them, after all."

Oh, meow. She's jealous. I'm absolutely loving this, mostly because it's clear what—or who—I do matters to her.

"I'm not so much into pictures. Maybe you'll give me a demonstration?"

"Stop provoking me," she warns.

I haven't even started yet. "Okay. If you're looking for a working definition, how about this: cheating is conduct with anyone else where sexual arousal or penetration of any sort is intended."

"All right. So, for instance, kissing. Obviously cheeks of friends and hands of old ladies don't count," she says.

"Right. But kissing like I want it to lead somewhere that involves heavy breaths, tasting of skin, and peeling off of clothes? That's a no-no."

I hear her swallow across the line. "This definition of cheating should also include any touching of body parts people generally cover in polite society, beach excepted. And no matter what anyone says, oral sex is, in fact, sex. Which means actual copulation—"

"Is just fucking someone else and is totally cheating."

She sucks in a breath. "Yes. So if you behave in any of the ways we just outlined, I win."

"All right."

"All right...what? Are you agreeing to the definition or the deal?"

"Both."

"Really? You didn't even think about that, Griff. Maybe you should. That will lead to fifty-two days without sex for you. Aren't you worried you'll go blind? Or crazy? That the top of your head will blow off? That you won't be able to handle it?"

Her sarcasm is thick. Sure, I could tell her that I have no intention of going without sex for that long. I'll have her, and I'll do whatever it takes to make sure she happily provides whatever gratification I want while I pleasure her so thoroughly and so often she won't have the energy to object—or think of Makaio. But just for grins, I should make this interesting.

"Don't you worry about me, angel. I'll manage. Neither of us will kiss, touch, or…what did you say, copulate with anyone else for the next fifty-two days. That's not going to be a problem for me. But if you can't resist Makaio, then I win."

I'm going to win anyway. I'll let her think she has a chance, but this is a slam dunk. Last time we were alone, she barely lasted five minutes without returning my kiss and climbing my body in silent pleading for more. There's no way she resists me for nearly two months.

"This is ridiculous. It… I can't. No. You and I aren't—"

"Those are your choices," I remind her. "I don't know what you're worried about. Since you threw away your stack of bridal magazines earlier, I'm assuming that means the wedding is already planned. If you love each other and you hate my guts, what could you possibly have to worry about?"

"You dug through my trash?"

How interesting that's the first topic she addresses, rather than her feelings for me. Not confirming that she hates me is almost an admission that she doesn't.

"It made a lot of noise. I couldn't help but notice. It's great that you've got the ceremony and the reception all nailed down. You always were organized, but wow. I have to congratulate you for—"

"Stop it. I threw them away because Makaio wants a traditional Hawaiian wedding, and he's asked me if his mother can plan it on our behalf. She really wants to."

Is she fucking kidding? Her fiancé cares more about his mommy's feelings than his bride's? It's cute, I guess. Well, it would be if he were Jamie's age. But any idiot knows that most women have been dreaming of their wedding since childhood. And Makaio doesn't seem to be thinking twice about taking that from Britta. All her planning, all her careful consideration, everything she's yearned for...all flushed down the toilet because he's a mama's boy.

I stalk my way to the counter and flip open the first magazine, riffling through until I come to a flagged page. She's circled a bouquet of tropical flowers. Another page has a margin note about bridesmaids' dresses in a color called cornflower. No idea what that looks like... Toward the back, I see she's starred an ad for a company that prints custom invitations quickly, themed for the perfect wedding. She's jotted down notes about timeframes and prices. I'll bet the rest of the magazines have more of her choices lovingly selected.

In fact, I'll bet Britta has already planned the perfect wedding in her head. Makaio stole her joy.

Asshat.

I hurt for her. I'm angry for her, too. But I don't let on. "Well, that saves you a lot of trouble, right? Much easier for you, less stressful."

"That seems to be the prevailing sentiment." She sounds pissed.

I can only imagine that's how Makaio pitched the idea of his mother planning their wedding. If he thought for one second that would make Britta's life better, he doesn't know my color-coding, calendar-keeping, deeply organized angel like he should if he intends to marry her.

I grin.

"Since you don't have to worry about that now, let's talk about our next eight weeks. I've already found a place for us. We'll take care of the childproofing tomorrow evening. Do you need help packing? I can come to the house right now and—"

"I've got it," she snaps out. "Griff, this arrangement is ridiculous and will never accomplish anything."

As far as I'm concerned, she's totally wrong. "Well, then you shouldn't have a care in the world. Be ready after work. We'll pick up Jamie and move into our temporary home together."

THE FOLLOWING DAY TURNS INTO hell. On the one hand, it works well that Britta and I are too busy to say much. Her response to my morning greeting was grudging and chilly. I feel hostility simmering under her skin. It's fine. I'm prepared for the fact that she'll send more my way before I break through the fortress around her heart.

I'm trying to shove all that out of my head when Maxon and I meet the representative for our potential mystery buyer at the Stowe estate promptly at ten a.m. She's a petite Asian woman who's got the stature of a domestic kitten but the bite of a shark. She gives nothing away regarding the identity of her client or even her feelings about the property. She simply takes snapshots and asks questions.

"The price tag seems a little steep," Lian comments. "When the estate last sold three years ago, it fetched just over ten million. I'm hard-pressed to imagine the value has tripled since then."

Our pricing was aggressive. Maxon and I both agreed to a listing amount on the high side that allowed for more negotiating room for one simple reason.

"There's nothing else on the island like it," Maxon supplies. "The acreage and expansiveness of the water views alone command a hefty price. But add in the fact that the previous owner significantly remodeled and updated the estate, that every room overlooks the ocean…"

I add to his argument. "The square footage of the outdoor spaces equal those of the interior. There are four infinity-edge pools, all on different levels of the property, connected via waterfalls. So no matter which you decide to swim in, you'll have the illusion of your water stretching out to the ocean. The estate has a chef's kitchen, detached ohana for guests or rental property, and flexible space for an exercise or media room, whatever your client wants to use it for. The grounds are impeccable. This is really the premiere property in Maui."

"But I can find most of these features elsewhere in Hawaii for less money."

"Not with this kind of privacy," I argue. "It's gated and it has a guard post in case your client would like the estate's security manned. There are no visible neighbors. Even the beach is private. Those factors, in some ways, make this place both unique and priceless."

She cocks her head like she's considering. "I'm going to walk the property again. You don't need to escort me, thank you."

Nearly two hours later, I'm guessing Lian has inspected every inch of the place once more when she finally saunters onto the lanai off the family room.

"Any questions for us?" Maxon asks, rising from a comfy chair.

I let him be the polite one. I'm not feeling terribly sociable. I'm itching to get back to Britta now, and have to bite my tongue from pointing out the mystery buyer is either interested in seeing the property for himself or he's not.

"No, but I need a moment to confer with my client." Lian excuses herself to make a call in the dedicated office space with stunning views of both the Pacific lining the front and the tropical gardens behind. Maxon paces between the kitchen and the family room, looking anxious.

I probably should be, too. Instead, I use the opportunity to walk the interior of the house again. I've seen it a couple of times, but I've looked at it from a Realtor's perspective, not a tenant's. Not as someone who will spend nights and weekends with his family here.

The bedroom on the top floor is an elaborate master suite with full ocean views from the bedroom, bathroom, and attached sitting area, the latter of which can be closed off from the rest of the room with an ornate pocket door. The remainder of the bedrooms are scattered around the property, mostly upstairs, on the far side of the floor from this amazing retreat.

For my purposes, the layout is perfect.

When I hear the opening of a door and the clacking of heels, I dash back down. Lian is clasping her phone and looking resolute. "My client would like to offer you twenty-four million. All cash. He insists on closing in exactly seventy-five days. Yes, that's a Sunday, but I trust you can make that happen. For this price, he also expects the estate to come furnished."

I somehow keep my jaw from dropping. Doesn't the client want to see it for himself? Sometimes investors don't, which I always think is a mistake. But I'm not about to blurt my opinion and throw a wrench into this offer.

Maxon and I exchange a glance, then fall back into old patterns. He talks. I evaluate our position. We'll compare notes before anything is signed.

"It absolutely comes furnished," my brother assures. "The current owners have already taken everything from the premises they want, so what you see comes included."

"Excellent. Have the papers drawn up. My client will sign. Once you present the offer to your sellers, they have twenty-four hours to respond."

At that point, Lian is clearly done. After a crisp thanks, she turns and leaves the premises. Because she insisted on coming in her own vehicle, she jumps into a sleek white Jaguar and departs. Maxon and I watch. As soon as the automatic gate closes behind her and she rounds the bend, he and I turn to each other and shout like rowdy teenagers.

Chest bumping and high-fiving aside, we scram back to the office to ready all the forms. Britta faxes them to Lian, seeming as shocked by the swiftness of this deal as we are. Maxon calls the Stowes. To say they're thrilled is an understatement.

This deal, if it goes through, is a sudden blessing. It's also a bit of a curse.

I thought I'd have more time to spend with Maxon before we had to decide whether to keep our respective businesses separate or merge again. But in less than two weeks, it looks as if we may have sold the biggest estate of our careers.

Decision time is upon us.

Maxon strolls in, wearing a smile. "I think twenty-five and a half is their bottom line, so if Lian's guy will come up another one-point-five, this is done."

The Stowes will make a huge chunk of cash off this transaction. The buyer will have an amazing home for himself and whomever he wants to share it with, along with all the privacy he can imagine. Maxon and I will both have money to spare and a basis to discuss our professional future. Best of all, Britta and I will have someplace to be with Jamie as a family virtually without interruption for the duration of our agreement.

The counteroffers fly back and forth, Lian signing with legal authority on behalf of the buyer's corporation. The Stowes push for a sooner close. After all, a bunch of their inheritance is tied up in this place until it's officially sold and money changes hands. But the mystery buyer is firm. On May seventh, he will close. That's nonnegotiable. In exchange, he agrees, after a lot of haggling, to come up to twenty-five-point-eight million. Not a penny more. At four p.m. Hawaii time, which I know is six hours later in Vermont, the deal is finally done.

"Let's go out for a drink!" Maxon says about three seconds later. "I'll call Keeley. We should raise a glass or two. This is great money we didn't have to work terribly hard for."

"Amen." I slap him on the back.

Rob is definitely in. If it involves quitting early and imbibing, he's all for it. "Where to?"

Only Britta demurs. "Thanks for the offer. I'd rather use this time at home to—"

"Nope." My brother isn't having any of her excuses. Good. I'm not, either. Maxon protesting thankfully saves me from being the bad guy today. "You're part of the team. We celebrate together."

Despite my silence, she shoots me a glare—about the hundredth for the day. I do my best to ignore it, hiking back to my desk to grab my car keys and shut down my computer. Through the internal window, I see Britta grab Maxon by the elbow and drag him into his office.

I can write the script on this conversation. I'm forcing her to move in with me. She already has to put up with me in the office all day and now under one roof all night. She doesn't want to socialize with the same rat bastard who will only end up fucking up her life seven ways from Sunday again, etc.

This is when it pays to know my brother. He can be both persuasive and stubborn. In less than two minutes, he's shaking his head, patting her shoulder, and leaving his office. Britta stomps out, looking ready to take off someone's head, preferably mine.

"Ready, angel?" By the front door, I toss my keys up and catch them as if I don't have a care in the world. "Let's get your suitcases and boxes into my Escalade."

Yes, I drove it today. I also installed a snazzy new car seat in the backseat early this morning. I'm a dad now. Jamie is going to be spending plenty of time with me. We'll be going on adventures. We're going to be close. I'll damn well work hard to be the dad he needs.

And I know Britta. Wherever Jamie is…she won't be far behind.

She insists on taking her own car. Fine. If it makes her feel more in control of the situation, I have no problem with that.

We all arrive at a nearby bar/restaurant on the ocean that serves greasy food and good times. Best of all, it's less than half a mile from Jamie's daycare.

Rob's live-in girlfriend, Alania, joins us. She's quiet and pretty, a good foil for the brash asshole we share an office with. Maxon arrives a few minutes later since he had to pick up Keeley to bring her over. They come in hand in hand, looking ridiculously in love. Their smiles are contagious. A ghost of something soft and envious plays at Britta's mouth.

I rise to hug my bestie. "Hey, gorgeous."

"Get the fuck away from my girl," Maxon grouses.

We laugh as Keeley hugs me back, then whispers in my ear. "You all right? Britta looks like she wants to kill me right now."

"She's right, bro. It's going to take a lot of fast-talking to keep you from crashing and burning with her."

I pull back and fist-bump my brother, glad my angel can only see my back. "It will be a bumpy ride for a while, but I'll work it out." Then I turn back to Keeley. "I need to talk to you when Britta isn't around. I need a huge favor."

Keeley smiles. "You got it."

We break apart and sit at a couple of small tables Rob pushed together. Maxon and I maneuver Keeley and Britta beside one another and exchange a glance. We're both hoping like hell that they become friends. Britta and Tiffanii barely tolerated each other, and that made for an uncomfortable Super Bowl party, tense cookouts, and a really crappy Fourth of July.

Everyone orders a drink and some appetizers. The place isn't crowded since it isn't yet five o'clock, so the silence, other than Rob speculating about the buyer's identity, is telling. Britta looks so taut, glancing at her phone and completely ignoring everyone, especially Keeley and me.

As soon as the waitress sets down our first round, Keeley swallows back some of her Crown and Coke, then shifts to face Britta head on. "I've never slept with Griff. I don't have any interest in hitting the sheets with him, either. Never have. You don't have anything to worry about from me."

I look over Britta's head at my bestie and I have to restrain a laugh. Well, that's one way to break the ice.

"I never said I…" Britta shakes her head. "What you and my ex have or haven't done doesn't make any difference to me."

I sense Keeley resisting the urge to give my angel a disapproving frown. She's pretty good at spotting lies, and I personally think this one is a whopper. If the tables were turned and Keeley was talking to me, she would give me a thorough dressing down. But I respect that she's not completely jumping on Britta all at once. Her opening maneuver probably feels like a headlock, but at least she didn't go for the body slam, too.

Keeley raises a dubious brow at Britta. "Did you know that I first met him because he was seeing a psychotherapist to try to work through his problems? He was a real mess."

Oh, shit. I didn't want her to spring that on Britta.

"What?" Britta turns to me with a frown. "You?"

I'm sure it's a shock that I was volunteering to talk about my feelings—or even admit I had them.

"Briefly. I only saw Dr. Wilson for a couple of weeks." I shift uncomfortably in my seat. This is not how I wanted to start my first evening with Britta.

"His stint in her office wasn't brief because Griff didn't need more therapy," Keeley clarifies. "He totally did. When he first arrived in the office, he'd barely slept in four months. His focus was shot and—"

"It was a patch of stress. That's all. I got over it without Dr. Wilson's 'help,'" I cut in before Keeley makes me sound any more like a head case.

"You're a liar. Zip it. This is my story," she scolds, then turns back to Britta. "Griff was suffering from way more than stress, and he was an absolute asshole."

Britta's face tightens with an acid smile. "*That* I can believe. Some things never change."

"He used to storm out of his therapy sessions because Dr. Wilson was too clinical and—"

"She had the compassion of a steaming pile of shit," I set the record straight.

"I'll give you that," Keeley murmurs with a nod. "Anyway, I overheard in his sessions that he was also suffering from an erratic heartbeat and what he called 'periods of anxiousness.' He was working twenty hours a day and picking up a new bed partner every three or four days, so I—"

Britta chokes on her wine, then shoots a stunned look over her shoulder at me. Her expression says that I'm the devil. "Are you serious?"

I glare at Keeley, silently asking *what the hell kind of friend are you?* "You're distressing Britta."

She gives me her most innocent expression. It's utter bullshit. She knows exactly what she's doing.

Of course, I plan to tell Britta everything about our time apart, including my "number," but not until she's ready to know. When she finally asks, I'll make it clear that every single one of those women meant nothing to me. It's the truth. But until then, she's not invested enough in the relationship to hear anything except that I screwed half of Maui or believe that I never forgot her.

"No, I'm being honest with her. I'm explaining how we met. It's important." Keeley focuses on Britta once more. "So he was playing a lot of musical beds, it's true. But the only woman he ever wanted to talk about was you."

Britta freezes. I wish like hell I could see her face now. I wish I knew what she was thinking.

She shakes her head. "Please don't think you have to make our relationship more romantic than it actually was. I don't care what he did after we separated. I'm getting married in April, and once he's done pretending he wants to be a daddy, then—"

"I'm not pretending," I lean in and growl in Britta's ear. "About Jamie or about you."

Keeley reaches around Britta to slap my arm. I'm grateful that Maxon seems to be distracting Rob and Alania or this entire conversation would be deeply humiliating.

"Shut up, moron. I'm telling her some things she needs to know that you're too proud and macho to say. You and Maxon are so alike sometimes..." She shakes her head. "I'm saving you at least two weeks of torment."

"Keeley..." I'm basically begging now. Short of gagging her or dragging Britta away, I can't stop this info dump.

Compassion crosses her face and she sends me a smile meant to comfort me. "Trust me."

"He's physically incapable of that," Britta scoffs.

I clamp my lips together and grip the arms of my chair. If I don't, I'll only do whatever it takes to stop this public lynching and prove Britta right. I can't deny that Keeley understands people and relationships. If anyone can improve this situation fast, it's her.

"I do trust you." I sigh, contradicting Britta's jibe. "This just isn't what I had in mind."

"I know." She doesn't say anything more. She simply waits for me to give her permission to continue or shut her down. "But it's your call..."

I look like a sex-addicted nut job if I let her continue or a control freak with something to hide if I don't. *Fuck me.*

With a wave of my hand, I tell Keeley silently to go on. It's not as if I'm going to be able to stop her for long anyway. And hell, maybe she's right.

She nods her approval before focusing on Britta again. And she's wearing an expression that says she understands my angel, woman to woman.

Britta turns to me as if she's surprised—no, totally shocked—that I'm allowing Keeley to smear my character. She blinks at me like she's desperate to figure out why.

"She's telling you the truth." I nod.

Still gaping, Britta turns back to Keeley. "What happened next?"

"I talked to him a few times before he slammed his way out of Dr. Wilson's office. I figured out right away that he was tightly wound. No one else was going to help him. He wouldn't let anyone try. He merely snarled like a lion. I think I'm the only one who saw the thorn in his paw, so to speak. I knew I could help, and I hate to see people hurting. Not only is doing nothing bad karma, I just…" She shakes her head. "I want everyone to be happy. So I struck up a conversation. Griff wasn't terribly forthcoming at first, but I started figuring him out. I realized he didn't need another lover. He didn't even require a therapist. I mean, it could only help him, sure… But what he needed most was a friend. He had no one."

"Because he left everyone," Britta points out.

I hear the defensiveness. I hear her saying that she would have stayed by my side and loved me with her whole heart if I'd given her a chance. It hurts.

"If you're going to do this, could you at least make me sound less pathetic?" I grouse at Keeley.

"Why? I won't lie to the woman. Geez…" She shakes her head and ignores me again. "I pointed out to him that sometimes it's easier to talk to a stranger, so he took me out for coffee. About five hours later, I figured out that he wasn't close to either of his parents. His sister was busy with school and lives on the mainland. And he had wounded the two people he loved most as deeply as they'd hurt him. Even if you and

Maxon actually had wronged Griff—though I know you didn't—he wasn't sure how to atone for leaving you both without a word. He was even less versed in apologizing, especially for an act so egregious." Keeley frowns as if the speech is about to get painful—as if it wasn't already. "He never knew about Jamie. And the endless parade of skanks was his attempt to find some sort of intimacy that he missed like hell sharing with you. I know you might not think he deserves a second chance, but if you don't at least listen to what he has to say, you're going to ruin him for good."

"That's enough." I can't hear this anymore. And I certainly don't want Britta's pity. "Let's go get Jamie and go…home."

While I can't say for sure what's going to happen if I don't intervene, I'm pretty sure the conversation would only get more excruciating and invasive. It's already beyond what I can take.

But when I grab Britta's hand, she yanks it out of my grip and glares at Keeley. "How dare you? You don't know what it was like to get naked pictures of the man I loved with a woman I despised mere days after he left me. What it was like to find out shortly after that my stomach flu was really pregnancy hormones. Or how it felt to have to call my mom, a single mother who always preached about having a husband before kids, and tell her that I was expecting a baby but the man was long gone. I moved alone. I gave birth alone. I've been raising my son alone." Britta's talking in a low voice, but she sounds shaken and angry. "Don't give me a speech about 'poor Griff.' He lost his temper, and rather than asking questions, he made terrible assumptions. He didn't trust me and wasn't man enough to apologize when he realized he was wrong. You can't imagine what I went through, so don't preach at me to take pity on him."

"You're right. I can't even begin to imagine," Keeley agrees softly. "I'm only speaking as someone I hope will be your friend someday. Adding more misery to this situation isn't likely to make either of you happy. At the very least, you have a child together. Jamie needs parents who can be cordial and provide him plenty of love. But honestly, I think you and Griff are both still in love with each other and need to give it a chance. If you don't, you'll always regret it."

CHAPTER ELEVEN

AFTER KEELEY GAVE BRITTA HER more than two cents, my angel takes an interest in wine—about three quarters of a bottle. She's always been a Pinot Noir drinker. The fact that she downs that much rosé of dubious distinction tells me she's confused and distressed.

I'm sorry I've backed her in a corner. But she's never going to come out unless I push her out. I wish things between us were simpler, that I could just wrap her in my arms, tell her I love her, and that she would believe me and openly love me back.

Those days are long gone.

Rob and Alania take off. They're late for dinner with her family. As they walk out, a guy schleps in with a bunch of equipment and starts setting it up in the corner. One look tells me it's a karaoke machine. I should have guessed that Maxon would bring Keeley someplace she could sing.

I turn to her. "You planning to sing at Gus's sports bar again?"

"Maybe." She shrugs. "I'm mostly hoping to sing for weekend entertainment once Maxon and I get moved into our new house and open officially as an awesome bed-and-breakfast. I've already got a spot for the yoga, and I'm working on recipes that use locally sourced food. You and Britta should come try a couples' meditation session. I've got a great spot."

Her little smile tells me Keeley is up to something. When she's got a scheme, she's a danger to be avoided at all costs.

That's my cue to leave.

"Angel…" I turn to Britta and put my arm around her. "You ready to go?"

"I'm finishing this glass." She drags her wine closer. "How else am I going to put up with you all evening?"

I ignore her jibe and the resulting pain. "We need to pick up Jamie in the next thirty minutes."

She looks at her watch, then blinks, panic tightening her face. "Is that really the time?"

I see the instant Britta realizes she's had too much to drink and can't drive.

"It's okay," I assure her. "I'm fine. Maxon can park your car at the office. We'll pick it up tomorrow."

That suggestion upsets her even more.

She covers her face with her hands. "I'm never irresponsible. Oh, my god…. What's wrong with me?"

I've rattled her, and she's seeking temporary escape, a release of her pressure valve. I have a better suggestion than booze, but I don't think she's currently in any shape to talk about sharing incendiary orgasms that will have her letting go of all her anger and unshed tears.

"Nothing's wrong with you. It's been a rough few days. I know." Just like I know I should have insisted she eat more than a pot sticker and a lettuce wrap before imbibing. I shove my half-empty beer away and stand. "I've got this. Let me take you home."

"You're really leaving now?" Keeley asks, looking a little bummed.

I rise and lean in to whisper in her ear. "I know you want Britta and me to have a happily ever after now, but FYI, she's not ready. We have a lot to work through, and I have to get started."

The clock is ticking against me.

"Have you made it through the CD I gave you?"

I know she spent a lot of time and energy to give it to me. "Not yet. I'm, um…taking it in small doses."

"Like Britta, you weren't totally ready, either. When you are, it's waiting." She kisses my cheek. "Now go."

When I look around, Maxon is helping Britta to her feet and giving her a hug and some speech of encouragement that ends with a brotherly pat on the shoulder. Keeley hands Britta her purse, and my angel stares at Maxon's fiancée as if she's not sure what to say. Finally, Keeley ends the awkward stare-down by grabbing Britta up in a hug.

"We're going to be friends, and I'm always going to be here for you. Maxon will give me your number, and I will call you soon."

"You're on Griff's side," she says. "So don't bother."

"I'm on love's side. Tonight…just remember that he wants what's best for all of you."

"If you think he doesn't have some control-freak vendetta—"

"He doesn't." Keeley shakes her head. "You won't see it until you stop being angry and afraid. He hurt you, and you're entitled to your feelings. But he's moved heaven and earth to give you a choice. You can either unleash everything you've kept bottled up inside on him or you can genuinely see if it's possible you two can make each other happy for the rest of your lives. You have to decide if you want to hate or are ready to love again." She squeezes Britta's hand. "Oh, and make sure you have a bottle of water and two ibuprofen before you go to bed."

"Thanks." I maneuver Britta behind me. I don't think she's in the mood to hear more wisdom just now.

After a manly chest bump with my brother, I wrap an arm around Britta's waist and escort her to my SUV. We're absolutely silent as we approach Jamie's daycare.

Ten minutes later, he's in my arms, looking happy—especially when I bring up pizza. I dial one of my favorite delivery places for those rare times I indulge in a pie. I know what Britta likes, so I make sure she'll be happy. Jamie gets a kid's cheese pizza all to himself. It will be delivered in an hour. When I give the restaurant the address, Britta is staring at me with a gaping jaw and wide eyes.

"You're taking us to the Stowe estate?" she asks the moment I hang up.

She might be tipsy but her brain still works.

"Yes. We're staying there until the end of our arrangement." I explain the estate's need for a caretaker. She already knows how I feel about staying at her house.

"There's so much water… The pools. The ocean! Jamie…"

"Shh… I'm a step ahead. You don't honestly think I would do anything to put our son at risk, do you?" I raise a brow at her. "I ordered a baby gate for the top and bottom of the stairs. We can put his toys in the spare room and keep him contained there with knob guards. He won't be able to wander out unless we open the door. The rest of the time, he'll be asleep or with us. If that's not enough, tell me what else we need to keep him safe. I'll take care of it."

Britta falls silent as we head to the property. "Why are you doing this? Really?"

I know she's not asking me why I want to protect Jamie. "Because I love you."

She clenches her jaw. "You love me so much you're going to force me to live with you?"

"I love you so much I'm willing to do whatever it takes to help you past your hurt, including taking your anger, which I fully realize I deserve, until you see that we belong together."

With a sigh, she clasps her hands in her lap. "You confuse me."

I don't think she'd be admitting that weakness if she hadn't consumed wine, but her honesty is more helpful than her blame.

"How? I've been very straightforward. The trouble isn't that you don't understand me; it's that you don't believe me. So this is me, trying to change your mind."

Britta doesn't speak again until we reach the house, but I can feel her thoughts turning. I wonder exactly what she's thinking, but I also know better than to force her to talk before she's ready. She's quiet, my angel. She often has to think alone, sometimes reflecting for days, before she's ready to reply.

By the time I pull all the suitcases and boxes of Jamie's necessities from the back of my SUV and stack them in the foyer, the doorbell is ringing. I collect the hot pizza boxes and drinks, then pay the delivery boy. Less than two minutes later, we're sitting down to gooey goodness at the breakfast bar in the rustic Hawaiian kitchen overlooking the peaceful tide of the blue ocean. I'm glad Britta included Jamie's booster seat in her packing so we can make it through this meal with relative ease.

His playpen will come in handy later, too.

Britta picks at her food, mostly fussing over Jamie. I take over coaxing the little guy to eat when it looks as if she's consumed less than a slice.

After he's chowed down half of his kid's plate and starts pushing at the counter, I clean him up and lift him into my arms.

"I'll give him a bath." Britta rises and grabs her plate, heading for the sink.

I grab her wrist and nudge her toward her chair. "Sit. Finish. I'll bathe him. After that, we'll set up his playpen so he can go to bed. Then you and I will talk."

She looks pointedly at her stool, silently refusing to sit again. "I'm tired of you telling me what to do."

"Then stop balking every time I try to lighten your load or meet you halfway."

I'm not going to stand here and argue. First, it's late for Jamie, and he's beginning to yawn and fuss. Second, I think I'm getting to her. She's being argumentative, picking fights, looking for faults…like she's trying to stay mad at me. Like she knows she's teetering on the edge of believing in me again.

Or like I'm thinking really fucking wishfully.

Right now, I'm pretty sure the score is me two, Makaio zero. Yeah, Britta might want to subtract a point from my total because I've twisted her arm, but I have to think that's less of a deduction than her groom telling her that his mommy is going to plan their wedding. So really, the banker is in negative territory, right? I should be good.

But I'm not taking anything for granted.

So I've got one more trick up my sleeve…

After I bathe my boy and find some pajamas in one of his suitcases, I unravel the mystery that is his playpen and set it up in the room adjacent to the master suite. Britta packed away his night-light, so I plug it in before I retrieve his favorite blanket. Then I rock him a little until his eyes droop.

"Hey, big boy. You ready for bed?"

I'm aware that Britta has wandered up the stairs and followed the sound of our voices. She now pauses just inside the doorway of the sitting room. I feel her eyes on me as I cradle Jamie and coo to him.

"No," he whines as he rubs his eyes again. "I not tired."

I try not to laugh. He's obviously exhausted, and it's already past his bedtime.

"Yes," I say firmly, kissing his forehead. "You are. Come on."

With a frown, he touches my cheek. His big eyes and a curious expression tell me he's trying to figure me out. "Daddy."

My heart stops. I blink at my son, hardly daring to move. Then I risk a glance at Britta, who's gaping at us in stunned silence. A resounding yes is on the tip of my tongue. It's one thing to push her to look past her resentment to see what's in her heart. But it's another to force her to allow Jamie to acknowledge me before we've both agreed the time is right.

"What do you want to do here, angel?"

She bursts into tears—something else I don't think would occur if wine hadn't happened tonight. "God, it's like you're a force of nature and I can't stop you. You invade every area of my life and wreak havoc—"

"I intend to put us back together," I swear. "You just have to let me."

I'm stunned that I'm getting choked up, too. I don't know whether it's because the three of us are finally under one roof together like a family or because it's so gratifying to think that, on some level, my own son recognizes me. You know what? I don't know why. I don't care why. Despite what my dad has preached my whole life, emotions don't always make a man weak. The flow of them makes the whole family unit stronger.

In this case, they're giving me the fortitude to push ahead when I'm sure a lot of people would tell me to back the hell off, so I refuse to judge myself now. I'm rolling toward our future.

With her body racking and her eyes leaking, she slowly approaches us, smoothing Jamie's hair from his face. "Yes, baby. He's your daddy." Then she looks at me. "Don't push me anymore tonight."

I hug him tight, kiss his forehead, and revel in a long second of bliss that my son knows the truth, that he'll call me Daddy for the rest of his life.

But as I hear Britta pace, I realize I can't let fear, resentment, or anger fester between us—or I'll lose her. "I didn't suggest to him that I'm his father or coach him to call me that."

She turns to me, frowning as if she's trying to hold herself together. I know this is a sensitive topic. And wine makes her emotions float closer to the surface. Always has.

Maybe that works in my favor tonight.

"The pediatrician told me it wasn't uncommon for kids without a steady father figure to start looking for one at some point. But until tonight, he's never done it. It blindsided me. I know in my heart this is both inevitable and best for Jamie. I just…" Britta doesn't finish her sentence, simply turns away.

I need to go after her. I need to figure out how to soothe her pain.

My first solution to make her feel good is sex…but that's easy. It's not going to fix a situation this complicated. I have to really use everything I've learned over the last couple of years and talk to her. I have to listen and try to say the right things.

I've never been great at that, but the stakes are too high to fuck up now.

"Good night, son," I murmur to Jamie as I lay him in the playpen.

"Daddy," he gurgles again as I hand him a stuffed bear.

"I'll see you in the morning. I love you." I kiss his head again.

As I slip out, I flip off the lights and leave the door cracked so Jamie isn't afraid in his new surroundings. Thankfully, he doesn't make a sound other than a sigh as he slides into sleep.

When I turn, Britta is on the lanai attached to the bedroom, looking out over the inky ocean and the silvery moon playing peekaboo with the clouds.

"I'm sorry you weren't ready for that," I say softly behind her, resisting the urge to touch her, offer her comfort.

She shakes her head. "I tell myself that I'm worried you'll crush Jamie if you walk away again. But I realize it's all wrapped up in my bigger anxiety. How do I simply trust you again? You can't fathom what you're asking of me. What—"

"Yeah, I can. You saved your virginity for the man you'd marry, and you thought that was me. I admit I seduced you. I admit that I wasn't a great boyfriend. But it was lack of skills, not lack of feeling. I loved you then. I love you now. I know that's hard to believe after everything I put you through, but I wish you'd try, angel."

"I'm in a terrible position. Everywhere I turn you're there, in my face, against my body, trying to barge your way back into my life. Memories I haven't thought of in years come out of nowhere to slap me." She breaks into sobs. "Makaio wanted me this weekend. I kept thinking about the first time you and I…" She shakes her head, tears now streaming. "And I couldn't."

The guttural, primal part of me wants to throw a party. She turned down sex with her fiancé because I barged into her thoughts—and crowded him out of her heart. She didn't admit that in so many words, but I feel it. I'm closer to breaking through than I even knew. Little by little, all my assurances have been wearing down her resistance. She just needs a few more signs, more proof that I'm here for her and I'm always going to be here for her.

On the other hand, I hate to see her so torn. Every moment of weeping she stifles into suffering silence is a blade to my heart. I'm furious that I have to finish ripping her apart before I can put us back together.

I grab Britta and fold her into my arms, soothing her with a hand down her back and a whisper in her ear. "It's okay."

"It's not! I'm engaged to another man but I'm letting the one who broke my heart comfort me because it feels confusingly right. I can't do that. I can't give you the power to hurt me again."

"I never will. That promise isn't just words I've strung together. I am determined to make you happy. I am committed to it. I *know* when I left it fucking hurt. And I know because I didn't just break your heart. I broke my own. Everything Keeley said tonight was true. I was a mess. I could have used a good therapist, sure. But I desperately needed a friend. I looked everywhere for something close to what you and I shared. In every bar, on every beach, on every app meant to facilitate a quick hookup."

She wrenches out of my embrace, and I let her. "I don't want to hear how many girls you fucked, Griffin Reed. I don't!" Her face looks crestfallen, her eyes so sad. "But I can do math. Now you want me to believe that you missed me so much that you had sex with hundreds of women while we were apart? How is that supposed to convince me that you loved me?"

"I don't know the exact number. I didn't keep track." But her estimate sounds about right. "I tried to replicate the way you made me feel. And this will sound totally messed up, but it should tell you that I never could replace you because—I realize now—you're everything to me."

Britta wraps her arms around herself and mulls my words over. "It does sound messed up. As much as I hate you for it and want to call you a liar, I can't. Because I tried some of that, too." She swallowed. "After making love with you, being with someone I didn't care about at all was one of the most terrible, hollow emotions I've ever inflicted on myself."

Her admission opens a fresh wound in my chest. I don't think for one minute that she's talking about her relationship with Makaio. And the last thing I want to hear about is Britta in bed with yet another guy. But I have to know that she actually understands. We both have to purge the past.

"What happened?"

She shoots me a sharp glance, then shakes her head. "The details aren't important."

"I don't need who, when, and where. Tell me what it felt like when someone else touched you."

"The first time?" She looks hesitant.

Of course there was more than one time, more than one man. We were apart for three years. I stupidly threw myself into the singles' cesspool about three weeks after our split and stroked all through the waters until I finally crawled out sixteen days ago. Britta is far more cautious. She would have waited, maybe hoped we could patch it back together. I wonder what made her finally decide to give up on me.

"Yeah." We can start there. If she needs to talk more, we will. I will attempt to suppress my homicidal urges.

"The night I received the naked pictures of you and Tiffanii, I went to some bar on Front Street. I don't even remember which one. I drank a lot, so I don't recall his name, either. He listened to me talk about our breakup for a few minutes, then asked me if I wanted to have sex. I said yes."

I close my eyes and try not to feel betrayed because I have no right. No, I try not to feel as if her words ripped my heart from my chest and squeezed out the blood with her bare hands. She had sex with someone else even before I did. "Why? Because you were angry?"

"Furious," she admits softly. "I wanted to hurt you. Not that you even knew when it happened, but I just... I don't know. I kept seeing the snapshots of you and that plastic bitch together. I know you've said you didn't voluntarily sleep with her—at least then. I can believe she rigged the scene since she was always jealous of what we had, enjoyed stirring up drama, and had no conscience. But that night, I didn't want to feel like the naive virgin you'd taken advantage of anymore. I didn't want to stand still like the clingy ex-girlfriend who couldn't move on. Maybe I needed to prove to myself that I'd be all right without you. I'm not sure anymore. I just know that, when it was over, I went to his bathroom and threw up. Then I gave him a fake number and cried all the way back to our apartment."

I clench my fists, but if I'm going to lash out at something or some-one, it should be myself. In a lot of ways, I did this to her. I forced her to confront the future without me when she was reeling and enraged and fucking lost.

"It hurt you," I croon in a soft voice that's somehow a small consolation to me, too.

"Yes. I couldn't sleep in our bed, so I sat up all night, waiting for you to storm back in, seething about what I'd done. To demand that I give you back the body that belonged to you because you'd always been so possessive. But hour after hour passed without anything except silence and regret. That's when I knew you were never coming back." Tears fill her eyes and spill again in a stream of sorrow. "I found out I was pregnant a week later. Once Jamie was born, I dated a little off and on. Sometimes, I'd sleep with someone to see if I was finally over you. But no... I went from feeling sick and stupid to being frozen and empty."

I understand. Most of my life, I've slept with women I didn't have an ounce of feeling for. That's how my old man taught me it was done. That's what life reinforced. I never really knew anything else existed—until Britta.

She shrugs. "Either way, I felt deeply alone. And god, I need to shut up. I'm giving you so many weapons to use against me. You're probably thinking gleefully about how sentimental and stupid I am and—"

"No. Never." I finally risk cupping her face. "I'm thinking about how I would do anything to change that week of our lives. But I can't. I can only ask for your forgiveness."

"I think I've forgiven you." She finally looks right at me, our gazes connecting in a snap I feel all the way to my toes. "I simply don't know if I can forget."

I want to kiss her. Right now. I want to imprint myself on her, show her exactly how I feel in a way I'm good at—certainly better than speaking a bunch of words. If I could show her the difference between the guy who randomly picked up women in a bar and gave them a good time because it temporarily masked how crappy I felt about myself versus the man standing in front of her desperate for the chance to make her mine because I love her, maybe she would understand.

I lower my head, inching so, so slowly toward her lips. She sees me coming, grabs my biceps, holds her breath. I feel her body tense. I dip closer. Her eyes slide shut.

Jesus, my heart is going to gallop out of my chest. We've made so much damn progress tonight. It must be a sign that she's working through her scars. Maybe, deep down, she even wants me back. I'm excited. I have hope. I'm—

"No." She steps back, shaking her head. She worries her engagement ring on her finger. "I'm committed to someone else. You and I have chemistry. I won't deny that. Some part of my heart still belongs to you because you were my first love. That part will probably always belong to you. But I've moved on, made different choices. You seem to want some fairy tale out of our time together. Griff, you're not Prince Charming, and you weren't around to rescue me from the tower, so I found my own way out."

Britta turns her back to me and heads into the house once more. Dismissing me.

"Makaio isn't going to make you happy," I call after her, following with soft footsteps. "He can't."

She stops, glances at me over her shoulder. I hover right behind her, absorbing the heat of her body as the tropical breeze kicks up. In those silent moments, I sense her hesitation. I smell her. I want her.

I'm not giving up until I have her again.

She whirls on me and backs a step away. "And you think you can?

"Yes."

"I don't need that crazy, consuming, dizzying sort of 'love' again. He respects me. We don't argue. We're looking for the same things in life."

I scoff. "Logic isn't going to fulfill you, angel. He doesn't love you. He doesn't challenge you. And he damn well doesn't excite you."

She presses her lips together and crosses her arms. But she doesn't say anything. She doesn't refute me.

"Tell me I'm wrong," I invite her. Fuck that, I goad her.

"Leave me alone."

"I'm not going to do that." Ever.

"Go to hell."

"I've been in hell for the last three years. Now that I'm with you again, I'm staying right here. You'll figure that out sooner or later."

"I prefer Makaio. He gives me space."

She's lying to herself.

I shake my head. "He doesn't care enough to do whatever it takes to earn your heart. He didn't take care of you when you were sick, and he doesn't give a damn that you have the perfect fucking dream wedding in mind. You're only marrying him because you think he's safe. Because you think he'll never leave you. Because he doesn't know or care that you'll never give him the power to hurt you. I won't make you admit that out loud, but you *know* I'm right."

She sighs. Her shoulders droop. "If I gave you what you wanted right now... If I said, 'You know, Griff, you're totally right. Let's get back together,' you'd be bored in under a month."

"No."

"You'd be sneaking away to add notches on your bedpost in less than six weeks," she goes on as if I didn't refute her.

I grit my teeth. "Hell no."

"You would. And you'd be gone from my life—and Jamie's—again in...three, maybe four months. What's the point? Am I your ultimate challenge? Does your ego need to see if you can win me back so you can dump me again?"

"Fuck no!"

I shouldn't touch her at all, not now, not when I'm worked up and she's feeling defensive. Cupping her shoulders certainly doesn't satisfy my need to have her next to me, under me, filled with me. But I want her used to my hands on her skin. I'm willing to start slow. I'm going to work a little more each day to erase the feel of every other man from her memory.

"Yes," she refutes. "You don't want to see that. Maybe you need to believe you've changed so you can live with yourself. Maybe you're looking for meaning or redemption or... I don't even know. Maybe you hit thirty last November and started to think about how sad it is to be unmarried and decided you should settle for the woman who once dreamed naively of the day you would commit and set up house and take meaningless vows—"

"None of that. Fucking son of a bitch. Haven't you been listening to a word I've goddamn said since I walked back into your life? I. Love. You. And if I was lying to myself about anything in the past, it was that. By burying that truth, I didn't have to admit that I was wrong or that I'd screwed up or that my loneliness was something I completely deserved. It would have been really easy to keep rolling along in life and blaming you for breaking faith first by stabbing me with Maxon's secret deal. I have plenty of reasons to know exactly how cutthroat women can be when it comes to money and power and…" I realize what I'm about to admit. It's actually on the tip of my tongue. But if Britta is horrified with me now, she'll be completely revolted by my dirty secret. "Whatever."

"Not whatever. Tell me," she demands. "What did I ever do to you but give you my devotion and believe in you?"

"We're not solving anything at this point. I'm done." I shoulder my way past her and stomp through the bedroom, heading for the stairs to find my suitcase in the foyer.

Britta marches after me. "See? That's just like you, giving up. Walking out. Thanks for proving my point, asshole."

God, she's pushing me. And pushing harder than I ever expected. On the one hand, it's a good sign. She'd be happy for my reprieve if she didn't care. On the other hand, I'm beginning to understand how she feels, why she's overwhelmed by what's going on between us.

"I'm not walking out. Get it through your stubborn head, I will *never* do that again. I'm stopping a destructive argument. I'm making sure we don't say awful things to each other, like we did the day we ended. I regret calling you a bitch. I regret letting you go, not being there for you and Jamie. Hell, I regret everything I've done in the last three years except the things I've done since I came to your engagement party."

I grab my suitcase. I spot her bag, too, and lift it by the handle, then lug them both upstairs.

"Where are you going?" She follows behind me.

"To our bedroom."

"Our…" She huffs. "What? No! You're out of your mind."

"I might be, but there is one bedroom on this side of the house beside Jamie. I haven't been there for my son since the day he was born, and I'll be goddamned if I'm not going to be here for him now. So I'm sleeping in the room closest to him. If you want another bedroom, it will have to be on the other side of the floor." I drop her suitcase at her feet. "You pick. I'm going to bed."

As I head to the master, I catch her grabbing her bag and chasing after me. "I'm not leaving my son without his mother."

"Then it looks like we're both sleeping there." I point at the king-size bed with the tropical white-and-blue comforter and the dozen pillows that make it look soft and inviting and luxuriously romantic.

"Don't pretend this is strictly about Jamie."

You know, she's right. Bullshit isn't my style. "It's not. But that doesn't change anything I've said. This is where I'm sleeping. How about you?"

"You manipulative bastard. You've cornered me again. So, of course, you win. Again. I'm sure that makes your ego feel all big and bloated."

"This isn't fucking about my ego."

"No matter what you say, everything is about your ego at some point, even winning me back." She rolls her eyes and heads to the bathroom. "I don't care. It won't be the first time we've shared a bed. Just stay on your side and don't touch me."

Now I'm just pissed. Or riled. Or frustrated. I'm not thinking, just reacting.

I drop my suitcase and snag her again, pulling her body against mine with a hand splayed at the small of her back. I dig my fist into her hair and force her to look at me. "I won't lay a finger on you until you admit you want me. Until you admit I'm the only man for you. Until you ask me."

"You're going to be waiting for the rest of your life."

CHAPTER TWELVE

I CAN'T SLEEP. I FEEL like the stupidest, most masochistic son of a bitch ever. I love sleeping next to Britta. But right now, I hate sleeping next to her. I smell her, hear her. I can almost touch her, taste her. I want her so badly I'm hard and sweating and aching.

I can't have her—yet.

Sharing a bed again is making me remember the morning sex, the good-night sex, our quickie nooners, and the lazy Sunday loving we once shared. Not going to lie, we got busy a lot. The difference was that, unlike other women, every time I was with Britta, I only wanted her more. I wanted her in a way that stemmed from somewhere deeper than my dick. I yearned to hold her when she cried. I couldn't wait to laugh with her when we caught the neighbor's crazy dog humping a fence post or landed a listing on a Hawaiian street with a name containing fifteen vowels we both had trouble pronouncing. And yes, I loved to indulge her in the most sinful, drawn out, claw-worthy orgasms while finding new ways to make her come.

Right now, I'd settle for her talking to me. After the end of our argument, she shut herself in the bathroom, took a long bath, then emerged in a shapeless T-shirt, palmed a sleep mask, and utterly tuned me out.

I might deserve it…but I don't know what to do about it. And I have to figure it out—fast.

I roll over and look at the clock—1:53 a.m. Yeah, I'm going to be worthless at work later today.

Reaching for my phone, I roll out of bed. Quickly, I peek in on Jamie, who's as sacked out as his mother, then I pace out to the lanai. The shadows of moonbeams dance over the water. I hear the crashing waves more than see them. I can almost feel them vibrating through my body as they churn loudly in the night that's otherwise silent—kind of like the turmoil rolling just under my skin.

Emotions. They fucking suck. But if I'm going to dive into that murky pit, I might as well wade in deep, make some decisions, and get it over with.

When I unpacked my car earlier, I brought Keeley's CD of song selections inside. Luckily, I don't have to wander the house for long to find a CD player. There's one in the bonus room upstairs. I probably shouldn't do this now. It won't cheer me up in the least. But I still cue up the next tune on the disc, then sink into a plush chair to listen.

From the very first strains, it's sad. No, haunting. A vocal realization that everything between this couple is tangled, confusing, and seemingly hopeless. A glance at the case tells me it's called "Breaking Ties" by some obscure band called OceanLab. No idea where Keeley finds this stuff, but she's dead on.

I *have* been fooling myself for so long, thinking I could live without Britta. I'm pretty sure she's been doing the same. I don't know how we could be both so right and so wrong. No denying that when I feel my mouth against her skin, she absolutely lights me from within. And it's been forever since I've felt that way because that's how long it's been since I've been with her. But right now, she's sinking like a stone. And just like the lyrics suggest, I need to be her parachute.

How can I do that? I'm not sure—yet. I'm certainly never allowing Makaio an opportunity to pull her rip cord and save her.

After the song ends, I silence the sound system. Ideas are rolling through my head. Big ones. Crazy ones. I'm pinging with them. Vibrating with them. I'll never fucking sleep.

I bounce my phone from one hand to the other, hesitating. Should I? Shouldn't I? I have to, don't I? Otherwise, I'll contemplate my uncertain future all night. Otherwise, nothing between Britta and me changes. The good news is, this won't be the first time I've called this late. The bad news? I doubt it will be the last.

With a sigh, I press a button.

Three rings later, Keeley whispers, "What are you doing up?"

"What are you doing up?" I counter. "I knew you wouldn't answer if you weren't awake."

She clears her throat. "Do you really want me to answer that?"

I cringe. "Shit. Please tell me that you and my brother aren't getting busy right now."

Keeley laughs. "No. I wouldn't answer the phone if we were. It's just fun to mess with you."

"Stop. I don't want to hear a word about his dick, joking or otherwise."

"I'll try not to offend your delicate sensibilities, Griff. So what's up? Out with it." Keeley sighs. "You only call in the middle of the night when it's really bad. I'm guessing you took Britta to the house and…what? Had a fight?"

Sometimes, I swear she's psychic. "More or less. It started off calm and reasonable…ish. Then Jamie called me Daddy."

"That's good, right? Oh, except it upset Britta, I'll bet."

"Some. Not as much as I thought, though. From there, we wandered onto the subject of our respective lovers after the split. That went less well." Much less.

"I'll bet she wasn't thrilled you'd been so…busy," Keeley predicted. "And you lost your shit when you found out she hadn't spent all her time alone."

"I didn't." Well, not visibly. "But I wanted to. That was one of the fucking hardest things I've ever heard. It solidified my resolve to make sure there's never another man in her life." Or her bed. "Then I might have screwed up by mentioning that Makaio isn't the right guy for her. She didn't want to hear that when she was wearing his ring. Things got uglier after that. Somehow, she's convinced herself that I'm full of hot air and me trying to win her back is all about my ego. Really? I'm not that guy."

"Not anymore," she corrects me. "Besides, I think that's her excuse. She has to attribute your actions to something, and if she lets herself believe you really are still in love with her, then she has to confront her feelings for you. And she's terrified to do that because she'll have to reevaluate the future she has planned."

Valid point. "I don't know how else to make her understand that I just want to—"

"Give her a better future? Make her happy? I know. But she doesn't. Think about this... What if she lets herself fall for you again and it doesn't work out? Britta is too smart not to realize she'll lose everything for giving in to her heart—her fiancé and possibly even her job. She will, of course, have to share her son going forward. And she'll have to live with that broken heart and a mountain of regret. Again."

I rake a hand through my hair. I hear what she's saying, but none of that is going to happen. "I keep telling her over and over that I love her."

"What did you tell her the first time you were together, Griff? How did you sweet-talk her out of her panties? Into your life, into your apartment, into her heart? And how much of that was a come-on?"

I didn't know how to act with Britta at first. I remember that. She seemed so different to me...but I fell into old patterns because that's what I knew. I told her she was beautiful. I "accidentally" brushed against her. I took her to posh restaurants and zipped her around the island in my expensive ride. I did and said whatever it took to tear down her resistance and wear down her halfhearted refusals until she gave me a date, a kiss, her trust, and finally, her virginity.

I probably was a dirtbag, but even before I truly understood how I felt, I treasured her on some level. I know I didn't want to ever let her go.

"So I need to prove this isn't about my ego, just about her."

"You do."

That's a relief. If Keeley thought I was making a mistake, she'd flat-out tell me so. "I'm not sure I know how. I have an idea, but you'll probably think it's unhinged."

"Is it underhanded and manipulative?"

I hesitate. "This *is* me you're talking to."

"True. Will it do anything to prove that you love her and want to make her happy?"

"If it comes off right, yeah. I think so." I sigh. "But I need your help. A lot of it."

"The favor you asked me for earlier?"

"You read me so well."

"Of course. You're male and transparent and have pure bastard running through your veins."

I scowl. "My brother isn't so different."

"I know. I'm still trying to figure out why I love him." She laughs. "Well, that's not true. Maxon sang karaoke to prove his love to me."

That's somehow endearing to her? "He can't sing."

"I know, and we've agreed he won't do that again. But he humiliated himself in public for me. And he was willing to give up the deal of his career and a few million dollars to make me happy."

Great for Maxon, but I can't give up now or I lose Britta and Jamie for good. I'll have nothing left but a career and a shitload of regret.

"My idea is a little more substantial." I pause, unsure how this is going to go over, but hey… I'm an all-or-nothing guy. "I want to surprise Britta with our wedding."

"What?" Keeley takes a minute to figure that out. "You mean plan it all and not tell her until the day you marry?"

Her skeptical incredulity isn't what I hoped for but doesn't surprise me. "Yeah."

"Are you fucking crazy?" she shouts, then yelps. I can hear Maxon stir beside her, then some rustling before she whispers again. "Seriously. Are you?"

"Probably." I explain Makaio's decision to let his mother plan their wedding, and the fact that Britta had lovingly hand-selected all the elements of her big day through those magazines, only to have the jerk flush it down the toilet. "So my idea is to give her the wedding of her dreams…along with the man who's devoted to her and the family she craves."

"Griff…" Her tone asks me to be reasonable. "Even if you gave me her stack of magazines, I don't know if I could figure out exactly what she wants. I mean, I've barely started looking and I've already seen ten dresses I love. I'll bet she's got her eyes on more than one of everything and—"

"Maybe you could help each other?" When she makes a sound of protest again, I wince. "Just hear me out. Please."

She sighs. "You owe me."

"Yeah, but I'm not being your maid of honor and wearing peach chiffon."

Keeley giggles. "But you'd look really pretty."

"Fuck you."

That incites more laughter, then a sound of exasperation—mostly at herself. "All right. Lay it on me. I'm crazy for even listening. I want that on record, by the way. And you're insane, too. That needs to be stated."

"Duly noted," I swear. "But this could be the perfect setup. Tell her you need help with your wedding, but that you're having trouble making decisions and would love her input. Britta has amazing taste, a great eye for visuals."

"Solicit her input for my wedding and use what she tells me for her own?"

"Exactly. Once you get the information out of her, pass it on to me. I'll take care of the rest."

"Actually…" She pauses. "I can't believe I'm going to say this, but it's not the worst idea I've ever heard."

"See?"

"And I can't believe I'm going to help you even more. The wedding Maxon said he already booked for Sunshine Coast Bed and Breakfast—that really has a nice ring, don't you think?"

"Way better than Maxon Maui Realty."

"Okay, I can't disagree with that. The point is, those people realized belatedly that it's Easter weekend and rescheduled for mid-May. So we have an opening."

It's the same Saturday that Makaio picked to marry Britta. Future anniversaries will fall on Tax Day, which is decidedly unromantic. But I'm not going to sweat that. I'll make future anniversaries amazing.

"Done. So you'll call her later, work your magic, and help me make her dream wedding a reality?"

"I should take my temperature. I must be stupid to agree to this. Not right in the head. Devoid of all my faculties."

"Is that a yes? Keeley, honey…"

"Don't honey-baby-sweetie-pie me." She sighs. "You don't need to. I think she loves you. I know you're absolutely besotted by her. So while this might be the craziest thing I've ever heard of, it's also one of the most romantic. All right. I'll help you."

TWO MISERABLE DAYS PASS IN which Britta is barely speaking to me. I'm eager for Keeley to get the ball rolling on the wedding planning, and I hope the nuptials I throw her will change everything. But until then, I need to make better use of my time with her so she actually *wants* to marry me. I need to ensure that all the days—and nights—I've strong-armed out of her aren't spent in chilly civility or I'm going to lose her for good.

The bright spot is my relationship with Jamie. Last night, I bought him a pair of floaties and a raft. We had a blast in the pool. He called me Daddy again before I set him down with toys. Not going to lie, that warmed my heart.

Then I helped Britta with dinner. And yeah, I probably brushed against her way more than I needed to in a kitchen that size, but she's right in front of me—all day, all night. How the hell am I supposed to keep my hands off her?

"Can you grab the roasting pan of potatoes from the oven?" she asks absently, then peeks into the adjoining family room to find Jamie with his trucks and blocks, making sputtering, slobbery noises.

"Sure."

She pauses to watch our son. "He looks happy."

I smile. "He really liked swimming."

"He's not as fond of the ocean, so I'm glad he reacted better to the pool." She hesitates. "I watched from the lanai. You're very patient with him. Thank you."

I grit my teeth. It burns me that she's thanking me for loving my own son. But I stifle it. I don't want to start a fight. This is the most conversation we've had since the night we argued. "He loved the pool. He's fun to be with and he's actually more competent in the water than I expected. But we need to watch him carefully. He was getting brave at the end. I don't want him thinking the pool isn't dangerous."

Britta pauses, her spoon hovering over the chicken in the pan. Her face tightens with worry. "Absolutely."

"We've got this. We won't let anything happen." I can't stop myself. I drop my hand to the small of her back and lean closer. "I promise."

She turns slightly, meets my gaze. My mouth hovers maybe six inches above hers. Her breath goes shallow. I see the heartbeat at the base of her neck flutter, mirroring the racing of my own. I could kiss her right now. She might let me. She might part her rosy lips and welcome me inside her mouth so I can worship her. She might moan, melt against me.

She might also kick me in the balls.

Willing to take the chance, I lean in. Jamie lets out a shriek and clangs two metal trucks together.

We jump apart, and I curse under my breath. It's not his fault. And maybe he did me a favor. As much as it chafes, with hot food cooking and a toddler watching, it isn't the time to make a move. And I don't think Britta is ready.

She jerks her gaze back to the stove. "Don't do that again, Griff."

As I drag the potatoes from the oven, I see her rubbing her engagement ring again like it's a talisman that will protect her from the temptation I'm throwing her way. I refrain from pointing out that I'm not going to make it that easy on her.

She'll figure that out on her own soon enough.

A few minutes later, we're all sitting down to a home-cooked meal. We eat in silence broken only by our attempts to help Jamie's spoon find his mouth and the clatter of silverware against dishes.

"Keeley called me this morning," Britta says.

I hear the note of confusion in her voice. "When she says she's determined to be your friend, trust me. That woman means it."

"I don't know why."

"You and my brother have always been close. They're getting married."

"True…" she concedes but doesn't sound convinced.

"And I'm sure it's because she's been my best friend for a couple of years and she knows how important you are to me. She knows I love you even if you don't."

Britta grabs her bottle of water to avoid looking at me. "Keeley asked me if I would help her plan her wedding. She said her mom is too far away and that she feels overwhelmed by the amount of planning to be done in a short timeframe. They're talking about getting hitched in two months. It's really fast."

"When you know it's right, why wait?"

She presses her lips together, then flips her engagement ring with her thumb—precisely where I can see the diamond glint. "Exactly."

It's tough, but I don't let her prod me. She's wrong about Makaio, and I think we're both aware of it. I could remind her that he skipped out on her when she needed him. I could also admit that I will never let him adopt Jamie because I'm not convinced he'd make my son's best interests a top priority. I could also promise her that, once we go to bed tonight, I'll be more than happy to show her what she's been missing between the sheets with Mr. Hawaii. He might look like a fucking underwear model, complete with stupid smile as he stands, hands on hips, showing off his cotton-clad junk. But I know I can make her want, orgasm. *Feel.* If she'll let me give her a reminder, I will be happy to help her compare notes afterward.

"Broccoli?" I pass her the dish, refusing to rise to her bait.

"Thank you." Naturally, she extends her left hand to me and grabs the dish. Her diamond gives me another mocking wink.

I manage to keep calm. "So what did you tell Keeley?"

She pauses. "I agreed to help. This will benefit Maxon, after all. I owe him for everything he's done for me over the last few years. Besides, I guess you told her I was organized?"

"And she's *so* not. Keeley is fun and smart, but she's a free spirit. Calendars and schedules and deadlines give her hives. Watching her flounder with all that would make you crazy, angel."

"I've told you not to call me that."

I send her a smile that tells her there's no way in hell she's stopping me. "What does Makaio call you?"

She pauses, then frowns as if she's giving my question a lot of thought. "He's not really the pet name sort."

Is she kidding? The slight furrow in her brows tells me she's not. And it doesn't seem as if she's sure how she feels about that.

I should probably shut my mouth but I'm really dying to know. "All right. What did he say to you when he proposed? What did he do? How did he give you the ring?"

"He didn't. Um, we were talking at my house a couple of Sundays ago. While barbecuing in the backyard, he pointed out all the reasons we're great together and asked me if I would do him the honor of marrying him."

Wait a minute. Hold up. She's given me a wealth of information there. First, why didn't the asshole make a big damn deal of proposing to her? It doesn't sound as if he even got down on one knee, much less hired a skywriter or something awesome. It was like... *Hey, since I'm in the middle of flipping burgers, I've got a minute to ask you if you want to spend the rest of your life with me.*

Fuck that.

The bigger nugget of fact I got out of her speech, however, is timing. He proposed on Sunday. When I barged into their impromptu engagement party, it was the following Thursday night. She said she'd just accepted his proposal four hours prior. So she made the bastard twist in the wind for four days before answering him?

I smile. I've got her. Right here. She's telling me without telling me that she doesn't love Makaio. What woman whose heart is filled with devotion waits four days to decide if she wants to share the rest of her life with him?

None.

I shovel chicken into my mouth and study her. The last forty-eight hours between us may have sucked, but life is definitely looking up.

"What is that expression?" she challenges.

"I don't know what you mean." My grin widens.

"That smirk. Why do you suddenly look so smug?"

I weigh the pros and cons of keeping this revelation to myself. But I'm not playing a long game. I don't have time for quiet.

Finally, I shrug. "I'm just thinking there's no way you're going to marry this guy."

"Excuse me?" She sounds shocked. "I am. I have no doubt."

I shrug like she's wrong, but whatever. Britta can't stand that.

"What is your problem? You can't have me, so you're going to try and talk me out of marrying him?"

"No. I don't hate that idea, but…" I shake my head. "He's got everything wrong. He has no special endearment just for you? He doesn't try to make you feel like the most amazing woman in his world?" I shake my head like that's a big fucking mistake because it is. "He didn't do anything awesome just for you, or even give you a ring, when he proposed? Then again, I guess that wouldn't be logical." I scoff.

Britta scowls. "It was very romantic."

"You're a terrible liar."

"It *was*," she insists. "And we shopped for a ring together after I said yes."

Because he wasn't going to spend money on her or any gesture of emotion until he knew he had to.

"And when he proposed, I'll bet he outlined all the reasons getting married made sense—you're both responsible, have good jobs, handle money well, like the same movies, and his picture-perfect family adores you. Right?" When she presses her lips together mulishly, I laugh. "Right. Then he talked about your lives together with all the excitement of a pile of compost before waxing boring about the requisite ten-minute coitus you'll share twice a week that he'll find a perfectly adequate expression of your shared passion. Am I far off the mark?"

She sputters. "Miles off, in fact."

"No, I'm not. That's why it took you four days to decide to marry the loser."

"You're wrong. And that doesn't mean I would ever marry you, Griffin Reed." Without skipping a beat, she helps Jamie by cutting another piece of chicken into smaller bits and sliding one onto his baby spoon, even as she rolls her eyes at me. "You know what? His proposal was way more romantic than yours because at least he asked. You had me for a whole year and never once broached the topic. You never cared about anything like that." She huffs. "You never even thought of it. So that puts him way ahead of you."

Jamie is about to toss a handful of potato across the table, so I grab him by the wrist and use my napkin to empty his hand. Then I stand and glare at Britta. "Wait here."

When I spin on my heel and head for the stairs, taking them two at a time, she calls after me. "Where are you going?"

I'm not answering. She'll see soon enough.

Two minutes later, I return, yank her barstool away from the table until she's facing me, then I get down on one knee and open the black velvet box in my grip. She gasps when she sees the engagement ring inside.

"I bought this on March sixteenth, almost four years ago. I knew the moment I saw this ring that it was meant for you and that I was meant to put it on your finger."

Britta presses her hand to her chest, mouth gaping like I've stunned her speechless, as she stares at the symbol of love I bought her years ago.

"Marry me." My heart is thundering, and I wish I had something more flowery and romantic to say. I could give her arguments about why I'm a better man for her. I might even be able to talk sweet and fast and whisk her into bed for an orgasmic glow that lasts a day or two.

It's all worthless if she won't admit she loves me. And if she needs proof I'm committed to this—and her—I don't know what more I can do beyond what I am right now.

"You're serious?" Her voice is shaking. She looks at me, blinks, looking frozen, stricken. She can't seem to find her voice, her breath. "You've had that..."

"For almost four years, yes."

"No." She shakes her head, her gaze bouncing between the ring and my face, like she's not sure where to focus. "We'd barely begun dating seriously. We'd barely begun..."

"Having sex?" I know that's what she's thinking, but she swallows the words down.

"That's not possible." She's shaking her head and looking at me like there must be some terrible mistake.

I'd be offended if I didn't understand that her accepting what I'm stating as fact means that she has to question everything—each past decision, all the anger she's carried, and that future she thinks she has planned.

I ease to my feet and pull the receipt from my pocket to set it on the counter so she has no doubt I'm telling the truth. It shows the exact date I purchased the ring and how much it set me back.

She scans it, then blinks at me in total shock.

I come closer, tuck her chin in my grip so I know she's paying attention to every word I say. "We started dating just before Halloween. I suspected our relationship was serious by Thanksgiving. I knew I was in love with you by New Year's. You finally trusted me enough to give me your virginity on March first. Yes, I remember the exact date. It changed my life because you changed my life. By the end of that night, I was sure you were it for me. When I saw this ring two weeks later, I bought it. And I waited for you to be a little older and a little more comfortable with me. I wanted you ready to say yes to spending your life with me. I intended to propose to you on my birthday. I had a plan. I might have been a shit, but I wanted to give you the best proposal ever. I knew it was important to you."

"And we fell a week short." The words tumble out of her mouth small, eked with pain, and filled with so much sadness.

"Yeah." I have to bear the responsibility for that. "But right now, you and I have the chance to erase the bad and start over, as a family." I ruffle Jamie's hair, then I can't help myself. I wrap my hand around Britta's arm, curl it around her elbow, and bring her to her feet against me. "I'm serious, angel. Marry me."

CHAPTER THIRTEEN

BRITTA DOESN'T ANSWER ME THAT night. Or the next morning. I already know she's going to leave me hanging more than the four days she made Makaio wait. And I'm okay with that for one reason.

She hasn't said no.

I'm calling that a win for now.

The day is a rush of property showings with clients, paperwork, and phone calls. Keeley taught yoga at the senior center this morning, then whisked Britta and Jamie away for wedding planning and girl time. I want details. I want to know what dress to buy her, what kind of flowers she wants, what flavor of cake—anything that will make our wedding seem more real.

"Are you sure you're doing the right thing?" my brother asks, approaching the door of my office. "You've always been ballsy, but planning Britta a surprise wedding…"

I look up from the late-afternoon sun sliding over the glimmering blue water in the distance. "I think so, but…no. I'm not entirely sure. You got better ideas?"

"If bad karaoke won't solve it, I'm afraid not," Maxon admits.

"The way Makaio proposed was so thoughtless it's almost an insult." I wish I'd done better, that I hadn't whipped out the ring in the heat of the moment to prove something. On the other hand, she knows now how serious I am—and always have been. "After what's happened, she needs to feel valued and loved, like I would crawl across glass, walk through fire, go to the ends of the earth to have her."

"Of course. And she deserves that. It just seems like there's a lot of potential to fuck this up."

"Yep. But is picking the wrong color bridesmaid dress really my biggest problem?"

"It's not," he concedes. "The fact you're forcing her hand is."

"She has to pick one of us."

"But you're not only making her choose a groom, you're wedging her into a position where she has two weddings on the same day and she'll have to pick the one in which she'd like to be the bride. That's messed up, dude."

I shrug. Maybe. Probably. "But fitting."

"What about a marriage license? You have to apply for one in person. Together."

"I'm already working on that. I can start the process online, which I've done. I had a client last year whose daughter is a marriage license agent on the island. I'm seeing if I can, you know, work the system."

"Of course you are." Maxon shakes his head, wearing a hint of a smile.

"What will you do if she ultimately says no to you?"

"Not an option."

Maxon shakes his head like I'm a dumb ass. "You need to start thinking about it. Not everything is always going to go your way."

"I've got a hundred ways to make her realize I'm the right man for her. I haven't even unleashed any of those yet."

"Uh-huh. I know you. Ninety-nine of those ways involve sex. You can't do that to her, bro."

Why not? "How do I reach her if I can't remind her firsthand about our chemistry?"

"I don't know. But remember the last time you kissed her? You freaked her out so much that she slapped those papers to relinquish your parental rights in your face. Even if you managed to seduce her, she's engaged to someone else. She wouldn't be able to handle the cheating."

Maybe he's right. I was hoping that, at some point—soon—Britta would find me irresistible. Once I got inside her and started giving her orgasms, Makaio wouldn't stand a chance. I wasn't going to push or rush her. I didn't think I had to. She wants me, too. I believe that. I feel it.

But Maxon is right. Britta is a stickler for honesty and fairness. I'm not sure she could live with herself. She might even resent me for leading her astray.

"Fuck."

"Probably not. You need to rethink your strategy because you can't use the most effective tool at your disposal." He gestures vaguely below my waist. "Your, um...tool."

It sucks, but Britta has to want to end her relationship with Makaio before she can be mine. That makes my "tool" useless right now. Damn it.

"Thanks for the insight. I'll figure it out." I've got to. "What about you two?"

"Me and Keeley? Thankfully, I don't have any competition for her affection, so my tool is getting lots of action." He winks.

"Eww." Lucky bastard that he gets to worship the woman he loves. "I mean did you two set a date?"

"Oh. Not yet. But I can't let you beat me to the altar."

We've always been competitive. Dad ingrained that into us. Maxon wasn't my brother; he was my competition, and I should want to squash him in all endeavors. But of course, since he's three years older than me, I'm not surprised he feels as if he has to do everything, including getting married, first.

"Yeah, I guess you better hurry up and tie the knot," I drawl. "You're almost eligible to apply for your AARP card."

"Oh, fuck you." He punches my shoulder. "I just don't want to wait. I know Keeley is the woman I want to spend my life with. I'm trying to convince her that we should do it on the beach in front of our new house before she gets too busy being an innkeeper to sink her teeth into a wedding."

"Makes sense. Britta really will help her."

"Speaking of which, I hope they had a good time shopping today. And that they're making friends."

We both know how uncomfortable our lives will be if they don't. Britta and Tiffanii mixed like champagne and turpentine.

"I hope Keeley vouches for my new and improved character."

Maxon is both rolling his eyes and laughing when Keeley breezes into the office with smiles for me and kisses for my brother.

"How was it?" I rush to ask before she's even had time to sit down.

"Actually, it went really well. Now that she doesn't think you're nailing me, she's very sweet." Then Keeley sends me a disapproving stare. "And very torn. She seemed all right when I talked to her yesterday morning. Today? Whatever you did to her, she's a mess."

"It's complicated." The engagement ring I bought is wearing a hole in the sock drawer in our bedroom. I'm waiting for the day I can slip it on Britta's finger, but I don't say anything now. Keeley will tell me to slow down and be gentle. I can't. "We'll have to work it out over the next forty-eight days. So what did you two do?"

"I know a subject change when I hear one." She reaches into her purse and pulls out a handwritten page, then begins pointing at each line as she hands it over. "This is the name of a bridal boutique we went to. Since the wedding is coming up so quickly, I encouraged her to try on some sample dresses—just for fun, you know."

Because Makaio's mother will have picked out traditional Hawaiian garb—a white muumuu—for Britta to wear. It's completely not her style. She likes clothes with structure and shape, more formfitting, that show the lean lines of her body. She's also not the sort who will want a crown of flowers in her hair or a lei around her neck. She won't want someone blowing a conch shell, either. It's no disrespect to Makaio's culture. It's just that he's not doing anything to accommodate her wishes or beliefs.

"And?"

Keeley's smile is full of excitement. "She found a sample dress in her size that looks ah-mazing. Which is great because she can buy it off the rack since you don't have the six months it takes to order from the designer. It needs a little repair on the beadwork, but the shop has a tailor on-site. Other than that, the dress fits perfectly. Call them quickly. I had them hold it for you. I'll pick it up Monday."

I lean in to kiss her cheek. "You're fantastic. Anything else?"

"The bridal shop recommended a photographer, a caterer, and a florist. I picked up business cards, so on my way over here, I made a few calls. I set up appointments with all these people to talk to you on the phone next week. During my lunch with Britta, I spread out all the bridal magazines available at the drugstore. I bought them last night so she could point out to me things she liked. So now I know what sort of arrangements, food, and cakes she's interested in. It was a really productive day."

I'm beyond pleased. "I can't thank you enough. This is going to work."

She nods my way. "It just might."

"Did you plan anything for our wedding, sunshine? You got the ball rolling for my bonehead brother, but you have an eager groom here…" Maxon all but growls.

"As a matter of fact, I did."

"I have to beat this asshole to the altar." Maxon points my way.

"How does April eighth sound? That's the week before his wedding…"

My brother pauses. "I'd rather do it in March. The fourth sounds perfect."

"That's next Saturday, Maxon," Keeley objects. "I'm already doing this last minute."

"Then why is it still taking weeks?"

We all laugh and discuss details a bit more. Since I brought the magazines Britta discarded, I quiz Keeley on things my angel seemed drawn to. The visuals give me a point of reference, and at the end, I'm sure I'm closer to making Britta my wife.

When the sun starts sliding toward the horizon and shadows begin to fill the office, I glance at my watch and frown. "Where are Britta and Jamie?"

Keeley showed up nearly an hour ago, and I didn't think they would be far behind. She mentioned a run to the drugstore earlier but…

"Oh, Jamie didn't go with us today. One of his daycare teachers agreed to watch him since a bridal shop isn't really a place to take a toddler."

I want to object that I could have spent today with him, that I would have been thrilled for the time with my boy…but I had to work. I grind my teeth at the missed opportunity. But Jamie is all boy, and the image of sticky hands and slobber on satin tells me Keeley is right. "Good call."

"Britta said she would meet you at the Stowe mansion later."

Not at home.

I know the building isn't actually our home. It never will be. But my home is wherever Britta is. Wherever Jamie is.

The conversation brings full circle the fact that she hasn't chosen me. It's possible she never will.

But that's not Keeley's fault, so I suck it up and smile. "Thanks."

The lovebirds leave the office hand in hand, still debating about a suitable wedding date. Maxon concedes that planning something as important as a ceremony commencing the rest of their life together might require more than six days. So he's willing to wait a whole additional week.

I laugh and head home, mentally prowling through the refrigerator to decide what we might have for dinner.

When I pull into the enormous garage and head inside the house, Britta is already there making something with salmon. I smell jasmine rice steaming.

I set my keys down as I watch her bustle around the kitchen and Jamie curled up on the sofa with her iPad and a cartoon, his thumb in his mouth. "Hi, angel."

She moved freely until I made my presence known. Now she seems guarded, sending me sidelong glances as she begins to toss a salad. "Hi. Good day? Did the couple from Seattle decide to buy a condo?"

"They said they'll call me Monday, but my gut says yes." I want to go to her, wrap my arms around her, kiss the nape she exposed when she lifted her golden tresses into a messy bun.

Maxon's warning that Britta won't be able to handle cheating echoes through my head.

I really am screwed.

"Good. Keeley and I had a great day. All my friends from college are on the mainland, and other than Emily, the woman you met at the park, my neighborhood wasn't exactly filled with single women I had a lot in common with. Girl time was nice. Really nice."

She actually smiles. I think that's the first time I've seen her happy in…well, since I barged into her life again. Sure, she's chatting to fill the space. So the silence otherwise isn't awkward? Or so I don't ask her whether she has an answer to my proposal?

"Good."

"Poor Keeley seems so lost about weddings. She really wanted my opinion on everything, like she'd barely given her ceremony a thought." She shrugs. "If I'm not going to get to plan my own, it's nice to…"

Britta falls silent as if she realizes what she's all but admitting.

"So you're marrying Makaio? You're choosing logic over love?" I try to keep my voice even and not reveal my absolute fury at the thought.

She tenses again, moving around the kitchen watchfully, as if she's steering clear of a wild animal. "I haven't decided anything."

I round the bar and invade her personal space. I don't touch her exactly. I can't or I'm worried I'll lose my self-control and be all over her. I pin her against the counter, anchoring my hands on either side of her, and manage to stop myself from dragging her closer. "What can I do to help you choose me?"

"Back off."

"Besides that."

"Nothing. I have to think this through. Last night was…a lot."

I can't dispute that. "Let's figure this out together."

That sounds calm and responsible. Mature. Not too demanding.

She's already shaking her head. "I need time to be alone with my thoughts."

That fucking grates on my patience.

"Give me one evening. Just one to imagine with me what our lives would be like if we'd been married for the last three years and if our lives were normal—"

"How do I do that? If we'd been married that long, you wouldn't have to force me to live with you. Jamie calling you Daddy would make me smile, not worry. We wouldn't be living here." She gestures around to the expansive mansion. "And I wouldn't be trying to decide whether I'm marrying another man in less than two months."

You're not, I want to growl at her, but I manage to bite back the words. "Britta... Angel. Give me a chance. I can't prove anything to you about us if you don't let me."

"Give me some space and we'll talk when I'm ready. I promise." She shoulders her way past me to take the fish from the oven.

As she sets the table, I clench my teeth. The old me would never have accepted that answer. She belongs with me. She needs to be with me.

But she doesn't believe in me yet.

The new me knows she's going to have to voluntarily choose me if she's ever going to stand beside me in a white dress and say *I do.*

We sit down to dinner in silence broken only by Jamie's antics. He's not a fan of salad tonight, and we both have to stop him from throwing lettuce. He decides to push salmon between a gap in his baby teeth. When he reforms his mound of rice into a snowball and threatens to throw it, Britta takes it away with a wag of her finger. Only the banana I peeled for him at the last minute seems to be a hit.

"He do this often?" I haven't noticed this behavior before.

She shakes her head. "Leslie, the woman who watched him today, is one of his favorite nursery school teachers, but she's in her sixties. I don't think they were running around the park all day. Sometimes when Jamie has energy to burn, he does this at the table."

It makes sense, and I have childhood memories of being forced to sit through a meal when I had something way more interesting, usually sports, on my mind.

I stand and untie Jamie's bib, then lift him into my arms. "Why don't you finish? We'll find some ball to chase for a while. If you'll put our food in the oven, I'll come back in a bit when we're ready to eat it."

She hesitates. "If you make him sit here long enough, he'll get it down."

"He's a boy. He needs to run. He needs fresh air. This is my department. We'll be back."

"Daddy," Jamie shrieks. "Let's play!"

As I lead him outside, I feel Britta's gaze on me, watching the two of us together. Is she assessing? Probably. I want to bristle a bit, but that's what this period is for, to determine how I would be as a father and husband. This is me.

I hope what I'm doing is enough.

After a half hour of running and giggling on the lawn, Jamie is panting. One thing I know about my son now? He's clever. He's determined. He doesn't mind being a little underhanded to get his way. He's definitely my kid.

But he's also kind and likes to laugh, and when I pretended to have a boo-boo, he didn't hesitate to come kiss it. He's caring, like his mother.

We enter the house again to find a spotless and empty kitchen. Britta slid our plates into a warming drawer, and I get them out, putting Jamie's food on a plastic child's plate so he doesn't burn himself.

"If you eat well, I might find you some ice cream, partner."

He claps his hands and digs into his food with gusto. Good, old-fashioned bribery works well. I can't help but laugh.

Despite the turmoil right now, the uncertainty of not knowing whether Britta will ever be mine, I can't deny how content I feel spending time with Jamie. Yes, he's fun and incredible. But every time I look at him, I'm amazed that I see my face and Britta's eyes. He's a perfect blend of us.

After a little contraband in vanilla/chocolate swirl, I give him a quick bath, then hoist him into my arms so he can get a kiss from his mother.

I find her in the media room curled up in a chair near the CD player, wearing noise-canceling headphones over her ears.

And tears streaming down her face.

I rush over to her. "Angel, what's wrong?"

She brushes the wetness from her cheeks and gives Jamie a falsely cheerful smile. "You all ready for bed, handsome man?"

"I want stories," our son insists.

Her grin turns genuine. "Of course you do."

When she stands and reaches out for Jamie, I hesitate. "You sure? I can do this."

She shakes her head. "I'm fine."

I don't think Britta means that, but she's stubborn and this isn't worth the fight. I hand him over. She hugs the little boy to her chest, eyes closed, her face a wealth of emotion as she holds him tight.

I can't stand seeing her upset. I lean in and settle my lips against her ear. "How can I make you happy, angel?"

She shakes her head and clutches Jamie. "I'll be back."

I don't like that answer, but I doubt she wants to risk upsetting our son just before bed.

"Night, little man." I kiss the top of his head. "Soccer tomorrow?"

"Yeah!" He cheers and grins. "Night, Daddy."

That still chokes me up. "Night, son."

As Britta takes Jamie from the room, I give her my silent support with a caress down her back. I'm here for her. I may not have been good at that the first time we were together, but nothing means more to me now.

Once she rounds the corner and disappears, I look around for what might have upset her. Britta is usually the quiet, suffer-in-silence type. So when anything makes her cry, I know she means it. I hate how often I've reduced her to tears in the last few weeks. But I'm even more baffled by what made her sad just now.

The only thing I see are the headphones on the table in front of me. The second I put them on, I realize she's been listening to the CD Keeley gave me.

I hear the ending notes of a song that tugs at me. I've heard this, I think.

I hit the BACK to start the last song she listened to over again. Instantly, I recognize it. Green Day's "Good Riddance." Most people think it's titled "Time of Your Life" or some similar crap, but that's just the sentiment of the song.

As I listen to the lyrics, so many things ring true immediately. It's about turning points and forks in the road, making the best of tests in front of you and learning over time. Yes. To all of that, yes. And if the last three years has taught me anything, it's echoed in the next line. What's happening is unpredictable, but being with Britta and Jamie? Despite the discord and the uncertain future, I *am* having the time of my life being with them both. So I'll preserve the still frames in my mind and tattoo the memories in good time. Whatever happens, this was worth all the while. Even if Britta chooses Makaio in the end, I will always have this period to look back on and remember.

Will it be enough if I wind up alone?

I listen to the song three times and imprint each word to memory. Keeley has always used music to process how she's feeling. I've never really understood why. It seemed like something a high-school girl does. But I'm seeing that at times—like now—songs help me understand what's in my head and heart when I can't exactly put everything into words. Or when I've buried my emotions so deep the right song will dredge whatever I'm feeling up.

I don't love the experience…but ultimately it's better than suffering without really understanding why.

When I see Britta come back into the room, she still looks red-eyed. I lift the headphones from my ears and pause the music.

"Now you know what had me stirred up." She gestures to the head-phones.

"Yeah. Did you listen to more of the CD?"

"I started at the beginning." She pauses. "Keeley made this for you? And these songs represent how you feel?"

"Yes."

In the past, I would have danced around the truth. Telling Britta too much about what was going on with me would be too revealing. Now I'm not afraid to express the tangle of thoughts and pangs, aches and desperation. I want her to know she has power over me. She always has.

"She must know you well." Britta sounds torn about that.

"She sees through me a lot. I'd like to be annoyed or weirded out by that. I was when we first met. But now, I admit it's kind of nice."

"Then I'm glad you two are friends. Keeley seems really lovely."

I take Britta's hands. "And that's all we are. That's all we ever have been. I wasn't sure how to wrap my head around it when she first got together with my brother, but now I'm happy I'll be calling her my sister."

Tears well in Britta's eyes. "Maybe we should talk about this."

"Keeley?" When she shakes her head, I lift the CD case. "The music?"

"No." Wisps of her golden hair come tumbling from her haphazard updo. "Us."

Oh, thank god.

Still rubbing her hands between mine, I nod and sit on the sofa. "Let's do that, angel. I'm here for no other reason than to convince you that I intend to make you and Jamie happy forever."

"I don't know if I'm ready to process that."

"I can't not tell you the truth."

Britta mulls that for a moment, then nods. "I'm just at a loss. I never expected to have you in my life again, much less as something more than Jamie's father. I have no idea what to do."

"I know I'm not making anything easy on you. I'm sorry. If you break things off with Makaio, I'll do my best to downshift so we can grow our relationship more slowly—"

"You can't expect me to end my engagement before I've even figured out how I feel." Her expression holds a hint of apology. She knows I want that—and more—from her and she's sorry she can't give it to me now.

"Then tell me how you and I can proceed, beyond what we're doing?"

"Can you give me a little breathing room?"

"No." I say the word softly. I can't candy-coat the truth or change the hand I've been dealt. "When he moved up the timetable of your wedding, he was putting me on notice. Did you realize that?"

She shakes her head. "He said he just didn't see the point of waiting and—"

"He also wasn't about to give me an opportunity to woo you away. He was letting me know that he's aware of my intentions. That date was a giant fuck you to me. I only have this small span of time to work with. So I have to use every moment of every day that I have to make you see how good being married to me would be. I'll bet he wasn't thrilled when you said you would be moving in with me temporarily."

She hesitates. "No."

"How did you get him to agree?"

"I told Makaio there was no other way to convince you to sign away your rights so he could adopt Jamie. He didn't like it but..." She wrings her hands in her lap. "Ultimately, he made me promise him something before he would agree to let me come here."

"What?" I have a suspicion and I don't like it.

"That I could never see you again."

I sit back, fists clenched, and nearly lose my temper. I take a deep breath and calm myself with two important facts: One, in Makaio's shoes, I probably would have wedged a similar promise out of Britta. Two, I understand his game completely. Sadly for him, I'm just better at playing.

"Then let's work things out so you don't make a mistake and marry him."

Britta bites her lip so hard it blushes bright red as she tries to hold back tears. "I've spent three years thinking I knew precisely who you were. Gorgeous, cocky, funny, possessive, sexy...and at the same time self-absorbed, aloof, quick to blame, slow to trust, even slower to commit. Last night, that engagement ring..." She shudders as she inhales to keep the tears at bay. "You made me question everything. I've spent our time apart believing that our relationship meant far more to me than to you, that you were never the sort of man who was going to simply love a woman for the rest of your life, that you could never care about me enough to stay and be faithful and—"

"You're wrong. Not about being self-absorbed. Or having difficulties trusting. But the rest..."

"Why? Why couldn't you trust me?"

I wave her away. If she can't handle the number of women I slept with during our split, the rest of my past will blow her mind. She'll never look at me the same. "Shitty childhood. You've met my parents."

She winces. "They're terrible people."

"Exactly." And hopefully that's all I ever have to say again about that topic. I couldn't stand it if she looked at me like some psycho-sexual monster. "But you're wrong about the way I felt back then. Our relationship meant everything. I did want to love you forever, faithfully. I wanted to marry you and..." Fuck, now I'm getting choked up. "I didn't know how to tell you then, and I'm trying to now."

"I just wish you hadn't waited until I was engaged to someone else."

Her whisper rips at me. I wish I had a good answer other than I should have pulled my head out of my ass sooner. But I don't. I can only try to move her forward with me.

"I didn't coerce you to live with me until your wedding day to make your life hell. I did it to prove that we belong together. If you didn't believe, at least a little bit, that I might be right, this situation would be easy for you. You would tell me to fuck off. You might acknowledge me as Jamie's father and make me fight out visitation in the courts, but you wouldn't have anything to do with me. We're here because what you feel for me is more than the remnants of first love. There's something else between us. Can you admit that much?"

She inches back on the sofa and crosses her arms over her chest, like she needs space between us. "If I do, you'll only come at me harder."

"But I'm right?"

No doubt she'll think I'm a pushy bastard, but Britta needs comfort and I think she needs it badly. From me. I take her hand and rub my thumb over her knuckles.

She grips my hand in return as she squeezes her eyes shut, silently affirming everything I've been thinking. "Yes."

We're finally getting somewhere. I sit up straighter and bring her closer. I want to put her palm against my skin. Hell, I want to put my hands all over her body. I live in a constant state of arousal fantasizing about it. But she's worth every moment of the agony.

"Thank you, angel. In order for you to figure out if you want me in your life, if what we have could work for you, we both have to be as honest as possible. I've been trying. I've been letting you in on everything I'm feeling and thinking—"

"I told Keeley today that you're so forthcoming I almost don't know who you are." She sends me a teary smile. "Sometimes I feel as if I'm waiting for the old you to show up. In the past, I spent half my time wondering if I mattered to you. Or if I even crossed your mind. Now I know. It's refreshing, on the one hand. Disarming on the other."

"If you'll let me, I'll tell you every day that I'm thinking of you. That I want you. That I love you. I'll never make you wonder again."

"What about the rest of our problems? I mean…you just left me that morning. I didn't even know what was going on so I could defend myself and tell you why you were misunderstanding the situation. You severed all ties before I could assure you that I knew nothing about Maxon's deal with that secretive prince."

I wince. "I know. But I'm getting better at trust."

Britta shakes her head. "That's not enough for me. We have a child now. Whatever anger you have? You have to think beyond it long enough to figure out what's best for everyone. This can't be about your temper and your pride anymore."

"You're right. Does it help if I make you a promise? If we ever seemingly reach the end of our relationship, I'll talk to you. And you'll talk to me. If we do that, I can't imagine that we'll ever call it quits again." I edge closer to her. "Britta, I was young and cocky. Angry and stupid. Immature. You've met my parents. That was my example of marriage. I knew I loved you. I was afraid to say it because that would be giving you power over me."

"But you had that power over me."

I nod, conceding the point. "You have to understand… I've seen one partner punish the other with their 'love.' The thought of reliving that wasn't something I could handle. But I'm telling you now because I know you'll never abuse it. Because I've lived years without you, and it made me fucking miserable."

She frowns like she doesn't understand me at all. I'm not surprised. Her mother is a doll of a woman who loves her daughter with all her heart. She chose a man who ultimately didn't stay with her because he went back to his ex-wife. But Eleanor knew her heartache was as much her lover's fault as her own. She's not resentful. Her maternal adoration shines in everything she does for Britta. My angel never saw two people tear each other up on a daily basis for the sport of it. She never gave her heart to anyone who crushed it simply for amusement.

"If you could promise you would never walk out on me again without a conversation—"

"Absolutely. Done. I will never, ever simply leave without a word. You won't do that to me?"

Britta frowns. "Whether we're together or not, you know that's not my style."

She's right. It's not. I'm a lucky bastard that Britta has never been the sort to try to make me jealous or angry or threaten me to get a reaction. Honest. Kind. Caring. Perfect. That's her.

"Okay, so that's one hurdle. I think…" She swallows. "We have to talk about all the other women."

"When we were together, I never once cheated on you."

"But you've hardly been a monk the last three years."

I want to protest. She can't hold against me what I did when we were apart. But she can't help how she feels about everything I've done since we separated any more than I can help how I feel about her crappy fiancé.

"If you'll say yes to me…" I dare to curl my fingers around her nape and make damn sure she's looking into my eyes. "If you'll marry me, I guarantee you'll be the last woman I ever touch. And I'll never give you a reason to want anyone else."

Much less someone like Makaio Kāle.

"I'm not ready to commit to that."

I try not to gnash my teeth. It's like we're having a circular argument. I don't know how to move her forward. I can't go back.

"Angel…"

"But your point about our time together makes sense. At the end, we should be certain of our decision to either get back together or split up for good. What if…" She sighs, collecting her thoughts. "What if you had the right idea earlier? Instead of one night of trying to imagine what life would be like if we'd been married all this time, what if we live that way the rest of our time here together? Minus the sex, of course."

Of course. That part doesn't thrill me, but the rest? I want to throw a fucking party. "Hell yes!"

That's a far better concession than I ever expected her to give me. It's such a relief to know I won't have to fight her for every conversation we share for roughly the next seven weeks.

The smile she gives me is halting at first, but it grows, reaches her eyes. It makes her come alive. It makes her look happy.

This is what I've been waiting for, fighting for, aching for.

Britta Stone is almost mine again.

CHAPTER FOURTEEN

IT'S NO SURPRISE THAT BRITTA isn't ready to break up with the butthole yet, so I have to keep working around him. No, it's not my first choice, but she's given a lot tonight. I don't know what magic words I used to persuade her to try the next forty-eight days my way, but I'll say it again and again if it will keep moving us forward.

I'd rather kiss her, make love to her, cement our bond right now. But until she ditches the most uptight Hawaiian I've ever met, I have to respect her boundaries.

We wander to the family room. I mention ice cream. She dishes us both a couple of scoops into a cup. And we smile. Talk turns to "Keeley's" wedding, and I press for details. My angel loves a good plan and she gets really excited.

"Do you think Keeley would be offended if I offered to take some of her tasks off her list?"

Because presumably she may never get to plan a wedding of her own. But this is genius because if she marries me, she will have unwittingly crafted at least a chunk of her own nuptials, which should thrill her to bits.

"I think she'd be both happy and relieved. You should do it."

She slides the gleaming spoon against her tongue, and I nearly lose it. Her lips are glistening and rosy, pillowy and sensual—and inches from mine.

I have to look away before I toss her across the counter, pull off her yoga pants, and do something she'll slap me for now or resent me for later.

"I will. Thanks." She glances at the clock. "It's still fairly early. If we'd been married for the last three years, maybe we would find a movie to watch to pass the rest of the evening?"

After the deep discussion we just had, I would insist on taking her to bed and making sure she feels loved, wanted, and secure. But...

I sigh. "Sure."

We climb on the sofa, maybe two feet apart, and turn on a numbing police comedy. There are a couple of suspenseful parts and a high-speed chase, complete with automotive acrobatics that strain credulity. When the cop's love interest is nearly killed for information, Britta edges closer and buries her head in my shoulder.

I smile. She's got a soft heart. She's never liked violence. And I'm not above using this moment to my advantage.

Wrapping my arm around her, I anchor my palm on her hip and slide her closer. "You okay?"

She's still tense. "Can I look now?"

I stare at the screen. One bad guy has cuffed this girl to a surgical table and another just picked up a cordless screwdriver. "Not yet."

"Why do they put this in movies? Can't they fade to black and tell me bad stuff might happen, then show me the outcome later?"

I laugh. "Guys like the aggressive, testosterone-driven scenes. Juices up the blood. Makes us feel manly. We imagine how we'd save our girl and all that." When she shudders, I can't stop myself from kissing the top of her head. "Not every movie can be *Love Actually*."

It's one of her favorites.

"I wish it could."

Twenty minutes later, the cop rescues his pretty damsel, who manages to run an awful lot in stilettos, and the bad guys all either died or went to prison. That's the ending I expected, so I'm good. I look down to find that Britta has fallen asleep against me.

I smile at the trust she's shown, the comfort she's allowed me to give her. I would love this every night for the rest of our lives.

Balancing her upright with one hand, I rise, doing my best not to jostle her awake. As soon as I'm on my feet, I lift her into my arms.

Her lashes flutter open. "What? Where…"

"Shh. It's late. You're tired. I'm taking you to bed."

She shifts in my embrace and tries to wriggle free. "I can walk."

"You don't have to."

I don't wait for any more conversation, just head for the dark wooden stairs that wind up to our bedroom. There's no way I can't not stare at her. She was always beautiful to me, but up close she's a masterpiece. And right now she looks so soft and sleepy and happy nestled against me, I don't want to put her down.

Inside the bedroom, I don't have a choice, so I reluctantly set her on her feet. She's blushing as she blinks up at me. "Thanks, Griff."

"Being with you in any way is always my pleasure."

She looks away with a bite of her lips, a flush to her cheeks. "I'm going to…um, take a soak in the giant tub."

It's just as well. If we climbed into bed together now, I don't know how I'd stop myself from crawling all over her. "I'm going to make sure the house is locked up and the coffeepot is ready for the morning."

I kiss her forehead again, then leave the room before the urge to slide my lips elsewhere on her skin overcomes me.

The next seven weeks are going to test the hell out of my restraint unless she ditches the banker fast.

After I make the rounds through the house, I return to hear the bathtub running behind closed doors. She's in there naked, and I would love the right to walk in and ravish her. Hell, I'd settle for merely looking at her.

Since that's not happening, I check on Jamie, who's fast asleep on his side with his blanket curled up in his arms. He needs a bigger bed. I make a mental note to bring that up with Britta tomorrow. The playpen just isn't cutting it anymore.

Clad only in my boxers, I pull the comforter down and slide between the sheets. The big bed feels empty. I've only been sleeping beside Britta for a few days, but I'm already used to her curling up beside me, to hearing her soft, even breathing. Sadly, she's not one of those women who wants to cuddle in her sleep. She doesn't need to seek me out for warmth in Maui. She doesn't require consoling for nightmares she doesn't have. And she's certainly not looking for nookie in the middle of the night.

I distract myself by scanning my emails. I read some agent feedback about one of my listings and agree the kitchen needs updating, but the seller isn't interested in sinking more money into the house. I have a web inquiry about another property and dash off a response that I'll call first thing on Monday.

Then I launch into my social media to check the stats of my active ads. I hear the water turn off in the tub. Britta is playing soft music via the high-end speaker in the bathroom. The tune is something soft and instrumental. Sounds like she's in for a long soak.

Over the music, I hear…panting? Must be background for the song. I grunt. I hardly need something more to work me up tonight.

But when I hear it again, I frown. Is Britta in distress?

I don't know, but I cock my head, listening more closely. Water sloshes. In between more of those heavy breaths, I hear a whimper. Pain? Sadness? Melancholy? Something else? I need to know if she's all right.

Slowly, I climb out of bed and head to the double doors on silent footfalls. I can't hear much better. But the crack between the doors shows me a shimmering shadow of water movement. I hear another high-pitched cry.

"Britta?" I call softly.

A gasp. A trio of harder pants. A strangled moan. "Griff…"

That's it. If she's sobbing her heart out in the bathtub, naked or not, I'm not leaving her there to cry alone. I can control myself long enough to comfort her. I think. And if I have to blot out the memories of her in the buff…that's one reason God invented Scotch.

I shove open the doors, expecting to see mascara running down her face and her eyes swollen with tears.

I don't expect to see Britta lying in the tub, head tossed back, hand between her legs.

"Don't"—she opens her blue eyes, which look heavy and sensual in pleasure—"come in."

Too late.

I can't move. I'm staring. Holy motherfucking hell. She looks amazing with her hair piled on her head, tendrils falling softly around her neck, trailing toward the bubbles clinging to the swells of her breasts. Her cheeks are flushed. Her lips are swollen.

She's aroused. I swallow hard.

"Griff." Britta shakes her head like I can't stay here, like she's denying me.

I don't know if she's embarrassed or worried or what, but I'm thrilled, turned on, and eager. Sure, I would have liked it a whole lot more if she'd come to me with her needs, but I can work with this.

"Don't stop, angel. Keep going." I lean against the counter a few feet away and lock gazes with her. "I'll watch. Nothing else."

"N-no. You can't. I can't."

I hold up my hands where she can see them both. "I won't touch you."

"You shouldn't be seeing me while I'm naked and…" She bites her lip like she doesn't want to admit precisely what she was doing.

"Masturbating?" I smile.

She sighs. "Just leave. It's humiliating."

"No, it's sexy as hell. Seriously. Do it, angel. Touch yourself."

"I can't do that with you in the room, staring at me."

"I'll bet you can. No reason to be shy. I've seen every inch of you. I've touched it, kissed it, worshipped it. Close your eyes and pretend…" *I'm touching you now.* "Whatever turns you on."

Her eyes flutter shut. "This isn't right."

"This is just for you. If we're going to act as if we're really married, me watching you self-pleasure wouldn't be any big deal. We've had a big day and a lot of important conversation. You need to feel good after all that. If I can't touch you myself or make love to you for a long, luxurious time, then let me be here for you while you make yourself feel so good."

She writhes, stretches. I see her pressing her thighs together. "Why do you do this to me? One look at you and I...want. It's almost physical. It hurts. I don't know how to stop it. I should. I try not to feel this way—"

"You don't have to. I won't do anything except talk to you. Close your eyes. Listen to my voice. Feel good. I want that for you so bad."

"What about you?" Her eyes flit open and she casts a long glance at the erection behind the fly of my boxers.

"I'll worry about me later." I'm doing my best to hang on to my resolve that my next orgasm will be one she gives me. But as far as I'm concerned, if being near me turns her on, I'm not putting a stop to that. If she really objects, I'll back off and give her privacy...but the way she's looking at me now, like she's eating me up with her stare, I don't think she wants to be alone.

She begins squirming in the tub again.

"That's it. Touch yourself where you need it. Are you wet, angel?"

She gives me a shaky nod.

"I know your pretty folds are still bare." The way I like them.

"Yes."

"They slick?"

"Yes." She's breathy again.

It's arousing as hell.

I want to cheer. Hell, I want to see for myself. The voice of sanity in my head—what's left of it, anyway—tells my libido to stick to the subject.

"Is your clit hard?"

Water sloshes. Her arm moves. She gasps. "Yes."

Everything about her is so fucking hot I'm overheating. I would give anything to drop to my knees and worship every inch of her.

Right now, I have to settle for what she'll give me.

"Good." I swallow hard. "Lift your other hand to your breast. Squeeze your nipple."

She does with a whimper. The movements under the bubbles pick up speed. Her back arches. She lifts her feet out of the water and braces her heels on the edge of the tub.

Yeah, it's getting serious now. I take a step toward her. Another. Last one, and I've closed the distance between us. Slowly, I lean in, brace my hands on the edge of the tub. My own breath is nearly out of control.

I won't touch her. I promised I wouldn't. I don't want to give her anything more to be tormented about. I just want to give her relief. And…if she thinks about me the next time she's feeling sexy, that's a bonus. It's been forever since I've been with her. She used to associate me with bliss. I want to build that connection in her head again. I want to hear her in climax. I want my ears to ring with the cries of her ecstasy.

"Griff…" Her voice is both a pant and a warning.

"I'm not coming any closer. I just couldn't stand anymore. You make me dizzy, angel." I drop to my knees beside the tub. "Your scent is swimming in my head. And I have to see you clearly to help guide you through the pleasure you need."

Sure, she knows how to find climax herself. She doesn't *need* me for this. And yes, I could turn up the lights to get a clearer view from afar. But I think she's less likely to relax enough to find her pinnacle with an LED blasting in her face. The low, golden haze from the canned lights on dimmers coupled with the pair of scented candles burning at the head of the tub are absolutely perfect. Her skin shimmers golden as her lips part. Her shoulders twist. She inhales a broken breath as her eyes slide shut again.

She's every fantasy I've ever had. She's everything I remember and more. She's the woman I'm going to spend my life with.

With every moment that passes, I die a little more.

"Oh, angel…" I croon. "Can you feel lips on your neck? A hand skimming up your thigh?"

In my head, that's me touching her, but if she needs me to keep this generic for her sanity, I'll grit my teeth now and prove my point later.

"Yes."

"Feel hot breath on your nipple?"

She's breathing so hard and the bubbles are dissipating with every moment that passes. I swear I can see the outline of her breasts under the shallow surface. I see the dark shadow of her areolas. The jut of their hard tips skim the surface of the water.

I grip the edge of the tub. I have to stop myself from reaching down and helping her along. I would kill to touch her now. I would love to be the one to give her release from all the stress and worry she's been under for weeks. But I can't risk alienating her because I was impatient, pushy, and horny. Well, more than I have been.

"Imagine a tongue dragging over those nipples. You like it, don't you? Yeah. They're sensitive."

She gives me a jagged nod. Her breathing picks up speed. Her back twists. I see the circular motion of her hand by the jerky movements of her arm. Her chest flushes pink.

She's seconds away.

"That ache building? Growing? Can you feel your blood racing?"

"Yes. Yes…" Her breathing is so hard I can barely discern her words. "Yes."

"It's going to be so sweet. It's going to feel so good. You're rubbing it, right? You going to come?" *For me.*

Her entire body tenses. She freezes—muscles, breath, words. I see the frantic shutter of her pulse at her neck and the frenzied motions of her arm before she opens her mouth with a pained cry that's music to my ears.

I sit back, watch, mesmerized. She is, without a doubt, the most sensual woman I've ever known. From the moment I first kissed her until the last time I made love to her, she's kick-started my desire like no one else. And this episode is tattooed in my mind indelibly. I'll never forget her sharp sounds, her female scent, the abandon in her movements.

Best of all, this moment is totally mine. I'm pretty sure butthole has never seen her this uninhibited. She gave a slice of her most secret self to me like a gift. I'll cherish it always. Someday, I'll thank her properly for it.

Right now, her sob of ecstasy is ending in a whimper. Her body goes limp. Her eyes flutter open. "Oh, my god. That was… I don't know what to say."

"Amazing?"

"Really damn good, yeah." A hint of a smile plays at her mouth. "I'm embarrassed."

"Don't be. I'm glad you shared with me. I helped, right?"

Her glance tells me I did, more than she wanted me to. "Don't push your luck."

"Need help out of the tub?" I grab her towel. "I'll dry you off thoroughly, angel."

Because I'll bet her pussy is still so wet. I bite those words back. My hard-on isn't her problem.

"Didn't I just tell you not to push your luck?"

Is that...? Yeah. She's teasing me. That's a great sign. After I took her virginity, she cried. It was emotional and that confused her. The fact that she's not caught up in anything but the afterglow gives me hope.

"Fair enough. What made you want orgasm? Why did you need it?"

Her smile falls. "Don't make me answer that."

Britta tells me without telling me that I'm the reason for her need. Exactly what I wanted to hear. I'm calling it a victory...but bowing out gracefully after my win.

I lay her towel on the side of the tub. "I'll leave you alone, then."

As I back out of the room, I watch her watching me. Our gazes connect. Her stare doesn't have the same hunger, but it's not lacking in intensity. I'm in her head, under her skin. I think I'm working my way back into her heart.

I cross the threshold. I know I should shut the doors, but I can't take my eyes off her.

"Close them, Griff."

So I can't peek when she rises from the water like a Venus. Damn it.

I find the strength to do as she asks. No doubt she feels as if she's stretched her boundaries enough for one night.

As I grab the doorknobs to give her some privacy, I glance at the counter and see her phone, lip gloss, and jewelry next to her sink. I see the piece from the banker glimmering and it makes me want to snarl.

"All right. But if we're going to act like we're a couple for the rest of our agreement, you can't be wearing his ring, Britta." My sanity and self-restraint won't be able to handle it. "That finger is mine."

"I know."

Thank fuck.

I sweep the doors closed and march across the room to open the sock drawer. She should be wearing my ring, by god. As I'm yanking the jewelry box from the back, her voice stops me. "But I'm not wearing your ring unless I'm going to put it on forever."

Damn it. Son of a bitch. I would have loved to see it on her finger at work. At breakfast. When we go to bed.

But I get it. I probably shouldn't get my hopes up, either, unless she's truly going to marry me.

I slam the sock drawer shut and stomp back to bed.

Five minutes later, Britta emerges in a soft, dark cotton nightie that says LITTLE BLACK DRESS and slides between the sheets next to me. "Thank you for understanding."

That she needed orgasm? That I couldn't touch her? That she's not ready to wear my ring? Probably all of it.

I can't be mad at her. I did next to nothing to accommodate her in the past. I have to give her everything I can now. "You're welcome."

With a light kiss on my cheek, she turns out the light and rolls over, dipping into a deep rhythm of sleep between one moment and the next.

I stare at the ceiling for a long time. Tonight notched the game up again. I'm more determined than ever to come out on top and win Britta back. I will make use of every single one of my remaining forty-seven-ish days so it's a foregone conclusion that she'll be mine.

CHAPTER FIFTEEN

WE ALL SLEEP IN THE next morning. It's not uncommon for me to hold a private open house on a day like this, but Maxon and I both agree we have a lot going on in our personal lives, and this is one Sunday we'll live without the potential new leads and lookie-loos.

Britta and I fix breakfast in companionable silence. There's an easiness between us that wasn't there before last night. But awareness also simmers in the air. She glances at me often. I see her smile my way more.

Maybe I should stop myself, but I can't not pile on the incidental touching. A caress of her shoulder. A hand at the small of her back when she's reaching up for something in the cabinet. A brush of her hair off her cheek. Yes, I'm pushing my luck. And I suspect where this sort of thing will lead eventually. But I want her to feel adored. I want to feel close to her. Is that so bad?

"Angel, I think we need to get Jamie a real bed."

"We could go to the house and pick up his crib. I need to check on my houseplants and my little garden—"

"Don't you think he's too big for a crib? He's almost as tall as the mattress. He climbs out of it. What's the point?"

"You mean…a big-boy bed?" She looks distressed.

I understand the resistance. She doesn't want her baby to grow up.

I give her a gentle smile and caress her cheek. "Yeah. Let's go out today. I want to give him a bed he can grow into."

"You're right." She concedes after a long moment. "Let me get ready.

I told Keeley I would call her. She texted me earlier and said she needed a minute of my time for wedding stuff. I should be ready about an hour after breakfast.

"Perfect." And if she's getting us one step closer to our wedding, even better.

After pancakes and eggs, Britta disappears by the pool, phone pressed to her ear. Jamie and I have a ball trying to clean both him and the dishes at once. I put him in his room with his toys to make sure he can't get free, at least while I hop in the shower. I'm climbing out with a towel wrapped around my waist when Britta sweeps into the steamy space and her eyes fall on me.

"Oh. Sorry. I didn't—"

"It's fine." I shrug. Does she think I mind her seeing me naked? "I'm just about done in here."

But if she's going to linger in the bathroom for makeup and hair, I can stand here—barely covered—for a while.

As I trim my beard, she doesn't hurry through her morning routine. I don't think I've ever seen her take twenty minutes simply to brush her hair and put it in a ponytail. But I totally notice her gaze sliding over me again and again. If I thought she wouldn't freak out, I would lose the towel and stalk across the bathroom, maybe lift her up and spread her legs so I could have my wicked way with her.

But I can tell by her furtive glances that she's not ready.

Finally, I hear Jamie getting antsy in his room. The sounds jolt us out of our mutual eye-fuck-fest, and we start dashing around to toss on clothes, grab our little man, and head out the door.

Big-boy bed is first. Britta sniffles as I purchase the double-sized bunk beds. I tell her I'm buying it bigger in case he ever wants a friend to sleep over, but I'm really thinking ahead. Someday, she's going to want more children. I'm sure of it. Just like I'm sure I'll be the one to give them to her. Our sons can bunk together. It's something Maxon and I did when we were little, and I loved that simple time before our dad tried to poison our minds against one another.

After we arrange delivery of the bed on Tuesday, we run errands—checking on Britta's house, then groceries, dry cleaners, pharmacy. I notice she isn't picking up birth control pills. I haven't noticed her taking them anymore.

What does that say? That she and butthole have had a next to nonexistent sex life? Or that since she's getting married soon, she's gone off them so she can get pregnant right away?

I'm searching for the right words to broach the topic when we get back in the car. It's none of my business—yet. Before I can find a subtle way to bring up my observation, my phone rings.

The display tells me it's Maxon. "Hey, bro."

"Hey," he says over the line. "Where are you guys?"

"On our way back to the house with groceries."

"Good. We're headed that way. I've got a surprise for you. Meet you there in thirty?"

I didn't really want company. I was hoping to talk to Britta. But Maxon on a mission is an unstoppable force.

I hold in a sigh. "Sure."

When we pull up about twenty minutes later, we settle Jamie with a snack and unpack all the groceries. I glance out one of the kitchen windows to see Maxon's SUV appear in the side yard. He and Keeley step out of the vehicle, wearing big smiles.

"They look happy," Britta remarks.

I noticed that, too. What the hell is going on? Did they elope or something?

Then the car's rear door opens and the last person I expected to see steps out.

"Harlow!" I shove the eggs in the fridge and take off running.

I haven't seen my baby sister in three years. She's funny, acerbic, and sharp as hell. And she's definitely more grown-up than the last time I saw her. But it makes sense. She was an angsty undergrad finishing her degree when she left Hawaii with my parents to move back to San Diego. Now she's twenty-five, completing her master's, and engaged to be married—to some guy I know nothing about.

As my sister pulls a rolling carry-on from the backseat, I reach her side and hug her tight. "What are you doing here? This is a real surprise."

"Hi, Griff. I've barely stepped out of the car, and you're already trying to interrogate me." She rolls her eyes. "I want to say hi to your way better half. How are you, Britta?" Harlow holds out her arms to my angel.

Britta steps into the sisterly embrace with a smile. "I'm good. It's been a long time. You look fantastic."

Harlow does. Her dark hair is in some haphazard twist that shows off the varying tones of browns, reds, and caramels. She's looking fit in a T-shirt that reads I'M NOT TRYING TO BE DIFFICULT. IT JUST COMES NATURALLY. Truer words were never spoken. Her white shorts fit like a second skin and her wedges are beige, high, and fairly impractical.

That's my sister.

"Thanks. You look as beautiful as ever," Harlow says to Britta with a laugh. "If you weren't so sweet, I'd really hate you."

My angel giggles in return.

"Come on in," I invite my sister. "Come meet Jamie."

I'm so proud to introduce my son to her. There's a swell in my chest and a lightness in my heart. I know nothing is settled or official, but I've made progress.

"Nice digs." Harlow glances at the mansion. "This place is…beyond. And huge. No wonder Maxon suggested I stay here with you."

I freeze and look at my brother. Is she kidding? By the apologetic expression working its way across his face, I'm guessing not.

Britta leads Harlow and Keeley inside, and Maxon sidles up to me. "Dude, I didn't have a choice. The house I bought for Keeley is being painted. We planned to move in after our wedding, but it's not habitable right now. So I've got twelve hundred square feet of condo, including my lanai space. It's a bachelor pad I'm sharing with my fiancée…who's a screamer."

I didn't need to know that.

Wincing, I turn to him. "I'll make it work. It's just terrible timing.

Britta and I have resolved to spend the rest of our time together acting like a normal married couple, as long as we're not doing anything that's technically cheating on her fiancé. We really need privacy and normalcy and…" I rake a hand through my hair. "I'll put her up in a hotel."

"I offered to do the same," he murmurs under his breath.

Neither of us wants Harlow to feel unwelcome. But shit, the timing couldn't be worse.

"She's not having it?"

Maxon shakes his head. "No. She says she's on the island to take care of wedding details. She wants peace and quiet to prep for her thesis defense, which is just before her ceremony. But she's really here to be with family."

It makes sense but… "Shit."

"Yeah. Keeley and I will help you all we can. So…what do you know about this guy she's marrying?"

"Nothing. Have you met him?"

Maxon shakes his head. "I was hoping you had."

"Other than Dad's rude drop-in a couple of weeks ago, I haven't seen any of the rest of the family since they moved away."

"Me, either. Harlow tells me that Dad introduced her to this guy."

That sets off a few hundred red flags. Finding out that Dad is hitching his only daughter to someone who is potentially similar is not welcome news.

"I don't like it."

My brother nods. "I don't, either. I'm hoping I'm wrong. I don't know anything about him but…"

"I'm not holding my breath. Simon. That's his name. The way she talks about him, it seems as if she's invisible to him."

I watch her laugh. She's not restrained in the least. Harlow is big and full of life. She's definitely buckets full of sass and sarcasm. Why would she marry some guy who doesn't see what's in front of him?

"If he ignores her, how long before she does something to raise brows? How long do you think she'll stay?" Maxon muses aloud.

I send my sister a measuring glance. She's already dressed like she wouldn't mind male attention, and I don't think her fiancé is anywhere on the island. I know how Harlow thinks. If she believes she's getting short shrift, she'll eventually fix it. She doesn't let grass grow under her for long. Her lack of patience is well documented. Her audacious behavior is even more legendary.

"We're in for a bumpy ride," Maxon whispers in low tones.

"I want to meet this guy before I pass judgment, but yeah. I suspect you're right."

We follow the women into the house. I catch up to my sister and lead her to Jamie, who's still sitting on the floor. He walked away from his animal crackers and found way more amusement tossing his trucks from Britta's organized basket and onto the tile.

I pick up the little man and hoist him onto my hip. "Jamie, this is Auntie Harlow."

My sister flashes a big smile. "That has a nice ring. Hi, Jamie. Can I get hugs?"

He looks at her uncertainly, then slants his stare over at me, silently questioning whether she's trustworthy. "It's all right. She's always going to be your friend."

Jamie hesitates a moment more. Harlow obviously planned for this possibility and pulls a big box from her carry-on containing six utility trucks. There's a crane, an excavator, a cement mixer... My son is going to be in heaven.

He obviously realizes it when he lunges at Harlow to get his hands on the goodies. Everyone laughs.

Maxon retrieves my sister's suitcases from his vehicle, and I schlep them upstairs, in the bedroom farthest away from the one I'm sharing with Britta, on the opposite side of the house.

As I head back down, I see everyone congregating in the kitchen, sipping iced tea, and eating raw veggies and sliced fruit with yogurt dip. There are smiles, jokes, laughter. It's really nice to have all the Reed siblings together. Well, the legitimate ones. Dad has two others close to our age, whom we've never met, and another one on the way. He's always paid for his children but never cared about any of them. I have no idea why—if he's going to fuck around with every assistant he hires—he doesn't get snipped.

Because he's a fucking idiot. And he married someone every bit as self-absorbed as he is.

I join the group and take the tea Britta proffers in my direction, then grab a slice of mango she cut off the tree out back earlier. "So how long are you staying, Harlow?"

Everyone laughs, my sister most of all. "You are so transparent. I'll try not to be a bother here in your palatial love nest. But I'll be here for about a month. I have to take care of wedding details before all this shit gets away from me. Simon can't help, and I'm over Mom and her 'boyfriend' right now. He's a young leech who wants her money but has no trouble hitting on me." She shudders. "I had to get out of there. I figured I can prepare for my thesis defense anywhere, so why not come to paradise?"

Why not? Except that a month is most of the time I have left with Britta. Still, I can't turn my sister away. It's great to see her, and I have the feeling she needs some time to decompress. Under her usual fun, flirty demeanor, she seems tense.

"Will we get to meet your groom before your big day?" Britta asks.

I'm glad she's quizzing Harlow. It saves me from asking the same question, and I'd probably sound a lot less polite since I don't like the sound of this guy.

"The way it's looking now, I don't think he'll make it to the island until the day before our wedding. He'll be working on a big deal in Amsterdam for the next few weeks."

I don't want to paint him with Dad's brush simply because they know one another, but showing up the day before tying the knot and not lifting a finger to help seems like a dick move and something Barclay Reed would do.

"Sorry to hear that. What does he do?"

"International finance. He brokers deals between overseas players, gathers consortiums for construction or infrastructure projects, finds investors from all over the world. That sort of thing. It's all boring to me."

Basically, what our father does, just on a global scale. I'm shocked Dad doesn't consider him a competitor.

Unless… "Is his firm bigger than Dad's?"

She shakes her head. "Smaller. Simon's company has only been off the ground a couple of years. He's gone a lot because he says the face time while he's establishing his business is critical. He's sure it will taper off soon."

Yeah, and monkeys will fly out of my ass before that happens. Dad wants to gobble up his new son-in-law's company. I'll bet you anything. Then he's going to send junior on the road indefinitely to make him more money. And Simon must like the travel. He might even like the exotic pussy he can sample all over the world. If he didn't, he would stay home more. Or at least stay home enough to make Harlow a priority. Sure, he's put a giant rock on her finger, but that doesn't hold her when she's sad or had a terrible day and needs a shoulder. And good ol' Barclay doesn't give two shits about his daughter's happiness. He's really only ever cared about money and sex.

Shallow. Trite. Predictable.

Even Britta smiles like she doesn't really believe my sister's line of crap. I'm worried, however, that Harlow does believe it—or is trying really hard to. What woman doesn't want to be happy with the man she's going to marry?

I suspect that's Britta's issue with Makaio…

The conversation wanders, and Britta leads the other ladies on a tour of the house. I kiss the top of Jamie's head as I set him down and help him dive into his box of new toys.

"Did you get all that?" I ask my brother.

"Oh, yeah. So much shit. How are we going to stop this?"

"I don't know right now, but I think we need to."

"Absolutely. I'll find some time to take her around the island and introduce her to people I know."

In other words, other agents and brokers. I can't think of any quality individuals who are currently single that I'd want to pair up with my sister, but I'm thinking that even the biggest dirtbag we know would be better than her current fiancé.

"It will do double duty," my brother continues. "She'll meet new people and I'll give you and Britta some privacy."

I appreciate him doing what he can. "I'll try to think of some people, too."

"Hey, what if we introduce Harlow to Makaio?" Maxon jokes.

If Britta is more woman than he can handle, my sister will run him over. Then back up, roll over him a few times for good measure, and leave him for dead. While that's appealing on some level, I don't want Harlow wasting her time.

"Ha ha."

Light, feminine laughter drifts downstairs. Maxon's face creases into a grin. "At least they have each other."

I smile myself. "Aren't you frightened, at least a little, by the mischief the three of them could get into?"

When his eyes go wide, I see he's finally realizing the possibilities. "Oh, that's bad. You and I need to marry our brides fast."

I couldn't agree more. I'm just not sure it's going to help. A sinking feeling in my gut tells me these three together will be very tight—and could cause a lot of trouble.

LATE MONDAY MORNING, BRITTA DISAPPEARS. I come out of my office after a series of phone calls that, if they all pan out, will lead to a shitload of transactions. Good news/bad news. The money is something I'll never turn down, but the timing sucks hard. Still, I can't exactly say no or they'll just go to the broker down the street. But that's the reason I didn't know my angel had left the office.

"Where is Britta?" I ask Rob, gesturing to her desk. She drove us in this morning, and I don't see her car in the lot now.

He shrugs. "She didn't say. Just grabbed her purse and left. Said to tell you she'd be back soon."

I frown. What, exactly, does that mean? She never said a word this morning about going anywhere over her lunch break today.

One thing I did notice? She didn't slip on Makaio's ring again.

I shrug and tell myself I'm overreacting. Maybe she wanted to grab a quick mani or is looking at something wedding related "for Keeley." It could be anything. Hell, maybe it's a surprise for Jamie. Or even for me. My mistake the last time Britta and I were a couple was my certainty that she was going to fuck me over, and it was just a matter of when.

I have to be careful not to fall prey to paranoia again.

Maxon and I grab a quick sandwich and bring it back to our desks.

"Keeley is taking Harlow around the island with her today. They're heading over to the bridal shop this morning to arrange for the tailoring of Britta's dress," my brother says as he unwraps his tuna salad.

"Our sister is now in on this plan?" I say as I take my first bite of a club.

"Did you really think we could keep her out of it?" My brother raises a brow.

Good point. I shake my head. "Thank your bride for me. I appreciate everything she's doing."

"I will. She's planning a lot of our stuff at the same time, so it all works out. But she told me to tell you that you don't get to see Britta's dress until the big day."

"I just get to pay for it." I laugh. "Of course."

"Naturally. She and Harlow are also meeting a deejay who's done a few of the community events at Keeley's last apartment complex. Apparently, he was pretty decent. She asked me to double-check that you have the appointment with the caterer and bakery this week."

"Took care of that this morning. She can check them both off."

"I think Keeley and Harlow would do better with the photographer and videographer."

Because what do I know about that shit? "Agreed."

"Good. Britta is meeting the florist on 'our behalf' later this week." My brother winks.

Flowers have always been important to my angel, and I want her to have whatever she wants for the perfect wedding. "Excellent."

"Keeley asked if you've got a guest list. Or know who you want in your wedding party. You'll have to make all the choices since you're surprising Britta."

"Um…" I'm drawing a blank, but I have to figure it out. "All right. I'll get on that. I'm thinking small. You'll be my best man?"

Maxon smiles and sticks out his hand. "Absolutely. Um, you're mine, too."

"Done. Glad that was easy." We fist-bump, then laugh.

"You inviting Mom and Dad to your big day?"

I wince. "I'd rather not."

Maxon sighs sadly. "Hell would freeze over before I'd invite Dad. I'm ambivalent about Mom…but I know you're not."

"This isn't about me." I shrug. "It's your wedding."

But if he invites her, I'll stand up with him at the ceremony and give the toast, but I'll avoid her at all costs. I don't know what the hell I'll do about family pictures. Because if I see her, I'm not sure how much fury I'll spew. Right now, it's packed down so tightly it could produce diamonds. But if it explodes…it won't be pretty.

"What did she do to you?"

My brother's question disarms me. I probably should have anticipated it. In some ways, I'd love to tell him. Hell, I want to unburden this shit. But it's terrible. Humiliating. It makes me ashamed. It's not my place to ruin Maxon's image of Mom, especially now that he and I are close again. Besides, if he's never had trouble with her, I'm not sure he'd believe my story.

"Ancient history. Invite her if you want to. I'll back you up, regard-less."

Maxon frowns at the finality of the closed subject, then consults the list in front of him. "All right. Officiant for your ceremony?"

I whip out my phone. "I need to add that to my growing list. Maybe we should hire someone to handle all the details."

"Like a wedding planner? It's not a terrible idea. Know a good one?"

I stare at him like he's just announced he's from Mars. "Why would I?"

"Yeah. Me, either."

So that becomes another possible item I add to my list of things to do. Fuck, it's getting long. And time is running short.

"Wedding bands?"

I bought Britta's when I picked out the engagement ring. I'll have to choose my own.

"I got that." I tap a reminder into my phone.

Maxon jots some notes himself, presumably to pass on to Keeley. "Bridesmaids' dresses? Invitations? Honeymoon?"

I blow out a long breath. "There's so much stuff to do."

"Yeah, and the first few people Keeley called for you on Saturday actually laughed when she gave them your wedding date, so...the sooner the better, bro."

If this wedding weren't so important to Britta, I would have scrapped the whole plan by now because I simply want to marry her. I don't care about the pomp and circumstance. But I refuse to take anything away from her fairy-tale dream.

"Keeley knows someone who will do hair and makeup the day of the ceremony. Tuxes?"

After an hour and a half of this crap, I feel as if I'm drowning in details. But I'm determined the ceremony and reception will be perfect.

And none of it matters if I can't persuade Britta to say yes.

Speaking of which, she's not back yet. I send her a quick text to ask if she's all right. A good five minutes pass, and I'm growing worried because she always answers promptly. I'm about to call her when she replies that she's driving.

With a deep breath, I sit back in my chair and relax.

"How's it going with her?" Maxon asks.

"We're making progress."

He slaps me on the shoulder. "Good luck. I'm here if you need anything."

"Thanks, man."

I still can't believe that we didn't speak a word to each other for three years. Now everything feels normal, natural. Easy. I'm never going to let my stupidity, temper, or petulance come between us again. I definitely won't let them part me from Britta a second time.

When she finally pushes the office door open, she's wearing big sunglasses. Her head is down. She's shaking.

I cross the office and take her shoulders in hand. "You all right, angel?"

"Fine."

That's a lie and I can hear it in her soft voice.

"Talk to me."

"Can we not do this here?" she whispers, casting a glance in Rob's direction.

Maxon's marketing guy is watching with great interest. So is my brother, for that matter.

I bite back a curse and usher her toward the door.

Britta digs in her heels. "No, not out in the parking lot, either. I just need some time to decompress."

I'm beginning to understand that's Britta-speak for keeping all her problems to herself. That's a no-go for me. It contributed to our demise in the past. Oh, I did all the heavy lifting by leaving abruptly and refusing to consider I might be wrong. But my angel also never told me when she was confused, when I hurt her feelings, when she needed more out of me. And I was too stupid to know.

"Not until you tell me what's upset you. I don't care whether we do this outside or in my office, but you don't have to carry this load alone."

She sighs and tears her shades off, shoving them in her purse, then looks at me as if she'd like to rip my liver out with her teeth. Instantly, I see that her eyes are red. She's been crying—and not just a little. Now that I look, her nose is powdery. She tried to cover the redness with her compact. Her lips are trembling. "Thank you but...can't you just leave it?"

I drag her to my office and shut the door. "Who or what upset you?"

She hesitates so long I'm not sure she's going to answer. "I had lunch with Makaio."

The bottom drops out of my stomach. First, because she saw him without telling me where she was going. Second, because he made her cry.

"Are you fucking kidding me?"

"He called this morning and said he wanted to share the details of our wedding with me."

So after last night, she's not even hesitating about going through with it? I probably shouldn't be stunned, but I am. I'm completely shocked. "What we have together doesn't mean anything?"

"I didn't say that..." She shakes her head. "Griff, I'm supposed to be choosing between now and mid-April."

"You agreed to spend this time with me so you'd know what life would be like if you and I were married. I guarantee you that if you were my wife, you wouldn't fucking be having lunch with your ex-lover to—"

She pokes a finger in my chest. "You're the one who told me that if I wanted to see him, to have lunch. I was taking you at your word."

I did say that. I meant it flippantly. Shit. Of course Britta listened and followed rules. She's a good girl at heart. I probably have no right to be pissed off—but I am, especially since she's been sobbing.

I grind my teeth together. "So what did Makaio say or do to upset you?"

"Nothing, except that he asked me a lot of pointed questions about you and I didn't know how to answer because I feel goddamn guilty about how deep my feelings for you are. He left angry, and I'm giving him some space, which I'm sure makes you happy as a clam. I don't want to talk about him with you. And I don't need you squeezing me for answers."

"But—"

"You have to back off and stop being an asshole."

Britta whirls on her coral-colored stilettos and, ass swishing in the off-white dress that hugs her every curve lovingly, she stomps her way out of my office.

That may be the most direct and assertive Britta has ever been with me. It's a good sign that she's freely telling me how she feels. But I can't stand her slamming the door in my face. I definitely won't tolerate that prick screwing with her emotions.

Come hell or high water, I'm going shut this shit down with Makaio for good.

CHAPTER SIXTEEN

THE OLD ME WOULD HAVE paid Makaio Kāle a visit and found out exactly what I could do to exit him from Britta's life. He doesn't deserve her if he's going to tear her apart. This me realizes that she has to willingly choose me as the man she wants to spend her life with.

Of course she's confused. This is a major life decision, and just because I know what choice she should make doesn't mean she does. If he's pressing her to commit now and making her cry, then I want to choose another tactic. I don't want to be *that* guy. I definitely don't want her lumping me in the asshole category again.

It takes every ounce of my patience and self-restraint, but I back off, focus on work and the wedding and making my relationship with Britta the strongest it can be. I try to push out everything I can't control, like that prick she's still engaged to.

Unfortunately, he's not my only problem. Why did work suddenly choose now to explode? Probably because everyone who's sick of long winters in snow-riddled states decides they'll dig out of the white stuff after another Snowmageddon and sell the family home in Connecticut or Wisconsin or wherever and move to Maui. Some of those people will stay. Some will realize it's too far from their family. Some will find out the hard way that the cost of living in Hawaii is high and they won't be able to afford to stay. Some will get island fever, end up feeling trapped, and move to another warm weather climate on the mainland.

It's usually fine. But I've never been busier. Same with Maxon. Long days are turning into longer weeks that run past me in a giant blur. I barely have time to breathe.

Unfortunately, Britta is running every bit as ragged, taking on duties my brother and I are way too busy to complete. Rob can't help since he fell in the shower two weeks ago and had to have pins and rods inserted in his ankle. He's working from home, but since he has to elevate and do physical therapy, he can't meet and greet clients or coordinate all the other crap that makes a good listing happen.

Evenings at home are short with all the work on our plates and a toddler under foot. I carve out time to give Jamie a bath every night, then Britta and I read him stories together before we tuck him in. He needs that. After that's done, however, we're both exhausted. Thank god Harlow is around to play with Jamie and help with dinner. She's been a godsend from that perspective, and I can tell my sister loves my son. She'll be happy with a couple kids of her own, I suspect.

With the little bit of spare time I have, I'm running wedding errands. I had a phone call with the officiant Keeley is going to use. He's a yoga teacher who performs nondenominational ceremonies as a side business. He's got a Zen vibe. Great. Fine. As long as it's legal, I don't care. Britta has never professed any religious preference, so I'm hoping she'll agree with my choice.

Provided she ever agrees to marry me at all.

I took a chance and ordered invitations. I don't need many since the wedding will be small. They arrived quickly and I made it very clear in the verbiage that the event will be a surprise to the bride. I fucking hope these twenty people, mostly casual friends and a few work-related folks, can keep their mouths shut. I mailed them yesterday.

We didn't have time to order bridesmaids' dresses, so Keeley and Harlow are coordinating on finding two dresses that are as close to that cornflower color—which I now know is blue—as they can find. I picked up a wedding band for myself, chose a tuxedo, then got Maxon, Jamie, and one of my college buddies to a fitting.

Keeley, with Britta's "help," has locked down all the visual elements of the ceremony. I have no doubt that will be perfect.

The marriage license situation is under control. If Britta will sign it before the ceremony, my former client's daughter will make sure everything gets done and legal.

I'm not sure what to do about a honeymoon. We live in Hawaii. How much better does it get? But I need to think of something. We deserve time to ourselves to cement our bond. We'll take Jamie with us since Maxon and Keeley will be newlyweds and won't need a toddler cramping their love life. Besides, I'm not sure I can do without the little guy for long.

Head spinning, I use one of the two spare minutes I have to rub together and call Keeley. She answers right away.

"Are you freaking out?" she asks without even saying hello.

The woman knows me well. "Yes. This wedding is in two weeks."

"I know. Mine is in eight days. Gah!"

"Sorry. I know you're under a lot of pressure, too."

"Yes, but mine is controlled. Everything is planned. So unless something goes horrifically wrong, I'll be fine." She hesitates. "Do you have any idea where Britta's mind and heart are?"

"No." And it's killing me. She's been reserved, harder to read, for the last month—since her lunch with Makaio. I regret that we've had so little time for us. I need to push everything else aside as much as I can or I'll forever regret that I didn't take full advantage of the one opportunity I had to win her back. "But I called Eleanor and talked to her."

Finding the courage to pick up the phone and talk to Britta's mother... I won't lie, that took some time, and I had to search for my balls. I could only imagine how much that woman resented what I had done to her daughter.

We talked for almost two hours. Initially, Eleanor was chilly to the point of being curt. I apologized, laid my cards on the table, and told her about the wedding with which I was planning to surprise Britta. After that, our relationship thawed to something almost friendly. Makaio, the idiot, hadn't even thought about incorporating Britta's mother into their wedding. Eleanor didn't have the money to fly to Hawaii. My angel didn't have it, either. And I know her. Not having her mother there for her wedding would be something she'd always regret. A woman wants her mom on her wedding day. Keeley assured me of that. Hers is coming from Phoenix, along with her stepfather, Phil. So I bought Eleanor a first-class ticket to Maui.

She'll see her daughter get married, regardless of which groom Britta chooses.

I simply have to push work aside long enough to figure out how to make that groom me.

"Why don't you send Jamie over here tonight with Harlow for dinner and a movie or something? You and Britta need a break."

Normally, I'd hate to impose, but I don't have a choice now. "Thank you. I owe you big."

Her light laugh is a familiar comfort in my ear. "I'll remind you of that someday when your brother and I need a babysitter."

Fifteen minutes later, my sister texts me that she and my son will have a grand time with Uncle Maxon and Aunt Keeley and she'll stay gone as long as she can.

I thank her. Then I start strategizing.

At the end of the day, Britta and I hop in the car. She looks beyond exhausted.

"Jamie is with the rest of the family. Maxon picked him up from daycare." Since he's on the approved list. I'm still not, and I try not to let that bother me. "It's just us this evening."

She sighs tiredly. "I'd be disappointed if I had any energy."

"I'm with you. Dinner?"

"Whatever you feel like."

I take her to a casual seafood place. It's not much to look at but the food is incredible. Best of all, it's not crowded, so it won't be too loud to talk and we shouldn't be distracted by anyone else.

After we're seated and we order, I don't waste any time. I feel as if I've pissed away too much of it already. "Tell me what you're thinking and feeling, angel."

"Besides beat down by the pace of work right now?" Her shoulders sag tiredly. "Overwhelmed maybe. What about you?"

I swallow. "Our time together is running out, and I'm not sure if you're any closer to knowing whether you can love me again and want to marry me."

The waitress sets down our drinks. Since we already ordered food, she slides away unobtrusively. I take a sip of my beer and watch Britta down half her wine.

"We are running out of time. I know." She licks her lips. "Let's be real. I don't think I ever fell out of love with you. I should have. I tried to. I just couldn't."

I sit up straighter and reach for her hands. "If that's how you feel, you can't marry Makaio. Because you know I love you, too."

"In the past, I've always made decisions with my heart. When I was young and didn't have responsibilities, that was great. In fact, what we had was magical and epic…while it lasted." She withdraws her hands from mine. "But maybe the time has come to think with my head. I need someone I can depend on. I need a family sedan, Griff. You're a Ferrari."

Is she saying no? After I've already planned our wedding? Granted, she doesn't know that, but I'm trying to go all out and prove how much she means to me. She's got to give me a goddamn chance. "A Ferrari still gets people where they need to go. I've been dependable as hell the last thirty-eight days."

"Yes, but it's barely a month. And we've been drowning in work for the last few weeks."

"I know. And I hate it. But that's not my fault."

"It's not," she assures. "I'm still hung up for some reason. Like I said, I've forgiven, but I can't seem to forget."

"After you saw Makaio and he made you cry, I didn't lose my temper or push you for more information. I've been trying to back off and let you make your own choice."

"I didn't say you haven't changed." She looks down at the table, tracing a pattern on the clear plexiglas. "But maybe I have, too."

Enough to marry a man who won't love her enough to put her and our son first? Nope. I won't believe that. "What am I not giving you that you need?"

Britta falls quiet and cocks her head as if she's debating the wisdom of her next words. "All of yourself."

I rear back. Of all the things I imagined she'd say, that wasn't it. "What? I'm with you all day. All night. By your side when we tuck Jamie into bed. I sleep beside you. I wake up next to you—"

"I don't mean your time."

"You know I love you."

She sighs. "I don't mean your heart. I mean whatever it is that makes you guarded and angry and keeps you from really trusting me. Despite all the time we've spent together, I'm not sure I know you any better now than I did three years ago. You know all about me, my life, my past. Since we moved into the Stowe estate, I've spent nearly every moment with you, risking everything to see if we could truly have a future. I've been thinking—hoping—you would open up and erase my doubts. You haven't once offered to tell me what makes you tick."

I sit back and stare, covering my shock with a swig of beer. She sees through me. Despite how well I thought I'd recovered or how thoroughly I've been hiding the decades-old crap, Britta isn't fooled. How much can I tell her without freaking her out?

It's clear I have to say something or she may walk out on me for good.

"Just before I turned seventeen, I had a relationship with an acquaintance of my mom's. Julia. She was divorced and had kids a few years younger than me. I started doing her lawn one summer...and she made it clear she wanted me to do her, too."

I still remember the forbidden thrill, the way she always made me feel like a man. I worshipped her. I didn't care that she was almost thirty-five. She was beautiful and smart and savvy. She ran her home-grown business and her personal life like a shark, and I admired the hell out of her for it. She taught me a lot about a woman's body, about sex. I'm sure people would call her a pedophile, but I was all too willing.

"So you did?" Britta grimaces as she asks.

"Yeah. I thought what we had was important to her. That it was real. By the time winter rolled around, she broke it off abruptly. No warning. No explanation. She told me off-handedly one day, after I put my clothes back on and she showed me the door, that she had hired a new lawn boy. I shrugged, thinking that if she wanted someone else to do the yard, that was fine by me. I was tired of the pretense. When I talked about being glad to see her somewhere other than her house, now that we'd ditched the cover story, she laughed at me as she explained in small words that it was over. It never once occurred to me that she'd been planning to do away with me for weeks and simply waited for the most expedient moment. After getting one more fuck out of me, of course. That was the end."

Well, not exactly. But the rest of the story won't shed more light. It will just make Britta pity me more. And make me choke again. But I've given her enough to help her understand…and the sad empathy flitting across her face is already warming my heart.

"Griff… She hurt you. You were so young and—"

"I learned a lot from the experience. I know now that I didn't *love* her. But at the time, it felt a lot like heartbreak."

"Thank you for telling me," she murmurs softly, giving me a quick squeeze of my hand. "Was it hard?"

"Yes." I squeeze back, not wanting to relinquish her fingers. "I've never told anyone, not even Maxon. I spent a lot of years being bitter. After that, I found myself questioning everything and everyone I'd always trusted. I decided that if I could just control the people and events in my life, I'd never get too attached to anyone again. I thought I'd be fine. And I was getting by." I blow out a ragged breath. It's hard to say this, but Britta deserves all I can give her. "Then I met you."

She blinks at me. "I didn't want to challenge or hurt you. I just wanted to love you."

I nod. "And I couldn't control that, just like I couldn't control how quickly I fell for you. I told myself you were sweet and innocent and that you would never go out of your way to rip my guts open. But you still scared the hell out of me. I spent so much of our time together waiting for the other shoe to drop."

"I was never going to betray you. I never would. Griff..."

"You seemed too good to be true, but I couldn't make my heart stop caring about you. I tried so hard to keep you at arm's length. But I seduced you because I couldn't stand not having you. I moved you in with me because I couldn't do without having you near me. Every day that passed, I began to think a little more that maybe you were real, that painting you with Julia's brush was unfair. Every day, I let my guard down more. I wanted to tell you I loved you. I wanted to propose. By the fall, I believed you were everything I wanted and more. I made a plan. I was going to give you the grandest gesture of love I could think of. Then that morning the listing agent on the prince's palatial love shack accidentally called me instead of Maxon and I heard about the deal. I lost it. My brother and I had always been competitive. I chalked him up to being too much like Dad. I decided that I couldn't be in business with a sneaky fucker like that. But you... I couldn't handle believing you betrayed me to help him, that I meant so little to you—"

"You meant everything." Britta sniffles. "I loved you so much then that I would have followed you to the ends of the earth. I would have stabbed Maxon if he'd intentionally been trying to cut you out of a deal. I would have married you, had your children, and held your hand forever. But you let go. Griff, I don't know what to do about that."

I close my eyes. If I keep looking at her, I'm going to fucking get emotional. We're at a restaurant, and now I wish we were anywhere with privacy. I want to hold her, kiss her, show her in some way how much she means to me. I don't want to fall days short of our happily ever after again. It fucking can't end this way.

"I'm going to regret that forever."

"So...all the women after we split up? They were—"

"Numbing. I could control everything about my time with them.

When. Where. How long. How much. How hard. How pointless. So much of it was basically anonymous. A bar there, a swipe to the right there. I'd undo it all for you if I could." I look across the table, willing Britta to believe me. "I don't know how to make you trust me again. I'm the last person who should preach to you about how long it takes to believe in someone. I'm sure it's doubly hard for you since I'm the one who first broke your heart."

"None of this has been easy. I'm still not sure what should come next for us."

"You know what I want."

She presses her lips together. "But that doesn't mean I can give it to you."

In other words, she's not ready to take a leap of faith. I didn't manage to our first time together, so I can hardly blame her. But that doesn't mean I'm going to stop trying to convince her.

"If you choose your head over your heart…" Jesus, she simply can't. "I know you. You'll be miserable."

"Maybe. But that's better than being broken."

I want to argue that I'm not going to break her again. But that will simply lead to a circular argument. I know better than anyone that wanting desperately to believe something doesn't mean you actually can.

"So where does that leave us?" I challenge her.

"We have two more weeks to figure it out. I'll keep searching my soul until I have an answer." She shrugs. "My mom always says that whatever is meant to be will be. I've always thought she's right."

It's not the answer I want, but I don't have any choice but to accept it. I destroyed us with one stupid act of fury and distrust. Now I may have to live with the fact that our future is beyond my repair. She may wind up with a man who won't worship her the way I do.

If that's the case, I will spend my life alone.

CHAPTER SEVENTEEN

THE DAY DAWNS BEAUTIFUL. BRITTA and I drive out to Keeley and Maxon's new house, which will officially be a bed-and-breakfast next week. They started moving in two days ago, but tonight will be their first night to spend here. Also their first as man and wife.

As I drive closer, I hold Britta's hand. My pants and shirt swish inside a garment bag hanging in the backseat, along with Britta's sundress. I'm not wearing a tie. Or a coat. Keeley wants a casual wedding. Hell, she even instituted a no-shoes rule. This will literally be a barefoot wedding.

I would rib my ambitious, traditional, bordering-on-stuffy brother about that, but he seems sublimely happy. I never imagined in a million years when my best friend sought him out to see if he and I could behave like brothers again that they would fall in love. But Keeley completes him, and that made all our lives come together perfectly.

Well, almost. I glance at Britta.

It's been just over a week since our last serious discussion. The following day was another explosion of work. When do we ever negotiate and sell six listings on the same day? Just insane. On Sunday, Britta and I caught up on paperwork while we took turns entertaining Jamie. Harlow breezed in late afternoon after meeting up with some of the friends from the private high school she once attended on the island. She waved our way, all smiles, then took a call and disappeared upstairs. After that, she glowered like a thunderstorm for the rest of the day and well into the following week.

Jamie got a tummy virus midweek, so that occupied Britta for two days. I offered to spell her, but she insisted I had a full schedule of showings and closings that we couldn't miss.

It sucks…but sometimes that's life.

Wedding activities started in earnest on Thursday, and we all began pitching in to get the house set up for the big event. Ditto Friday. We finished less than ten hours ago. Throwing together a last-minute wedding was a mountain of work, but Keeley wants something simple, almost homemade. Maxon just wants to marry her ASAP.

When we pull up, I'm awestruck by how inviting the cheerful house looks sparkling in the morning sunlight. On the lawn, we laid a pair of crisp white sheets, sprinkled them with petals from all kinds of flowers we found on the grounds, and topped that with folding white chairs we managed to rent. Thankfully, we barely need more than a handful. There are white covers on the chairs, tied off with bows that match the ocean waters.

Maxon found a tall lattice archway on the property, all but languishing in the garden. He and I moved it to this spot, overlooking the vast, crystal-blue Pacific that's calmly rolling onto the white sand. We painted it, then everyone pitched in to decorate the arch with fragrant flowers that Keeley, Britta, and Harlow strung together. It looks perfect, like it's meant to be here.

If everything works out for me and Britta, I'll be in this very spot next week, staring down a similar setup, taking a deep breath before I—hopefully—slide my ring on her finger for good.

We park.

Two seconds later, Keeley darts up, makeup half-done, hand out for the punchbowl Britta rummaged from her kitchen this morning. "Thanks. Do you need help unloading the car?"

I snatch the plastic bowl back. "I got this. Go finish getting ready. Maxon and I can do the rest."

"Oh, please keep him occupied," she begs. "The ceremony starts in ninety minutes, and he's asking me why we can't just start now."

Laughing at that is unavoidable. My brother has never been patient. For that matter, neither have I, and I can only imagine how I'm going to feel in seven days' time, surprising Britta with the wedding she envisioned and wondering whether she'll finally say yes.

Strolling inside, I set the bowl on the island and glance around at the covered dishes. The ladies cooked some last night. Maxon and I catered the rest, and the food in plastic dishes has already arrived. There's also a cake on a stand waiting in the dining room and champagne chilling for the twenty-five guests.

Everything is heartfelt. And beautifully simple for this momentous occasion.

Maxon marches in, looking at his watch, obviously prepared to do next to nothing to keep busy...and stop himself from beating down Keeley's door.

"You look awfully impatient. You going to make it, man?" I ask, brow raised.

He scowls at me. "Oh, the things I want to say to you right now..."

But he doesn't. Instead, his gaze flips over my shoulder, toward the folding glass doors that have been drawn open, to see Britta coming through, holding Jamie's hand and wearing a pensive expression. When she realizes my brother is looking her way, it quickly becomes a strained smile.

Somehow, I hold in my grimace. I haven't asked her if Makaio still thinks she's marrying him. He doesn't faze me. *She* matters. I should find out if she still wants to be the Hawaiian banker's bride, but I'm afraid to hear her say yes. I still have seven days to convince her to pick me. I'm going to use every moment I can to my advantage.

Despite my brother giving me a hard time about how antsy I am with all the uncertainty in my personal life, I smile. "But you can't right now. So sorry..."

He sends me a snarky glance. "Fuck you."

I laugh, then glance around and realize who's missing. "Thanks for not inviting the parents. I'm sure it was a hard decision for you to get married without either Mom or Dad present."

"Probably not as much as it should have been. But after Keeley over-heard Dad rant at me a couple of weeks ago, despite how peace-loving and forgiving she is, she refused to have him around. And Mom… Apparently Harlow told her I was getting married. She decided to head to Cabo with Marco so she could come back in a few weeks, all refreshed for our little sister's nuptials."

I want to say how much her decision completely sucks, though I'm hardly surprised.

"But"—Maxon goes on—"I've got the people who are most im-portant to me here. Thanks for standing up with me, man." He hands me a small, flat box from inside his pants pocket.

I open it to find a sleek brushed-silver keychain with my initials on one side. On the other, he engraved the words MY BROTHER, MY FRIEND.

I'm choked up that, despite my stupidity, we somehow managed to pick up exactly where we left off—very close. We exchange a manly hug, and I know that, regardless of what happens with Britta, I'll always have Maxon and his lovely wife in my life.

"Thanks, man. I have something for you, too. I was going to give it to you next week but…" This seems like the perfect time.

I pull a business cardholder from my pants pocket. As a good Realtor and broker, I never go anywhere without them. At the back of my stack of cards, I find what I'm looking for, pluck it up, and hand it over.

REED BROTHERS PROPERTY ASSOCIATES is emblazoned across the top. It looks almost exactly like the cards we had back in the day. Updated, of course. I had them made when I ordered the invitations for my wedding. I've given this thought and I realize that, three years ago, I was on the right track with life. Then my stupid ass jumped off. Now I'm hoping Maxon thinks I've earned his trust back and that he wants to be partners again permanently.

I watch him scan the card, then look at me with a question in his eyes.

"What do you think?" I ask.

"You sure?"

"More than positive. I'm sorry for screwing everything up. I'd love to work with you again, build our business—the way we should have."

Maxon's face breaks out in a massive grin. "Hell yeah!"

We hug, slapping backs with manly thumps to disguise the fact we're both more emotional than our masculinity allows in the moment. "Fantastic. We just need to take that terrible tarp off *our* sign next week."

He laughs as he steps back, looking away until he finds his composure. "First thing Monday."

"Get real, dude. You're not coming to work on Monday."

With a sheepish grin, he flashes me something wry and full of white teeth. "Probably not. Maybe Tuesday…"

I'm not holding my breath on that, either.

Before I can call Maxon on it, Harlow strides through the room, wearing a salmon-colored dress that's almost not okay with me. Sure, it's high-necked and there's no cleavage. And technically it covers all the essentials—but barely. It's so short I worry what I'll see if there's a stiff breeze. The waistband is a thick strip of transparent lace that accentuates her small waist. I can't believe I'm looking at naked skin on my sister's torso. There's also no way to miss that she's got boobs in this getup. I didn't need the reminder.

"What are you wearing?" I ask.

"A dress." Harlow looks at me like I'm an idiot.

"Doesn't she look pretty?" Keeley's mom, Patty, asks as she starts putting some of the catered food in the bulging refrigerator.

I hate the dress but I keep my mouth shut because I like Patty.

I finally met her and Keeley's stepdad last night. Instantly, I could tell they were great people, and I see from whom Keeley gets her beauty—and her red hair. They oohed and aahed over Jamie, then looked at their daughter as if the clock is already ticking. When Maxon joined in the chant for babies, I suspect I may have a niece or nephew this time next year.

We all bustle around, trying to get everything ready for incoming guests. Britta might have the softest voice of everyone here, yet she's organizing the troops, scanning the site for any task that has been overlooked, and efficiently assigning it to the nearest warm body so nothing falls through the cracks.

With thirty minutes to spare, it looks as if we're finally finished. Harlow and Patty head back to check on Keeley. Britta makes to follow.

I grab her wrist and pull her close. "You did good, angel. I know my brother and his bride appreciate you."

She gives me a tight smile. "I was happy to help."

She doesn't seem happy at all.

I squeeze her hands. "What are you thinking? Do you want to talk about it?"

"I was just realizing…" She pauses and bites her lip. "This could have been us."

"This? Getting married?" I pull her closer. "Angel, it still can be."

A little frown worries between her brows. It's her thinking face. "We've been living together for a few weeks, and it's been good. But I'm—"

"Britta, quick! Keeley needs another opinion." Harlow sticks her head out the bathroom door and motions my angel into the all-female domain.

"One minute." She turns back to me with something obviously on her mind.

"Hurry!" my sister shouts.

Britta glances at the ladies, then looks back to me apologetically. "I should go. I guess it's urgent…"

If the crisis involved anyone but Keeley, and if it weren't her wedding to my brother, I would gladly tell my sister to zip it until Britta could share her feelings with me. She seems ready to talk—or close to it.

"Just tell me one thing. Are you any closer to saying yes to me?"

She tilts her head and gives my question a long moment of consideration. "Since we moved in together, I've had days where I think we can't try to relive our past. I've had other days where I see a possible future for us so clearly it makes me want to cry."

But neither side has won over her heart and mind for good or we wouldn't still be having this conversation. "And where are you now?"

"I've been thinking a lot about what you said when we talked last. It told me so much about you and why you find trust so difficult. I needed that, so thank you for trusting me with your secret. But the reality is, you'll never be able to control how I make you feel. Are you truly ready to handle that? Or would you eventually push me away again, like you did before?"

It's a fair question. I'm glad we're getting to the root of her hesitation. "I'm—"

"Britta!" my sister shouts again. "Hurry! Guests are starting to arrive, and we may have a problem."

"I have to go," my angel murmurs.

And just like that, thanks to Harlow's big mouth, the moment is broken.

"We'll talk after the ceremony?" I ask, but it's not really a question.

She hesitates for a moment, like she wants to say something—do something—important right now. But ultimately, she nods, then turns away and disappears into the master bathroom with all the ladies and the cloud of hair spray.

With a curse, I head outside. The officiant is strolling along the edge of the lawn. He's a tall man with crow's feet, laugh lines, and the sort of belly that says he likes good food and good times. He's wearing a big smile, a red-and-beige Hawaiian-print shirt, and a pair of khakis, sans shoes.

"Lono?" I ask.

"Griffin?" He's clearly guessing, too.

I get a positive vibe right away. Keeley did well.

"Yeah. Just Griff." Normally, I don't like when other people call me by my full name. It reminds me of my Dad shouting at me as a kid to do better, be better, crush everyone—even Maxon.

"Is your bride here?"

"With the ladies." I try not to wince. "She still doesn't know about our wedding."

He shoots me a puzzled glance. Yeah, he thinks I'm a crazy bastard. I probably am. But instead of saying that, he cocks his head. "Everything will work out. I have a sense for these things."

I have no idea what "a sense" means, and it's probably bullshit meant to calm me. But I still smile, shake his hand, and confirm that he'll be here next Saturday morning for what I'm hoping is another Reed wedding.

After a little more conversation, guests start milling around the lawn, and Lono says it's time for the ceremony to begin.

With a nod, I head into the house to round everyone up. Britta, Harlow, and Patty all emerge from the bathroom, looking perfectly coiffed. Jamie looks bored and comes running at me full speed. His expression says he's hoping I'll have something more male and amusing to occupy him.

With a laugh, I pick my boy up and hold him close. I ruffle his hair and promise to set him up with toys as soon we finish marrying Uncle Maxon off.

When I look up, Britta is watching, silent. She looks teary-eyed and moved. Love is all over her face, and I hope like hell some of that is for me.

But there's no time to talk now or to find out what's rolling through her head. So I grab Maxon, now pacing like a madman, and haul him outside.

Behind the rows of chairs, we pause until Harlow and Britta catch up and take Jamie by the hand. I lead my brother to the altar, then file in behind him, hands clasped in front.

The processional music suddenly sounds over speakers hooked up to Keeley's wedding playlist. Harlow gives Jamie a little nudge. He's carrying a ring pillow with the bands tied in a bow at the top. We've coached him to walk in slow, measured steps to deliver the goods on a waiting table. But he's a boy, so he runs to the altar. When he realizes that everyone is looking at him, he tosses the pillow vaguely toward Maxon's feet and darts to the first familiar face he sees, Keeley's mom, and buries his head in her skirt.

The small gathering laughs. With a grin of her own, Harlow starts down the aisle, clasping a simple bouquet of lilies, roses, and plumeria. Besides the brief, skin-showing dress, she looks lovely. I wonder if she's thinking about her own wedding, just a few weeks away.

Britta comes down the aisle next, carrying a similar bouquet. She's wearing roughly the same soft peachy-pink as Harlow, but her dress sits just off her narrow shoulders and has a thick strip of lace at the bottom. It's a little shorter than I'd like, and I glance around the gathering to see who among the male attendees might be checking out my woman. Thankfully, I don't see anyone I'll have to kill. Just a lot of smiling people and couples holding hands. Happiness floats everywhere.

Finally, a slight breeze kicks up, and the music changes. The familiar strains of Andy Williams' version of "Ke Kali Nei Au," also known as "The Hawaiian Wedding Song," fill the air. Yes, this is the moment. Leave it to Keeley to choose a tune that's traditional yet offbeat. It's relaxed and romantic and meaningful because I believe they will love each other longer than forever.

For them, this tune is perfect.

Then Keeley strolls toward us carrying a bouquet centered by a giant stargazer lily, ringed by soft pink plumeria, and surrounded in white blooms. Her pristine, gauzy dress has spaghetti straps and a handkerchief hem that flirts with her shins and flows around her with every step of her bare feet like the most graceful hula dancer's.

The smile on her face beams with how blessed she feels. It's more profound than any expression I've ever seen on her. Or possibly any bride. She might not have waited long for her day to come, but she knows she's marrying the right man. A glance at my brother floors me. I've rarely seen Maxon emotional about anything, except maybe Super Bowl XLII when the Giants upset the Patriots. But he's wearing his naked love for Keeley all over his face and looking at her as if he'd make a lei out of stars for her if he could. It might sound sappy, but the devotion flowing between them is a stunning sight to behold.

Lono starts the ceremony quickly. Her mother gives her away. Keeley and Maxon speak their vows, light candles, and stare into each other's eyes.

It's funny how a few words can be so meaningful. Those same words spoken in another order, in any other context, would have a totally different meaning. But with a few sounds and syllables, bolstered by the feelings in their hearts, they tie themselves together forever.

I'm really happy for them. And really fucking envious. I glance at Britta, wondering if I'll be full of joy—or grief—this time next week. I can't tell from looking at her face...but she's teary. She's moved by the ceremony.

When Lono pronounces Maxon and Keeley husband and wife, they pause, stare at each other as if they can hardly believe their dreams have come true, then move in for a soft kiss. They cling together, and the embrace seems to go on and on until Keeley's stepfather finally clears his throat. When they break apart like guilty teenagers, everyone laughs again.

"Maxon and Keeley Reed, everyone!" Lono shouts to the revelers.

As the gathering claps for them, Maxon takes his wife's hand and they dash back down the makeshift aisle.

It's done. They're married. I'm so happy for them.

Since Rob couldn't hobble up the aisle to be Maxon's other grooms-man, I do double-duty, escorting both Britta and Harlow away from the altar. I squeeze my angel's hand, and she looks over at me again with barely repressed emotion haunting her blue eyes.

What is she thinking? Goddamn it, I wish we'd been able to finish our conversation... Does she realize that if she marries Makaio, she won't be getting the kind of love she saw exchanged today? Or does she think I could never love her this wholly and she should back away from me?

Fuck, I sound like a pubescent girl, running through what-if scenarios and trying to anticipate what my crush is truly thinking. I have to be patient, wait for some privacy. I have to keep believing that we're building something good.

The sun sets as everyone pitches in to tear down the folding chairs and put away the sheets. In three minutes, we assemble the portable dance floor Maxon rented. Keeley loves to dance, and as much as it makes him cringe, he'll do it for her.

Soon, the deejay has his space set up. Earlier, the men set up banquet tables around the dining room table and on the attached lanai. We tied floral-print cloths to the legs to dress up the situation. Now, ladies bring out the food and punch, and when the music starts, we have a party.

Through the afternoon, the celebration gears up. Dancing ensues, along with bouquet tossing, garter throwing—I caught it, thank you— and lots of pictures, laughter, and toasts.

Finally, the deejay announces the last song of the night, mostly because we're losing the sun and didn't have any lights to string—not to mention the fact that Maxon is losing patience waiting to be alone with Keeley. It's an Elvis classic, "Can't Help Falling in Love." While Harlow is playing tag with Jamie on the lawn, I grab Britta, despite her protests that she intends to clean up this mess for Keeley and Maxon so they can enjoy their wedding night without stress.

I pull her against me. "I've missed you all day, angel. And to answer your question, yes. I can handle not controlling how you make me feel because it's *you*. I welcome it. The two of us together are stronger than either of us alone. It took me three years to believe that, but now I know it to my core. How can I help you believe that, too?"

"Griff...you're asking me to take a leap of faith. It's not that some part of me doesn't want to jump with both feet, especially today with the wedding and everything. I just... Let me process that for a little while, okay?"

"Sure." I don't love it, but I have to respect it.

I've done my best not to touch her in any way that pushes her comfort level. I know I can't force her to be ready to open her heart, and she can't handle cheating. But I can't handle not being with her right now. I want to touch her in any way—every way—she'll let me that will show her how much I love her.

As we sway to the music, I wrap one arm around her waist. My other hand cradles hers. She puts her head on my shoulder. I absorb the moment. Other than sleeping, it's the closest we've been in weeks. I'm loving the hell out of this. I miss her like mad. I want her so badly I can barely stand it.

"Britta?"

When she lifts her head and blinks up at me, lashes fluttering, our gazes fuse. She doesn't answer me, just stares, as into the moment as I am.

I kiss her forehead, her cheeks, her temple.

"You're pushing me."

"What's new?" I joke.

"Nothing. And everything." When I brush my lips over her bared shoulders—first one, then the other—she shivers. A breathy protest follows. "That's against the rules."

"Hmm." I rub my cheek against hers. "Just showing you how good we are together. Besides, we agreed that it's not cheating if the intent isn't arousal or penetration. I just want to worship you. You have to admit, this isn't sexual."

"No," she says softly, painfully. "It's romantic."

"You didn't tell me I couldn't be romantic." I smile as I turn her around the floor in my arms, then kiss her face again, this time dangerously close to her lips.

She pulls back. "What are you doing to me?"

Her voice is both jagged and pleading, but she doesn't sound distressed. I'm curious about that. Fascinated, in fact. Something is brewing in her head, in her heart.

"I'm loving you. Is that all right?"

I kiss her jaw. I kiss her neck. I hear her draw in a sharp breath.

"I can't exactly stop you…"

She can't. "Would you like me to, angel?

"No."

Oh, that's almost victory. My gut tightens. My pulse races. Yeah, you can guess what my cock is doing.

"Then what would you like me to do?" I murmur in her ear.

"I think… Maybe you're right. We are stronger together." Her feet stop. Her lips part. She lowers her lashes for a moment, then meets my stare head on again. "You love me?"

Every muscle in my body seizes up. She wants to know for a reason.

"I always have."

Britta swallows, then lifts her hand over my heart and eases closer. "Then take me home and show me how much."

THREE MINUTES AFTER BRITTA SOFTLY delivered her bombshell, we're speeding down the road in my sister's rental, heading home. Well, to the Stowes' mansion. Harlow spent last night with Keeley at the house, drinking wine and giggling, so she had her own ride at Keeley and Maxon's place. Britta joined them for a few hours so they could give my bestie a mellow sort of bachelorette party. Tonight, my sister offered to drive my SUV to the house later and bring Jamie with her. Something about my expression or my urgency to leave the reception must have given my intentions away. Harlow offered to give my son a bath and have a slumber party with him tonight in her room.

I'll thank her profusely tomorrow.

I clutch the wheel in one hand and clasp Britta's with the other. Adrenaline roars through my system. And questions are hitting my brain.

The primal part of me wants to forget them until we've been as close as two people can be and sated our desire all night. Until we've cemented our bond again for good. The logical part of me is aware that probing for answers now could bite me in the ass. But I have to know.

"What changed your mind?"

"A lot of things," she murmurs. "Mostly time and seeing how different you are. Things you've said. How honest you seem now. How willing you've been to work through our problems without burying them under sex. But you're still pushy," she scolds with a grin.

I send her a wry glance. "I can't change every part of me, angel. Some things are just too ingrained."

Her trilling laugh fills the car. "I wouldn't know what to do with you if you weren't forever challenging me to step out of my comfort zone. It's one of those things that both infuriates and excites me. We're so opposite."

It's true. I'm forever fascinated with how considerate and compromising she can be while gently but firmly standing her ground. Not barging and shoving is an art form I simply never mastered. I probably never will.

"And Keeley helped me clarify," she goes on, confessing. "She gave me this song to listen to last night. Odd that music I've never heard could move me so much, but this tune perfectly summed up my situation. It helped me to acknowledge feelings I've had but couldn't put into words. I've been playing it over and over since then."

"Can I hear?"

She nods, then launches the song on her phone and flips the screen in my direction. "Lies" by Trifonic.

It's sad, haunting, with an air of finality. This woman has been denying how much she wants her man because he left and she's convinced he's no good for her. Regardless of all that, she realizes she has to stop lying to herself and embrace her sweetest sin.

Me.

"That's how you feel?"

"I have for a while. I just…didn't know how to face it."

"And now you're sure about us?"

"Yes."

She doesn't even hesitate. Triumph spikes. I press my foot down on the accelerator a little more.

"You're done with Makaio? You're not marrying him?"

Britta unbuckles her seat belt and crawls across the console, lying over my lap and plastering her chest to mine. She cups my cheek. "He doesn't belong between us anymore. Now shut up and kiss me."

Yeah, I'm not turning that down.

As we roll to a red light, I dip my head and seize Britta's mouth, shoving her lips apart and tasting every corner of her sweetness. It's like coming home but better. Just being near her turns me on, but this... I hold her tight against me with one arm, wishing like hell I didn't need the other to drive. My tongue sweeps in, meeting hers, tangling until my heart threatens to thump out of my chest.

Someone honks behind me, and I look up to see the light has turned green. I slam on the accelerator, cursing the few minutes between here and our bedroom.

I half expect Britta to slide back into her seat for the rest of the trip, but no. She glides her plush lips up my neck, brushing them across my jaw, against a spot just below my ear that makes me shudder and the blood rush to my cock. When she unbuttons my shirt enough to skate her fingers along my hair-roughened skin, her mouth follows. Her tongue traces a loving path over my chest that makes my blood jet and my need soar. I want her so bad I almost can't see straight.

"What are you doing to me?" I groan.

"What you do to me with nothing more than a look," she murmurs softly in my ear.

My whole body shudders. "Oh, fuck... Angel."

"Hurry."

If I drive any faster, I'll be speeding way too recklessly to stay on the road. "Two minutes."

"Good." She tugs at my bottom lip with her teeth as she caresses her way past my chest, to my abdomen...then toward the waistband of my pants. Her fingertips are flirting in dangerous places, and I'm trying to hold myself together. I have not waited over three years for this woman to lose my patience now, pull over on the side of the road, and snatch a quickie in the backseat of a compact. At six foot three, I don't even think I'd fit. I definitely wouldn't have the room to make love to her the way I want, to spread her out underneath me and leave her no question how *deeply* I feel for her.

I groan as Britta's fingers find their way just inside my boxers. I swear she grazes the head of my cock.

"Griff..." Her voice itself is a seduction as she presses her lips down my neck, then nips her way back up to my mouth, delving into me.

I suck in a breath, try to keep my head on straight. Fuck yes. In every way, yes.

With a jerk of the wheel, I careen into the driveway. I lift my hand and stop steering long enough to raise the garage door. I refuse to let go of Britta.

Once I pull the car inside, I jam on the brakes. The vehicle lurches to a stop.

We bounce back into the seat, and I kill the engine. We stare, breaths coming hot and loud in the small space.

"I'm going to spend all night inside you, angel."

"I was hoping you'd say that."

Her answer makes my cock even harder. I didn't think such a thing was possible.

When Britta cups my face again and leans in like she intends to kiss me, I grab her wrist to stave her off. "Not here. I'm on the edge. It's been almost fifty days since I've had an orgasm—for any reason. I haven't gone that long without since I was sixteen, and I can't vouch for my self-restraint. Let's get inside the house."

She blinks, frowns. "Why?"

Why haven't I exercised my sex drive? She really has to ask?

I take her face in my hands and will her to understand. "I was waiting for you. I only want you."

Britta melts against me softly, sweetly. "I've been waiting for you, too."

I want to know how long it's been for her. Did she really not have sex with Makaio when they went away for the weekend? But I don't ask. I refuse to have him in bed with us—in any way—tonight or ever again.

I manage to wedge my hand down enough to release my seat belt, then shove the car door open. Britta eases off my lap and makes it out the passenger's door. We leave everything else in the trunk. It will wait.

When I hold out my hand, she takes it. I shove open the door to the house, and we enter the dark hallway. There's a soft light on over the top of the stove and another on a timer in the adjoining family room. I contemplate the sofa for a long minute, but Harlow won't be far behind us. I stifle my urge to be inside Britta right now in favor of having privacy all night.

But everything between us needs to happen faster. My sanity won't last otherwise.

Without a word, I turn and lift Britta into my arms, clutching her to my chest. She yelps in surprise, then winds her arms around my neck and locks her gaze with mine as I stomp my way up the heavy stairs. "Griff?"

Is my impatience upsetting her?

I frown. "I've got you. I'll take care of you."

"I know," she breathes. "I was just going to point out that if you had let me walk, I could have gotten undressed at the same time."

I love the way her mind works.

I run double time until we're in the bedroom we've been sharing for the last month and kick the door shut. I immediately attack my shirt, unfastening one button after the other and quickly shucking it onto the floor. "You could, but then you'd deprive me of unwrapping the perfect gift. How attached are you to that dress?"

She shakes her head, a slow smile spreading across her face as her eyes eat me up. "Not at all."

An answering grin curls up my lips. "God, I love you."

I grab a handful of the garment with my fist and tug her closer, then whirl her around to shove the sleeves down her arms. A moment later, I yank down the zipper while I'm jerking the garment down her hips. I'm hasty. I'm not even trying to be careful. The sounds of ripping fabric fill the air. The primal beast in me rejoices.

Once the little pinkish garment is in a heap on the floor, I glide a palm down Britta's hip and use it to pull her against me. She must feel my erection prodding her back. She can't be surprised by the fact I'm aroused as fuck. The only thing that's keeping her from being completely naked is a pair of lacy, nude-colored panties barely covering her taut ass and a matching bra I can undo with one hand.

"Griff…"

I want her naked. I want that now. I want inside her, too. But I want to make her ache every bit as badly as I do first.

"Yeah, angel," I murmur in her ear as I wind my hand around her waist, down the flat of her belly, under the waistband of her little panties. I skate my fingers over her bare sex, slick and plump and ready. Touching her again is a beautiful agony. I wouldn't trade it for a hundred anonymous women.

I was being straight-up honest when I said I only want her.

When I walk my fingers between her folds and settle them over her clit, I have to grit my teeth to bite back a groan. Dragging my lips across her neck, I start rubbing her most sensitive spot slowly enough to ramp her up…but not nearly fast enough to provide relief.

Her entire body stiffens. Her back arches. She tosses her head against my chest and grabs my thighs, fingers digging in.

"Like that?" I croon.

"Yes…"

"Want it? Need it?"

"Yes," she pants. "God, yes."

I love hearing the desperation in her voice. She's always been responsive to me, putty in my bed. But this is sweeter, somehow new all over again. Maybe in the back of my head, where I'm trying not to want to hunt down every guy she's ever fucked, I'm aware she finally has a point of comparison so she can be sure how good I make her feel and this is what she wants.

"I've missed you like hell, angel. One thousand two hundred fifty-four days without you felt like eternity."

She stiffens in surprise. Yeah, I counted.

Then she seems to melt against me again. "I've missed you, too, Griff. No one makes me feel the way you do. No one."

Her confession pumps my blood, my need. Impatience to get inside her claws at my restraint, and I try to keep it together. This isn't about me. This isn't even merely about her. Sure, I could make her come in the next few seconds, then throw her on the bed and tear off those teasing undergarments before affixing my tongue to her sensitive clit and wring another orgasm from her two minutes later. Then I could start the process all over again. If there's one thing I've learned well in the last fifteen years, it's my way around a woman's body.

But I don't simply want to make Britta feel good. I want to make her mine. I want to make the two of us one again.

"You close?"

"Why do you ask when you already know?" Her tone pleads.

She's reached the end of her restraint. I've reached mine, too. It's been too long. I want her too deeply. We have too much at stake.

I grab the thin strings at the sides of her panties and give a vicious tug. They break apart in my hands. Britta is still gasping as I tear her bra off. It's probably ruined beyond repair. I don't give a shit. As I cradle her naked breasts in my hands, I doubt she does, either.

I kiss my way up her neck. Jesus, the smell of her skin mixing with her arousal is making my thoughts hazy, my blood savage. "Get on the bed."

She turns, looking at me with big eyes like a blue beacon in the shadowy room, lit only by silvery moonbeams filtering through the folding doors. The waves crash, mingling with the sound of her audible breaths as I jerk my pants down and grab a condom from the nightstand.

I planned ahead. I've been hoping for days, weeks, that we'd be busier. I'm well equipped since I suspect she's not on the pill anymore. If I had my preference, I'd go in bare. I've never had sex condomless with anyone except Britta, and I can't deny that I would love the chance to get her pregnant again so we could grow our family and I could see it all this time, be with her from the first little plus on the home test all the way through her final contraction and beyond.

Later. Soon. Hell, maybe even tomorrow. Once I get my ring on her finger, I'll open the conversation and—

Britta stops all coherent thought when she lies across the bed, props herself on her elbows, throws back her head, and spreads her slender thighs.

I kick off my trousers with a curse. In my haste to tear them off, I think I broke the zipper. Who gives a fuck?

With my teeth, I open the packet and roll it on as I balance my knee on the edge of the bed, catching myself above her, cradled between her legs.

"This is going to go fast. At least the first time…" I growl. My voice sounds like I've been on an all-night booze-and-sex binge. "Ready, angel?"

She wraps her arms around my neck, plants her feet on the mattress, and lifts her hips to me as if she can't wait another second. "Stop talking."

If I could spare a second or a brain cell for amusement, that would make me smile. But I can't. Instead, I reach down and line up the crest of my cock against her opening. She's so fucking wet, and my eyes nearly roll back in my head at the sensation, at the thought that I'm almost inside her again.

I stretch my body out on top of hers, sliding my palms up her arms until I'm curling our fingers together. We're touching foreheads, bumping noses, tangling breaths. Britta lies beneath me, pinned to the mattress, unmoving, watching, waiting…

I brace my knees for leverage, then thrust inside her with one deep stroke. Instantly, she gasps, twists, arches. I can't stop my invading surge. Straining and undulating, she squeezes my fingers, gripping hard, and moans my name.

When I'm finally in to the hilt, totally submerged in her tight heat, it's all I can do not to pummel her like a jackhammer. She feels beyond anything I remembered, everything I've ever wanted.

I pause, drag in a breath. I have to keep myself together and make this good for her.

"Did I hurt you?"

"No," she gasps out.

But she can't seem to stay still. I'm gritting my teeth, trying not to rock with her yet so she can adjust to the feel of me inside her. And yeah, I'm savoring this hard-won moment.

But she's killing my control.

"What's the problem?" I murmur.

She tosses her head, neck arching. All that sensuality I remember awakening once upon a time unfurls for me again. She's beautiful, graceful, and so much woman I can't wait another moment.

"Fuck me. Please…" Britta sounds like she's in pain with wanting.

I'm not rejoicing at her demand. "I used to make you say that when you wanted me, but not anymore. That's not what this is about. I'm making love to you, Britta. That's all I'm ever going to do."

Sure, we'll get raunchy and desperate and hungry sometimes. We'll be in the mood to fuck, and there's no way I'll say no. But under it all, I'll be making love to her every single time she'll let me.

Britta bucks up against me as she squeezes her eyes shut, then opens them to stare, gauge my expression. I feel her in the telltale tingling at the small of my back, which tells me I'm too aroused to hold out much longer. I feel her all the way down to my balls, already aching and full. I definitely feel her in my heart, where she's filled every corner with herself and the promise of tomorrow.

She's mine again—body and soul.

I'm going to take her so thoroughly she'll never forget it.

In the silvery shadows, her eyes soften. "Love me, Griff. Always love me."

"That's all I've ever wanted, angel."

Then we don't need words anymore. I cover her lips with my own and find my way inside even as I fill her with slow, controlled thrusts. Quick withdrawals, unhurried plunges forward. Methodical. Rhythmic. Torturous.

Beneath me, Britta goes wild, heaving and wriggling as she whimpers and pleads wordlessly for more while giving me her all. It was always good with her, every single time. But this pleasure is agonizing, honed like a knife's edge. It's excruciating as it opens me up, takes me apart. And with every thrust, I don't care. I have Britta, so I have everything I need.

Beneath me, she's fierce as she fights for the ecstasy we've worked so hard to share. It's the bliss I plan to experience with her for the rest of our days.

My senses zero in on her. Concentration narrows until there's nothing and no one else. My thoughts scatter. My body takes over. Restraint evaporates.

I turn animal.

Propelling inside her with all the force in my body, I hammer her again. Again. Again. The bed sheets bunch. The mattress jumps the frame. Her nails dig into the backs of my hands. Her keening cries split the air. I feel her tightening. It's getting serious. Dangerous. Inevitable.

"Give everything to me," I demand. "Give it. Now."

Her body jolts, freezes, then bucks wildly as I feel her clamp down on me, seizing me, as she shouts out a climax that comes from deep inside her. Sweating, I push through, plunging in, one stroke after another, as desire pools at the base of my cock, heats until I swear she's burning me, then zips through my body in an explosion that not only staggers my libido but destroys my soul. I've just lost everything to this woman— body, head, heart. It's all hers now. And forever.

That makes me smile.

My thrusts slow, along with our breathing. I finally release my harsh grip on her fingers and gather her up in my arms. I don't want to move. I just want to stay entwined with Britta, attached and attuned to her.

But I'm probably crushing her.

I prop up on my elbows and look down at her face, caressing the skeins of her fair hair away from her honeyed face, glowing with a supreme look of satisfaction.

"That was…" I don't even have words to describe it. "Beyond."

"And more." She nods with a suddenly shy smile. "It was everything I wanted."

"I feel so close to you, like we've managed to work past the walls dividing us."

A little frown that bothers me settles between her brows. "I hope so."

What else could there be? Sure, maybe we've both got some details we haven't shared. But they're not important now. We've taken the risk, found the courage. And held tight to one another again. "I know so, angel. We've been through a lot, but it was worth it. I love you."

She smiles softly at me once more, and my whole heart flips over in my chest. Everything about being with her—minus any of my usual barriers—has scraped me red and raw.

"You're right. Now…can we do that again?"

CHAPTER EIGHTEEN

THE SOUNDS OF WAVES CRASHING and the tapping of a keyboard wake me the next morning. I roll over and open my eyes with a scowl. I don't want to face the real world after such a delicious night with Britta, of being inside her over and over. We made love in bed, on the lanai, against the wall... I couldn't let her get two steps away from me without tangling myself up with her again.

About midnight, I crept down the hall to make sure Harlow and Jamie made it back. They were both curled up in the queen-size bed, Jamie in a pair of Spiderman pajamas we had in his diaper bag, sacked out. I don't hear noise now, so I'll bet they're sleeping in. We all should be.

So why is Britta sitting across the room, typing and clicking on her laptop?

"Angel?" My voice cracks from lack of sleep. "If I didn't wear you out enough, come over here so I can try again."

She gives me a nervous giggle, then shoves her laptop away. "Just taking care of a few last-minute things... But if you want to muss me up, I should shower first and give you the chance to do it right."

When she rises, she's wearing a clinging white silk robe. Through it, I see the beads of her nipples, the cinch of her waist, the curves of her hips, the delta outlined between her thighs.

I already had morning wood, but now it's not a reflex; it's for real and ready. This woman does something to me every time I see her.

"Come here…" I coax, crooking my finger and looking at her like I want to eat her for breakfast, lunch, and dinner. Actually, it's not a bad idea.

She flushes sweetly but shakes her head. "What if I play hard to get?"

"What if I pin you down and fuck you again?"

"What a bad man, always saying things to tempt me…" She shakes her head, tsking. It's all playful, flirtatious as she walks past me, casting a come-hither glance over her shoulder.

"I always will." I rise from bed to follow her. I don't care that I'm stark-ass naked. My raging erection is like a divining rod following her wherever she goes.

I should be sated. Hell, I should be sore. Nope. I just want Britta again.

"After my shower," she insists, batting her long lashes. "You want me to smell good, don't you?"

She knows putting me off only makes me harder. We used to play this game. I called it *one more thing…* She would invent a task she needed to complete before we could make love. Then another and another—until I held her down, tore at her clothes, and fucked her breathless. I've missed this. I've ached to play with her.

"You smell fine now. Like sex. Like a woman. Like I've been all over you. I told you to come here."

She reaches into the walk-in shower and flips on the water, then doubles back with a ghost of a smile. "You did. Oops."

Oh, she's going to pay for that. The too-innocent expression she's wearing tells me she knows it—and is looking forward to it.

But as I saunter toward her, I see something else I couldn't at a distance. The set of her eyes is taut. So is her mouth. She's nervous. Worried.

The games can wait. I close the distance between us and take her hand. "What's wrong?"

"Nothing."

The lie is too fast. Something is definitely troubling her. After the night we just shared, how could she possibly be upset?

I rack my mental checklist. She knows I love her. We're great together. I gloved up every time. Jamie is fine, and if Britta was awake before me, I'm sure she checked on him. In my head, that only leaves our past…or our future. The former feels as if we've put so much of it to rest. How could it be a problem anymore? She finally believes I'm sincere about wanting only her for the rest of my life. And she has a functioning understanding about the reasons I've had trouble trusting.

"I'm fine," she offers and drops her robe.

As it pools on the tile floor, I gape at her body. I don't mean to. It's just unavoidable. I see the girl who became a woman in my arms. I also see the changes in her body pregnancy wrought. Most of all, I see perfection.

She scrambles my brain even more by leaning in and kissing me. It's not a simple peck. Her kiss is a long press filled with something I don't understand. Anxiety pours off her. Now I'm really worried.

I pull back and take her shoulders. "Britta?"

The smile she gives me is totally false. She's hiding tears as she cups my cheek. "I love you, Griff."

I stop, stunned utterly silent. Is that what's unnerved her, telling me? I've waited nearly two months to hear her say that to me again. "Oh, angel…"

She wriggles gently from my grasp, gives me one last smile that isn't happy at all, then disappears into the shower.

And she leaves me standing there, so confused. I want to be thrilled right now. Fuck that, I should be exultant. But I can't feel anything except gnawing worry until I know what's troubling her. If it's not our past, it must be our future. Does she think that, after last night, there's any way I'm not putting that ring on her finger?

I stride out of the bathroom and head straight toward my sock drawer. I can fix this. And I'm going to. The last thing I ever want is for her to worry again about the two of us. We're solid. I'm hers. And I'm beyond eager to make it legal.

As I round the bed, I see the bright screen of her laptop shining in the shadowed corner. Did something she read upset her?

What's on her screen is a hotel reservation. The Four Seasons. One phrase in big, bright text snags my attention: HONEYMOON PACKAGE.

What the hell is she up to?

I walk past it, turning the conundrum over in my head, and reach for the knob of the sock drawer. But those words keep poking my brain. Whose honeymoon? Maxon and Keeley have decided they would rather spend a few days alone in their new house than leave the island to enjoy their newly married bliss. Britta has no idea I've been planning a surprise wedding for us in six days, unless...

I march across the room and snatch up my phone. Yes, I know Keeley and my brother just tied the knot yesterday. I'll make my intrusion short. And I'll do something deeply apologetic later.

I dial Keeley. After a few rings, my bestie answers, sounding a little hoarse and breathless. "Griff?"

Guilt hits me. I'm being selfish. I'm being an ass. Sometimes, it's a reflex. "Sorry. One question. Did you tell Britta what I have planned next week?"

"No." Her answer is quick and emphatic. "I swear."

I believe her. Keeley is a lot of things, but a liar isn't one of them. "Nothing slipped out? There's no way she might have guessed?"

"Impossible. We mostly talked about the frogs we kissed before we met our princes. Hey... Maxon!"

I hear rustling, laughter, a growl. That's my cue. I have what I need anyway. "I'll let you go. Thanks."

More rustling, then something that sounds a lot like a male snarl. "Hey, asshole. Piss off until I say otherwise, okay? Love you, bro."

Three beeps fill my ear, then silence.

I shake my head. I can't not smile at Maxon's craziness...but this mystery is bugging the hell out of me. If Britta doesn't know about our wedding next weekend, what is she doing looking at honeymoon packages at a swanky hotel online?

With a sharp glance back toward the bathroom, I see the steam still rising. I hear the water still running.

Yeah, I'm a rat bastard when it comes to my woman. Sue me.

But I'm going to get to the bottom of this now.

Stalking back to Britta's computer, I pry the lid open more and sink into the chair as I read her screen.

She confirmed her reservation for the honeymoon suite at the Four Seasons next Saturday night. Why? I frown. She doesn't know she's marrying me next weekend. Keeley just confirmed that. How does she know she needs a honeymoon suite for the night of the fifteenth?

Unless she's still planning to marry Makaio that day, like she has been for months.

Maybe the time has come to think with my head. I need someone I can depend on. I need a family sedan, Griff. You're a Ferrari.

The bottom falls out of my gut. No. Fuck no. She's not serious. She can't be. She spent all night with me. Together with me in every way. She finally told me she loves me.

Maybe, dumb ass, that was her way of saying good-bye.

My head is buzzing with shock, but I can feel anger stretching, growing, rising like the pressure of a volcano about to spew lava. No, there must be some explanation. She wouldn't do this to me. Britta isn't the sort of woman to lead someone on. She's done with Makaio. She said so...

He doesn't belong between us anymore. That's all she murmured when I asked if she was marrying the moron.

I blink at the computer screen, stare, trying to wrap my brain around the obvious. She didn't actually say she was done with him. She certainly didn't confirm that she wasn't marrying him.

So what she really said was that Makaio doesn't belong between us anymore because she's going to surf off into the sunset with the Hawaiian banker and leave me for good.

The water from the shower cuts off. The door opens. "Griff? I forgot to grab my towel. Can you help me?"

I stand rooted in disbelief. How did the best night of my life become the worst morning ever? I get this slippery sense of déjà vu. I've been here, Britta squeaky clean and dripping as I realize the enormity of her betrayal. But last time I was dead wrong. I was a flaming idiot who jumped to all kinds of conclusions.

I roll through my logic again, but it all snaps together like snug pieces of a perfectly obvious puzzle.

She never had any intention of not marrying Makaio. Oh, she took off his ring to humor me. But she refused to wear mine. She lived with me because I didn't give her a choice. I convinced myself she had one. I assured myself there was no way she would choose that dipshit over me. And why? Because I didn't want to believe it. Just like I didn't want to believe she could string me along.

I never wanted to believe Julia could, either. Look where that got me.

Is this resentment? Is this her payback? Or did she just never really give a shit?

Goddamn it, I won't be Britta's fool.

I stomp into the bathroom and grab a towel off the counter. I toss it at her with a snarl and try not to notice how naked she is. "How fucking dare you?"

She doesn't act at all surprised as she wraps the terrycloth around her. "You saw my computer?"

"You're damn right I did. When were you going to tell me?" I get up in her face and scowl. "Friday night while you were packing your bags to run off and marry another man? Or did you plan to fuck me one more time, *cheat* on him like you did last night, then get up Saturday morning and speak your forever vows to him?"

She doesn't say anything, just stares, lips pressed together like she can't speak.

"Well?" I prod. "Did you enjoy it? Did you laugh? Yeah, I'll bet you did. I made an ass out of myself. I turned both our lives upside down to be with you. I tried to open up and be romantic—all the things Keeley said you needed from me. I fucking told you things I've never told anyone."

I still can't believe it. She's stabbing me in the heart—for real this time—and it doesn't make any sense.

Please explain it away. Please tell me I'm wrong. Please…

"That's what you think?" Tears well in her eyes, then fall down her freshly scrubbed face in silvery tracks.

She looks so young. Hell, so innocent. What is happening here? "What the fuck else do you want me to think? Britta…if I'm wrong, tell me I'm wrong."

"No."

Shouldering her way past me, she makes for the bedroom and shimmies into panties and a bra. I watch, dumbfounded. "That's all you have to say? No, what? No, I'm wrong? Or no, you're not going to tell me anything?"

Silence.

"Goddamn it, I've been fighting for us. I've done everything I know to make you love me again. To make you believe in us again. And this is what you do?"

She opens the closet. Her back is facing me, but I see her shaking. I hear the sobs. She's heartbroken, but I don't understand. I haven't ripped us apart. She has. She wanted me to see her computer, planned it that way. Why the hell should she suddenly be verklempt?

After pulling down the first two garments in front of her, she tosses on a pair of capri pants and a T-shirt, then storms past me again, towel in hand, and heads to the bathroom. Tears stream in earnest down her face.

She's behaving as if I've somehow wronged her. I don't understand. She never intended to stay with me. She led me on. She basically admitted it. What can I possibly be missing?

I grab her arm. "Talk to me."

"I think you've said enough for both of us." Britta wrenches free from my grip, then makes her way to the bathroom woodenly, on autopilot. She shoves her hair in a wet ponytail, then grabs her suitcase from the linen closet.

My jaw drops. "You're leaving?"

"Give me one reason not to." She blinks at me, waiting, looking so desolate.

I'm confused as shit. Does she want me to slice my heart open and bleed for her one more time before she marries someone else?

To hell with that.

I toss my hands in the air. "I think I'm all out of them, angel. I've done everything I know to win you back, and apparently you'd already made up your mind. But hey, at least we had a night of great sex before you decided to fuck off."

"So that's what you think? And you're done?"

What the hell? I look at her as if she suddenly spoke Greek. That's how much I comprehend her question. "What else do you want? I can't do it all for both of us. I sure as hell can't keep twisting your arm to be with me. I can't keep telling you I love you when you don't care in return. I can't—"

Suddenly, I choke. Emotion is closing my throat. My eyes sting. I can't speak. I will not cry in front of this woman. I refuse to cry for her again.

"Am I a backstabbing bitch?" she challenges, eyes narrowed.

That's what I called her three years ago before I walked out. She's baiting me. Why? Something inside tells me not to take it, but my temper grabs my tongue. I'm so angry. I feel so fucking betrayed. How could she do this? How did I not see it? Just...how did we wind up here, again a week short of being together forever?

"Yes. Goddamn you!"

"Well, you're a bastard, Griff." She opens the suitcase and sweeps everything on the counter inside. Bottles and tins rattle and clink to the bottom. Then she dumps it on the ground, opens the cabinet, and tosses everything under the sink on top. I watch in disbelief as she zips it shut with angry jerks. "I believed in you this time. I did the first time, too. But you think I would have learned. Nope. I'm still the stupid girl who falls for the same asshole who already hurt her once. Fool me once, shame on you..." She yanks up the collapsible handle of the suitcase. "Guess I'm the one who should be ashamed this time."

"Seriously? *I* hurt *you*? You're the one marrying someone else. What the fuck do you think I did this time?"

"It's not what you did. It's what you didn't do. You couldn't give me the thing I needed from you most: trust. Without it, we have nothing." She rolls her bag out the bathroom and through the bedroom.

I follow. "Trust?"

"This time, just like last time, when you saw something that looked damning, you didn't ask me to explain. You just assumed. You accused. And you ended things between us." She shrugs. "I'm just beating you out the door this time."

I freeze. Tell me I didn't fuck up again. Please tell me I didn't make the same mistake twice.

"So you're not marrying Makaio next Saturday?" I ask, my voice so muted I barely recognize it.

If she says she is, I'll have been right. But it's a small fucking consolation. If she says she's not, I'll have fucked up. Again. I will have to live with the fact that I screwed up in exactly the same way.

But either way, she'll be gone.

I shut my eyes.

"I'm not," she says finally.

Her voice is like a death knell on my heart. Her sniffle puts the final nail in the coffin I shoved the lid on with my own two hands.

I almost demand to know why she simply didn't tell me that I was wrong, that Makaio wasn't in the picture. But I understand the answer now. She wanted me to trust her. She needed to know that I would give her the benefit of the doubt, not automatically convict her in my mind. She needed me to believe in us.

I failed.

"I'm sorry," I blurt. "I lost my temper. I didn't think. I—"

"And I have no reason to think it wouldn't happen again. That you wouldn't simply assume the worst. If I wasn't leaving right now, you would have beaten me to it and walked out on me again." I open my mouth to protest, but she holds up a hand. "Don't lie to me. Or yourself. Griff, I can't let you break my heart anymore. And I won't let you break Jamie's. I'm leaving now. Don't stop me."

She turns away, reaching for the knob of the bedroom door.

I don't have any illusions. Once she walks out, I will be at less than square one with Britta. I will be nothing to her.

Air freezes in my lungs. My thoughts race. What can I do? What can I say? How can I stop this shattering of my heart?

My hand shakes as I reach out, drop my palm on her shoulder. "Please. Don't go."

Nothing else comes out. I've told her I love her. I've said I'm sorry. I've tried to explain.

Too little, too late.

"Griff…" She shakes off my touch.

I need to keep her talking. I need to understand.

I drag in a deep breath, and my temper finally downshifts. Logic kicks in. "When did you decide you weren't going to marry Makaio?"

"It doesn't matter now."

"It does. Help me understand."

She hesitates, then glances at me over her shoulder. "In the beginning, I didn't think you could do or say anything to change my mind. I was so angry at you for barging into my life and trying to screw it up again. But you explained Tiffanii and your failure to acknowledge Jamie. Then you caught him at the park. And you kissed me. God, after that I was so furious at you for making me think about you and want you again. But I couldn't seem to fight it, no matter how hard I tried." She clenches her fists. "But then, I caught bronchitis and Makaio refused to take care of me. He left me to cope. Left Jamie exposed to my germs. And I kept thinking, if we're going to be married, doesn't 'in sickness and in heath' mean anything? And if that vow is meaningless to him, what else will he shrug off?"

"You were having second thoughts eight weeks ago?"

She turns to me finally and nods. "I was still undecided, teetering, but you kept pursuing me. You wanted me—and Jamie. You wouldn't take no for an answer. You seemed so different, like the man I needed you to be all along."

"Then what?" I rasp.

"When you proposed, I was shocked that you actually did love me back then. I never knew. I wanted and hoped… And I'm so touched that you held on to that ring, like you subconsciously hoped you would marry me someday. That night, I knew I had to stop resisting you simply to protect myself. That night, I knew I couldn't marry Makaio."

Her voice is shaking, and I want to touch her again so badly. I didn't see any of this. Why was I so fucking stupid?

"Then you kept being wonderful, helpful, understanding. And okay, ruthless. It probably sounds weird, but you forcing me to move in with you reinforced how much you wanted to be with me. The night you didn't touch me in the tub told me you were really trying to be good for me. I know that was hard."

"Not to touch you? Torture."

"But you respected my feelings."

I sigh, my shoulders falling with my breath. "I wanted to be a better man for you."

She doesn't acknowledge my comment. It's silent subtext that I failed. "The following Monday, I had lunch with Makaio—"

"You were crying." Suddenly everything makes sense. "You ended the engagement. You gave him back his ring."

"I did. We haven't been engaged for weeks."

Incredulity roars through me. Elation followed by despair crashes in next. Finally, confusion settles in. "Why didn't you tell me then? Or anytime since?"

"Before I could completely commit, I needed to know if you really, truly had changed…or if you were simply a smoother talker than you were before. I needed you to understand how it felt to wonder if I loved you, even after you gave your all. Even when we lived and worked together as a couple. I needed you to let all your barriers go and give yourself wholly, without exception or hesitation." She casts her stare to the ceiling, and I know she's fighting fresh tears. "I needed you to know how I felt three years ago so you wouldn't do it to me again. So you wouldn't hurt your own son. And you passed every test, one after the other, so I let myself hope. So I gave you every bit of myself last night and went to bed praying that—"

She breaks into a sob and hides her face in her hands.

I bend to her, wrap her in my arms. "Britta, angel…"

"No!" She surges away from me. "No. Keeley told me last night that I should plan something special for us next Saturday night, so I did. But I woke up this morning so in love…and with so many niggling doubts. What if I was wrong? What if you left me again? So I left my laptop lid up to see what you would do." She chokes on a sob. "Now I know."

Her eyes look so bleak, inconsolable. Her world is falling apart. She didn't see it coming. She believed in me.

God, I hate what I've done. Who I am right now. I won't ask what the fuck is wrong with me. I know the answer.

I don't know what to say to Britta, but I know that saying I'm sorry won't mean a damn thing. I can't unbreak her heart.

So what can I say? A thousand thoughts blaze across my brain. *I'll be better. I'll try harder. I'll love you more than any man ever will.*

Right now, with her emotions shattered all over the floor, none of that will matter to her.

"I'm going to grab Jamie and go. I'll make arrangements to get the rest of my things later. I'll call Maxon tomorrow and tell him I've resigned. Tell your sister and Keeley I said good-bye. Have my lawyer call yours to work out visitation." More tears fall down her cheeks. "I hope someday you come to terms with whatever's haunting you."

By the time I blink back a sting of wetness from my eyes, she's gone.

CHAPTER NINETEEN

MY LIFE IS OVER. NOT literally, of course. But life as I dreamed of it? I doubt there's much I can do to revive that. It's been five days since Britta left me and the palatial paradise we shared, taking my son with her. As promised, she hired someone to retrieve the rest of her things, along with Jamie's clothes, toys, and necessities. The house has felt like over ten thousand square feet of pure emptiness since then. Sure, my sister is still here. She means well. She tries to talk to me, cheer me up.

It's not helping. Nothing is.

On Monday, Maxon lost his shit when Britta quit. I guess he didn't believe me when I forewarned him. In fact, he and Keeley spent most of the Sunday afternoon following Britta's departure with me. I'm sure dealing with my catastrophic breakup is not what they wanted to do on their first full day of marriage. But I'm grateful they came.

"I don't think what Britta did was fair to you," Harlow insisted just last night. "She laid landmines in front of you, then got angry when you stepped on them. She set you up to fail."

It's sweet that she wants to be so loyal and take my side. But she's wrong. I didn't see the landmines because I didn't even stop to look. I made the same mistake now that I did three years ago by treating Britta with distrust before love. And, righteously cloaked in all my wronged fury, I cut her because she made me bleed.

I don't have the energy to argue with Harlow—or anyone. I haven't slept in days. I certainly can't lie in the bed Britta and I shared. I can't find any peace.

Hell, I don't think I even deserve it.

My phone buzzes in my pocket. I pry my eyes open and realize the sun is coming up at my back. I wince at the brightness of the cloudless dawn. I have a splitting headache, and my back is killing me. But drinking Lagavulin out of the bottle and falling asleep at two a.m. on a lounger splayed across the lanai will do that. All I can think of is that my dream wedding should have been tomorrow. If I'd been smart, I would have cancelled everything and gotten what refunds I could. That might have saved me a small fortune. But I couldn't bring myself to do it. Some stupid part of me can't stop hoping...

The phone buzzes again. I fish it out of my pocket to turn it off. I don't want any more well-meaning texts and phone calls. Especially since I don't know yet what to say or do. I want to fight for Britta...just as much as I'm sure she'll hate me even more if I do. I don't need my tribe's feel-good chatter telling me to give it another go.

With a sigh, I look at the screen. Keeley has been texting me for an hour. Call me. Call me now. Call me, damn it.

I can't accuse her of being inconsistent.

Moving like someone a few days shy of becoming a centenarian, I unfold myself from the lounger and head inside, empty bottle in hand. I feel like shit. I'm sure I look like it, too. I can't remember my last meal. I don't even miss food.

I don't miss anything except Britta and Jamie.

God, I sound pathetic. And hungover. Definitely that.

When I walk in the house, Harlow is standing in the kitchen, coffee cup in hand. She watches as I toss the bottle in the trash. Shaking her head, she gives the steaming mug to me, regarding me with a disparaging glance. Yes, I'm sure I look sketchy. I probably smell it, too.

"Want to talk yet?" she asks as I grab the cup and take a sip of the wickedly black brew. She makes java unapologetically strong.

"Do I have a choice?" I force myself to swallow. That shit could acid-wash the chrome off a bumper.

"Not really."

Didn't think so. "Is it just you or the whole intervention team?"

"Just me...for now."

I don't ask for clarification. If Harlow can reason with me, she won't call for reinforcements. Got it.

"Can I shower first?"

"Are you finally going to do something today besides drink, beat the shit out of the punching bag upstairs, and sulk?"

"Gosh, Harlow. You really have to stop sparing my feelings. Just say what's on your mind."

She laughs. "Well, if your sarcasm is back, I hope that means the rest of you will be soon, too. Shower. I'll make you breakfast. You're going to eat it. Then—"

"I need to decide whether I'm going to give up and be a miserable bastard for the rest of my life or fight—again—for the woman who will always own my heart. Is that what you were going to say?" I raise a brow at her.

Her green eyes flare in surprise. "Something like that."

I sigh. There's no escaping her pep talk. I have to suck it up. And maybe...maybe it will be good for me to have another female's perspective. Though with a bastard of a father and two competitive older brothers, Harlow's feminine outlook on life ranks somewhere between auto mechanic and rugby player.

"I'll be back in fifteen." I head for the stairs.

"Make it ten," she shouts after me.

I acknowledge her with a wave of my hand and find a bottle of ibuprofen in the medicine cabinet. As I start the shower, I try not to look at Britta's empty counter or remember her swiping everything in her suitcase as, tears rolling, she left me for good.

I'm not very successful.

After a punishingly hot shower and a few more sips of caffeine, I feel marginally better. My brain even starts to kick in again, what-iffing and unfolding scenarios. How much will I always regret it if I give Britta the moral victory and simply leave her alone? How shitty will I feel? A lot. Terribly. But this isn't about me. How unloved will Britta feel if I don't even try? How bitter? What about Jamie? He needs a father.

And I can't leave everyone shattered because I didn't have the balls to try again.

Harlow is shouting that my time is up when I toss on a pair of clean shorts and a T-shirt, then run my electric razor vaguely over my stubble. I slide into flip-flops and run down the stairs. My headache protests, pounding until it feels as if my brain is trying to push my eyes out of their sockets. I grimace and cradle my head as I enter the kitchen.

"Maybe that will teach you to stop substituting Scotch for dinner."

I glare her way. "A beacon of compassion... What did I ever do to deserve such a wonderful sister?"

That makes her laugh. "I am wonderful. I'm going to straighten your shit out." She shakes her head. "Men are so dumb."

She's plating eggs as I toss myself onto a stool at the breakfast bar and nurse more coffee. "I'll ask you what that means only because you'll tell me whether I want to know or not."

Harlow pauses, hand on hip. "Stop being snarky."

"Sorry. Predictably, I'm not in a great mood. But yes, I know I need to do something today. I know I can't walk away forever and prove to Britta once and for all that I'm an incredible shithead."

"I was going to say dumb ass, but the rest of the speech is about right." She flips a couple of pancakes onto my plate, then slams butter and syrup down in front of me. "You weren't an asshole, Griff. You were stupid. I still stand by my statement that she set you up. But given your history together, I would have needed some proof to take back the dirtbag who crushed me once, too. This is a heap of complicated."

"Yep." I shovel in some eggs because I know I'm going to need energy later. "I don't know how to simplify that."

"This is why men are so stupid." She shakes her head. "There's a reason you keep doing the impulsively idiotic thing. Something makes you believe the worst. Do you do that to all people or just women? You don't even have to tell me. But you need to tell Britta. Whatever it is, no matter how ugly. Unless you come clean, she will never understand you. If you don't and if she gives you another chance, you will be doomed to repeat this cycle again."

Leave it to brutally honest Harlow to cut through five days of my confusion and lay it all out in a few sentences while forking in some pancakes. Granted, I'd somewhat arrived at this conclusion last night in my Scotch-induced stupor.

But it sucks.

Telling Britta about Julia gave her the power to hurt me. Telling her the rest... She could utterly destroy me.

Then again, can't she already, simply by not being with me?

"I know."

"Then why are you sitting here with me?"

"Because you told me to," I remind her. "And because I'm actually hungry."

At that, my sister smiles, whipping a mass of dark curls off her shoulder and behind her back. "Glad to hear it. You need to go get your woman back. And you need to convince her to marry you tomorrow."

Because that won't be challenging at all. I smirk at Harlow. "Thanks, doc."

"I'll send you my bill later."

"If you're so damn smart, why are you marrying a man you don't love?"

She freezes, fork filled with eggs halfway to her mouth. Slowly, she lowers it. "We're compatible. Simon is easy to get along with...and easy on the eyes. We both want kids. He'll never demand attention if I'm busy working. He's a logical choice."

But his behavior just before the wedding... He's utterly ignoring her. Doesn't she care? "Twenty bucks says he's cheating on you."

Harlow tries to shrug but falters. "I know he probably does when he's on the road. But is that really the most important thing in a marriage? He's kind. He'll never do half the shit Dad did to Mom. And I won't fall in love with him so he can't break me."

I stare at her like she's lost her mind. "So the most he has to recommend is that he won't be asshole enough to hurt you but you won't care because he's not interesting enough to fall for? Why get married at all?"

My sister glares at me and scoops up her plate. "I don't want to be alone. Simon is fine. It will be…fine."

Fine? "A pretty day is fine. Vanilla ice cream is fine. Flowers are fine. Love should be more than that."

"I'm not looking for it. I'm glad that you and Maxon found it but…" She dumps her plate in the sink with most of her food still on it. "Yeah, that shit's not for me. I'm going to…"

When she seems to search for words, I swallow my next bite and try to help her. "Run on the elliptical? Take a shower?"

She shakes her head. "End this conversation. Putting me and love in the same sentence gives me hives. Hey, I need to know if we should keep all the wedding plans tomorrow as is or start bailing on what we can?"

"Leave it. I'll do my best to get Britta there. If it doesn't work…" At least I'll have gotten to see it, and I'll be able to close my eyes and imagine our perfect wedding for a brief, bittersweet moment. If I can't have her anymore, at least I'll have that memory.

"All right."

Her expression tells me I'm crazy. Maybe I am.

She waves as she heads up the stairs. "Good luck."

Yeah, I'm going to need it.

HOW THE FUCK DID I get here?

An hour after breakfast with my sister, I sit outside of Britta's little blue house. There's a FOR SALE sign in the yard.

My heart still stops at the sight.

The longer I sit in my Porsche and stare at her door, the more I refuse to give up on her without one last attempt. If she doesn't want me—us—even after I've given her every part of myself... Well, there's nothing more I can give her.

I check to make certain I have everything I need in my pockets, then I head to the front door. Her car is under the carport. There's a sign in the window proclaiming it for sale, too. Yes, she might have decided it's time for a new car. It sounds more likely that she's decided to leave Maui.

Guts twisting, palms sweating, I knock and wait the longest thirty seconds of my life for her to open the door.

Finally, she cracks it. Her golden hair is slicked into a ponytail. Her face is as bare as her feet. She's wearing a pair of short denim cutoffs and a too-big Hawaiian-print blouse with the tails tied at her slender waist. I can't go down the rabbit hole of being aroused by the sight of her. I've got too many important things to say. But I can't help being a man. I think of the perfect night we spent together last weekend. I wish to fuck I could go back there and do it all again and make different choices the next morning.

But I have to play the hand I idiotically dealt myself.

"Griff." She bites her lip. "What are you doing here?"

"I'd like to talk to you." I glance across the yard. "You're moving off the island?"

"Yeah. The landlord called me on Tuesday and told me he'd decided to sell the house. So it seemed like the right time to head back to Chicago."

She's not just leaving the island; she's leaving me. Her mother has always tried to tempt her to go back home. Maybe, with nothing to tie Britta to Maui anymore, she's relented.

My gut seizes up. If I don't succeed today, I'll be lucky if I see Jamie once a year. I'll be a name, a picture, and a voice to him at most. Britta will only speak to me through lawyers. But if my gamble doesn't pay off, I won't even have that.

"You hate Chicago."

She stifles whatever is on the tip of her tongue. "What else do we have to say? I'm pretty sure we said all we needed to the other morning."

"I just want one conversation. Can I come in and talk to you? That's all; just talk."

When Britta blocks the entry through the door with her body and looks like she's going to refuse me, I blurt, "I have something you want."

"You don't." She shakes her head. "You don't have a damn thing I want anymore, Griffin Reed."

I dig into the pocket of my shorts and take out the papers she gave me weeks ago to force me to relinquish my rights to Jamie. "If you give me thirty minutes, I'll sign them. And you never have to see me again."

It guts me to offer her that. Hell, to even think it. The thought of never seeing Britta or my son again is a physical ache twisting my stomach. My chest is on the brink of imploding. I'm making the biggest gamble of my life. If I lose, I can't even imagine how it will decimate me.

I never wanted to sign the papers. Normally, I would refuse for the rest of my fucking life. But it's literally the only way I know to persuade Britta to listen. To save us.

Finally, she sighs and opens the door wide enough to admit me. "Thirty minutes."

"Is Jamie here?" When she nods, I look around for my son. "Can I see him before the clock starts?"

Before Britta can even call him, he comes toddling down the hall, holding a book in one hand and a truck in the other.

"Daddy!"

I run to scoop him up and hold him close. He smells like baby powder and peanut butter and sunshine. Grief twists my insides when I think this may be the last time I hold him. I can't imagine it. This can't be it.

"Jamie, boy," I manage to croak out. "I missed you, buddy."

He wriggles out of my grip and tries to hand me his truck. "Can we play?"

"Not right now, young man," Britta says softly. "You're supposed to be taking a nap."

"Don't want my crib," he insists. "I want da big-boy bed."

It's still at the Stowe estate, in the room adjoining the master. It's the only thing in there that reminds me Jamie once slept feet away from me. Everything else of my son's is gone.

"I know. How about if I let you sleep in my bed?" When Jamie looks unsure, Britta throws in a sweetener. "And ice cream for dessert."

"Yeah!" the little boy cheers, then looks my way. "Can we play later?"

Britta sends me a warning glance. Don't make promises I can't keep. Right.

"We'll see," I say finally. "I hope so."

"Go on." Britta shoos him down the hall and into her room. I hear a fan engage. Then she shuts the door behind her.

I stand awkwardly in the foyer, waiting. She glances at her watch.

The clock is ticking.

"You can't talk your way out of what you did, Griff. You can't apologize. I know you love me...in your way. I love you. Unfortunately, that doesn't change anything. I can't trust you to trust me." She meanders to the sofa and sits with a heavy sigh. "You're broken. And if I stay, you'll break me, as well."

I follow and sit beside her on the couch, gripping my thighs so I don't give in to the urge to touch her. "That's what I want to talk to you about. I want you to understand why. Even if it doesn't change anything between us, at least you'll know the reason I broke us apart twice, and maybe you'll see that I never meant to hurt you."

She crosses her legs away from me, arms wrapped around her waist. Everything about her body language screams at me to keep my distance. I'm on my end of the sofa, doing my best to respect that.

"I'm listening," she murmurs.

"I told you about Julia."

She nods. "I know she hurt you but—"

"She wasn't the problem, just the final straw." I swallow, feeling like I'm going to choke on the boulder of my past. It's stuck in my throat, suffocating me. "It started months before that. When I turned sixteen, my dad thought it would be a great rite of passage to get me laid, so he brought me to his office and set me up with his assistant and mistress, AnnaBeth. She was twenty-three. She couldn't type at all…but my father hired her because he wanted her to bang out more than correspondence. I didn't know her. I didn't even like her."

"He *told* you to have sex with her?"

"What he said was that he'd made the same offer to Maxon with his previous assistant, Danielle. My brother passed on the opportunity to 'become a man.' Dad mocked Maxon and made his life hell from that day forward. He constantly referred to my brother as a coward and a pussy. I didn't want Dad's needling and contempt. So I told myself losing my virginity was no big deal." I shrug. "After all, I was sixteen and horny. Sex with her was better than randomly choosing some girl at school to deflower. I was happy to skip the blind-leading-the-blind thing. If not AnnaBeth, it would have been someone else. I had a lot of excuses for why this was okay. My dad always said relationships were a waste, and after seeing him and Mom constantly at each other's throats, I didn't want one."

"They're toxic together," Britta agrees quietly.

I nod. "They feed each other's worst tendencies. I'm glad they're finally getting divorced and ending their thirty-five years of lying, cheating, and misery."

"I can't disagree." Her face softens. "So you had sex with this woman?"

"A lot of it."

Britta looks somewhere between stunned and horrified. "She just…let you?"

"She was happy to. She said having sex in the office was way better than working."

My angel's expression asks me if I'm kidding. She must know I'm not. "What a—"

"Yeah. But Dad was glad to have a 'real man' as a son, so he hired me to work after school. I thought I wanted to follow in his professional footsteps. According to him, I had the killer instinct. And the market was volatile that year. He claimed he wanted to train an analyst the 'right way.' What he really meant was that he was traveling a lot and wanted someone to keep AnnaBeth thoroughly occupied whom he could control."

"You," she says, her voice painfully quiet.

I've barely started, and she's already nearly mute. Believe me, I'm not thrilled about my sordid sexual past, either. "Exactly."

"Your dad wasn't any sort of responsible father. You weren't even old enough to consent. That woman raped you repeatedly."

I give her an ugly scoff. "I never saw myself as a victim. Hell, guys at school thought I was downright lucky. Sex anytime I wanted it with a woman who knew how to please a man? They envied me." I frown. "I won't say the pleasure wasn't great, especially at first, and I won't lie and say I ever turned her down. I kept..." I reflect, trying to put that time of my life into words. "I kept thinking there had to be more. Physically, it was fine. Great. But every time we did it, I felt less for her and more... I don't know. Empty is the word, I guess. I kept waiting for it to mean something. It never did."

"How long did that go on?"

"About six months."

"And all that time, your dad was still having sex with her?"

I really don't want to answer that. I'm nauseated when I think of it now. "Yeah."

Every time I think my angel can't look more shaken by something I say, I open my mouth again.

"Oh, my god." She lifts a trembling hand over her lips.

If she thinks that's bad, I'm just getting started.

"And you weren't having any sort of...relationship with her?" Britta is still having a hard time wrapping her brain around what I'm admitting.

"We didn't date, if that's what you mean." Having a relationship with AnnaBeth would have been as cozy as cuddling up to an octopus. If she wasn't bending herself over my desk or bobbing her head between my legs, I never saw her. "We didn't even talk. In fact, I didn't really attempt more than casual flirting with someone my age until I was almost nineteen."

"So, you're saying she warped you and that's why you are…the way you are?"

"No. I had to explain AnnaBeth because, if I didn't, you couldn't comprehend what happened next. One day, I was too wrapped up in what she was doing to me orally to realize I should have been in a meeting. The firm lost a client. The pressure from other partners was too much and Dad had to fire me."

"After letting his mistress abuse you, he threw you under the bus?" She blinks at me incredulously.

"Actually, I was relieved. I didn't have to see AnnaBeth anymore. I didn't have to have sex with the gossipy, catty, and vindictive shrew. It was for the best—or it should have been. Everything would have been all right—mostly—if she hadn't decided she wanted to be the next Mrs. Barclay Reed. You see, when my mom asked why I got fired, I told her that I'd been goofing around. It was kind of true. Dad happily went along with it."

"Of course he did." Britta scoffs. "That way he didn't have to take any of the blame."

Precisely. "But AnnaBeth knocked on our front door one day while I was in school, just before the end of my junior year. She told my mother everything. Every. Single. Thing."

Britta's jaw drops wide. "What a heartless, horrible…"

Bitch? Yeah. "She was. When I got home, my mom confronted me. I thought she was going to be furious with my dad. I thought she would scold or ground me for not telling her sooner—or telling anyone who could put a stop to it. I had visions that she might even call the police. I expected something. But AnnaBeth went on and on about my prowess. And my dad's, too. She was probably just looking for any blade in her arsenal that would stab my mom in the heart."

Little did she know that Linda Reed had grown an iron shield around hers years ago. I discovered that ugly truth.

Easing to the edge of the sofa cushion, Britta leans closer. "What did she do?"

"My mom? First, she asked me what happened."

"What did you say?"

"I confessed to everything. I knew she was already aware of my dad's hookups, affairs, and mistresses. But I thought she would be shocked by what had happened to me. I thought she would make sure no one used me again." I duck my head because I can't look at Britta right now. I might not be able to look at her for the rest of this confession. "Instead, my mom cooed and awwed, like she was comforting me. Then, once I'd gotten my emotions under control, she asked me if I would help her get voted onto the country club's social committee—a really prestigious honor in her eyes. According to her, she'd always been snubbed because she came from a dirt-poor Nebraska farm, and that made her blood less blue."

Britta drops her hand on my knee. I didn't realize she'd come that close. I had no idea she was going to touch me again. I jolt when her warmth seeps into my skin. It's as if I'm alive again.

I find the guts to lift my head and meet her stare. Is this the last time I'll ever be this close to love—to her?

"What did she mean?"

"Well, if I could just be a good boy and 'persuade' the committee members she'd make a fine addition…"

Britta's horrified gasp guts me, and I look away again. Yeah, I never wanted her to know just how fucked up I was. But I couldn't shove it down forever. One way or another, my damage was going to ruin us. At least now she doesn't have to wonder if she somehow contributed to our problems.

"She wanted you to *sleep* with them?"

I nod. "I didn't know that at first. She simply told me to visit them. I had better manners than Maxon, you see. Once they met me, of course they would understand how she could add to their community."

"But what she meant was, scratch their itch until they were convinced to let your mom onto the committee?" Britta looks outraged. Or is that disgusted?

"I think blackmailed would be a better term."

"Oh, my god… She's your *mother*."

"I don't say this lightly, but she's a self-serving bitch."

"How many committee members were there?" Britta's voice shakes.

Once I tell her, I can't take it back. She'll know what a man-whore I was as a teenager. The kind of man-whore who became exponentially more practiced as an adult. "Twelve. I started on her 'project' in mid-May. By August, I made sure she was not only on the committee but she was the chair."

"And you were *sixteen*?"

I risk another glance at Britta. She's gone ghost white, pale lips pressed together. "Yeah. I think what hurt most was that my mom knew I wanted more than empty sex. I found the courage to tell her that's what I hated about being with AnnaBeth. But…"

"She set you up to have more of it." Britta shakes her head, looking dumbfounded and numb. "A lot more."

"A summer full, yes. Dad found out, of course. He clapped me on the back and congratulated me on my 'hot dozen hussies.' His words, not mine. Maxon had already escaped to college. Harlow probably knew something was up, but I did my best to shield her from everything ugly." I sigh, wishing like hell I was at the end of the story.

"I don't think she knows," Britta assures.

One small blessing. If my sister knew, she would look at me like a monster. The same way I fear Britta is going to look at me by the time I finish.

"The only one of the committee members I was with more than the few times it took me to 'convince' them to give my mom a seat at the table was Julia. She came across as nice. She actually talked to me. She seemed to care."

"So you didn't mow her lawn?"

"I did. That was my cover story for all of them. A free mow, some conversation, a smile, an invite inside for a drink since it was so hot outside and…" I was between their legs in under thirty minutes.

"Didn't any of them care that you were just a kid?"

"I was six feet tall, one sixty, with a full beard. A kid wasn't what they saw. And these were people used to getting their way at someone else's expense."

"You should have called the police."

Probably. "I was too ashamed. I couldn't imagine going to school and everyone finding out I had cried rape." Life in high school was already vicious enough, constantly fighting off guys who were already jealous of all the pussy I was getting. All I wanted to do was crawl out of my skin. "Julia came in the middle of the bunch. By then, the whispers had started. She knew why I was knocking on her door. Unlike the others, she didn't make me go through the motions. She just sat me down and asked me how I was doing. How I felt. I don't know what possessed me, but I told her that I wasn't very happy." I drag in a deep breath and let it out in a shudder. This part is going to be harder. "I told her I was lonely. She said she was lonely, too."

"She connected with you emotionally. You thought she understood you?"

"Yeah."

"But she still used you?"

"Absolutely." I scrub a hand across my face and stand. "I thought I was in love with her and that she was the one person I could trust, who would always be on my side. She dumped me just before Halloween, laughing like it was a great joke because she had already replaced me. You know the rest."

"Griff…" Britta stands, easing beside me, compassion welling in her blue eyes.

"Don't cry for me, angel. I've cried enough." It's hard for me to admit that. "It's over. And I admit I've let it fuck me up for far too long. When I met you, my first thought was that you were an angel." A little smile creeps across my face.

"I thought you were the most handsome devil," she whispers. "Your brother warned me…"

"But you didn't listen. He warned me to leave you alone, too." I shrug. "But I couldn't. When I first kissed you, I was sure you were too good to be true. I guess… I was afraid to let myself believe you were beautiful, inside and out. That I could trust you with my whole self until it was too late."

Her chin wobbles as she tries to hold in tears. I hope she doesn't regret me for too long. What we've been though is gut-wrenching torture, but I wouldn't trade my time with her for the world. She's changed me, made me better. Maybe after this—someday—I can have a normal life. Oh, I'm still going to make my last-ditch pitch to win her. But I'm not holding my breath that she'll say yes.

Now that she knows how fucked up I am, why would she ever marry me?

"Do you have any questions?" My voice almost sounds normal.

She frowns, searches her thoughts as she holds back tears. "Now that you've told me, do you feel any better?"

"Um…" How do I answer that when I feel as if I'm dying inside? "If you understand me better, I'm glad. But my adolescent shit cost me my son and the only woman I've ever loved. And trusted. I didn't show it last weekend, but I do trust you, Britta. Sometimes I have to remember not to be an ass, that not everyone is out to get me. I just spent a lot of years feeling that way." I press my lips together. Emotion clogs my chest, tightening my vocal cords. I grit my teeth to hold it back. "I know it's good to unburden, as Keeley would say."

"Does she know any of this?"

"I've never told a soul."

She looks touched that I chose her. "Thank you for telling me. For trusting me."

I can't imagine ever telling anyone else. "I know it's a lot to digest."

"It is. But all of this helps me understand you."

I nod. "Then, yeah, I feel better. You got a pen?"

Britta seems perplexed by my request when she meanders to the bar between her family room and kitchen. I follow as she produces a pen and a pad of paper.

I set the pad down again and withdraw the document relinquishing my parental rights. With my chest buckling, I grip the pen tightly and sign my name everywhere her lawyer has laid a tape flag. My hands are shaking when I set the pen aside and leave the paper behind. "There. Now you're free of me."

"Oh, god. Griff..."

I don't know what she's thinking exactly, except that she's feeling sorry for me. I don't want her making decisions on that kind of emotion. This is the last time I'm ever going to lay my heart on the line. She's the only woman I'll ever do this for.

"Shh. I've said everything I came to say except two things: First, if Jamie ever wants to know his father, I will welcome him with open arms. I'll be the best dad I know how."

"You were wonderful with him." I hear the tears in her voice.

I look up to find them pouring down her face. I wipe a path dry with my thumb, more than grateful when she doesn't flinch away. "I love him. Would you tell him that for me?"

She doesn't answer, just dissolves into sobs that shake her entire body.

I want to take her in my arms, soothe her, kiss her, tell her everything will be all right. But I won't lie to her.

"Angel... Don't do this." *Please don't make it harder.* "I'm not worth it."

"Don't say that." She lays her hand on mine and clasps our fingers together.

I close my eyes and savor her touch for a sweetly sharp moment. But I'm barely holding it together now. I need to say the last thing I came to, then leave.

"Second"—I reach into my pocket and pull out the box containing her engagement ring and wedding band—"I want you to have these. I bought them for you. I know you probably won't wear them. But...maybe you'll look at them and think of me sometimes. Or not. I just know these don't belong with me anymore."

She presses her hands to her chest, as if her heart will fall out at my feet if she doesn't. "I can't take these from you, not like this."

"Hey, I'd love to insist that you wear them for real... But unless you want to marry me, I don't have that right. My offer still stands, though. I would marry you tomorrow. I will—if you want that." When she opens her mouth, I press a finger over her lips. "Don't answer me now. I want you to think. Without me here, without my interference. I want you to comb through everything I've said and everything we've been through. I'll never be an easy man to live with. I know that. If you still want me, come to Maxon and Keeley's house tomorrow about noon. If you can't spend your life with me, if this is good-bye...then it's been my pleasure and my honor." I lean in to kiss her cheek softly, working my jaw to hold myself together. "And I will love you always."

CHAPTER TWENTY

Britta

THE DAY BEGINS WITH A hushed anticipation I can't shake. I'm not even sure what I'm waiting for. To see Griff again? Sometimes I think I look forward to that more than I should when we just hurt each other so much. At least I finally know why.

Now that the truth is between us, can we stop it from happening again?

I roll down the car window. The trade winds are gentle. The skies are clear.

I wish I could say the same for my mind.

Gripping the steering wheel, I head north. I'm not exactly sure what I'm going to say. Griff gave me so much to think about yesterday. I spent most of the night turning his confession over and over. I finally fell asleep about four this morning, still shocked. When I woke, only two things were clear to me: I've spent so much time wrapped up in my own anger and hurt, carting around my own baggage, that I never stopped to ask myself what thousand-pound monkey Griff might be carrying on his back.

I regret that utterly.

His behavior about so many things makes perfect sense to me. Initially, we dated for months before we had sex. Sure, some of the wait was navigating office etiquette. But he kept asking me to be sure—really sure—before we took that step. He always said he didn't want me to have regrets. I'm guessing he didn't sleep with Tiffanii for months because she reminded him too much of one of the country club women—shallow, self-absorbed, completely unconcerned for anyone's feelings but her own. It also explains why he might have taken her to bed once in a moment of loneliness or weakness, then resolved to never do it again.

Griffin Reed has been looking his whole life for love, acceptance, someone he could trust.

I feel so terrible that I didn't give it to him when he needed me most.

The second thing I know for sure? When I tried to force him out of my heart, I found it impossible. I will always love him, too.

Tears pool in my eyes again. I've been crying off and on for hours— for what he's survived, for how it's shaped him, for how it's torn us apart. For the turmoil of not knowing exactly what to do next.

But at least I know now what I want.

Last night, I stared at the engagement ring and wedding band he left me for at least an hour. I took them out of the box. Put them back inside. I imagined wearing them for the rest of my life. I considered what life would be like if I never once put them on my finger.

"Mama, you cryin'?" Jamie asks from the backseat.

"I'll be all right." I wipe away a stray tear that falls down my cheek.

He frowns. "You got a boo-boo?"

Yes. A gigantic one, breaking my chest in half at the thought of all Griff has been through. At all the ways he tried to overcome his past to learn to love me like I wanted him to. At the thought of never being with him again.

"I'll be fine." Maybe. I hope.

My phone rings in my purse. Is it Griff, wanting to know if I'm coming to see him? I admit it, I have a thousand questions. Yet…what's really left to hash out between us? Everyone who should have protected him as a kid warped his innocence and broke his trust. I want to understand more about how he felt, how he coped, but that's me trying to fill in my head with the details so I can empathize the best way possible. For him, answering would probably only be another twist of the knife.

When the cell trills again, I pull myself from my thoughts and rummage through my purse for the device. I glance at the screen. Keeley.

She's called every day for the past week. I haven't answered. I know she only wants to help...but I don't know what to say.

Maxon is lucky to have a wife who's both soft enough to give him all the feels and strong enough to make that difficult man toe the line. They're perfect together. I'm happy for them.

The device rings a third time. I silence it. She wants to do whatever she can to help her best friend be happy, and I commend that. But I have to be the one to tell Griff what I'm thinking, not whisper it to his pal to pass on to him like seventh-grade gossip.

I pull off the highway and turn up the radio, hoping it will occupy my mind. All I get is talk and commercials, so I turn it off again.

In the silence, broken only by Jamie's gurgling truck noises, my thoughts wander again. My son looks so much like his father. More every day, in fact. Sometimes, I used to resent the way just looking at my son would remind me of Griff. Now...it touches my heart. I'll protect Jamie the way Linda Reed never sheltered Griff. I already know he's the kind of father who would never let anything happen to our boy.

I'm pretty sure I know what kind of stepfather Makaio would have been. Logical and slightly removed. It's how he treated everyone, even me. He would never have become a roaring beast the moment anyone tried to harm my child—or any others we had together.

He would have been all wrong.

I've known that for weeks. I'm glad Griff finally made me admit that to myself.

If he hadn't walked back in my life, I would be putting on a flowing white tent of a dress that Makaio's mother picked out and listening to the wail of conch shells as I headed toward the altar to marry a man I respected...but didn't love.

Whatever else Griff and I say to each other today, I have to thank him for saving me.

A few minutes and a few turns later, I pull up in front of Keeley and

Maxon's big, sunny house. As I stop and put the car in park, I see the front lawn is set up for another wedding, very much like last weekend's. Vaguely, I wonder who's getting married today…but I'm way more focused on making sure everything I need is in my purse.

I grab the straps and sling them over my shoulder, then climb out and reach in the backseat for Jamie.

My heart is pounding so hard I'm sure it's going to bruise the insides of my ribs. It gets worse once I stand up, cradling my son, and see Griff prowling toward me in ground-eating steps, a silent question shouting across his face.

I close the car door, lock it. I can't take my eyes off him. He's…everything. He always has been. A glance tells me he hasn't slept. His eyes are red-rimmed. He looks pale and unshaven—and still unbearably handsome. I can't take away the agony he survived, but maybe—if he'll let me—I can help crowd it out with devotion and love.

"You came." He cups my cheek, then abruptly jerks his hand away. He covers the gesture by ruffling Jamie's hair.

The boy smiles. "Daddy!"

I'm not sure if Griff uttered those words because he's talking to me or reassuring himself. It doesn't matter. He allowed me to make this decision. The man who's spent the last fifteen years controlling everything so that no one could ever hurt him again gave me total dominion over our future.

I'm going to set it right.

"I had to. I thought about everything you said yesterday. I ache for everything you told me. I admire who you've become."

He flinches. "I'm hardly perfect."

"I'm not, either. Far from it. The fact that you could open yourself up to tell me your darkest memories simply to help me proves your strength and compassion and—"

"I couldn't leave you to wonder anymore. Not explaining was cruel."

"You were protecting yourself, Griff. You probably learned to do that a long time ago because no one else did."

He frowns, drops his head. He doesn't have to tell me I'm right. I know. And every bit of me aches for him.

"Why did you come?"

The question takes me aback. He told me to. At noon. I'm five minutes early. Did he change his mind overnight?

Dread clenches my belly. "I wanted to see you. I wanted to talk about us."

Over Griff's shoulder, Harlow runs out of the house and adjusts all the blue bows on the folding chairs. She drops more tropical petals on the white sheets underneath. "There's another wedding here today? Is this Keeley and Maxon's first official day open for business as a bed-and-breakfast?"

He pauses. "Not exactly. Maybe Jamie can run around with Auntie Harlow while we talk?"

"Sure."

Griff calls out to his sister, who dashes our way, wearing a beaming smile and a full face of makeup, which seems odd for this early on a Saturday. Maybe she's got someplace to go later?

She hugs me tightly, which surprises me even more. "Glad you're here. We're—"

"Going to talk," Griff cuts in. "Can you entertain Jamie for a few?"

Harlow's smile falters but she nods. "Sure."

When the pretty brunette carries my son away, I watch. She's an interesting woman. I hope she doesn't marry the guy she's engaged to, but it's none of my business. She's not my sister-in-law. I don't even know if she considers me a friend right now. The mixed signals are confusing.

Then again, I've got a mountain of problems in front of me. Harlow is a smart cookie, and she'll make the right choice. I hope she finds love someday...but I'm pretty sure her outlook on happily ever after matches the one her brothers shared for years. Her heart won't go down without a fight. Vaguely, I wonder what secrets are lurking in her closet after growing up in the Reed household, but Griff takes my hand, distracting me.

"Is this okay?" He squeezes my fingers. "To touch you like this?"

"Of course. Griff, I'm here because I love you. And I'm here because I don't want this." I extricate my hand from his and reach into my purse for a small manila envelope, then pass it his way.

He scowls at it. "What's in here?"

"Look inside."

Prying open the lip, he stares down into the contents. "Is that confetti?"

"It is now. It was the papers you signed yesterday relinquishing your parental rights. I can't keep you from your son any more than I can bear to stay away from you myself. What you told me changed my outlook—and mind—about everything between us. You told me your past because you wanted me to understand your behavior. But what you really needed was for me to understand *you*. So I could be with you. So we wouldn't repeat this terrible cycle again. So we could commit to each other with whole hearts." I swallow nervously. "Am I wrong?"

He crushes the envelope in his fist, then shoves it in his pocket. "No. You're right. So right. About everything."

His voice isn't quite steady, and I'm touched down to the soul. This man has walked through fire and stripped himself bare for me. I can't do any less for him.

I reach into my purse again and withdraw another form, the one he had drawn up voluntarily establishing his parental rights. I swiped it from his desk at the office on my way over here.

With a deep breath, I hand it to him. I understand this is forever—and that makes me so happy now. "Here. I've already signed this. If you do the same and give it back to your attorney, you'll be Jamie's father in the eyes of the law."

Reverently, he takes the paper from my hand and unfolds it. After a quick scan, he breaks out in a big smile and starts looking for a pen. Luckily, I come prepared and hand him one out of my purse.

He smooths out the form against the car and adds his name in all the places marked FATHER. Then it's done. My heart feels lighter already.

"Thank you. Really. That means the world to me."

I shake my head. "You don't have to thank me. You're his father. And I know you'll be a great one." I dig into my purse again. "I also brought you something else."

After a little searching, I finally find the black box containing the rings he bought me so early in our relationship and held on to because he couldn't let me go. I put the velvety square in his hand. "I also came here today because I finally have an answer to your proposal."

He glances at the box, then yanks his gaze to my face, as if he's desperately trying to read my intentions. "Angel?"

"Yes." I cup his jaw and look into his beloved hazel eyes. "Unequivocally, most certainly, wholeheartedly yes. I want to marry you." I break out into the tears I swore I wouldn't cry. "Finally."

"Thank god." His voice crumbles. "I love you, angel."

"I love you, too."

Griff wraps his fingers around my nape and hauls me closer like he can't get to me fast enough, slanting his mouth over mine. There's hunger in his kiss, but I taste the relief and the devotion. We've only been apart for a week, but it's felt like an eternity. I press myself against him. He's solid, strong. His heart beats against mine. This feels right. We feel right.

We share a love—and trust—we can both count on. I'm convinced of that all the way to my soul.

His fingers are in my hair. I grope for his shoulders. He moans. I melt.

"Get a room!" Maxon yells across the yard.

We jump apart guiltily. I give a nervous laugh.

Leave it to Maxon to say the most inappropriate thing at the most inappropriate moment.

Griff turns to him with a snarl. "I'm going to kill you."

"Nah, you look like you're going to be too busy to mess with me." He winks, then waves at me. "Hi, Britta. Your job is still available..."

I giggle through my tears. "I'll think about it."

"Later," Griff adds to his brother. "Go the fuck away. Don't you have things to do?"

"*Now* I do." He salutes us. "I'm on it."

Then he disappears inside the house again.

"What was that about?"

Griff clears his throat nervously. Why he should be worried now that I've said yes is a mystery.

"Let's get this engagement ring on you."

I'm beyond ready. "Please."

He flips open the box, and I'm struck again by how beautiful the stones and setting are. It's something I would have been drawn to. If he had turned me loose in a room full of rings, I have no doubt I would have chosen this one. He knows me so very well. Finally, that's a comfort.

He lifts the ring from its pristine perch. I hold out my hand. Together, we work to slide it on my finger. It fits perfectly, and the unfamiliar weight clenches at my heart. I'm his—now and always.

"It's beautiful," I murmur.

"I really believe it was made for you." He pockets the box containing the wedding band. "I'll keep this until the right time. You're happy?"

More tears flow, and I have to laugh at myself. I never considered myself a crier until Griffin Reed walked back into my life. "What part of me bawling doesn't say happy to you?"

Finally, his face breaks out into a blinding smile. "Just checking, angel. I have a couple of surprises for you if you'll come with me."

I try to think through that. "But you didn't know I was coming."

"Not for sure…but I hoped."

With that, he takes my hand again and leads me into the main house, where everything is a bustle of activity. I see a wedding cake on a stand in the dining room that looks eerily like one I fell for in a bridal magazine. Same pale blue fondant, same classic white trim. White lilies and plumeria decorate the three tiers.

It's even more breathtaking in person.

I try to stop and stare. I'd love to take a picture for our wedding, hopefully soon. But Griff keeps dragging me toward the master bedroom.

What is he up to?

I'm about to tell him we can't make love in Maxon and Keeley's bed—then ask if there's another one free in this house—when I see someone I didn't anticipate seeing for weeks. "Mom?"

She rushes forward in a formal cocktail dress in a coral shade that looks beautiful on her and embraces me. "Baby Britta..."

No one calls me that except my mom. I smile at all the childhood memories those two words evoke. I didn't grow up with a father, but I grew up sheltered and loved. My mom is the best ever.

I squeeze her tight, then lean back to look back at her. "What are you doing here? When did you arrive?"

"Thursday evening. Griff called me a few weeks ago and asked me if I'd like to come to your wedding."

I spin around to face him in shock. "A few weeks ago, you thought I was marrying Makaio."

Slowly, he shakes his head. I look up and see a wedding dress hanging on the front of the door, one I tried on with Keeley weeks ago—that I fell in love with—all pressed and repaired. I see a satiny pair of shoes I pointed out to Harlow when we did some window-shopping.

"A few weeks ago, I knew you had plans to be marrying him..." Griff begins. "But I was hoping you would marry me instead."

I glance between my mom and the dress. I remember the cake, Harlow's polished makeup, and the chairs set up outside...

Oh, my god.

"You planned us a wedding for *today*?" I gape at Griff.

He nods. "Three o'clock."

My mother reaches up to kiss my cheek. She soothes my back. "Your engagement ring looks lovely. Congratulations, baby. I'll let you two talk."

She leaves and closes the bedroom door behind her. I hear impatient feet and hushed whispers just outside the bedroom.

"Keeley, Harlow..." Griff calls. "Can you give us a minute?"

"Ugh. If the wedding is on, we need to start hair and makeup," Keeley insists. "Oh, the caterer is here. BRB."

"You suck, big brother. Hurry. You need to make sure Jamie's tux fits, and we have to try on Britta's dress in case she needs any last-minute alterations. Oh, and it's way past time to hug her and welcome her into the family."

"Soon," my groom shouts. "Scram."

They might do so reluctantly, but the duo scampers off. I'm staring at my now-fiancé in blinking shock. "You and all the people I love... You did this?"

"For you. I couldn't stand the thought of you marrying Makaio, of course. I wanted you to marry me. But I wanted you to have the wedding you'd been planning, dreaming of... You deserved that. So I took your magazines out of the trash can and gave them to Keeley and Harlow. We all took note of your preferences, then the girls took you wedding shopping on the pretense that Keeley needed your help for her big day."

"Oh, my... I kept wondering why they both seemed so interested in what I thought of everything. I mean, it was her wedding. Or I thought it was."

"No, it was for ours. This is all for you." He stares into my eyes, his sincerity making my heart catch.

The tears won't stop falling now, but they're accompanied with smiles. I throw my arms around Griff, and he pulls me in, holding me against his body for a long embrace. He kisses my forehead, my temple. I reciprocate on the top of his shoulder, his jaw.

"This is the most amazing, beautiful gesture..." I'm moved beyond words.

"So you're okay with becoming my wife in less than three hours?"

"Okay?" I take his beloved face in my hands. "I can't wait. I'm going to love and honor you. And I'll protect you always."

"I'll do the same. And I vow to trust you, no matter what."

We kiss softly, sweetly, a lingering expression of the devotion we feel.

The rest of the family comes in to break it up with smiles, good-natured ribbing, and champagne. Griff and I are separated with Harlow's stern, "It's bad luck to see the bride before the wedding. Your turn to scram."

Maxon tries to pull Griff out of the room, who hangs on to the doorjamb. "Hey, did you cancel that honeymoon suite you booked?"

"No." I couldn't bring myself to do it.

"Excellent. Maybe we'll have some freaking privacy tonight," he shouts as his brother tugs him out of the room. "See you at the altar…"

I giggle. "See you then!"

The next two hours are a whirlwind of preparations. I get three seconds alone for a hot shower, then the hair and makeup artist pounces. Finally, my sisters-to-be, now dressed in beautiful cornflower-blue dresses—just like I pictured—help me into my wedding dress, which fits perfectly. A woman tiptoes in and asks me to sign the marriage license. Griff has already put his bold scrawl on the GROOM line, so I add my signature where it says BRIDE.

It's real now. We're truly getting married… I'd tear up again at the enormity of all he's done for me, but I don't want to destroy my face. The poor woman who fixed it already spent a lot of time trying to make me look as if I slept great last night and haven't cried a tear. Luckily, she's talented. I can't remember a time I looked more radiant.

The girls shepherd me to the dining room to line up for the ceremony. At the open door to the lanai, Jamie is waiting for me in his precious tux, along with his uncle Maxon.

I bite my lip to hold in those pesky tears. I'm about to pledge my life to the man I love, to join together with my son's father into the most beautiful group of siblings and friends… I'm beyond blessed.

"You two look so handsome," I tell them.

"Of course. This gorgeous redhead I know tells me every day how hot I am…"

Keeley rolls her eyes with a laugh. "Maybe I won't tell you that today."

"Maybe I'll make you pay later," he growls.

"Eww. TMI, guys." Harlow scowls, then points at Jamie. "Young ears in the room. Hey, buddy. It's you and me tonight. Got any movie requests?

"How to Twain your Dwagon!" he shouts.

"It's on my iPad at the house," I assure Harlow.

She nods and looks down at her nephew. "Got you covered, pal. Twaining Dwagons it is…"

We all laugh, then Keeley hugs me. "Don't be nervous."

Oddly, I'm not—at all. "Everything is beautiful."

"I picked out the perfect song for your wedding. 'Wrapped in Your Arms' by Fireflight is an unconventional choice, but it's about once walking alone, then finding home with your love and—"

"If you chose it, I'm sure it's perfect. I couldn't be more thrilled. Thank you to all of you. So much."

"You can repay us by babysitting," Maxon quips.

"Hey! I'm not even pregnant." Keeley gapes at her new husband.

"Yet."

Everyone laughs until my mom comes bustling out of the kitchen, carrying two things. She hands me my bouquet. All white and spilling almost to the ground, it's still cold from the refrigerator. I grip the handle. I *feel* like a bride.

"Thanks, Mom."

She nods, then walks behind me and settles a pearl pendant around my throat. "This is the one gift I have from your father. I'm sorry he won't be here and he doesn't know what a beautiful woman you've become, but I want you to have this and be happy. And don't ever think about moving to Chicago again."

I touch the pearl dangling at my throat. It's already been an emotional day, and I know there's more to come. I drag in a deep breath to keep myself together. If I peek around Maxon, I see Griff pacing around the altar. He's anxious, beyond ready. Like me.

"You know, you could always move here," I say to my mom.

She smiles as if that's a lovely impossibility. "I don't have a job."

"You cook. You bake!" Keeley sounds thrilled. "I'll hire you."

We all laugh, but Maxon's bride is very serious. My mom sends her a considering glance, then looks around the big, happy house. "I just might do that…"

"It's time!" Harlow shouts, then bends to Jamie. "Remember last week, buddy?" When my son nods, his aunt straightens his bow tie. "No running. Just carry the pillow calmly to the table next to Daddy. He'll do the rest, okay?"

"Otay." He turns to me and opens his arms for a hug.

It might wrinkle my dress but I don't care. I bend to hold him close, rejoicing that we're going to complete our family circle.

"Pretty Mommy." He pats my back.

"Thank you, Jamie. I'm going to go marry your daddy now, okay?"

"Yeah!" He skips around.

Maxon joins his brother at the altar. I see the officiant waiting. The bridesmaids begin their trek down the aisle. Then the swell of music starts. And that's my cue to begin my future with Griffin Reed. After I float down the aisle, hearing a soft voice swear that nothing can separate us, we grip hands and exchange vows that have me near tears again. Finally, we slip wedding bands onto each other's fingers. The words and symbols are meaningful…but it's our kiss that seals our forever. My heart fills with joy and certainty because I know we'll spend every day for the rest of our lives totally in love.

The End

Read on for an excerpt from Shayla Black!

Look for the continuation of the More Than Words series on February 13, 2018 with Harlow's book, MORE THAN LOVE YOU.

MORE THAN LOVE YOU
More Than Words, Book 3
By Shayla Black
Coming February 13, 2018!

I'm Noah Weston. For a decade, I've quarterbacked America's most iconic football team and plowed my way through women. Now I'm transitioning from star player to retired jock—with a cloud of allegation hanging over my head. So I'm escaping to the private ocean-front paradise I bought for peace and quiet. What I get instead is stubborn, snarky, wild, lights-my-blood-on-fire Harlow Reed. Since she just left a relationship in a hugely viral way, she should be the last woman I'm seen with.

On second thought, we can help each other…

I need a steady, supportive "girlfriend" for the court of public opinion, not entanglements. Harlow is merely looking for nonstop sweaty sex and screaming orgasms that wring pleasure from her oh-so-luscious body. Three months—that's how long it should take for us both to scratch this itch and leave our respective scandals behind. But the more I know this woman, the less I can picture my life without her. And when I'm forced to choose, I realize I don't merely want her in my bed or need her for a ruse. I more than love her enough to do whatever it takes to make her mine for good.

MORE THAN WANT YOU
More Than Words, Book 1
By Shayla Black
NOW AVAILABLE!

A fresh, sexy, and emotional contemporary romance series by Shayla Black...

I'm Maxon Reed—real estate mogul, shark, asshole. If a deal isn't high profile and big money, I pass. Now that I've found the property of a lifetime, I'm jumping. But one tenacious bastard stands between me and success—my brother. I'll need one hell of a devious ploy to distract cynical Griff. Then fate drops a luscious redhead in my lap who's just his type.

Sassy college senior Keeley Kent accepts my challenge to learn how to become Griff's perfect girlfriend. But somewhere between the makeover and the witty conversation, I'm having trouble resisting her. The quirky dreamer is everything I usually don't tolerate. But she's beyond charming. I more than want her; I'm desperate to own her. I'm not even sure how drastic I'm willing to get to make her mine—but I'm about to find out.

This book is the first in the More Than Words series. The books are companions, not serials, meaning that backstory, secondary characters, and other elements will be easier to relate to if you read the installments in order, but the main romance of each book is a stand-alone.

This book contains lines that may make you laugh, events that may make you cry, and scenes that will probably have you squirming in your seat. Don't worry about cliffhangers or cheating. HEA guaranteed! (Does not contain elements of BDSM or romantic suspense.)

"THIS WILL BE OUR LAST song for the set. If you have requests, write them down and leave them in the jar." She points to the clear vessel at her feet. "We'll be back to play in thirty. If you have a dirty proposition, I'll entertain them at the bar in five." She says the words like she's kidding.

I, however, am totally serious.

Keeley starts her next song, a more recent pop tune, in a breathy, a capella murmur. "Can't keep my hands to myself."

She taps her thigh in a rhythm only she can hear until the band joins during the crescendo to the chorus. Keeley bounces her way through the lyrics with a flirty smile. It's both alluring and fun, a tease of a song.

Though I rarely smile, I find myself grinning along.

As she finishes, I glance around. There's more than one hungry dog with a bone in this damn bar.

I didn't get ahead in business or life by being polite or waiting my turn. She hasn't even wrapped her vocal cords around the last note but I'm on my feet and charging across the room.

I'm the first one to reach the corner of the bar closest to the stage. I prop my elbow on the slightly sticky wood to claim my territory, then glare back at the three other men who think they should end Keeley's supposed sex drought. They are not watering her garden, and my snarl makes that clear.

One sees my face, stops in his tracks, and immediately backs off. Smart man.

Number Two looks like a smarmy car salesman. He rakes Keeley up and down with his gaze like she's a slab of beef, but she's flirting my way as she tucks her mic on its stand. I smile back.

She's not really my type, but man, I'd love to hit that.

Out of the corner of my eye, I watch the approaching dirtbag finger his porn 'stouche. To stake my claim, I reach out to help Keeley off the stage. She looks pleasantly surprised by my gesture as she wraps her fingers around mine.

I can be a gentleman…when it suits me.

Fuck, she's warm and velvety, and her touch makes my cock jolt. Her second would-be one-night stand curses then slinks back to his seat.

That leaves me to fend off Number Three. He looks like a WWE reject—hulking and hit in the face too many times. If she prefers brawn over brains, I'll have to find another D-cup distraction for Griff.

That would truly suck. My gut tells me Keeley is perfect for the job.

Would it be really awful if I slept with her before I introduced her to my brother?

ABOUT SHAYLA BLACK

Shayla Black is the *New York Times* and *USA Today* bestselling author of more than fifty novels. For nearly twenty years, she's written contemporary, erotic, paranormal, and historical romances via traditional, independent, foreign, and audio publishers. Her books have sold millions of copies and been published in a dozen languages.

Raised an only child, Shayla occupied herself with lots of daydreaming, much to the chagrin of her teachers. In college, she found her love for reading and realized that she could have a career publishing the stories spinning in her imagination. Though she graduated with a degree in Marketing/Advertising and embarked on a stint in corporate America to pay the bills, her heart has always been with her characters. She's thrilled that she's been living her dream as a full-time author for the past eight years.

Shayla currently lives in North Texas with her wonderfully supportive husband, her teenage daughter, and two spoiled tabbies. In her "free" time, she enjoys reality TV, reading, and listening to an eclectic blend of music.

Connect with me online:
Facebook: https://www.facebook.com/ShaylaBlackAuthor
Twitter: http://twitter.com/Shayla_Black
Instagram: https://instagram.com/ShaylaBlack
Website: http://shaylablack.com
Newsletter: http://shayla.link/nwsltr
Goodreads: http://shayla.link/goodreads
Google +: http://shayla.link/googleplus
YouTube: http://shayla.link/youtube
Amazon Author Page: http://shayla.link/AmazonFollow
BookBub: http://shayla.link/BookBub

If you enjoyed this book, I would appreciate your help so others can enjoy it, too.

Recommend it. Please help other readers find this book by recommending it to friends, readers' groups and discussion boards.

Review it. Please tell other readers why you liked this book by reviewing it at the book retailer of your choice. Thank you!

OTHER BOOKS BY SHAYLA BLACK

CONTEMPORARY ROMANCE

MORE THAN WORDS

More Than Want You
More Than Need You

Coming Soon:
More Than Love You (February 13, 2018)

CONTEMPORARY EROTIC ROMANCE

THE WICKED LOVERS (COMPLETE SERIES)

Wicked Ties
Decadent
Delicious
Surrender to Me
Belong to Me
"Wicked to Love" (novella)
Mine to Hold
"Wicked All the Way" (novella)
Ours to Love
"Wicked All Night" (novella)
"Forever Wicked" (novella)
Theirs to Cherish
His to Take
Pure Wicked (novella)
Wicked for You
Falling in Deeper
Dirty Wicked (novella)
Holding on Tighter

THE DEVOTED LOVERS

Coming in 2018!

SEXY CAPERS

Bound And Determined
Strip Search
"Arresting Desire" (Hot In Handcuffs Anthology)

THE PERFECT GENTLEMEN (by Shayla Black and Lexi Blake)

Scandal Never Sleeps
Seduction in Session
Big Easy Temptation

Coming Soon:
Smoke and Sin (September 12, 2017)

MASTERS OF MÉNAGE (by Shayla Black and Lexi Blake)

Their Virgin Captive
Their Virgin's Secret
Their Virgin Concubine
Their Virgin Princess
Their Virgin Hostage
Their Virgin Secretary
Their Virgin Mistress

Coming Soon:
Their Virgin Bride (TBD)

DOMS OF HER LIFE (by Shayla Black, Jenna Jacob, and Isabella LaPearl)
Raine Falling Collection (Complete)

One Dom To Love
The Young And The Submissive
The Bold and The Dominant
The Edge of Dominance

Coming Soon:
Heavenly Rising Collection
The Choice (Fall 2017)

THE MISADVENTURES SERIES

Misadventures of a Backup Bride (October 17, 2017)

STANDALONE TITLES

Naughty Little Secret
Watch Me
Dangerous Boys And Their Toy
"Her Fantasy Men" (Four Play Anthology)
A Perfect Match
His Undeniable Secret (Sexy Short)

HISTORICAL ROMANCE (as Shelley Bradley)

The Lady And The Dragon
One Wicked Night
Strictly Seduction
Strictly Forbidden

BROTHERS IN ARMS MEDIEVAL TRILOGY

His Lady Bride (Book 1)
His Stolen Bride (Book 2)
His Rebel Bride (Book 3)

PARANORMAL ROMANCE

THE DOOMSDAY BRETHREN
Tempt Me With Darkness
"Fated" (e-novella)
Seduce Me In Shadow
Possess Me At Midnight
"Mated" – Haunted By Your Touch Anthology
Entice Me At Twilight
Embrace Me At Dawn

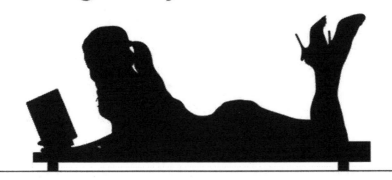

Made in the USA
Lexington, KY
05 January 2018